Rain

Rain

BARNEY CAMPBELL

MICHAEL JOSEPH
an imprint of
PENGUIN BOOKS

MICHAEL JOSEPH

UK | USA | Canada | Ireland | Australia
India | New Zealand | South Africa

Michael Joseph is part of the Penguin Random House group of companies
whose addresses can be found at global.penguinrandomhouse.com.

First published 2015
001

Set in 13.5/16 pt Garamond MT Std
Typeset by Jouve (UK), Milton Keynes
Printed in Great Britain by Clays Ltd, St Ives plc

A CIP catalogue record for this book is available from the British Library

HARDBACK ISBN: 978–0–718–18125–3
OM PAPERBACK ISBN: 978–0–718–18126–0

www.greenpenguin.co.uk

To Mum, Dad, Poppy and Rosie

I have made for you a song,
And it may be right or wrong,
But only you can tell me if it's true.
I have tried for to explain
Both your pleasure and your pain,
And, Thomas, here's my best respects to you!

Rudyard Kipling, 'To Thomas Atkins'

PROLOGUE

'O Lord, you know how busy I must be today; if I forget you, do not forget me.'

Every morning, in a hundred deserts, his mantra, his ritual. Everyone has one. Irrational, pathetic, but a blanket. If he says it, things will be all right. Over and over he whispers it, blind in the bitter darkness, and reaches down his chest and kisses the St Christopher.

'O Lord, you know how busy I must be today. If I forget you, do not forget me.'

He still has five minutes before reveille, five minutes to meditate on creeping out of the safety of night and heading north into the light, floating in and out of sleep and barely minding the icy condensation dripping onto his sleeping bag, the breaths and snores. In his cocoon, in his trance he buries himself from the outside world but can still not escape his stomach's terror. On the spectrum of human emotions, when you are stuck on that left edge, the fear and hopelessness of knowing that this day you will risk destroying everything dearest to you, that is a lonely place. *Golgotha.* He remembers a poem to himself.

> Pulse nigh to pulse, and breath to breath,
> Where hushed awakenings are dear . . .

Hushed awakenings . . .

'Boss, boss. Reveille. 4.30. Let's get ready. It's fucking freezing.'

Lance Corporal Miller shakes his shoulder and he grunts

assent. His brain starts to shed the fog. Struggling out of the sleeping bag, he gets out of the little canvas shelter at the side of the Scimitar. Pitch black, biting wind. He can hear the murmur and stumbling of the rest of the boys getting up. He joins Miller and Davenport and they fumble with the tent, packing it all away on the side of the wagon. Davenport checks her over – track, running gear, oil levels – and starts the engine. Miller jumps in the turret and fires up the radios.

He leaves to go and check on the rest of the compound. An officerly check on the troops, in fact a cry for company, a scream for help. He needs someone to talk to, who will tell him it will be all right.

Please can everything be all right?

He comes to Corporal Jesmond's wagon. The two crews were leaguered together that night with their Scimitars while his other two car commanders, Sergeant Trueman and Corporal Thompson, were in another compound, ready for their part in the day.

'Morning, boss! It's gonna kick off big time today, I reckon. We're good to go, hundred per cent. Cocked, locked, ready to rock. Sleep well?'

Relief, his crutch. Chatting with Jesmond amid the boys getting themselves and the wagons ready, he is dragged from the left of the spectrum. 0500. Thirty minutes to H-Hour. He steals up to a camp bed next to a crumbling wall.

'Clive?'

'Hmmm?'

'Morning, mate; it's five. Another day in paradise.'

'Hmmm. Thanks, bud. Any news?'

'Nothing, mate, quiet as the grave. The boys push up in half an hour.'

'One day we'll remember this with fondness, I suppose.'

'Yeah, mate. What a farce. What the fuck are we doing here?'

What are we doing here?

Moving on. The first weak light, just a film of it, starts to halo the hills to the east. It would be on them soon, sunlight searing across the globe, valley by valley. Where was it now? It would have passed Tibet, have eaten the Wakhan Corridor and would now be nibbling Kabul before vomiting that out into day. *Please delay. Please leave us.* Light meant action. He struggles up a rickety ladder to the rooftop, and finds the infantry sniper eyeing the gloom to the north through his night sight.

'Morning. You OK?'

'Not bad, sir, not bad. Just looking forward to it kicking off, to be honest. Morning, Talibs. My name's Dr 7.62 mm, and today I'm going to give you a lecture about bullet wounds – to the face!'

With deft, blind ease, the sniper's own ritual begins. He unloads his rifle, thumbs the rounds from the magazine onto a rag and oils up the breech.

'You'll be OK though, boss, in those Scimitars of yours. Safe as houses, them.' He grins sarcastically.

'Yeah, cheers. I'd rather be in a baked bean tin; that'd be more use when you're about to drive through a medium-density minefield.'

'Bet you're looking forward to unleashing that 30 mil.'

'Honestly, I'll be delighted if bugger all happens. Keep an eye on us anyway. What's the phrase? Rather be tried by twelve than carried by six. Get my drift?'

'No probs, boss. I got your back. Any fucker comes into this scope while you fellas are in contact they're getting it. '

The halo grows bigger and the undersides of the cirrus, way up high, start to reflect the light in flames of red and yellow. Rosy-fingered dawn again. Pure epic.

Was this epic?

Twenty past five. Not long now. He picks his way back to the Scimitar. The pitch blanket has slowly been drawn back, and the sky is rich purple. As he passes the infantry, all around is a hive of battle preparation. Rifles being oiled, grenade pins checked. New batteries on radios, spares checked for power. Crucifixes kissed. One rifleman reads a passage from his Bible to his mates. They all listen. Last gulps of water slugged, biscuits crammed down. Nervous smiles, black humour. Extra tourniquets handed around by the medics and stuffed into pockets. A corporal checks all his section's morphine syringes are in their left thigh pockets, with secondaries behind their body armour in case their legs are blown off. Vallon metal detectors 'sing' as their users test them on the metal eyeholes on their boots. Endless belts of machine-gun rounds are piled into rucksacks, draped around necks. Some young soldiers are carrying so much weight they have to be lifted to their feet by their sergeant and then left to stand there, panting, bent double. They can barely see from beneath their helmets, eighteen-year-old boys ripped from their mothers and today off to kill other mothers' sons. A sardonic crow watching all this from a wall cackles. *What are these men doing?*

He climbs onto the turret next to Miller. 'All right, Stardust, how are we? Radios?'

'Dropped in, boss, and radio checks done with Three One. Sights are up and running, laser's gleaming, ECM's all in.'

'Good lad! Dav, engine?'

'No dramas, boss. She's held up OK.'

'Thanks, lads. Top work. Dusty, let's load her up.'

They drop inside the turret to load the Rarden. In a wordless drill Miller elevates the barrel to give him more room as he draws up a clip of three rounds from the centre rack and slams them into the feed tray. He winds the loading handle on.

Dunk, dunk . . . gaDUNK. The first round clunks in the breech and he slams another clip into the feed tray. The familiarity of the drill and the sleek shells embolden him and help get some blood flowing around freezing hands. He loads and cocks the machine gun.

'Awesome, Dusty. We're looking good.'

Scrabbling out of the turret, he looks at Jesmond behind them, who gives him the thumbs up. He's been good to go for ages. His gunner, GV, next to him in the turret, wags his trigger finger with a grin. He can't wait. The best gunner in the squadron, he will be busy today.

Slowly, slowly, he leaves the left of the spectrum.

Through the gloom the night starts to spill its secrets. Fast Pace lies to the north in bland, poker-faced silence. How many IEDs does it hold? The Farad gardens, which they fought through two days ago, lie to the south behind them. Their tall pines and cypresses tower over the poorer families' crops.

The radio bursts into life; it's the commanding officer, needing to know if the Scimitars are ready to go. 'Hello, Tomahawk Three Zero, this is Minuteman Zero Alpha. Callsigns leaving my location now. Confirm you are ready to move north to support when they are engaged. Over.'

He seizes up. He is lost, frozen.

'Um . . . Hello . . . er . . . Minuteman Zero Alpha, this is Tomahawk . . . er . . . Three Zero. Yeah . . . er . . . roger . . . er . . . Wait.'

Snap back.

Come on!

'Tomahawk Three Zero, roger my callsign. Complete at

immediate notice to move and will push north once Vixen are in contact. Your intent understood. Over.'

That's better.

'Hmm. Bit of a crowbag there, wasn't I, Dusty?'

'Don't worry, boss; the lads will have loved that!'

Nothing. They wait. Over the radio come sitreps from Vixen, pushing up with the ANA to Fast Pace. When they come into contact the Scimitars will storm up to support them. The radio gives encouraging news: progress is good, all quiet, no Taliban. No IEDs found so far. He starts to shiver in the turret. Stamping his feet on the seat, he cocks, unloads and then loads again his pistol. Cock, unload, load. Cock, unload, load. Miller hums to himself as the purple turns ever bluer.

Gunfire to the north.

'Hello, Minuteman Zero, this is Vixen Three Two. That's us now in contact. Small arms, RPGs. Wait out.'

We're on.

'Hello, Tomahawk Three Zero, this is Minuteman Zero Alpha. Vixen callsigns in contact. Move now, move now. Acknowledge. Over.'

'Tomahawk Three Zero moving now, making best speed. Out to you. Hello, all Tomahawk Three Zero callsigns, this is Tomahawk Three Zero. Move now, move now. Out.'

Up north the crickets' croak of automatic fire intensifies after the first, tentative fumblings. Tracer bounces off walls and arcs into the sky before fading like shooting stars.

Where will the bullets land?

'OK, Dav, let's go.'

The wagon complains through the gears. He looks back at Jesmond and gets another thumbs up. He reaches the gate.

'Left . . . left stick . . . and again . . . You're on now, Dav . . . Steady . . . steady . . . now right stick . . . Good lad . . . Now you're clear . . . Foot down, pedal to metal, drive it like you stole it. Let's fucking go for it.'

The engine screams as Davenport floors the accelerator and they burst down the track towards the sun. The flame is just at the horizon now, and the east is bathed in gold. At the track's end they turn north and plummet back into the dying twilight.

Do not forget me.
Do not forget me.
Please don't forget me.

ONE

On a sunny morning in August the parade ground is full. Young men and women in dark blue stand nervously, fiddling with their belts and caps and swords, making sure there is no fluff or dust on them. 'Right, brace up. Show the movement!' barks a voice. All fiddling ceases, and caps are put on hurriedly as more and more butterflies make them nauseous. The academy sergeant major, with rapid screams that their bodies seem to hear before their ears, petrifies them from nervy fidgeting to poised, chest-out attention. Not long now. Two minutes to march onto the parade. Colour sergeants, who have spent every day of the last year breaking these men and women into military service, take a last inspection, going past the rows and making last adjustments, like tigers licking dirt off their cubs. One of them stops at a cadet with straw-coloured hair and whispers to him, 'Well, Mr fuckin' Chamberlain, who'd ha' thought it? Next time I see ye I'm goin' to have tae call you sir.'

'That so, Colour Sergeant?'

'Aye, but it don't mean ah'm goin' tae enjoy it. Or fuckin' mean it, ye little wretch.' He grins fondly and moves on. The cadet and his friends laugh but are quickly silenced by his mock-serious glare. Thirty seconds left.

The academy sergeant major shouts, 'Ladies and gentlemen, in my regiment we have a motto: "*Quis Separabit?*" It means, for those ignorant pikeys of you unfortunate enough not to have had a classical education –' he waits for the laughter to die before continuing '– it means, "Who shall separate us?" Just remember that. Every day of your lives. After this year no one, nothing, can separate you. Be you in Afghanistan or Iraq or Kosovo, or whichever next shithole it is that Her Majesty decrees that you go to in order that you might lead her men, if you live to be a hundred or if you die tomorrow no one can break the bond you have forged this year.' He pauses to let it sink in. He sees them all thrust out their chests an extra inch. He loves military theatre. 'Now, march to the beat of the drum, get on the heel, hold your heads high; today you are kings of all you survey.' Pulses quicken, sweat trickles down necks. A band strikes up, and they march onto the parade ground.

Fifteen minutes later they stand immaculate as the band plays the 'Radetzky March', and an elderly retired general totters around inspecting the rows of cadets, mere hours away from joining their regiments as fully fledged junior officers. The general looks at them with envy – for their youth, for their straight backs and lean faces – but with sadness as well. Some of these boys and girls will not be alive in a year. As he passes the ranks of puffed chests and neat, clipped hair he looks at them and thinks of his own friends who are no longer alive and remembers his own commissioning parade. He sighs with tiredness and regret as he completes his inspection and shuffles his way back to the dais to begin his address.

The cadet with straw-coloured hair cannot stop himself from smiling, breaking the pattern of stern arrogance on everyone else's faces. He has freckles on his nose, and raises his chin so sharply that he seems three inches more than his five feet nine. He sees his mother in the crowd, wearing a hat so large that those behind her are hidden entirely from view, and his smile breaks into a grin, which he quickly suppresses.

In the crowd he can also see a wheelchair, its occupant's

chest sparkling with medals hovering over a gap where legs should be. His mind suddenly moves away from the parade ground and far away to Afghanistan. The sweat that trickles down his neck now is not from heat. He glances back at his mother, almost to check that she is still there, and this time he doesn't smile. A sadness comes over him.

They begin the slow march past. As they wheel across the parade ground in unbroken line, he can feel the fragility of his friends' flesh as they press against each other.

He sighs. No turning back.

Who is this boy, with his dancing eyes?

Tom Chamberlain was born to fight in Afghanistan. That does not mean that he was a natural soldier, although he became a very good one; simply that the circumstances of his family history, birth and upbringing meant that for him joining the British Army was an absolute inevitability. Just as when a boy kicks a ball in a garden it is only going one place, smack bang through a window, so his mother acknowledged the moment he put on his father's old army helmet aged four and started to march around his bedroom that he would end up, not just in the army but in a war with it.

As a boy he was never happier than when playing soldiers. Gardens were the Burmese jungle, any beach was Omaha or Utah, any street Stalingrad or Caen. A simple stick would become a pistol, flame-thrower or bazooka. As a six-year-old in 1991 he ran downstairs every morning before school to watch coverage of the Gulf War. It looked amazing – Scud missiles shooting gold up through the pitch-black screen and tanks screaming through the desert – and he sat transfixed and square-eyed.

However, while he idolized the army and anyone who had served with it, an unspoken fear gnawed away that if or when the time came and he found himself not just in a fight but with the responsibility of leading men in that fight, he would prove unequal to the task. He just didn't think he would ever be up to leading men. How could sergeants and corporals, veterans of past conflicts, ever look to him for guidance? Would he be a popular officer, trusted and liked by his soldiers, or would they take against him? Could he cope? Always these shadowy doubts lay beneath the outward bravado.

The main shadow, the only shadow, cast over Tom's childhood was the death of his father when he was eight. Leonard Chamberlain was a fine-looking man: tall, with a Roman nose and two uncapped chipped front teeth, giving him an oddly noble but friendly appearance. He was guilty of an aversion to hard work where charm and procrastination sufficed, and devoted himself to a blissful – if financially ruinous – life of Epicureanism. What he inherited when he was eighteen had by the time of his marriage to Constance dwindled to just enough cash to buy a farm cottage on the estate of an old army friend of his in Kent, near Chatham.

People often described Leonard as a wasted talent, and correctly, but he was more complicated than that. The army friend – Tom's godfather Sam Hockley – and he had joined the same regiment together when they were nineteen and just out of school, and had cavorted, gambled and drunk-driven their way through service in Germany, Belize and Cyprus via a succession of hair-raising and improbable escapades, the stories of which became all the better for their frequent and ever more baroque embellishments. But one day, as he explored the attic, six-year-old Tom came across an old photograph of his father on a Belfast street corner, more angular but unmistakably him, talking urgently into a radio while a dead soldier was carried away in a body bag. Tom kept the photo in the drawer of his bedside table and would often look at it long after he had been put to bed by his parents.

A few months later Tom was helping Sam out on the farm and, as they put some cattle feed in a trough, asked him, 'Godfather Sam, did you and Daddy ever have to fight baddies in the army?'

Sam paused, ambushed, pondering whether to obfuscate or to tell the truth. *Bugger it, the boy would have to learn sometime.* 'Well, you see, Tommy, and promise me not to tell your father I said this, will you?' He waited until he received a solemn nod. 'Your dad and I were together in a town called Belfast. And it wasn't very nice. A lot of people were doing horrible things. And of all the people with me out there, I'd say that your dad was the bravest. He had some tough times out there, but all his men loved him, and he made sure that a lot of them got home.'

'So was he a hero then?'

'Yes. Yes, he was.'

'Were you a hero?'

Sam took off his flat cap and pushed back his thinning sandy hair. 'Well Tom, I don't know if I was a hero. But I was certainly surrounded by them. Now, you promise me to never tell Dad what I just said, OK?'

What Sam didn't say was that Leonard's problems – his alcoholism and spiral into near bankruptcy – had begun just after that tour of Belfast in 1979. Sam had seen his friend change from quite a serious-minded young man into a reckless, live-for-the-minute rogue. Leonard left the army in 1981, much to the chagrin of his superiors, who were grooming him for rapid promotion, and embarked on a three-year binge which knew no bounds and certainly every casino in the West End. Three years later, his inheritance down the drain, he woke up one morning next to a girl, had decided by lunchtime that he wanted to marry her and did so six months later.

She was Constance Rowley, a secretary at a law firm in London, heaven-sent for the undeserving Leonard. She took him out of London, away from temptation, and with Sam's help and generosity – borne more out of irrational loyalty than financial sense – they moved into the Old Mill on his estate. Constance got a job with a firm of solicitors in Rochester, but Leonard never rediscovered the appetite for work he had once had. It was very strange. Even when Tom was born in 1985 he was disinclined to finance their lifestyle, which although comfortable was not luxurious, any further by getting a job. Constance let it stand. She slightly suspected, for one thing, that all was not well with him. As indeed it wasn't. On Tom's first birthday, a quiet March day with a grey clanging arch of sky hanging over the house, Leonard told her that he had been diagnosed with cancer of the liver. It was a hereditary condition, apparently, but both couldn't help wondering whether it had been accelerated by the excesses of the past few years. They kept it very quiet and hoped desperately that Leonard would live as long as possible.

Leonard spent his days inside armed with a history book and a bottle of wine or whisky. Whenever Tom, who had only the vaguest notion of his father's fragility, came in Leonard would look at him with a sparkle and challenge him to a game of chess or backgammon, or tell him to sit next to him as he read him passages from histories of the crusades and the fall of Byzantium. Tom didn't fully understand but was enthralled by the exciting names and the thought of entire cities being sacked.

When the end came it was swift. Seven year after his diagnosis, Leonard deteriorated in a couple of weeks; finally his immune system abandoned its long rearguard action. Tom

18

was woken one morning at eight o'clock not by Constance crying but by the silence from downstairs. He tiptoed out of bed and down to the kitchen. It was all quiet; nothing had been touched. He felt the kettle. It was cold. Then he heard broken sobs from upstairs, and his fear vanished and numb realization hit him. He knew as surely then as he did a minute later when he opened the door to the bedroom that his father was dead.

The next week they buried him, Tom walking with Constance behind the coffin. There were no more tears from Constance; she had long known this was coming, and after the first shock, save for dabbing her eyes occasionally at the funeral more out of form than necessity, she did not weep. She still squeezed Tom's hand though, all the way through the service.

'Stop it, Mummy, you're hurting my hand,' he whispered.

'Oh, I'm sorry, Tommy.' She smiled at him and relaxed her grip, but only for a moment before unconsciously squeezing it again, even more tightly this time.

After the wake, Constance ushered everyone out of the house and she and Tom sat forlornly in the kitchen, slowly getting used to the unwelcome quiet. Breaking the empty silence, as if seized with a sudden idea, Constance leaped up, went to her bedroom for a moment and came down with a letter in her hand.

'Now Tommy, your father wanted me to give you this when you were fourteen or fifteen, but I'd like you to read it now. You should read it now, I think. You're old enough. Daddy wrote it to you just last week. Would you like to read it by yourself? If you want to I don't mind, but if you want me to be with you then of course I will.'

Tom's heart felt light as she handed him the stiff ivory-white envelope, bare save for 'To My Darling Boy' in his father's beautiful spidery handwriting. He gulped.

'Um, don't worry, Mummy. I'll read it outside.'

Tom walked outside and Constance shut the door after him, ruffling his hair as he passed her. The letter felt heavy, heavier than the paper in it. He climbed over the fence and walked to his den, cut out of the middle of a large rhododendron. The setting sun bounced off the undersides of the leaves in yellow and gold. He fingered the envelope for some minutes, before gently prising it open. He unfolded the letter.

My Dear Tom,

Please forgive this letter. I so very much wish that I could have said all of the following to you in person. Face to face is so much better than the cold written word, but at least you will, should you want to, be able to keep this letter for a while. I am afraid that I did not talk to you before I died for two reasons. First, aged eight you are too young, I think, to deal with the concept of speaking to a man about to die, and I want to keep you young for as long as possible. You will be annoyed with me for not treating you as a grown-up, but I hope you will understand. The second reason is that I could not have brought myself to have spoken to you; I simply would not have been able to witness your reaction. So there you go; half out of concern for you, half for me. Please forgive my cowardice: I hope you understand it.

Tom, by this stage you will know all there is to know about looking after your mother and being the man of the house. I know you will have done a superb job, but I am just so sorry that a boy so young has had to grow up so quickly, too quickly. I know that you and your friends are impatient to grow up, but one day you will realize that it is a magical thing to stay young for as long as possible.

So I will not lecture you about looking after Mummy; you will be doing that already and as I head towards death (gosh that is strange to write!) her safety is mercifully not on my list of worries (though the future of the English cricket team and your tree house surviving a storm are). You are a brave boy, Tom; I have always known that. Mummy may have told you that you were very ill when you were born; you actually very nearly died and the doctors and nurses had given up hope. One doctor told me, when you were at your worst, that you would not survive the night.

The next morning that doctor came and saw you. Not only were you still there but you had somehow, from the night, drawn from some great invisible reserve of strength. The doctor was amazed; no baby had ever made such a recovery in that hospital, and all the nurses after that fawned over you, saying that you were their little hero.

I wish I could have spent years and years writing this to you. I wish I could put down every single bit of advice I have ever heard myself, but I will limit myself to the following, in no particular order, but as they come into my head, apart from the last one, which is the most important advice I have ever been given. Some of it you will understand now, some you will understand later, some you will think is just rubbish!

1. *The eleventh commandment. Never get caught. If you obey this one you don't have to worry about any of the other boring ten. Apart from 'Honour your father and mother.' You must do that!*
2. *Always, always say please and thank you. It will amaze you how many grown-ups do not do this.*
3. *Never be rude to girls.*
4. *There is no such thing as a stupid question. If in doubt, just ask!*
5. *The ancient Greeks had a great saying, 'Nothing in excess.' I have no doubt that you'll see what that means later on in life. Unfortunately, probably only because you will have done something to excess or gone too far. But learn from it!*
6. *You will do well to learn this quote from Walter Scott about the mess you will get into if you start telling lies: 'O what a tangled web we weave, when first we practise to deceive!' Never a truer word spoken.*

7. *Have a child. It is the best present in the world. But not for a few years at least!*

8. *I don't know who said this, but like virtually every other good quotation it was probably Johnson, Wilde or Churchill. 'The harder I work, the luckier I seem to get.' Tom, I never worked very hard, and as you can see I haven't been that lucky.*

9. *You were born into a family which, if not wildly wealthy, at least does not struggle. Remember to look after those who have not had the advantages of a loving family and a good education and relatively secure financial background that you have. This will become clear later in your life. You will come to understand what I mean.*

In terms of university, jobs, exams, etc. I have two things to say.

1. *From me, your father. You must do very well and get a first at university. And then you must join the army, and after mastering that you must be in the cabinet, having made yourself (legally) into a multi-millionaire.*

2. *From me, Daddy. As long as you are happy, Tom, and add value even to just one other person's happiness, do whatever you want to do. If you don't want to go to university, don't. If you don't want to touch the army with a bargepole, don't. If you don't want to work, don't. But always add value.*

Goodness me, Tom, I know I will wake up tomorrow and reread this and think it is all drivel. But I don't think it is. In any case, I am putting it in the envelope and sealing it now. I must go now; goodbyes are better short and sharp.

Tom, I do wonder how you are going to do, but I am not scared about it.

God speed, and with love, with all the love in the world to you, my brave, brave boy,

Daddy

Tom noticed that there were splodges on the paper, some old ones that were dry and some new ones his own eyes had made. Fearing for the letter's survival, he folded it up into its envelope and hugged it to his chest. Tears were now streaming down his cheeks, and he ran back to the house, scratching himself on thorns, running, running through the dusk's purple towards the light of the kitchen door, which was already being tapped by moths. He hurled the door open and threw himself into Constance's lap, where he stayed for an hour crying his eyes out. He didn't feel very brave at all.

Leonard's financial legacy was not impressive. They were able to stay – just – in the house, and while they weren't ever exactly poor, Tom was denied the holidays and treats that his classmates had. But he was very popular at his primary school, where he always came top of the class while managing to be one of the chief mischief-makers. Constance was sad that she wasn't able to afford to send him away to boarding school, but while Tom accepted having to go to the Henry VI Comprehensive in Chatham, a low, sprawling, prefabricated structure whose grim facade hid some excellent teachers, Constance seemed dumb with embarrassment every time she had to admit to one of her old friends that he wasn't at an independent school. Tom, however, true to form, settled in without a problem. He was still the same old Tom, still climbing trees just out of curiosity to inspect the birds' nests at the top, still unfailingly generous-spirited to all who met him, and he fitted in with his new classmates with consummate ease.

Due to the combination of his father's charm and his mother's brains and ability to work hard, Tom eased into Cambridge, securing a place to read English at Sidney Sussex College. When he put the phone down after hearing his A-level results he hugged her, almost lifting her off the ground. 'Thanks, Mum. If it wasn't for you this would never have happened.' Constance was thrilled. As he ran off with his lurcher Zeppo through the woods to go and tell Sam she flopped into a chair. *So far*, she thought, *Tom's doing all right.*

Three years later, after his final week at Cambridge, Tom took the entrance exam for the army. To his great relief he passed; he had made absolutely no provision for anything else. Halfway through July, after a month of helping on Sam's farm, he got his results: he had got a first. To celebrate, in August he left with his girlfriend Cassie Foskett to travel around Europe by train.

He had always felt insecure around Cassie; he couldn't ever really believe that she was going out with him. They had been in the same college at Cambridge and had shared tutorials since the start. It was only at the end of the first term that Tom had summoned up the courage to talk to her properly outside a tutorial, over-engineering a meeting in a coffee bar to talk through 'bits of Austen that he was having trouble with'. She humoured him, and Tom soon found that behind a cool, fierce exterior lay a warm smile and an infectious, cackling laugh.

She was funny, Cassie. She seemed to Tom otherworldly, almost timeless, indefinable. She was a chameleon, both in looks and character. Sometimes she would wear floaty dresses and put flowers in her hair as though she was at Woodstock – what she wore around her college friends, when Tom thought she was at her most liberated and best. Sometimes though, when she was with friends from other colleges who knew her through the octopus-like public-school network that permeated the university, she would dress and act differently: immaculate hair and expensive, fussy clothes combined with a haughty, icy air. He didn't mind this, but it puzzled him. As he got to know her better, it meant that Tom always felt that just when he was on the brink of really understanding her she would slip away from him.

Halfway through their second year on a warm March day they were lying on the banks of the Cam sharing the earphones to an iPod, listening to 'American Pie'. The lyrics woke Tom out of his slumber near the end of the song. He brought himself up onto his elbows and looked at Cassie. She was asleep, or dozing, and he wondered how on earth he was going out with her. Messy hair tumbled over her face. She couldn't have looked more beautiful, and he lay there transfixed. He was right there, right next to her, and his arm could feel the soft, near imperceptible rises and falls of her chest, but he still didn't know what was going on inside her head, what exactly she thought of things, how exactly she saw herself. How she saw him. When he got close to her she always slipped away into the mist. Always turned away at the last moment.

She opened her eyes, green and soft, and stretched like a cat.

'What you looking at?'

'Nothing. Just trying to work you out. Riddle wrapped inside an enigma.'

She laughed almost derisively, and then her expression switched into sweetness and innocence. 'More chance of getting the theory of relativity than of getting me. Sorry, buster.'

He looked hurt.

'Don't worry, silly. It's not an insult. I just don't think you need to worry about it. I love you, you know. And anyway I don't understand you and I don't lose any sleep about it.' She smiled and stroked his cheek. 'Come on. Lie down. Chill.'

In the third year they didn't see as much of each other, as she lived out of college in a flat with some of her public-school friends and they both busied themselves with revision for their finals. Sometimes she asked Tom to house parties, invitations which he always found reasons not to accept as he found her friends quite intimidating – cocaine addicts dripping with privilege who would at best barely register and at worst baldly resent his presence. But they still shared tutorials, and Cassie spent a lot of time with him in college, occasionally accompanying Tom on visits to his mother.

A further complication was her parents, whom he found almost unbearably awkward. Her mother Lavinia at least talked to him, although as if he were an interesting curio rather than a realistic marriage prospect. Her father Jeremy, on the other hand, a successful QC as short of charm as he was long of wallet, acted as though Tom's sheer presence in a room with Cassie sullied his daughter's character. Still, Tom was unfailingly polite, and while he would occasionally, even often, make Lavinia laugh, he had no such luck with the old man, who was obviously desperate for Cassie to get her act together and ditch him at the first opportunity.

All this meant that throughout their final year, while Tom found himself falling more and more in love with her, the fear was growing within him that he would never be able to keep her, that she would slip from his grasp. But over that post-university, pre-army summer he had Cassie all to himself for four weeks.

And he loved Europe, being taken around all the great cities, churches and museums by Cassie, who seemed to know everything about everywhere they went. Tom had not been on many holidays and was initially embarrassed about his ignorance, but she laughed it off and took to her role as his guide and teacher with huge enthusiasm. Tom had never been happier, but sometimes at night when they were both drunk or when he looked at her during the day across a stuffy train he thought he could see something. What was it? Sadness? Coldness? Blithe indifference? But then she would look at him, remember herself and smile, blink sparkle into her eyes, and all his worries receded until the next time he caught the look.

Their travel plan was simple. Bouncing around cities and towns that took their fancy in guidebooks, they plotted a rough circle, going south through France into Switzerland, down into northern Italy, up to Austria and then beginning the route home from there. They stayed in dingy youth hostels and used the money they saved to go to the best restaurants in town. It worked like a dream.

One night, money nearly exhausted, they stayed in a hostel down a back street in Graz, with domestic arguments from nearby tenements and barking dogs a discordant lullaby as they tried to sleep. Tom, sweating in the late-summer air, lay in the dark watching a decrepit fan wheeze its way around above them. He heard her quietly crying.

'What's wrong, Cass?' he prodded unhopefully.

'Nothing,' she stonewalled.

Tom sighed, picked up his book and tried to read by the bright moonlight; he would wait this one out.

Suddenly she sprung up onto her knees. 'It's just . . . What are you doing, Tom?'

'Um . . .'

'I mean, look at you for fuck's sake.' Tears streamed down her cheeks, mixing with her mascara to form black streaks that clung to her cheeks in the pale darkness. 'You've just got one of the top firsts at Cambridge University and you could walk, I mean walk, into any job out there. You would be snapped up, tomorrow, by anyone, and instead you're joining the army. The army?'

'But I've always wanted to join the army.' Tom tried to take in what was happening. All he could think was that her father had put her up to this.

'Look, Tom, we've all heard about the fucking army. Army

this, army that. Well great, I'm sure there are some great guys in there, but look at you, Tom.' That was the second time she had said that, and he fought down his anger.

'What do you mean, look at me?'

'I mean just that, Tom: look at you. You've got a brain the size of a planet, friends who love you, a mother who's devoted to you, and you've got two arms and two legs, and you want to go and piss it all down the drain just to fulfil a childish fantasy.'

'It's not childish, Cassie,' he bleated.

Gaining momentum she went on. 'Oh shut up, Tom. Treat yourself as a grown-up for Christ's sake. What are you going to do in five years' time if, and that's a big if, you ever get through this Afghanistan stuff, probably with some kind of drink problem and an inability to engage with anyone who hasn't been in the sodding army, and that's assuming you've even got any legs to walk on. No one, Tom, is going to care about it because deep down they'll know that while you were dicking around they'll have got themselves set up for life.'

'I don't know if I want that life.' He suspected, deep down, that Cassie had a point.

'Yes, you want that life, Tom. Why are you going to waste it?'

The street lamp outside flickered and the fan shuddered from a power surge as Tom's throat went dry. *You know what — bugger it.* He decided to fight fire with fire.

'I'm not wasting my time. Yes, I could go and work for whatever twats those tossers at all the milk-round events fawn over. I could go and make friends with a calculator and a spreadsheet instead of real human beings. But I'd look at myself in ten years' time, Cass, with a massive, massive regret that I hadn't done the army. It's a young man's game; anyone can be a banker, anyone can hang out with a calculator whether they're seventeen or seventy. If I don't do this now, Cass, I'll never do it.' He stopped, knowing this was only going one way, what she was about to say. It was her only logical move. And he wouldn't have an answer.

'If you do this, you lose me.'

'Well Cass, I can't expect you to stand it. If you want to go, just go. I can't stop you.' With that, Tom realized that she would go; he'd lost her for ever. At least her parents would be pleased, he thought bitterly. He sighed. 'Come on, let's tidy up your face.' He rummaged in his rucksack for a T-shirt, crumpled it up and dabbed at her eyes. 'You look like one of the living dead.'

She giggled just for a moment but then hardened and pushed his hand away.

'We'll talk about this in the morning,' he said. 'We need to sleep on this.'

She lay down again, the argument dying as quickly as it had started. Tom never heard her stir the whole night; he just kept looking at the fan.

They didn't talk about it in the morning. For the next four days they limped back through Berlin, then Strasbourg, then Paris, more out of polite obligation to their original plan than any enthusiasm. Tom thought about suggesting a detour through the First World War battlefields but thought better of it. Probably not quite the time. Back in London they split at St Pancras, Tom to go home for a final week before Sandhurst and Cassie going on to a festival with some friends.

Waiting in the queue for her cab, Tom looked at her as she scribbled down his Sandhurst address. The late-afternoon sun bounced off high windows above them and lit up her hair. He knew that she'd probably only write him one letter at Sandhurst. He knew he'd never see her again.

She got into the taxi and kissed him on the cheek. 'Bye, Tommy. Take care, please take care.'

'I will, don't worry.' He felt completely alone.

'I'll write.'

'Please; it'll be such a boost.'

He leaned into the taxi and pressed twenty pounds into the driver's hand.

'Tom, don't be ridiculous . . .'

'No, I insist. I'm not going to be spending much in the next year or so, am I?'

He gently closed the door, smiled at her, turned and walked away. He didn't look back. Cassie watched through the rear window as the taxi pulled away, willing Tom to turn his head. He didn't. If he had, she would have seen him crying.

A week later Constance took Tom to start at Sandhurst. Her battered old Ford Focus heaved with the paraphernalia that he had been instructed to bring, from twenty wooden coat hangers to shoe-cleaning kit to an ironing board that was so large it could fit in the car only if Tom removed his headrest and almost crouched in the footwell. Leaving the house was a frenzy of nervous laughter with Zeppo trying to jump in the car with him, Tom fretting about not having all his kit and Constance worrying about whether she was wearing a smart enough dress.

Sam came to wish him goodbye.

'Well boy, I wish your old man was here for this. Best of luck.'

'Thanks, Sam. I hope it's not going to be too bad.'

Sam flashed his teeth in a throaty laugh. 'Oh, it'll be worse than anything you could possibly imagine. But then, just when you think you can't go on, you'll start to love it. You'll make friendships that you'll never lose. Oh, one thing. You could have bothered to get your hair cut.'

Tom's face went pale. 'Oh bollocks! Mum, we need to go to a hairdresser. Right now.' He felt his hair. 'Oh God, they're going to crucify me.'

In the car on the slog around the M25 it felt like he was off to live in Australia for the rest of his life. Tom's throat was dry, and the closer they got to Sandhurst the more monosyllabic and terse he became with Constance's eternal questions and worries. She kept glancing over at him, her eyes sad with losing her son and having an empty house again.

At Sandhurst Constance was ushered straight into tea with the commandant, the general who commanded the academy, while Tom unpacked the car. The boot had jammed shut, so he had to wrestle the ironing board out through a window. He was sweating in his suit and getting into an ever greater panic. As he trudged up the steps to Old College laden down like a pack animal, two colour sergeants, rampant in their service dress, death-stared him. They knew that while the parents were having tea they could torment their new prey with impunity.

'Fuck me, wha' the fuck is this? Fred fuckin' Karno's Army or wha'?'

'I give 'im five days before he runs away screaming.'

'Nah. Two, max. Ah Christ, just look at that hair. I'll bite it off for him.'

Tom finally got all his kit into his room and went to find Constance. They went outside together, passing the now silent vultures, and walked to the car in the afternoon sun. She kept finding excuses to touch him, straightening his tie or flicking bits of dust from his shoulder, and he felt himself welling up. After a strangling farewell hug he watched the car wheeze away, not even daring to imagine what a state Constance would be in that night at the house. What had he done? He tried to harden his heart and took a deep breath but found nothing in there. He waited till the car disappeared from sight, gave one final, unnoticed wave, turned and walked up the steps back past the vultures.

'Eh, wee man, why so fuckin' weepy? Eh Trev, ah think he's greeting.'

'Yeah well, Robbie, if I had a suit like that I'd cry.'

'Two days. Max.'

Tom turned to face them. Might as well be polite. 'Good afternoon, Colour Sergeants. Nice day for it.'

The Scottish one looked at him aghast. 'Eh son, speak when ya fuckin' spoken tae, ya lippy cunt. We were talking aboot ye, not tae ye. Now FUCK OFF!'

That night in Tom's platoon lines the same man, Colour Sergeant Robbie Laidlaw, the midwife of their army careers, introduced himself. He cut an immediately impressive figure. Hovering just above six feet, with crew-cut black hair splashed at the temples with grey, beneath his immaculate uniform both his arms were sleeved in Japanese-style tattoos. Broad Glasgow accent soft in conversation, when he raised his voice to admonish or to bark a drill command on a parade ground he seemed to rise to six foot six. He had crow's feet laughter lines at his eyes, and back in his battalion had already been marked out as a superstar. At battalion he got on well with the officers – he liked their self-deprecation and their keenness to help the young soldiers – but when he was posted to instruct at Sandhurst he swore not to show this fondness; the harder he treated these kids the more he would be helping them in the end. He was going to push these boys, and push them hard, but only so they didn't get themselves killed when they eventually got into the ulu. And certainly so they didn't get any of their lads killed.

Laidlaw filed them all into a classroom and made them sit in a circle and introduce themselves. When his time came, Tom mumbled. He was rather intimidated by the rest of the platoon, half of whom seemed already to know each other from private school or university. He hoped that his shaking legs wouldn't show under the cavernous green overalls. He noticed two of them catch each other's eyes and barely suppress smirks when he told them about Henry

VI Comprehensive. Cambridge got their attention though. Typical.

Always the same with public-school boys, Tom thought: their ears are trained to filter vast amounts of information and names and schools, ignore 95 per cent but prick up immediately a famous name or establishment is mentioned. This signifies to them that the speaker might be worth knowing. So Tom wasn't surprised when later that night, as they were all sorting out their kit in the way that Laidlaw had told them to, the smirkers put their heads round the door and introduced themselves.

'Hi, mate,' said one, tall, thickset, with raven-black hair and a rugby player's jaw, whose burly appearance was offset by his spectacles. 'Will Currer. You haven't got any spare coat hangers, have you?'

'Ignore him.' The other one, just shy of six foot and with an easy drawl, grinned. 'The stupid bastard didn't follow the instructions on the packing list.' He held out a hand with a signet ring on the little finger; clearly he had ignored Laidlaw's instruction to remove all jewellery. 'Clive Hynde-Smith. Right, now that Jock maniac's buggered off, I'm going outside to have a smoke. Want to join us, mate? Tom, isn't it?'

They chatted happily outside on the fire escape, Tom fielding their questions, perfectly friendly ones at first glance, but each concealing a probing dart designed to work out exactly how to take this Cambridge boy.

The next day they had their heads shaved, and in their boiler suits their homogenization was now complete; they had lost the final visible distinction between them. The routine quickly established itself. They slept on the floor so that they didn't crumple their beds for the 4 a.m. inspection. When they woke they would parade in the corridor, sing the national anthem, do forty press-ups and then drink a litre of water without drawing breath. Someone always then vomited. They would then go back into their rooms and crawl all over the floor with Sellotape wrapped around their hands to remove any dust before Laidlaw inspected. This he did wearing white gloves, and when he wiped something, if the glove came away with dust on it he would calmly tell the occupant to trash his room.

'What do you mean, trash my room, Colour Sergeant?' Tom asked on his first inspection, instantly regretting doing so.

'I mean turn yer bed upside doon and rip yer clothes off the shelves so yous learn how to fucking tidy it properly, yous fucking twat. Here ye go, I'll start yous off,' Laidlaw screamed as he chucked Tom's immaculate drill boots out of the window into a patch of mud. He watched on as Tom then dutifully turned his bed upside down and pulled out his drawers and emptied them on the floor.

They were exhausted. They would sleep standing up or sometimes even as they marched. And they marched everywhere in a group and never, ever by themselves. They ate, drank, pissed, crawled through mud, breathed each other's breath and ironed their clothes till 2 a.m. together. This lasted for days. Tom would wake at 3.45 just to lie in silence for the precious few minutes of the day he would have to himself and despair. Maybe Cassie had been right.

Slowly though, all the hardship began to fade away. Knowing grins and in-jokes, shared torture and common slang became their glue, and as they saw each other pushed to the brink of mental and physical collapse, so all barriers crumbled. Each of them was at some point laid bare in front of everyone else, bare to their souls and buttocks. They could hide nothing from anyone, and Tom realized that he knew these men better after mere weeks than he did most of his university cohort after three years. They would bicker, laugh and chatter like a tribe of gorillas picking nits out of each other's hair. They became very fit, developed extraordinary stamina and could sleep within five seconds of being told to do so.

Cassie's letter, when it came, was as bloodless as Tom had expected it to be. He found it in his pigeonhole after the platoon got back from a ten-mile march, and while the rest of them showered and fought over the washing machines Tom sat on his bed and stared at the envelope. He sniffed to see if there was any perfume on it. None. Resignedly he started to read. It was nothing he hadn't already heard tens of times before in his idle faraway speculations. She hoped he was well, that he was being treated nicely and had made lots of friends. It was as though she was writing to someone in prison. She was really enjoying her new job at a hedge fund in London. Tom didn't even know what a hedge fund was. She had loved Europe and all the time at Cambridge but reckoned it would be best for them to move away from each other, at least for the moment; her new job might take her to New York. Who could say? She'd no doubt see Tom again, but with travel and the rest, who knew when?

Tom read it without a flicker, walked out of his room and pinned it to the noticeboard, already half full, that Laidlaw had put up for such letters.

As the months went on and the cadets learned more, Sandhurst became less like a penal institute and increasingly like a dressing room before a boxing match. They were being primed and honed for their soldiers and to get on the ground. Every lecture on leadership banged this home to Tom, every range session or final assault of a company attack came with the exhortation, 'Come on, Mr Chamberlain. That cunt's just killed your fucking mate! Shoot him where it hurts, in his fucking Taliban FACE! In the FACE! In the FACE!'

Their generation had, amazingly, been picked to go and fight in the hardest place, in the hardest fight since Korea. And in Afghan, Helmand. And in Helmand, they had to be in the worst area, the most kinetic base. The most contacts. All the cards had to fall exactly in to place.

Almost a year later, in April, Tom and Clive walked into the officers' mess of their regiment, the King's Dragoons, based in the outskirts of Aldershot. Filthy, with matted hair and sallow cheeks, they had just finished a three-week exercise on Salisbury Plain. After Sandhurst they had been thrown straight into the exercise with a squadron preparing for a tour of Afghanistan in September. The learning curve had seemed almost beyond the vertical, and they had never felt so tested. Clive went up to have a shower, and Tom went into the anteroom, took a can of lemonade from the fridge and sprawled over a sofa. He put his head back and dozed.

The pair of them had arrived late to the exercise, fresh from their troop leaders' course, and had hung around an empty Westdown Camp on the edge of Salisbury Plain for a whole afternoon, kicking their heels and wondering if anyone in the regiment knew they were even there. They sat down on a grassy bank next to their bergens and spent the afternoon chatting, reading or just in companionable silence, enjoying the springtime sun. They were pretty much joined at the hip now, each eternally amused by the other's character and linked by the invisible umbilical that Sandhurst had created between them. Where Tom was shy, terrified of being embarrassed and with a quick dry wit, Clive was brash, bumptious and happy-go-lucky. They knew each other now better than they could ever have wished to know anyone, and loved winding each other up and poking at each other's flaws, while turning swiftly protective of the other and rounding on a critic or a threat. The afternoon passed in lazy if faintly nervous anticipation of what they would face when they met their soldiers for the first time.

A rickety Land Rover pulled up next to them in the early evening and a bored voice asked them, 'All right, sirs? If you're the new officers I've got to drive you to C Squadron. Jump in.'

Twenty minutes later their sullen driver, one Trooper Livesey, pulled to a halt and pointed up a low hill towards a dark wood. 'There you go, sirs,' he said disdainfully. 'C Squadron. Middle of the wood.' They got out, and he drove off, leaving them bewildered and struggling to see in the drizzly gloom.

Labouring with their bergens, tramping through brambles and making a din of snapped branches and stumbling, eventually they were challenged by a sentry and led into the squadron harbour. They were immediately impressed. A squadron's worth of Scimitar reconnaissance vehicles had been skilfully camouflaged, and the only noises were the quiet snores of those asleep in tents put up at the sides of the wagons and the drivers' muffled and deliberate tinkering with the tracks and running gear of their wagons. Tom couldn't make out anyone in detail, but his eyes, now attuned to the dark, could register blurred shadows moving softly around, breaking no twigs or branches – unlike his and Clive's clumsy steps.

The sentry led them to the middle of the harbour and pointed to the dark bulk of a tent attached to a Sultan command vehicle. 'There you go, sirs. I don't know if they're expecting you,' he whispered.

Pulling back the flaps of the tent, dingy with the rain and years-old damp, they found inside an organized chaos of map boards, radios sending out clipped instructions mingled with bursts of static, mugs of steaming coffee, one man sleeping on the floor and three others huddled around the board, the steam from the mugs condensing against the glass of their red-filtered head torches. They looked up at the newcomers with irritation.

'Well well, look what the cat dragged in. You must be Clive and Tom.'

The tallest of the three, swept-back hair and looking immaculate, even elegant, in the less than chic surroundings, grinned and thrust out his hand. 'Chris Du Boulay, squadron leader. Just call me Frenchie. The commanding officer said you'd be coming over. Afraid we haven't got much of a welcome for you. You're in the lions' den here – all the head honchos. This is the 2ic, Jason Gates.'

A burly figure verging on the overweight crouched over the map board threw them a glance with tired eyes and grunted before turning back to plot symbols on the map.

'Don't worry about him. He's got a raging chest infection. He wouldn't stand up if you were Kelly Brook and Carmen Electra. And this –' Frenchie indicated the other man '– is Sergeant Major Brennan.' Completely bald and very short, three gold teeth glinted at the back of Brennan's mouth.

He growled rather than said, 'All right, sirs. Welcome to the squadron.' He looked them up and down before turning back to the map with a shrug, which Tom wasn't sure was a sign of acceptance or rejection.

Frenchie continued, seemingly finding the others' visible lack of interest rather amusing: 'Sorry, guys. If you were expecting a big welcome speech and pep talk, or ritual debagging or whatever, you're not going to get it. My plan for you two is simple – in at the deep end. Just as long as you don't kill anyone on this exercise, I'm happy for you to make your own mistakes, and I, Jason, the SSM and your threebars will sort you out. It's the only way you'll learn. Tom, you've got

3 Troop, with Sergeant Trueman. Don't piss him off. Clive –
4 Troop, Sergeant Leighton. He's new as well as you, just
picked up from full screw, so you can both fumble around
together. Expect me to bite your heads off at regular intervals
over the next few days, but don't worry, it won't be personal.
At least,' he paused, 'not yet. Right, you might as well go and
meet your troops, and the other troop leaders as well. Two
Troop is Scott Lanyon and One's Henry Bell. Learn from
them. If you don't, I'll sack you, and no tour in September.
There's plenty of others who can fill your spaces. So, no
pressure then, eh? As for what I expect from you, just be
damn good at your jobs. I don't really give a monkey's whether
you're funny, kind, clever, played rugby for England, wear a
dress and call yourself Susan at the weekend or what name
you call the loo, just be hot stuff at soldiering. Capiche?'

They nodded simultaneously, eyes on stalks.

'Right, see you back here in two hours for orders.' They
turned to leave before Frenchie bade them look back in.
'And fellas, cheer up! It ain't that bad!' They smiled wanly
and headed out into the pitch-black forest to find their
troops.

That was their introduction to the tribe, as Frenchie called
C Squadron. Tight-knit, rife with impenetrable slang and
in-jokes, its soldiers took themselves not very seriously at all
and their jobs very seriously indeed. They looked down with
disdain not just on the rest of the army, but the rest of the
regiment as well.

The sense of loyalty to the squadron was tangible, and
some of the boys had a C tattooed in Gothic script on a
shoulder blade. It wasn't unknown for soldiers in C to turn
down promotion if it meant having to leave to join A or B
Squadrons. Nothing gave them more pleasure than putting
one over A or B. And they all loved soldiering. The better

you were at soldiering, the slicker your skills and drills, the higher you were in the social hierarchy of the squadron. Experience filtered down all the way from Brennan, a veteran of the first Gulf War. He and the SQMS, Staff Sergeant Grant, had been in the same squadron together as troopers in that war. Beneath them were the sergeants, all with their eyes on Brennan's job, and all competing to control the mood of the boys.

But if anyone was the C Squadron archetype, whose mood was both the bellwether and the creator of the squadron's state of morale, it was Martin 'Freddie' Trueman, Tom's sergeant. Middle-height with a friendly round face and a squashed nose, mousey brown curly hair, and thirty years old to Tom's twenty-four, he was the beating heart of the squadron. He knew it, Frenchie knew it, Brennan knew it and all the boys knew it. Nothing on tour ever happened without his involvement.

Ever since Bosnia, right out of depot and from a broken childhood of serial truancy before that, wherever he went, action followed in the remarkable way that it tends to with certain soldiers. But unlike those soldiers who are catalysts for action and sometimes get those around them hurt, Trueman was lucky. When things happened to him and around him everyone else seemed to get out OK as well, and he was worshipped for it. He had his faults: he was inclined to be a barrack-room lawyer; his innate grasp of the immediate tactical battle sometimes obscured an appreciation of the wider picture beyond that firefight; he could be a hothead who let his emotions get the better of him and whose moral compass was as sensitive as his fists were willing to right any perceived wrong. But Frenchie, who had had him as his driver when he was a troop leader in Bosnia, seemed to adore him.

Luckily, Tom and Trueman got off to a good start after

Tom's first set of orders, where Trueman was impressed by Tom's robust, no-task-too-hard attitude.

Frenchie himself, a rising star among his peers and whose easy manner hid a razor-sharp ambition, skilfully harnessed the boys' exuberance to produce an excellent performance on the exercise. Tom and Clive had, after predictable frictions at the start, come through their test with flying colours and had each gained if not yet unconditional love from their soldiers then certainly a benign acceptance.

At the end of the exercise the squadron was washing down the vehicles on the dustbowl in Westdown, desperate to go home for the weekend, when Frenchie shouted over to Tom and Clive: 'Right, you two. Laurel and Hardy. Over here.'

They detached themselves, sensing trouble, and as they approached Frenchie noticed their nervousness. Somehow managing to look as well turned out as if he had been in an office for three weeks and not among the drizzle, dust, mud and no showers of Salisbury Plain, he relaxed them immediately.

'Don't worry, maniacs. Not a bollocking. I just want to say well done. Top effort for the last few weeks. And look, you've made mistakes which you're never going to make again. Result, eh? You might have thought that when you pitched up in the tent at the start of the exercise that we were treating you callously. Well, we were. Tough love. View it as if we were a family of gannets on some massive cliff. The only way you're going to learn to fly is by me kicking you out of the nest. If you're good, you'll figure out how to fly before you hit the bottom. If not, splat! Anyway, you two gannets managed to fly. Congratulations.'

And so as Tom lay on a mess sofa later that evening, looking forward to a long bath before supper, all seemed fine when Jason came in. 'Ah, one of the two amigos. Well done, fella – good effort on the plain. I'd better go see the wife and try to rescue our shambles of a marriage. I tell you, never get married in this job. More trouble than it's worth. See you tomorrow. These were in your pigeonhole by the way, Tom. Blueys from Afghan.'

Tom sat up straight and caught the two letters that Jason threw at him. 'Thanks,' he said absently as he saw that they were from Will Currer.

Tom went up to his room with the letters, like a small boy carrying unopened presents. He sat on his bed and opened the first one, wondering how his friend was. Tom had seen him, but only for a brief drink, a couple of weekends before Will was due to go out, back in February.

Ridiculously hot evening
The Bastion Naafi
28th March
Mate,

Here we go! The last few days have been mental. I arrived at Bastion yesterday, and have been hanging round doing RSOI, which is a barrel of laughs; ranges, IED lessons and med lessons teaching us all how to treat someone who has just had their head blown off. You know how I told you I was going to be a spare bod at Battle Group HQ, stagging on the radios, making the brews, etc? Well all that has, surprise surprise, been thrown out of the window. One of the platoon commanders, Jimmy Dalton, fell off the back of a Chinook last week and smashed in his knee, and is being lifted back to the UK tomorrow. I'm taking over his platoon. Oh lucky me. I went to see him in the hospital (which, by the way, is grim. Lads in clip all over the place.) So I went to banter Jimmy and pick his brains. The platoon's tour has been pretty quiet, but there was a Cat B the day before he got injured. He was gutted to be out of action, but he was really reassuring about the platoon. Apparently they're awesome, and the sergeant, Adams, is a legend. I think my drama will be that he'll just treat me as I am – i.e. a total crow. Quite how I'm going to win him over is a mystery to me. Help!

I can't believe it's happening like this, ridiculously quickly. You suddenly realize here what we've let ourselves in for. The dust, the heat and the noise of the helicopters coming in bringing in casualties are a million miles from Sandhurst. Big boys' rules, and, not going to lie, I'm not quite sure I'm big enough for this game. Obviously don't tell any chicks that! Better go now to the scoff tent (scoff's all right out here by the way) before a lesson tonight about more med stuff, this time probably about how to stuff your own intestines back into your stomach cavity. Take care, mate; send me lots of blueys and parcels, and sneak over some grog, please! I reckon I'm going to need that. Having said that, knowing how slow the post is you'll probably get this only after you've visited me in Selly Oak after I've been minced.

Gotta go; no rest for the wicked, unlike you war dodgers back home . . .

Knew that would wind you up!
Will

Tom smiled as he thought of Will and wished that he could be out with him. He picked up the second bluey, written in pencil this time in spindlier handwriting and grimy with dust. He fingered it open, taking care not to allow the hastily licked brittle gum to tear too much of the body of the letter.

Mazeer
28th April
Dear Tom,

Wish I could put a brave face on this, but I've landed in the middle of a nightmare. Please can you not say too much of the following to

46

anyone. You are the only person I can write to with any degree of honesty. I certainly can't write anything approaching the truth to Mum and Dad or any civi mates, especially girls. You should see my letters to them! They are masterclasses of euphemism. I say things like 'things have got a bit tasty out here' when you know that means 'things are beltingly horrific out here'; 'the boys' morale is sky high' meaning 'well at least they're not slitting their wrists yet'; 'the Afghan Army are quite an amusing bunch', for which read, 'They are utter fucking retards, and quite how we're going to be able to trust this bunch of muppets when we eventually leave them to their own devices is beyond me.' I just need someone, anyone, to unload upon; I hope you understand.

We (3 Platoon) are based in PB Mazeer, a compound about the size of two tennis courts about 200m from the FLET. We are in contact every day; whenever we get out the gate, there are IEDs all over the shop. Sergeant Adams was killed on my fourth day out here – IED. He just evaporated in front of me. Don't want to talk about it any more than that. Since him we've lost a single amputee, Mercer (left leg), and one of the Fijians, Tirinaqakalaika (T for short), got shot in the foot. T thought the whole thing was hilarious, and couldn't stop laughing throughout his casevac. A doc told me that it would have been the adrenaline that made him do that. I'm not so sure; he was pretty wired to the moon in the first place.

Every step you take is horrendous, and your heart leaps the moment you put your foot down and don't find yourself ripped to shreds. The boys have got some banter – 'Try the Mazeer diet; tread on an IED and lose half your body weight in half a second.' It's just a hornets' nest. When we go out the gate now we're fired upon before we've even reached 200m. No civilians want to talk to us; our relations with the community are non-existent. We must look like aliens to them.

Mazeer itself is a womb, the only place where reason and order exist. Outside is just shit Afghan, some dumb failed state whose only

47

concessions to modernity are the motorbike and the machine gun. I'll leave it for you to find out for yourself when you get here what 'manlove Thursday' means. In for a treat there, pal.

I feel sick every moment thinking about going out again. When you get back in after being out you get this amazing elation for about half an hour, but then the sickness starts to build again, and by the time of the next patrol you want to vom your guts out. Corporal Thomas (my acting sergeant since Adams died) and I have to go down the line of the boys as they're checking kit before we go out. Some of them are crying, not bawling just weeping gently but still steadfast; others are just pumped to the max, bouncing their heads up and down like they're listening to trance music, just amped about getting rounds down. Those are the ones I'm most worried about; how they're going to cope with being back home is beyond me. They just LOVE the violence. Others are being sick from fear or dry-retching. The other day Thommo and I had to drag one boy, Croxley, out the gate and kick him down the road for 10 metres as he sobbed and wailed just to get him going. But when the contact started, he was in the zone; amazing, loving it, drills immaculate, calm as you like. It was extraordinary. And they're so young as well. For some of them this is their first time abroad. I've promised them that abroad's not usually this bad.

We have four months left out here. I get R & R with only four weeks to go before the end of tour. Please can I see you for a drink when I'm back? The thing is I just can't see how it's going to happen without me getting hit. I don't want to sound like O'Neill in Platoon (!) but I just have a really bad feeling about this whole thing.

I caught my reflection yesterday in some broken glass in a window frame. Three weeks ago I couldn't have looked more crow. Now I'm allyer than Andy McNab. Op Bronze is well underway, my kit is as dusty as you like, even my pipe-cleaner arms are turning into guns of steel because of the pull-up competition we have every night, and I've got a bit of a beard coming on because there's no water to shave with.

I put my foot down a bit though and have a rule that we shave every five days and always when someone comes to visit, i.e. the brigade commander, who's coming tomorrow. Apparently he's a stickler. Get the razors out, lads!

I don't know how this is all going to appear when I look back on it. Can you keep this letter so at least I have some kind of document to remind me. I'll try to write again soon mate, better go and radio the OC and give him the 1600 sitrep. Looking forward to a pint or thirty, mucker,

Will

PS. Make that forty.

The letter drooped in Tom's hand. Will had changed completely, irreversibly, and he wondered how he would be able to talk to him when he saw him next. Part of Tom was appalled that he was thinking of Will with a degree of envy – even if only half of what he was saying was true, then he must be well on the path to some kind of decoration. To be put in that situation only days after finishing his training and not only surviving but actually seeming to be the only thing holding his platoon together virtually guaranteed some sort of medal at the end of tour, a Mention in Dispatches at the very least. Tom felt appalled that he had been so indoctrinated to feel this envy. What was this universe he had entered? What cult had he joined, where proportion could be so distorted that you looked upon suffering with envy and guilt that it was not you on the firing line? He looked out the window, eyes lost in the dark blue as the afternoon faded into dark.

All the summer C Squadron were bounced around the country on various exercises preparing them for tour. In June they were in Northumberland, firing their Scimitars in support of a series of huge infantry attacks down a valley in the training area at Otterburn, safety margins squeezed to the minimum to inoculate young soldiers to friendly rounds cracking metres over their heads. The weather was glorious, and between battle runs Tom and Sergeant Trueman would park the four wagons up on the crest of a hill and let the lads sunbathe. When they got really bored, Trueman introduced them to one of his favourite pastimes, a left-handed throwing competition. He found this hilarious, seeing all the boys attempt to throw stones and rocks while looking like utter incompetents. Tom took part bashfully.

Tom found that on exercise he got to know the soldiers far better than he ever did in camp. He discovered he was harder and more remote from them than he thought he would be, never using a nickname and hating letting himself be seen to be wrong. The boys didn't really mind this apparent stand-offishness, as Trueman found out by accident one evening. He discovered a half-finished letter Tom was writing to the father of Lance Corporal Miller, in which he introduced himself as his troop leader and said that if Mr Miller needed any information or reassurance about how his son was doing in training or when they got to Afghanistan he should write. Trueman asked around and found that two of them had already had their parents receive such a letter from Tom. Trueman was amazed; he had never had an officer do this before. He thought Tom a bit square if very professional, but knowing about the letters started to forge a bond to him that no one would break.

In the last week of July the squadron was in the west of Wales on Castlemartin Ranges, their last chance before deployment to fire the Scimitars and practise vehicle movement. In between range runs they practised barma drills over

and over again, and got lessons from the medics in tourniquet application, hemcon bandages, first field dressings and
morphine use, until they could do everything in the dark with
Trueman firing full magazines of blank rounds next to them.
Tom shuddered at the tourniquets, both fascinated and
repelled by them. A black strap with thick Velcro on it, it was
put around an injured limb or a stump as tightly as possible,
and a plastic rod turned to squeeze it so much that blood
would, like water from a tap, stop flowing out of it. There
was nothing clever or delicate about it, as it treated the human
body like a plumbing system, not as a repository of thoughts
and hopes.

Trueman and Tom endlessly made the boys practise filling
out the MIST and 9-liner cards that they would use in
Afghanistan to organize casualty evacuations. After the first
session Trueman said, 'Thing is, fellas, I hate practising casevac. It's like you're accepting that it's going to happen to one
of us out there. I agree, it's not fucking nice. But if we don't
get this now, if something does fucking happen out there,
then the lad who may just have survived with a bad injury
will fucking die. I mean it. I've seen it in other regiments on
Herrick 6. If some dumb cunt sends the wrong information
up the net or doesn't do it rapid-like, then they send the
wrong heli which can't land at the HLS, or they don't bring
the correct kind of stretcher or whatever. So that's why we're
rubbing your fucking noses in it now, yeah?'

At first the boys were awful on the radio, completely
unaccustomed because of their junior role in the troop to
talking on one accurately and concisely, but by the end of the
week they were delivering multiple casualty reports with ease.
Tom led the boys through the lessons, watching in wonder at
the sick reality they were entering as Davenport, an

eighteen-year-old who still only had to shave once a week, calmly rattled off a double casualty report as though it was the most normal thing in the world.

'Hello, Zero, this is Three Zero. Stand by for MIST for two casualties. Casualty 1. Mike – explosion. India – double amputation. Right leg amputated above the knee, left leg at the ankle. Fragmentation to genitals and abdomen. Sierra – breathing 12. Pulse 40. Catastrophic bleed. Tango – morphine, two tourniquets and hemcon applied. Roger so far over? Casualty 2. Mike – gunshot wound. India – shot in the knee, femur broken. Sierra – breathing 12. Pulse 80. Some blood loss. Casualty going into shock. Tango – morphine, tourniquet and FFD applied. Over.'

Tom patted him on the back. 'Good job, Mr Davenport. Let's just hope that you don't have to do that in theatre, eh? Who's next? Ellis, your turn. Three casualties from an RPG: one guy's blinded, one guy's hit in the gut and the other's lost his arm. 9-liner and the MIST. Three minutes to prepare and then go.'

After the final attack of the exercise, an apocalyptic array of destruction rained down upon targets for two hours by Scimitars, Javelins, mortars, artillery and air strikes, the squadron parked up their wagons in neat rows. Tom jumped out of his wagon, climbed onto Trueman's and grinned at him. 'Well, Sergeant, what do you reckon? With a performance like that there won't be any Taliban left, will there?'

Trueman scrunched up his nose and looked out down the range, where smoke still rose from destroyed targets and fresh craters. 'I dunno, sir. This is good for the lads' morale this, but it's a turkey shoot. No twats shooting back. No IEDs. This exercise has been good, don't get me wrong, but it ain't reality out there. Promise you.' He saw Tom looking crestfallen, his cheerfulness dented, and tried to make him feel better. 'I see what you mean, sir – it's good crack – but I'm just saying so you know, yeah?'

Tom pursed his lips and nodded. 'Got it, Sergeant. Sometimes I run away with myself.'

'That's OK, sir; that's what you're meant to do. And I'm meant to rein it in. And then one day it'll be vice versa.'

On the bus back from Castlemartin the officers sat at the front reading and trying to snatch some sleep in anticipation of the night out in London they had planned. In the back were the likely lads, led by Trueman in his customary place, the middle seat of the rear row, who did impressions of every member of the squadron in turn, officers included. They were very funny, and Tom couldn't help laughing as Trueman gently poked fun at his own staid manner. All the bus was roaring, but it wasn't mean laughter, and Tom was almost sad when Trueman switched to Clive, whose matey manner with his soldiers was completely the opposite to his. Clive and his sergeant, Leighton, even went to the pub together – something Tom would never dream of doing – and he never seemed to use rank when talking with his lads, immediately giving them all new nicknames when he took over the troop. He was content just to be addressed as the informal 'boss', where Tom was never anything other than 'Mr Chamberlain' or 'sir'.

Tom's phone buzzed. He was delighted to see a text from Will.

'Guess who's back in town?! Got back to Brize a couple of days ago, now very much in the smoke, keen for a session tonight. Nuclear alcoholocaust. Keen? House party Wandsworth Bridge Road 9ish. Come along! Babes coming too. Get involved. Callsign Weakdrinker!'

Tom tapped back, 'Oi oi matey, the wanderer returns! Defo bevvies tonight; we're doing a captains and subalterns' session in Ken High St so I'm fixed there until 2200.'

Will replied in an instant: 'Ace fella; buzz me then and we'll meet up.' Another text then followed from him, this one suddenly less happy. 'Thanks for this, mate ... really need to speak to someone about it all. So weird to be back. Am properly darked out by this city for some reason.'

Tom frowned, put his phone back in his pocket and went to sleep.

Back in the mess they met the A and B Squadron subalterns, who had been back for hours and were champing to get into town. The de facto kingpin among the young officers, rakish, beanpole-thin Operations Officer Jules 'The Menace' Dennis, shouted at them, 'Come on, slackers; minibus leaves half an hour ago; get upstairs, get your poof juice on, and let's offski, schnell machen. Go!'

They needed no further encouragement, and soon they were on their way, twelve of them crammed into a minibus, chanting songs as they whizzed up the A3 into London, swigging cold lagers and laughing and singing.

They gathered in their usual pub, just off Kensington High Street. They arrived at eight, dived straight into pints of beer, and by nine they were tackling shots of vodka and tequila. Half an hour later three of them had already been kicked out, another two were about to be, and Jules Dennis was lying beneath the bar as Clive poured a bottle of sambuca with unerring aim into his mouth. Tom, who had tried with only partial success to keep a grasp on his senses, decided to make his escape by pretending to go to the loo and then slipping out a back door. As he left a hand grabbed his collar. It was Jules.

'Where you going?'

'Just for a piss.'

'Bollocks. You're pulling Op Cat Flap, aren't you?'

It was no use lying. 'Um, yes. I've got a mucker from my platoon at Sandhurst who's back on R & R tonight, and I need to see him.'

Jules' tone changed. 'Why didn't you say? Of course you've got to see him. Before you go though, I just want to say one thing.'

Here it comes, Tom thought. Jules, who had already done two tours, one of Iraq and one of Afghanistan, both of which had seen heavy fighting, and who now as operations officer was the commanding officer's right-hand man for the tour, was famous in the mess for telling new officers exactly what he thought of them.

'Before I get too pissed, although to be honest I think I passed that mark some time ago, I just want to say that you're doing an awesome job.'

'Thanks, Jules. Er . . . that's very kind of you.'

'Shut up, crow. It's not about being kind; it's about being truthful.' He dragged Tom closer and continued, conspiratorially, 'Trueman was in my troop in Iraq. He tells me everything. And he likes you. Which is impressive because he's one of the hardest NCOs to win over in the whole regiment. He says he's never met someone who cares more for the lads. Good job. Keep it up, Tom.'

They were interrupted as a group of men swarmed past them on their way into the pub and they had to step back. Jules muttered under his breath, 'Tossers.'

The two at the rear of the phalanx stopped, surprised and aggressive.

'What's that, mate?' one said, burly and wearing a Harlequins rugby shirt.

Jules took a long drag on his cigarette and said, with innocence writ across his face, 'Nothing, pal. Nothing. Sorry, just wondering, are you guys in the army?'

The man sneered at him. 'Are we fuck, mate. Bollocks to that.'

Jules nodded and said, again innocuous, 'Oh. Sorry. Just wondering, that's all. My mistake.'

The man, puzzled, went inside the pub to join his friends, and Tom looked at Jules quizzically. 'What was that all about?'

Jules smiled. 'Nothing really. Just wanted to stir some trouble, gauge what those blokes were like. And there you have it: most people in this country, most blokes anyway, think we're mugs. He said it himself.'

Tom left Jules, went to the house party and was let in by a horsey-looking girl wearing a hairband. Tom hadn't seen anyone with a hairband since he was eight. Someone thrust a thimbleful of lukewarm wine into his hand. He mumbled his thanks, realizing that he was by quite some distance the drunkest in the room. He talked to a few people. Everyone seemed to work in banking or for hedge funds. *For fuck's sake*, Tom thought, *can everyone just stop working for hedge funds?* He'd now asked about twenty people what they were, and even he, a relatively sentient being, hadn't been able to understand the explanations.

At least, he thought he was the drunkest until Will came staggering in, having just been sick. The raw and beaming smile that tore over Will's face was glorious, and he ran forward, and he and Tom hugged each other. Tom could smell the vomit on his breath, but he still clung to his friend with fingers driven into his back. He couldn't believe how much he had missed him. The rest of the room looked on nervously. Tom quickly felt self-conscious, and he and Will went out to the garden to smoke and escape the oppressive sitting room.

'I know what you're thinking,' said Will as he lit a cigarette. The small flame threw a glow over his dopey eyes. '*Why the hell has Will dragged me along to a party that makes chess club look like Ibiza?'* He grinned.

'No, mate, not at all . . . '

'Don't worry, they're all right.' He flicked ash into a plant pot. 'They're some maniacs I went on a cookery course with in my gap year. They always have this annual reunion. They were dull then and they're duller now, and normally I fuck it off, but the thing is there are these two absolute babes who are meant to turn up later on, and I'm just thinking that if civvies lap up Afghan as much as they say they do, with this Help for Heroes malarkey and everyone wearing some kind of military wristband, then I can't fail to slay. What do you reckon?'

'What about the others?'

'You kidding? Did you look at any of them? I wouldn't touch them with a telescopic barge pole. Not even Afghan makes you that desperate.'

They both laughed – callous, self-righteous, arrogant.

'All right, mate,' Will continued, 'before we get stuck in I've got to give it to you on Afghan.'

His mask dropped, his tone changed, he lost the sparkle in his eyes and he fixed Tom with them. He started to speak as though he was talking not to his friend but to one of his soldiers. He was quite violent in his manner, and he had small tears in his eyes. He unloaded on Tom, telling him for almost twenty minutes what had happened to him, smoking cigarette after cigarette, taking long, urgent gasps. When he had to light another, if he couldn't work the lighter at the first or second attempt, he clicked his teeth and swore under his breath. It was horrible. The letters had merely been the start of it. Tom listened as he went on, horrified. Then, hearing the hubbub from the sitting room start to move through to the kitchen and threaten to come out and disturb them, Will

57

wound up his diatribe almost as quickly as he had begun it, hurrying out his words.

'Mate, I can't tell you how bad it is. It's minging out there. Just make sure your lads are as prepped as possible before they get out. If your drills aren't 100 per cent up to scratch, lads will die. They have to be all over it. There's no room for fuck-ups, no room. One mistake, one slack drill, boom.'

The door to the garden opened, and a handful of guests poured out. Will put his mask back on, stubbed out his final cigarette and turned to hug one of the girls.

After half an hour the party started to fill up, the music got louder and, it seemed to Tom, the guests got a bit edgier. Back inside, Will liberated a bottle of vodka from somewhere and they tackled it; they were only interrupted by the arrival, Tom was amazed to see, of the same man in the Harlequins shirt who Jules had confronted outside the pub earlier. He didn't recognize Tom. Evidently he was also one of Will's gap-year cookery gang. Will greeted him with no particular enthusiasm and they were forced to talk to him, or rather listen to him, trapped in a corner by his boorishness. Tom got restless. Who the hell was this bloke? As if he had heard him, the man thrust out his hand. 'Sorry, chap. Didn't say hello. Jonty Forbes.' Tom winced. He hated being called chap. He squirmed his hand forward and had it crushed by his new acquaintance.

Jonty changed tack: 'What say we get this party going, amigos? Your nostrils as hungry as mine?'

Tom watched as Jonty grabbed a fold-out table, wrestled with it and finally succeeded in erecting it with an undignified grunt of triumph. Drawing up a stool he cut some cocaine into lines using a credit card, ostentatiously wetting his forefinger, dabbing it on the powder and then rubbing it onto his gums. Will was encouraging him: 'Wow, thanks, mate. This is really kind of you. Is it good?'

'Good? The best, pal!' Jonty looked at his deftly drawn lines with pride.

Will egged him on: 'Go on, Jonty, we're in. Put some more out. I'm good for the cash.' Delighted, Jonty emptied out a packet to form a little mountain of white powder on the table. Out of his wallet came a twenty-pound note, which he rolled into a tube.

'Right, who's first?'

'No, after you,' said Will.

'OK. Get your skis out, lads, because here comes a blizzard!' announced Jonty as first one, then two lines disappeared up his nose, reminding Tom of films about aliens coming to earth and beaming up unsuspecting humans. Manfully, Jonty was about to tackle the third line when out of nowhere Will kicked the table away, seized him by the throat, lifted him up and slammed him back against the wall.

'You twat! Do you have no idea that your fucking drug money goes back to fund the same cunts who blow up my soldiers?' he screamed at him, eyes blazing with unblinking hatred, mad in his skull. He looked to Tom as though he thought he was back in Helmand in a firefight with the Taliban, in a one-track mania to kill. Jonty's own eyes bulged out of his sockets, his eyelids unable to close around them. Will drew his head back as if to butt his quivering victim, and Tom winced in anticipation, but then he stopped, blinked and said quietly, in a low snarl of contempt, 'I'd headbutt you if it wasn't going to kill you. You make me sick, you piece of shit.'

He threw Jonty to the floor, where he choked and spluttered, his face pasty with dribble and cocaine. Will looked around him and calmly addressed the cowed crowd: 'Sorry, everyone. I think I've ruined this party. Oh well. Come and visit me when I'm in Selly Oak lying in bed with no legs. Or come to my funeral and pretend that you were my best mate. Enjoy your spreadsheets and calculators. I'm going.'

As Will turned away, the hapless Jonty, with a speed that belied his girth, leapt to his feet and charged at him. As if on autopilot Tom stepped over the fallen table, drew his fist back, threw it forward and smashed him back to the floor again. 'And stay down, prick,' he snarled, amazed at how infectious Will's anger was. He turned to leave.

Will clapped him on the back, and as they pushed through the onlookers Tom stopped dead, rooted in front of a girl who had arrived just in time for the fight. She was still wearing her coat, and her hair was wet with a rain shower that had caught her on the way to the party.

'Tom?'

'Cassie.'

Why now? Why had she come back into his life at this moment, when his brain had at last completely expelled everything about her from his memory? A sudden love for her bounced itself to the front of Tom's head before a strange hatred hit him too. She had always dismissed the army. He remembered her loathsome father. He saw Will in the street through the open front door, standing in the rain. He should be looking after him, but he wanted to be with her.

He heard himself say to her, polite and distant, 'I'm sorry, Cassie; I must go with my friend. Hopefully see you soon.' He left her and walked out the door. At the end of the road beside a bus stop Will collapsed in tears.

Tom knelt and hugged his friend. 'All right, mate, all right. Everything's going to be all right. Everything's going to be all right,' he whispered over and again as Will sobbed into his shoulder. Tom looked back up the street towards the party, but the houses were blurred in the dark and the heavy rain.

Pre-tour leave began, and Tom went home. Constance surprised him by announcing that she had rented a cottage on the Devon coast for a week. Tom found the total peace down there the tonic he had needed all along in the testosterone-fuelled last few months. It wasn't Las Vegas, where Clive and Scott had gone, driving from San Francisco in a rented Mustang – far from it – and Tom could only imagine what they were getting up to, but he was pleased he was in Devon.

It was like being a boy again. In the mornings Tom and Constance would go round nearby National Trust properties and castles, then have lunch in a pub and go back to the cottage, where Constance would read. Tom would go with Zeppo for walks along the cliffs, wind picking the sweat off his face and emptying his brain. There was a cove a quarter of a mile down from the cottage, completely secluded, where an Edwardian swimming fan had had a seawater pool dug into the rocks. It was straight out of an Agatha Christie novel. In the sun it warmed up quickly, and Tom spent hours swimming in it.

His favourite activity, which he soon came to do with a haunting addiction, was to jump in from a rock above the pool. As he plunged in, the thousands of bubbles that he brought down with him into the water then began to rise, and Tom dreamed, holding his breath for twenty or thirty seconds, that these bubbles were the dust and shrapnel thrown up by an IED he had stepped on, his body engulfed in the cloud of sparkling light, lost in weightlessness. The bubbles rose past his chest, tickling it on their way to the surface, as he hung in suspension and looked up from the bottom of the pool to the dancing mercury underside of the water. He did this again and again, wondering if an explosion could possibly trick a shocked mind and screaming nerve endings into feeling comfortable. Would it feel sore? Or would it be like a dream, with you borne away in silk blankets?

Early one evening, as the late-August sun lit up everything in gold, Tom jogged up the sandy path from the cove to the house. He walked through the garden and saw through the window that the television was on. A news report announced the names of three soldiers who had been killed in Afghanistan the day before. Their pictures appeared on the screen. A sergeant and two privates. Then the scene changed to Wootton Bassett, to where the bodies of another four men had been repatriated that day. Constance was kneeling just two metres from the screen. She didn't notice Tom at the window as he watched her watch the television and cry.

He stepped away from the window and went to catch his breath. Fifteen minutes later he walked into the house and Constance greeted him: 'There you are, Tommy! Now what are you going to get me for a drink? I think a glass of wine, please!' As Tom opened the fridge and uncorked the bottle a terrible feeling swept over him. What was he doing? What was the point of this wretched game?

That night at supper Tom did his best to keep conversation away from the army. But at the end of pudding, just as Tom was finishing off his ice cream, his mouth full, Constance took advantage of the fact that he couldn't give her any more flannel and told him, 'Now Tom, I know you will hate me for this, but when you are out in Afghanistan no one will think any the less of you if you don't always take risks. You don't have anything to prove.'

'I know, Mum. I promise you, nothing unnecessary.'

'We're all very proud of you, and nothing will change that, so don't feel as though you always have to be the hero.'

'Look, Mum. I'm going out with the best soldiers and the most experienced NCOs. I promise you they will look after me. I can't wait for you to meet them.' He had made sure Constance, who had a ready ear for gossip, was always up to date with the ups and downs of his troop, and she was always amused by tales of what the soldiers got up to, the ill-advised tattoos they had got or their brushes with the law.

Tom was about to start a story about one of Miller's tattoos, just to steer the conversation away from Afghanistan, when Constance stepped in again, seeing straight through her son's plans to obfuscate.

'You see, Tom, and I do not at all want to put undue pressure on you, but a mother must say this: you are all I've got. I know you know that, and you have known it ever since your father died, but I must be allowed to say it again. There, I've said it. Please, Tom, come back. Don't try to be a hero.'

Tom's throat seized up and his eyes strained. After what felt like minutes he managed to croak out, 'I know, Mum. I know. I'll be OK. I promise.'

After Constance had gone to bed Tom sat up for hours with a glass of whisky, on a stool in front of a fire that fought the cool night, looking through the flames as though he were fixed on a point a hundred metres away, as the logs slowly burned out into grey skeletons of ash. Finally he stood, put the fireguard up and pulled his way up the bannister to bed.

On the final day of leave he said a sad goodbye to Sam, and then Zeppo, and then finally Constance, after a tea of cakes and scones. He couldn't eat them all – she had made a vast spread – and so she gave Tom a full tin to take back and give to 3 Troop the next day. She made the parting mercifully brief, but as Tom pulled away from the house and saw her in his rear-view mirror as she waved him off, he was again almost overcome with waves of guilt. When he got back to the mess that night, he walked into the TV room to be greeted by the other subalterns, looking just as gloomy as he was, slumped on sofas and beanbags and pretending to be interested in a film.

'Tom!' Clive piped up. 'How was leave?'

'Great, pal, really great. The drive back was miserable though.'

A sea of nods agreed with him. 'Too right, mate,' Scott Lanyon answered. 'I've felt like slitting my wrists ever since I left home.'

'I know; the central reservation never looked so tempting.'

'How was leaving home? Dreadful?'

'Yep, pretty much. I've never felt like that in my life. It made the first day at Sandhurst feel like going to a fairground.'

'I know. And all those KIAs out in Afghan didn't help, all through fucking leave. My ma and pa were just glued to the TV. I just felt like a total bastard.'

They all grunted agreement.

That was the Monday night; they were to deploy on Saturday morning. The week was a whirl of administration and rituals. On the Tuesday morning Tom helped Trueman to check that all the squadron's bergen rucksacks had a small blue and black marker painted on them, to identify them as King's Dragoons bags in the airports at Brize Norton, Kandahar and Bastion. Then in the afternoon he had to help the guys make out their wills, as well as write his own. On the Wednesday morning they had an eight-mile run and that afternoon lessons on the Vallon metal detectors, and then they practised their barma drills. That night Tom and Trueman took 3 Troop out for a curry and few drinks, but nothing spilled over into a particularly late night.

On the Thursday morning they packed up their rooms,

putting all their kit, posters, pictures, books and trinkets into boxes and leaving them in the middle of the bare rooms, so that if they were killed it would be easy to get all their property back to their next of kin. In the afternoon they were issued their dog tags – lining up in the gymnasium to receive them from the regimental clerks – as well as their medical documents, and had all their passports checked. It all started to feel as though they were going on some kind of extreme package holiday.

Immediately they got their dog tags Tom and Clive debated how they were going to wear them. They came on a beaded metal necklace, and detailed in shallow punched capitals the bearer's army number, his initials, blood group and religious denomination. There was great mileage in discussing how one wore these millstones of mortality. The rule was that they were to be worn around the neck, but there was an urban myth that it was bad luck to do this, as what would happen if your head was blown off and they were both lost? So some soldiers had one tag tied to a belt loop of their trousers or strung on one of their bootlaces.

Tom, always content to take the path of least resistance, had his around his neck and thus avoided exasperating Frenchie. Clive went with what the allyer soldiers were doing, stringing one on a bootlace and hanging the other around his neck, substituting the metal necklace with a piece of coloured string. 'This is what they'd have done in 'Nam, mate,' he told Tom before being discovered by Frenchie and then rather pathetically having to scrabble around in a bin for the necklace so he could wear them properly.

Tom was amused at how much attention soldiers devoted to these bits of trivia. No one ever seemed to talk about the rights or wrongs of Afghanistan, still less about the picture on the ground in the country. They just knew that once they got there Brigade would give them a task, and they'd just crack on and do it; the tour would look after itself. What they did spend all their time doing was debating things like how to make their helmet look cool – how much scrim netting to put on and whether or not to surreptitiously Vietnamize it with slogans. How much sniper tape to put on their rifle, GPS, torches. Where to keep pictures of wives and children – down the front plate of their body armour or in the padded lining of a helmet? What tattoo they would get to commemorate the tour. What tattoo everyone in the troop should get if someone was killed.

On the Friday morning they paraded again in the gymnasium and everyone had their 'death photo' taken; this would be released to the media if they were killed. Frenchie and Sergeant Major Brennan stood behind the photographer and checked each photo, making sure no one had pulled a silly face or was looking too vacant. As Tom stepped onto the podium and stood in front of the regimental colours – the backdrop – he looked as white as a sheet, and Frenchie said to him, 'Come on, Tom; it's not that bad! Try to look a bit more cheerful.' Tom flashed a bit of a grin, but still felt that the result, when he saw it, made him look as though he was on day release from prison. Clive, on the other hand, posed and pouted for the camera, saying, 'Still need to impress the chicks from beyond the grave.'

After the photo session they formed up, all the administration now done. The buses collecting them from the barracks to begin the journey to Bastion were due at midnight. Frenchie spoke to them. 'Right, fellas, that's it all done. Go home now and get some final time with your families. I know that that's only going to help those who live on the patch; as for the others, do whatever you want. Go to the cinema, go to the pub, have a few drinks, but only a few. I

66

want you all back here, good to go, at 2300. If any one of you cocks up and doesn't make it, or gets arrested, or whatever, then I will formally charge him. And then make him lead Vallon man for the duration of the tour. With no batteries in the Vallon. See you tonight, boys.'

Most of the squadron were delighted by this, many being able to spend a final few hours at home, but the officers moped around pathetically. They couldn't get drunk, they couldn't go home, and the idea of watching films in the mess for twelve hours was too depressing for words. Just as they were contemplating a trip to Thorpe Park to stave off boredom for even a few hours, Tom decided to strike.

'Guys, actually, I can't do this. I'm going into London to meet a friend.'

'What mate? Who?'

'I need to go and mend some bridges. See you guys tonight.' He sprinted upstairs, threw on a shirt and a pair of jeans, and Scott drove him to the station. In the car he texted Cassie: 'Hi Cass, it's Tom. This is so out of the blue, but I am about to go away and it would mean so much if I could see you today for even five minutes. I understand if impossible. I can come wherever.' He sent it, arrived at the station and got the train into London.

No reply came. The train went on into town; still no reply. He was going to feel very stupid if nothing came of this. The train wheezed through Clapham Junction and then sidled along the Thames past the MI6 building, Tom glimpsing the Houses of Parliament, the Ministry of Defence, the buildings that were responsible for him going to Afghanistan tonight. The train pulled into Waterloo and he sighed. A wasted journey. The train halted. His phone buzzed. He looked at it in his sweating palm, expecting it to be abuse from Clive or Scott. It was from her, and he almost dropped the phone. 'Hi Tom. Yes please, I'd love to see you! On gardening leave anyway. Yippee! Zero's behind Sloane Square at 1?'

He texted straight back, 'Great news; see you then! Tx.'

He was hardly able to breathe. Soon though his excitement gave way to fear. How on earth was he to play this? How the hell was he going to be able to reintroduce himself to her after what had happened over the last two years? He crossed the river and made his way down Whitehall to Parliament Square, turned along Birdcage Walk and passed Buckingham Palace, not noticing the hordes of scuttling tourists and working out what he was going to say to her. He arrived at the restaurant ten minutes early, went to the bar and sank a gin and tonic before ordering a bottle of white wine and being shown to a table in the middle of the crowded brasserie.

For a moment he regretted ordering the wine – what if she wasn't going to drink? But then he'd just have it all himself, he decided. He sat down and waited, losing himself in the chatter, trying to store it all up to remember in Afghan. It felt surreal. He was woken from his trance by Cassie standing over him wearing a blue dress and a mock-serious frown.

'Well, well, Thomas Chamberlain, I hope you're not going to be punching anyone to the ground this time. You'll definitely get arrested if you try it here.'

Tom squirmed from his chair to stand and kiss her on the cheek, but he was so shocked that she had actually turned up that he only managed to semi-headbutt her. At first he was lost for words. 'Oh . . . er, hi, Cassie . . . You look amazing,' he fumbled, feeling like a dying fish. Then he broke into a grin. 'Glass of wine?'

'Yes please!'

She sat down and Tom poured her a glass, trying not to

spill any and cursing the gin for making him feel so clumsy, though at least it had helped to knock a bit of edge off the whole thing. She looked at him, tilting her head to one side like she used to do in tutorials while pondering a question. 'You know,' she said finally, as though she had just examined a strange object in a museum, 'I'd never have recognized you. In the street, I mean, out of context.'

'How do you mean? Have I changed?'

'Changed? You look completely different. The hair for one; where has it all gone? Did they make you shave it off? Your face has changed shape, and there's not an ounce of fat on you; you just look like one big lean muscle now. You're a bit gaunt though. We must feed you up this lunch. Christ, I sound as though I'm your mother.' She paused and drank her wine. Tom noticed she took somewhat more than a sip; clearly she was needing some help too. At this rate they'd be on to a second bottle even before the food arrived.

'Look, I'm so sorry for the other night. You see—'

She interrupted: 'What, for shattering Jonty Forbes' nose or for completely ignoring me?'

'Well, for the punch too, I suppose. But to be honest he had it coming. No, I wish I'd been able to stay, honestly, but I had to go with my friend. He was in a really bad way. But I wish I'd stayed. I must have looked so rude.'

'Well, it was quite amusing you guys taking that oaf down a peg. He can be a pillock sometimes.'

'What happened to him?'

'Well, after trying to scoop up what he could salvage from his cocaine supply he stormed upstairs, spitting daggers about you both, to clear himself up. I saw him at another party the other day. His nose is completely healed – just a tiny scar – and I overheard him trying to tell someone that he got it playing rugby. No one believes him, obviously; the real story spread like wildfire. But I almost think he believes it himself now. He's that kind of boy.'

'What, the absolute twat kind? If I were his parents I'd be ashamed to have produced something like that. What a waste of space.'

'His father's my godfather.'

There was silence for a few seconds before she tossed her head back with a huge laugh. 'You idiot. I've missed you so much. You are so good at putting your foot in every situation that ever comes your way.'

After that it all flowed. The other bottle of wine duly followed, and they found themselves caught up with memories and news and jobs in London and thoughts on Afghanistan all tumbling out among one another. As their puddings were cleared away and coffee put in front of them and they paused for a moment's breath, Tom said, 'Cass?'

'Hmm?'

'Can I ask you one thing? Like, a big thing. Don't worry; I'm not going to ask if we can go out again.'

'OK', she replied softly, trying to look amused and curious when in fact her heart was racing. She wasn't sure whether or not it was the coffee.

'It's just that now I'm about to go away, in about –' he looked at his watch theatrically '– oh, all of nine hours, I can't get out of my head what you said to me back in Graz. When you said I was wasting everything. Whether what I'm doing isn't just me taking every single bit of love that has ever been thrown my way and throwing it into the gutter. There is a very real, very real chance that something might happen to me in Afghanistan. That's not me being special; it's the same for about six thousand other blokes in the brigade who are going to get out on the ground. You have to acknowledge it as a possibility. Everyone does.

'But, you see, and this is where I think you were right, I'm an only child. If one of my soldiers dies and leaves his parents having to bury one of their children, at least they have the consolation that they probably still have maybe one or two other children to love. But in Ma's case there's none. None at all. What am I doing?'

He sat back, looking into space over Cassie's head and speaking as if to himself. 'Sometimes I look in the mirror, and I don't see what I used to see, which is what everyone else sees in a soldier – an upstanding pillar of society, a selfless young man who is going off to fight for his country blah blah blah and lead men blah blah, and they hold parties in our honour and everyone says how great we are. When I look in that mirror now, I see a scared little boy who's doing not something great and selfless but something so selfish that he's about to rob his mother of the only thing left in her life. And not because our country's in danger, because it's not. The Taliban aren't ever going to be goose-stepping down Whitehall. Me going out to Afghan won't protect this country one bit. The only reason I'm going there is to try to look like a man because I'm not imaginative enough to think of another way. As soldiers we think we have the monopoly on heroism because we wear a uniform that's dripping in history and we have medals and things that everyone in society knows about, like the Victoria Cross, Trooping the Colour, Dunkirk, H. Jones . . .

'But we don't have that monopoly; that's bollocks. We're no different from militias in the Sudan – drugged-up little twats who cruise around burning straw huts to try to impress the girls back in their shit little villages. No different to gang members in some council block in NW18; they have their own slang, their own hierarchy, their own uniforms, just like us. The only difference between us and gangs is that they're

71

hunted every day by the same police who provide the protection for our medal ceremonies in Buckingham Palace. But the motivation of a fifteen-year-old who joins a gang is the same as mine was to join the army: he wants to be part of a club, and get kudos from his mates and girls. And by scratching that itch, that little boy probably gets stabbed to death in some concrete jungle five miles north of here and I probably get shot through the face in some desert five thousand kilometres away. It's just the same. At the end of the day we'll both be rotting flesh and leaving families who have been destroyed by our selfish stupid wish to join a gang.'

He stopped for a moment, snapping back to look at Cassie, who had an almost shell-shocked expression on her face. Tom felt bad that he was subjecting her to this tirade. He picked up his coffee; it had gone cold but he drank a huge gulp all the same. She stayed silent, and so he went on.

'The same applies to Afghan. The guy firing that AK-47 at me has probably had no education; he probably doesn't know what electricity is, and the only contribution he will ever make to society will be not raping some young boy too often. He has a battered old assault rifle; I have Apache gunships and the US Air Force on call. But me and that Taliban lad, we're the same in why we're doing what we do. We just felt as though we had to impress people. And now I'm here, about to go out, I don't want to impress anyone at all. I just want to stay here.'

'But your soldiers. You speak of them with such fondness. Surely they'll look after you?' she replied pleadingly.

'That's it. They're the only thing that keeps you from jacking the entire thing in. That's the genius of the army: your desperation not to look like a coward in front of the lads only just beats your wish to throw in the towel. That's why it works. But I still don't know how it's going to work for me. I literally have no idea how I'm going to behave when it kicks off. No idea. At the moment I just feel like a selfish little boy who's in far too deep and is about to destroy everyone who's ever loved him and that – and this isn't particularly eloquent, I'm afraid – is a really shit feeling.'

He again reached for his cold coffee, and drained it. He had never spoken like this about the army. It felt good to get it off his chest. He hadn't realized he felt those things almost until he found them coming out of his mouth.

'Cass, I'm so sorry for that. I don't know what came over me.'

'Tommy, not at all. I mean, it's shocking, utterly shocking. I don't quite know what to say.' She had never known that Tom had so much going on in his head, that what he was going through could be so complicated. And the thing was, halfway through his rant, as she looked at him gesticulating and speaking as though he were arguing with himself, she realized that she still loved him. She didn't know why – and he certainly had clearly moved on from her – and she didn't know whether she was just feeling sorry for him because of what he was about to do. This could be the last time she'd ever see him. She hadn't missed him in the past two years; to be honest once she'd written the letter dumping him she'd put him out of her mind altogether, or thought she had. Why had he come back now? For a moment she hated him, resenting him barging his way back in and demanding time with her. But she could have ignored the text. She could have refused to meet him, but something had made her.

After much protesting from her, Tom paid the bill and they walked down to the river and the Albert Bridge. She might as well accompany him to Clapham Junction, she thought, and they walked along together, settling back into small talk. The tide was right out, and the river was stripped to its bones as though there was a drought. She liked the river when it was like this, it was as though its smaller channel and dirty gravel littered with detritus was like a confessional, before the tide rushed upstream and the city put her make-up back on.

It reminded Tom of pictures he had seen of the Helmand River, streaking its way across the desert. The sun hit the water, shattering into a hundred glints, and he thought they might be what muzzle flashes would look like. As they crossed the bridge he turned to her and said, 'Cass, I'll let you go here. Don't come to the station, please. It'll be dreadful, like some recreation of *Brief Encounter*. Please let's say good-bye here.'

'What, as if it's any less of a cliché saying goodbye on a bridge?'

He grinned. 'Oh come on, we're over it, aren't we? OK, let's make sure.' He held her hand, and they walked twenty metres into Battersea Park. Tom stopped next to a bollard and held her elbow with his right hand and her waist with his left. He could feel goosebumps on her arm. 'Thank you so, so much for coming to see me. I can't tell you how grateful I am. I have no idea what you must have cancelled to come or how much you wanted to pretend you didn't get the text.'

She bit her lip.

Tom laughed. 'Ha! I can still read you like a book. No, really, Cass, thanks so much. It means more than you can ever know.' He squeezed her waist. 'Better go. Take care. I'll write and tell you how it all goes. Fingers crossed I'll break my ankle coming off the plane and be back in a few days.'

She didn't know why she let herself, but she was crying. Tom looked hurt, and she saw his eyes decide to close the conversation.

He stroked her cheek. 'Look what I've done to you. You must go.' He kissed her gently on the forehead with dry lips and said, 'Goodbye, flower girl.' He smiled, turned and walked away through the park.

'Tommy.' He looked back. 'Take care,' she croaked. He smiled again. This time she turned, and walked back over the bridge.

That night the clock ticked erratically, sometimes slowly, sometimes quickly, as the squadron prepared to leave. There was too little time to do anything meaningful, and too much time to go and sit miserably by the buses outside the gym. The officers were in the mess skimming newspapers or spread out on the sofas throwing a tennis ball around. In the soldiers' block some played computer games, some made last-minute adjustments to their kit.

On the patch some of the soldiers shared a last supper with their families; others sat watching television. Brennan had put his children to bed and was working out how he could say goodbye to the dog. He opened the door to the garden and kicked a ball out into the dark. The dog ran out, and when it came back in, having discovered the ball in a flower bed, found its master had gone, the chain still jangling on the door. Outside, Brennan pecked his wife on the cheek, businesslike, just as they always did before he went away. 'Fucking hell, Ads Brennan –' she spoke sadly '– this is separation number seven for us. You'd better come back OK. Or else.'

'I will, love; I've got to. Everyone's going to be looking to me this time. See you when I see you. Ha! If you saw that eighteen-year-old again you'd run a mile.'

'Too bloody right. Come back safe, eh?' She kissed him again. 'Now go on. See you when I see you.'

Brennan got into his car and drove to Trueman's house, who was upstairs until the last, reading stories to his two girls even after they had finally gone to sleep. Brennan's car horn tooted outside. He closed the book, kissed the girls, drew their duvets up to their shoulders, closed the door gently and tiptoed to his bedroom, to his wife, who always went to bed early when he deployed anywhere. He crept over and kissed her on the side of the head while she pretended to sleep. He left the room and ghosted down the stairs and out of the house like he had never been there. The journey with Brennan was silent. This happened all through the estate that night, houses sleeping and preparing to wake up to six months without a father against a guilty symphony of softly shut doors.

The officers dragged themselves out of the mess, going out to the buses and trying to put on a cheery face in front of the soldiers, counting kit and rifle bundles and double-checking that everyone had their passports. Under the sickly orange lights slowly the group grew, now away from the small cells of their families and coalescing into a larger unit. The commanding officer was there with the RSM, both wearing civilian clothes as they were to remain in the UK for a couple of weeks before bringing RHQ out. Tom watched the CO, in a scruffy pair of cords and a tatty old shirt, chat easily with the boys, who looked at him like a god as he bantered with them. The RSM came over to him. 'Evening, Mr Chamberlain! On a scale of dreadful to dreadful, how dreadful are we feeling then?'

'Um, yep, pretty bad, RSM, actually.'

'Don't worry, sir; when you get on the plane everything clicks. If it doesn't, well –' he came closer as if imparting a secret '– just bung a couple of knitting needles up yer nose, a pair of boxers on your head and pretend you've gone mad. Got it?'

Tom grinned. 'Yep. Thanks, RSM. See you in a couple of weeks.'

'Safe journey, sir. Look after the boys for me, will you?'

'I promise.'

A few wives and girlfriends had come to the buses to see them off. Through the crowd of tearful hugs and last-minute photographs Frenchie's wife was there with their sleeping daughter and young son Alex, who was posing for photographs with some of the soldiers and trying to hide in the great pile of bergens and black grips. Frenchie scooped him up and said, 'Right, young man; time for you to stop making a nuisance of yourself.' His voice lowered to a confidential whisper. 'Look after your mother and your sister. Be a brave boy. Keep the house safe.' Alex nodded. Frenchie hugged him to his chest one final time, wishing he could keep him there for hours, and whispered, 'Goodbye, my darling boy.' He handed him over to his wife, pecked her lips and drew back with an apologetic smile.

Frenchie stood at the door of the first bus, and Jason at the door of the second, counting and ticking off every man as they filed on. At last all the boys were on. Frenchie stepped on board and sat at the front, next to Tom, who was staring blankly out the window. Midnight on the dot. Frenchie tapped the driver, 'Right, chum, no time like the present. Let's go.'

The buses moved off past the guardroom, where the sentry smacked his rifle hard with his hand, saluting his friends. Through the town they swept. Streetlights threw an eerie light over the buses as they passed bars and nightclubs filled with those who had no idea of the blood tribute that was passing them. Only in the corners of their eyes did they register the buses bearing boys who would have killed to be in those same bars and to have woken up the next day with a hangover, pondering how to fill a weekend. Only the occasional traffic light, delaying their progress for a few tantalizing seconds, seemed to acknowledge them, winking at them like evil eyes. As they left the town and slipped anonymously onto the motorway Tom felt as though they were the country's shame, not its pride; the nation's best sent off without fanfare in the dead of night to hurtle wide awake into long-nurtured nightmares.

TWO

'Tell that fucking idiot to stop arsing around that IED, unless he wants his feet blown through his face,' said Tom in exasperation to Solly, his interpreter.

'Yes, Mr Tom, but I think he's trying to show his friends how brave he is,' said Solly, before shouting over to the Afghan militiaman, who was being egged on by his friends to see how close he could dance to an IED. The Afghan ignored him. Tom sighed and gritted his teeth as his rucksack bit into shoulders still getting used to the weight he was carrying: radio, spare radio batteries, five litres of water, ten magazines, a belt of link for the GPMG, schmoolies – all on top of the suffocating plates of his body armour. He went into the compound through the blue-and-orange-painted corrugated-iron gate to find Trueman, who was positioning Ellis and Miller with the GPMG on the roof of one of the compound outbuildings.

'What do you reckon, Sergeant? These maniacs are going to top themselves.'

'Wait one, sir. Dusty, you set? Good lad. Any cunt tries any funny business, brass him up. Right, you got me now.' Trueman jumped off the ladder back into the compound, took off his helmet and lit a cigarette. His bandana was dark with sweat. 'Sorry sir, what are these crazies doing? Dancing on an IED? Yep, sounds like them all right. Where are they?'

They walked through the compound, straw on the ground, chickens squawking and running around a tethered goat, its ribs sticking through its hide. The men of the family whose compound it was were huddled in a corner, sulking at the militia, sometimes chattering in low hurried tones to each other. The boys sat in the shade of a wall, trying to escape the heat of the sun and pouring water down their throats. Already Livesey from SHQ had been casevaced back to Bastion with heatstroke after only two days on the ground, and Brennan had warned that the next time it happened he'd let whoever had collapsed just lie and die there without treatment as punishment for not looking after himself. As they approached the gate Trueman put his helmet back on, and they walked out to see the Afghan now urinating around the IED.

'Solly, what the fuck?' said Tom.

'I'm sorry, boss; he just won't listen. Think they've all been smoking weed as well.' Solly, a cheery angular Kabuli, working as an interpreter to fund his plans to go to university in India, looked apologetic. Tom nodded. He liked Solly, who had a lot more in common with 3 Troop than he seemed to with the militiamen.

Trueman finished his cigarette, threw it on the sand and rolled his eyes at Tom. 'Well, I suppose that's one way to tackle an IED. Not seen it in no manual though.'

'I need to get where Frank Spencer is to mark the grid for the 10-liner. I could do without him dancing around me while I'm trying to do it.'

That was the reason for them being in the compound. C Squadron, a week after arrival in Bastion, had moved by helicopter up to Loy Kabir, base of Battle Group North East, in the far north of Helmand Province. They had almost immediately been sent to the town of Shah Kalay, ten miles to the east of Loy Kabir, partly in order to give the squadron something to do, as due to complications with vehicle upgrades their CVR(T)s were going to be stuck in the workshops at

Bastion for a couple of weeks, partly because it was a good chance for them to get out on the ground, and partly to assure the local militia that ISAF was interested in helping them out.

There was another reason. The governor of Loy Kabir, a wily old ex-Taliban defector called Gumal who had swapped sides in 2006, was originally from Shah Kalay, and as its richest son – he had immense wealth compared to most of his countrymen, mostly created through foul means rather than fair – he was paying the militia out of his own pocket. He professed to be doing this out of love for his home, ever keen to show his new American and British masters that he was making a personal contribution to the war against the Taliban. In reality though, the Shah Kalay militia were his security against his immediate murder whenever the Westerners left. If he could provide a two hundred-strong army to any future overlord, then he'd likely avoid assassination, at least for the time being, buying him time for, in the worst case, an escape to the West.

Gumal was pretty sure he would be OK; he was well versed in the rituals of dropping – and sometimes killing – old friends and earnestly promising unwavering fealty to new ones. He had worked with CIA agents against the Russians in the 1980s, had been the Taliban's most zealous governor in Helmand during the 90s, had personally executed a French charity worker kidnapped in the area in 2006, and then jumped on the ISAF bandwagon three months later. He was a natural survivor – garrulous, gregarious, with an engaging glint in his eye – and an almost mythical figure in the area. There were rumours that he personally gouged the eyes out of any Taliban prisoners brought to his house for questioning and kept in his labyrinthine basement a harem of seven boys, one for every day of the week. The dinners he hosted were many and extraordinary in their largesse. Every month he would invite the entire battle group staff to his house for a five-hour extravaganza of food, music, speeches and cases of Johnnie Walker Black Label.

Gumal's militia, given legitimacy by his wangling them permission to wear the uniform of the Afghan National Police, had fallen into the arrogance and cruelty that corrupts any group of personal favourites. The Taliban in Shah Kalay, a quiet cell not much bothered by ISAF whose only military activity hitherto had been to provide food and accommodation to any foreign or out-of-area fighters coming to the district, had recently roused themselves into action, and there had been a spike in the number of attacks and IED emplacements, and so it was that Gumal had prevailed upon the battle group to send a sub-unit to the town in order to bolster the crumbling image and confidence of his militiamen.

Thus C Squadron had come, cramming into Mastiff troop carriers for the journey over, arriving at dusk on the Thursday and securing the huge compound the militia used as their HQ. At dawn on Friday Frenchie sent out four troops to the four corners of the town, with SHQ and the REME section guarding the compound. Three Troop had been given the south and were due back that evening. They were to go with the militia to the positions of known IEDs, mark them and note their locations, not step on any themselves, and get a feel for the atmospherics in the town.

The militiaman was still jumping up and down around the IED. His colleagues, who now weren't bothering even to half-heartedly conceal their dope-smoking, were doubled up with laughter. He couldn't have been more than fourteen years old, and Tom and Trueman had raised their eyebrows at each other when they had met him that morning. He wore jet-black, very finely drawn mascara, and when he shook their hands his skin was soft and delicate. He walked in the most exaggeratedly feminine way and was constantly being stroked on the face by the other militiamen. He wore a garland of wild flowers around his neck and had a perfect red rose sticking out of the muzzle of his AK-47. The rifle itself was filthy, and when its magazine had fallen off Tom noticed that it only held two rounds. He was pretty sure it was the same with the rest of them.

Leaving the militia compound and heading south as the last traces of dawn streaked overhead, they had made an incongruous party. Three Troop walked in column ten metres distant from each other, meticulously scanning left and right, all the while with an eye on the dry earth beneath their feet for any ground sign of IEDs. Lance Corporal Gatunakaniviu – known as GV as the boys could never get to grips with his Fijian name – walked at their head with the Vallon, sweeping it from side to side just like he had done two years ago on his previous tour. Now and again one of the boys would halt, get down on one knee and look through his rifle sight at something on the horizon. All this nervous professionalism was undone, however, by the bizarre behaviour of the militia, who minced along ahead of GV's Vallon, holding hands and singing. This caused much amusement among the boys, especially when Tom's increasingly livid efforts to control them through Solly were ignored.

They continued like this for a kilometre south, with Tom sending in sitreps over the radio when he could get a word in edgeways. With the whole squadron out on the ground for the first time, the net was constantly busy. It was the first time SHQ had wielded four limbs, the first time on the ground for four keen young troop leaders all competing for Frenchie's approval. With myriad other frictions caused by slack voice procedure, comms blind spots and operating in an unfamiliar area, Tom couldn't hear what anyone was saying around him, as his left ear was so busy trying to distil the huge amounts of mostly useless information from the radio. It sounded as though the other Troops were having similarly shambolic experiences.

At ten o'clock they arrived at the site and the militia barged their way into the nearby compound that was now their temporary base. Tom had been so overwhelmed with the morning's assault upon his senses that he hadn't even smiled, let alone apologized, to the family as they walked in, treating them like ciphers in a computer game as opposed to humans. Trueman, for whom the learning curve was less steep, was much better with them, immediately establishing a bond with the children and offering cigarettes to the men. They accepted them readily enough, if without thanks, but looked at the militiamen with mute acceptance and hate in their eyes.

Now though Tom was feeling better, standing outside the compound with Trueman, Jesmond and Solly as they watched the boy continue to prod and gesticulate at the area around the IED.

'Don't worry, sir,' Trueman piped up. 'I'll get rid of that twat for you.' He marched over and, in front of all the militiamen, grabbed him by the scruff of the neck and dragged him back from the IED. There were actually two devices, each marked with a little pyramid of white-painted stones. The boy squirmed, and Trueman flung him bodily into the crowd of the militia, where he hung back, embarrassed. Trueman strutted back over to Tom. 'Right, sir, that's my part done. Yours is a bit harder. Didn't get too close to them myself, but it looks like they're marked OK.' He saw Tom gulp and tried to cheer him up. 'Don't worry, sir; if that bummer can dance around them for ten minutes and be fine then you'll be all right. And besides, this is what you lot get your pop-star wages for, ain't it?'

Tom smiled weakly and headed out to the pyramids. He had to step as close as he dared to the devices, use the GPS to get the ten-figure reading that would pinpoint to the nearest metre each location, write that down and then step away and compile the 10-liner. Simple. The small stone pyramids were only twenty metres from him but seemed miles away. Tom wished for some of the militia's hashish to slow his frantic heart. Blood was pulsing in his ears, and he could feel the artery in his neck swell to his heart's drumbeat. He edged closer. The radio crackled in his left ear, and he turned the volume to silent. He didn't want any distractions. Now he was four metres away, and he peered even more fixedly. His eyes were straining. This was it, his first time looking into the face of one of the devices that had killed so many. It felt as though he was approaching the edge of a cliff but despite every urge to step back he couldn't; he had to look closer.

Inch by inch he moved, now in a low shuffling crouch up to the first pyramid. Just ten centimetres from it a bit of earth had been scratched away, and Tom could clearly see part of a crumpled white plastic bag buried in the ground, the waterproof covering for the pressure plate of an IED. He had no idea where the main charge was buried. He could well have been standing right on top of it. He got about a metre away, almost forgetting to breathe, and then held out his wrist-mounted GPS straight in front of him over the pressure plate. He looked at its face and wrote down the grid reference with a white hand in a notebook balanced on his thigh.

With a desiccated throat he didn't bother to get up from his crouch but shimmied the three metres to the second one.

This time any vestige of colour in him drained away. Nearly the whole main charge had been exposed, and was lying there like a half-buried corpse. That meant that the pressure plate could be anywhere around him. He stayed there for ages. *How did that boy dance around it and not hit it?* Almost for want of something to do, and terrified to move, he did the same trick with the GPS and then, grid written down, took a deep breath and squirmed back, knowing he should search the earth with his fingertips or his bayonet but just wanting away as quickly as possible. The crunch of the grains of sand and gravel under his boots sounded like rocks falling down a mountain, and the sinews in his neck were taut as he braced himself for the explosion that had to come. Finally though, somehow, he found himself three metres away and straightened up. As he did so, he got a head rush and felt as though he was about to faint. He walked back to Trueman, who was looking at him astonished, another cigarette burning in his mouth with an inch of unflicked ash at its end.

'Fucking hell, sir. I thought you were going to mark their location, not try to shag 'em. Why in fuck's name did you get so close? Me and Jessie were going to come and drag you out, but the only reason we didn't was that you looked so in the zone that if we surprised you, you'd probably have jumped onto it or something.'

Tom was amazed at how coolly he replied; his whole body was tingling. 'Well, Sergeant Trueman, always got to give the ATO the best possible information.'

'Aye, sir, but remember you ain't a fucking ATO, so don't go behaving like one.' He smiled as the tension left him. 'Fuck me, Jessie; we got real ice blood here!'

This made Tom swell with pride, but he didn't want to show any emotion in front of them, so he kept his distance and replied with a formal, 'Well anyway, enough of that.

88

Right, Sergeant Trueman, I'm going to send a sitrep to Zero.'
He went inside the compound, took his helmet off and wiped
his hand over his crew cut, sending a spray of sweat off it. He
wriggled his rucksack off, sat next to it with his back against
a wall and took a drink of water, pouring a few glugs over his
forehead. It didn't work; the water was so hot it just felt
clammy and made his saturated shirt feel as though he'd just
sweated into it some more. He checked his map, checked his
GPS, wrote up the two 10-liners, rehearsed them in a whisper, went through in his head what he was going to say to
Zero and mopped his brow with his sweat rag. At last a lull
on the net came.

'Hello, Zero, this is Tomahawk Three Zero. Sitrep over.'

A harassed voice crackled back. SHQ had been overwhelmed with flannel all day, and Jason, suffering from
D & V anyway, was railing at the vast amount of rubbish
pouring over the net.

'Zero Bravo send over.'

'Tomahawk Three Zero sitrep as at 1030 hours. My callsign complete now static in 4 Sierra Romeo compound 42.
Enemy activity none. Friendly activity: we have gone firm in
compound, and have been shown two IED locations.
10-liners to follow with 10-figure grids roger so far over.'

'Zero Bravo roger. Get on with it over.'

'Three Zero roger. My intent to stay here and dominate
surrounding area until we collapse back at— CONTACT.
WAIT OUT!' he screamed down the net as a whoosh and a
sharp bang from over the wall tore through his head, making
his brain feel as though it was pushing against the inside of
his eyes.

Unmistakably – as he'd heard them a hundred times in
films – an RPG had just been fired at them. It was just so
much louder than he thought it would be. His brain raced.

What the fuck? What the fuck? He had to find Trueman. He threw on his rucksack, put his helmet on, backwards, and sprinted, kit jangling behind him, across the compound screaming, 'Sergeant Trueman, Sergeant Trueman. Contact! Where's the firing point?' he yelled up to Miller and Ellis on the sun-baked roof with the gimpy, who were looking around desperately. 'Watch your arcs, lads. Where's the firing point? Where's the firing point? I need the firing point. Say what you see.'

The rest of the boys, sitting at the foot of the wall, were looking shocked as well, fumbling with their kit. Tom shouted to them, 'Right fellas, kit on, look sharp. I'm going out to check out what's happening. Wait here.' In his ear Jason was saying for the fourth or fifth time, 'Three Zero roger. Send contact report over,' with increasing violence. Tom hared out of the gate, bracing himself for carnage, and blanched when he saw Trueman and the militia boy both on the ground, about twenty metres apart. Trueman was writhing around, and the boy was on his back looking straight up at the sky. But there was no blood on either of them, and Trueman seemed to be laughing. Tom looked to his right and saw dust settling near where the IEDs were, and then saw the rest of the militia looking on in drugged-up bewilderment.

What in Christ's name was going on? Only Jesmond seemed to have any hold on reality, and Tom shouted to him, 'Right, Jessie, get these fuckers inside. We're in contact! We're in contact! I'll get Freddie; you cover me.'

Tom was mad with adrenaline, but before he could start dragging Trueman inside the compound Jesmond thumped his shoulder and shouted, 'NO. Sir, sir, NO CONTACT. NO CONTACT. ND with an RPG. I promise you, I promise you. No enemy action.'

'What?' Tom didn't understand what he was saying.

'Sir, LISTEN! The boy used the RPG to fire at the IED and blow it himself. He missed and got thrown back by the explosion. He only aimed it about five metres from where he was standing. We couldn't stop him; it all happened in about a second. That's why the sarge is laughing. I promise you. Stand down, stand down the contact report.'

Christ. Tom could imagine Frenchie and Jason flapping inside SHQ and quickly blurted over the net, 'Hello, Zero Bravo, this is Three Zero. Cancel that contact report. It was a militia NDing an RPG. Understand? Over.'

It took about ten minutes for everything to be pieced together, for Trueman to stop laughing, for the militia boy to be dusted off and given some water, for Tom to reassure a panicked SHQ, and for the boys, who were convinced they were under attack, to get their breath back.

Trueman filled him in. 'I'm sorry, sir; I just couldn't help it. When you went back inside to speak to Zero that bum-bandit boy got an RPG off his mate and started fucking about, pretending to fire it at the IED and stuff. To be honest I didn't think he had a clue how it worked. Anyway, suddenly everything goes quiet, and he only goes and fucking launches it. It were like slow-mo. The grenade explodes literally about from where that goat is to me now in front of him, completely missing the fucking IED, and he gets hurled back by the explosion. I swear that was the funniest shit I have ever seen, and then when you came tearing out the gate like John Wayne I just couldn't stop meself.' He looked at Tom and saw that he was still angry. 'I'm sorry, sir, but it were quite funny, you have to admit.'

Tom looked at him, wanting to be annoyed but for some reason finding it impossible not to laugh himself. He let out a quick chuckle that soon turned into a fully fledged fit. The militia looked at Tom and Trueman and Jesmond, who were soon all unable to speak. Now it was their turn to be bemused.

That evening, after having pushed out a bit further south in the afternoon and finding no sign at all of the Taliban, 3 Troop headed back to the SHQ compound. Half the militia had melted away back to their families, and the boy had been taken home by one of the older men, prompting jokes among the troop. 'Hey, boss,' said Davenport, as they did a final kit check before patrolling back, 'as if that twat hasn't had enough of a shit time already today, he's now about to get bummed as well. What a day!'

Tom looked up from putting a new battery on the radio. 'Yeah, I know. Strange bunch, aren't they? Slightly different from Croydon, I imagine.'

'Well sir, depends who you ask. Everybody's got a price, know what I mean?'

'Right. Thanks for that. I think we'll stop the conversation there. Now get on and get packed up, you wretch.'

They left the compound and started the trek back. The sky blazed with orange in the west, and a perfect round sun hung just above a huge teeth-like range of hills. The village – parched and bleached under the midday sun – started to gain a kind of beauty that Tom had heard people talk of before about Afghanistan. With its compounds spaced a few hundred metres apart, it was deserted as they walked through it, and although in a couple of hours it would seem spooky, a ghost town, just now bathed in the soft light everything seemed safe and fuzzy, as if nothing bad could ever happen there, or had ever happened. It was like they were walking, twenty-first century, post-9/11 robots, through a landscape meant for Moses.

Tom reflected on the day. The highlight had definitely

been the boy's ND, but there were a few other things to think about. First, the fearful reaction of the family to the militia, and with what contempt the militia had treated them. Second, how he had called Jesmond Jessie in the heat of his panic and referred to Trueman as Freddie, breaking one of his cardinal rules. He'd have to work on that. Mostly, however, he was filled with quiet satisfaction that when he had heard the RPG explode he hadn't crawled into a ball, and despite looking like an idiot when he ran outside, he'd at least shown everyone that when the shit hit the fan he would go out and try to face it. And so when he walked back into the SHQ room inside the main compound, now home to the eighty-strong squadron, he had a smile on his face and was looking forward to hearing how the others had got on.

He had left the boys in a corner of the huge expanse, almost the size of two football pitches. A wall about seven feet high ran around it, with towers at each corner. Brennan had sorted the security plan, and 3 Troop were to sleep that night under the south-east tower and stag on from the tower roof. Four Mastiffs from the Loggies remained from the fleet of sixteen that had brought them to the town; one was positioned next to each of the towers, adding the firepower of either a grenade machine gun or a .50 cal.

In the middle of the compound was a two-storey building, the only one in the village, which was the militia base. It looked as though it could have been built forty years or four months ago. There were no windows, and reinforcing steel bars stuck out from unfinished concrete pillars around it. The building reminded Tom of Henry VI Comprehensive, and on a whim he took a photo of it to send back for the school newsletter. The entrance to the building was via a porch, open on three sides, up a small flight of steps. Hanging from the ceiling of the porch was a hook, and the boys were already talking about this being the site of torture and beatings by the militia. The concrete beneath the hook was a dull dark red, and Tom shivered as he imagined what had gone on here. He walked through the building, lit with cyalumes taped to the walls, and pulled back a curtain over a doorway, relieved to see all the officers inside with Frenchie leading the laughter directed at Jason, who was lying on a camp bed in the far corner with a sick bowl next to him.

Frenchie looked up. He was wearing a T-shirt and baseball cap, with his Osprey perched next to him. 'Tom! Welcome back. Glad you didn't get any more dramas from that RPG fool. Bet that gave you quite a shock.'

'Too right, Frenchie. I thought the world had caved in.'

'Well, good to have you back. Sounds like your experience with the Keystone Kops was pretty similar to everyone else's.'

The other troop leaders nodded in unison, with their head torches throwing red beams up and down the walls. They were all still wearing their body armour, each with different accoutrements clipped to the front. They looked a year older than they had the night before, and Tom could recognize his own exhaustion in them.

In the corner Jason groaned and heaved into the bowl.

'Yeah, sorry about him,' said Frenchie. 'His D & V's got worse. Mind you, it might help him lose some weight.'

'Bugger off. Just wait till you lot get this, and then you won't find it so funny,' came the groan back.

'He'll be all right by the morning. Just don't breathe the air too freely.' It was a ridiculous sight, Frenchie and the four troop leaders huddled in one corner and Jason sprawled in the opposite one, naked save for soiled boxer shorts, his sweating chest covered in a film of vomit-speckled dust. Frenchie continued: 'Right, fellas. So far, so good. Well done today; all my gannets back safe and sound. It's not going to be the hardest day on tour, but it was your first time out and about on your own, so remember the mistakes you made and don't do 'em again. Before anything else, sort your bloody voice procedure out. That radio needs only about 20 per cent of the waffle that was coming over it. Especially you, Moyles – Radio Clive.' He looked at Clive, who shrivelled in the beam of the torch. 'Yeah you. I'm not interested in what the clouds are looking like or whether you've just had a chocolate bar, OK? Keep the chatter and claptrap off the net.

'The big news is that we're not going back tomorrow. Minuteman Zero Alpha wants us to stay here for another four days. Officially it's so we can suck up to Gumal and claim that we're mentoring the militia. Unofficially, it's because the CO wants to get to the bottom of this militia issue – just what they're doing to the local population, how reliable they are, how professional they are, yadda yadda. I agree with him. From what I heard you guys say today, they're doing more harm than good.'

Scott stopped him. He shifted nervously, his wide eyes apologetic for interrupting. 'Sorry, Frenchie, for butting in, but they're worse than that. I didn't say over the net because I didn't want the rumour to spread among the boys, but I was talking to a few elders in a compound – 4 Sierra Papa number 35, I think it was, that one with the white gates – about the spike in Taliban attacks in the last week and this old guy said it was because one of his granddaughters, who's nine years old, was gang-raped five days ago by the militia in this building here. They just lifted her out of her home one afternoon, dragged her here in the back of a pickup truck and did it. Apparently they could hear the screams all over the village. They almost killed her. She's now in hospital over in Now Zad. And these guys weren't lying; I could just tell. And my terp believed them as well, and he knows bullshit when he sees it. I swear, these guys are animals. I'm sorry, I should have told you earlier, but you know what the boys are like when they hear something like this.'

A hush descended. Clive murmured, 'Christ, and we're on their side? What kind of fucked-up logic is that?'

Frenchie rubbed his forehead for a few seconds while he worked out how to approach this. 'Thanks, Scott, that's good int. You lot sit tight on this, all right? If the fellas find out about this kind of stuff then the whole thing's going to blow up. They'll refuse to soldier; you know what they're like. As for you lot, well, welcome to operations. It's not black and white; it's shades of grey. The art lies in trying to find yourself nearer the lighter shades than the darker shades. Don't think this kind of thing doesn't happen elsewhere. In Bosnia it was just as bad, having to protect fuckers who you knew had done the most horrific things. Sierra Leone, Iraq as well. I'm sorry, guys; it's just what we do. I don't like these tossers any more than you do, but we're stuck with them.' He was speaking to them fiercely now; he knew he had to harden their hearts to this. 'Just stomach it, yeah? Talk to each other about it and crack on, but not a word to your troops. As I said, it's grey, and don't think the local Taliban are a bunch of saints either, because they're not. If it's not one, it's the other, like those nobbers in Ulster. Both as bad as each other. Capiche?'

Again four head torches bobbed up and down, Tom and Clive looking at each other through the dim light, reading each other's minds: *What in God's name are we doing here?*

Frenchie moved on, knowing that he had to snap them back to the mission. 'Anyway, as I was saying, we're here until 1200 on Wednesday, at least. We'll get a heli resupply tomorrow, and – who'd have thought it – we're even going to get sent a REST and an ATO to deal with the IEDs. Read into that what you will. Someone, somewhere, is on a serious "Let's charm the pants off Gumal" mission. So, as I said, no funny business with his militia. Clearly, boys on a much higher pay grade than any of us want to keep him onside, and so they're ripping out one of the most important assets in theatre and giving it us for two days. Let's make sure we return that asset back safe and sound.

'So, tomorrow, when they get here, you're going to take the ATO to the IEDs you found today. And then he's going to destroy them, sod off back to Bastion, and then all the militia are pleased. We then skedaddle ourselves, and everything here becomes a land of milk and honey. You know, I know, the world knows, it's not going be like that, but that's the mission. Suck it up. Right, go and get some scoff or whatever it is you perverts do to amuse yourselves around here. Full orders back here at 2200. Bring your threebars.'

They got up to leave, Jason still groaning in the corner, the room now reeking of vomit. 'And we won't have it in here either. We'll let misery guts over there have this boudoir all to himself. And fellas –' he paused to ram the message home '– as I said, it's shades of grey here. Just keep the guys on the missions we get from higher. We can't afford to be judge or jury out here. We're just the blunt instruments of the state. Cheer up! At least we don't have to think!' The troop leaders filed out of the room. Frenchie waited for their low, excited story-swapping to disappear down the corridor and looked over to Jason. 'You hear all that, Jase?'

'Yeah. What a cluster.'

'I know. I hope I wasn't too hard on them, but you know what they're like. When they're that junior their moral compasses are so sensitive they make a Jesuit look like Jessica

97

Rabbit. Puritans, all of them. Just like the Taliban. Now there you go; if it's irony you're looking for, there you have it. And I bet you the boys have found out already about the gang rape. Jesus Christ. Well I for one can't wait to get out of here. This place gives me the creeps.'

It was late the next evening, and 3 Troop were in a compound a hundred metres away from the one they'd been in the previous day, now with the REST. They lined the wall, peering over at the activity around the IEDs, which were about to be destroyed by the ATO. The militia were outside the compound, keen to see the explosion from as close as possible. Tom and Solly had long given up trying to look after them.

The ATO was lying over the second IED that Tom had marked, having prepared a circuit that would blow both of the devices simultaneously, and after putting the finishing touches to it he got up, dusted down his trousers and walked over to the two Mastiffs that had brought the Brimstone team down. Staff Sergeant Hotchkiss was a short man, a career-long bomb-disposal expert with a cleft chin, an easy if introspective manner and yellow teeth and yellow finger-nails, who reminded Tom of the kind of person back home who would come and get rid of rats or mice.

He prepared his trigger and signalled a thumbs up at Tom, who was standing on a crate looking over the compound wall. 'Ten seconds, lads,' shouted Tom, who jumped off the crate and stood against the wall next to Jesmond and put his fingers in his ears – only halfway though; he wanted to hear how loud the bang would be. The seconds passed, and then even with the refraction of the wall the air shot out from Tom's lungs as the device blew. The explosion was so much longer than the RPG blast had been, a great reverberating boom as opposed to a quick crack. It almost felt friendly, a great big enveloping haymaker as opposed to the sharp jab of industrial explosives. Tom walked through the gate to look at the damage. A dust cloud was now dispersing, fifty metres up in the air. The ATO walked nonchalantly over to admire his art and whistled to Tom.

Tom followed the yellow spray-painted safe lane marked from the Mastiffs to where the two devices had been. Behind the two craters was the compound with the orange and blue gate. Hotchkiss was chomping on some gum and standing between the craters, each about two metres in diameter. All the dust had now settled, and they looked as though they had been there for centuries, like meteorite strikes on the moon.

Hotchkiss grinned. 'Well there you go, Tom. That's two less in this shithole. Only another five thousand to deal with. Nasty fuckers these ones. That first one had an anti-lift device on the pressure plate as well. Pretty fucking good, I've got to say. Ain't seen handiwork as good as that before out here. Not even in Sangin, where they know their stuff. I mean, not Northern Ireland good, but still pretty damn hot. I got a lot of good int as well – DNA, eksetera, that kind of shit.' He motioned to a clear plastic bag that held the pressure plates and battery packs that he'd disconnected before blowing the main charges.

'Christ. Thanks, Staff. What was the second one like? How close was the pressure plate to the main charge?'

'About a foot away from it. You say you were mucking about near it yesterday? Well, you were fuckin' lucky, I gotta say. I mean, what was that one, about 10 kg? Yep, would have ruined your fuckin' day, that's for sure.'

'Dead?'

'Depends. Both legs at least. But it didn't blow, Tom, so forget about it.'

Tom didn't mind being called by his first name by Hotchkiss. The ATOs could behave almost as they wanted. There were stories of them squaring up to colonels. Everyone knew that their job was the most dangerous around and treated them slightly like rock stars. When they had first arrived in Bastion, and he, Jason and Clive had been having a coffee in the Naafi one evening, they were amazed when an ATO walked in and everyone in the room stopped and stared at him, before about eight people got up and offered to buy him a brew.

Tom, despite himself, was more amused by his escape than afraid. 'Well, someone must be looking out for me. Fingers crossed they keep doing it.' He offered his hand and the ATO shook it. 'Well, Staff, thanks for today. I can't promise you a proper drink, but what about a brew and some scoff back at SHQ?'

'Sounds good, let's do one.'

And so they began their move back northwards to the militia building, the huge Mastiffs trundling ahead of those walking. Tom looked back at the craters, again struck by the red glow that settled on the area at dusk. He glanced at the orange and blue gate, now ajar, of the compound they had been in the day before and noticed a shadowy figure peering out. Tom raised his rifle to look more closely through the sight. The figure was dressed in black, with a white dish-dash around his face. He raised his hand, very slowly waved it at Tom as though mocking him and then disappeared behind the gate. Tom frowned and took his rifle out of his shoulder. Whoever it was, the figure was the only Shah Kalay local he had seen all day. He turned back and carried on walking.

The next day Hotchkiss and the REST were called away to another task in Musa Qala while the squadron continued to patrol the village. The troops' AOs were shifted clockwise around the village so they could get a feel for its different parts. Tom found the place more and more eerie as the days passed. They barely saw any locals at all, and if they did it was only snatched glimpses of them scurrying behind doors as the British soldiers and the militia appeared. The militia continued as they had started: wild, undisciplined, late, rude. One of them was caught by Brennan trying to steal a box of grenades from the back of a Mastiff. Another was found on the roof of the main building during the third night, flashing a torch towards the village. Frenchie told the troop leaders that they had to be prepared to react to the militia suddenly turning on them, either in a premeditated attack or in a drugged-up moment of fury at some minor altercation. The interpreters agreed with this warning; Solly had never trusted the militia since the start of the op. At first, Tom thought Solly simply looked down on the provincial Helmandis but soon realized he was afraid. Tom was starting to feel uneasy as well.

On the final night, news came over from battle group that a rogue policeman in Kajaki had shot and killed two American soldiers. The story rippled through the boys like every other tale of disaster from elsewhere in theatre, but this time with added piquancy brought by living with the militia. The atmosphere, if not yet poisonous, was febrile. They couldn't wait to leave.

That night a half-moon shone over the village as Dusty shook Tom awake at 0200 to go on stag up in the tower. 'Sir, wake up. Stag. Sorry!'

Tom whispered jokingly, 'Corporal Miller, don't apologize when you wake someone up for stag. All the sorries in the world won't stop the bloke being woken up from hating you for ever.' Tom had been only dozing anyway. It was still too hot to sleep the whole night through, and he had been lying there looking up at the stars in his shirt, rolled-down sleeves his only concession to the slightly cooler night air. He put on his Osprey and helmet, both still damp with sweat, picked up his rifle and climbed the ladder at the side of the tower, where he found Jesmond scanning the village through a night sight next to the gimpy.

'Evening, Corporal Jesmond. Nice night for it.'

'I dunno, sir. This place is fucking weird. There's just something about it.'

'How do you mean?' Tom looked out, the moon capturing in precise detail all the compounds as far as he could see, picking them out against the white sand and midnight-blue shadows.

'I dunno, boss – I mean sir – just everything. We ain't seen no fucking locals, and the militia are just fucking weird; they freak me out. And listen.'

Tom strained his ears. 'What for? I can't hear a thing.'

'Yeah, exactly. Nothing. In every other Afghan village I been to on Herrick 6 – ask the sarge as well; he'll say the same – in every village there was always stuff happening at night. Farmers going to look after crops cos it was the coolest time of day; dogs barking – not loudly or very often – but there was always a bit of noise through the night. Here though, there's fuck all. It's like a ghost town. I reckon half these compounds aren't lived in. It'll have a lot to do with these crazy militia, sir. They're fucking evil.'

'Yeah, well, I agree with you. But we're off tomorrow, and then we can forget all about these maniacs and start the joys of taking over the wagons. Before you know it, when we're stuck into our umpteenth set of vehicle docs, you'll all be wishing you were back here. Hey, look at that.'

Far to the east, over Loy Kabir, illumination shells cracked open as a firefight started. Faintly, very faintly, but accentuated by the unbroken night nearer them, Tom and Jesmond could hear the low beat of gimpys being fired and the crack of illum as the artillery fired off salvo after salvo. It looked beautiful, and they watched it and forgot all about Shah Kalay until Jesmond went to go and wake Ellis to take over from him. Tom sat on the roof, momentarily alone, and wondered about Cassie – where she was, what she was doing.

In the morning, the squadron prepared to leave as a column of Mastiffs started out from BGHQ to come and pick them up. As a parting shot, Frenchie sent 3 Troop south and 1 Troop north to show a bit more presence and pick up any final int. Clive went back up north, and Tom retraced his route south to the IED site, with the now familiar drill of immaculate patrolling from the lads and the militia mincing and smoking on the flanks.

The militia boy was up to his usual tricks, though this time with a pink rose in his AK, not a red one. He kept on coming up to the boys and stroking their faces, picking on Davenport in particular. His colleagues found it hilarious; the lads, who had found it amusing a couple of days ago, were now bored rigid by him. He was wearing more make-up than normal today, and his fringe, dripping with gel, was combed down to cover one eye. His perfect white teeth, unusual for an Afghan, shone between sickly red lips. Tom thought he was grotesque, almost like a whore from a painting by Breughel.

When they arrived at the craters they kept their distance from the immediate area and took up fire positions in a long line to Tom's left and right. It was only 0930 and already boiling hot. Tom could tell the boys were losing patience. Even Trueman and Jesmond, usually razor sharp and motor-mouthing banter at each other, were sullen.

Frenchie came up over the net: 'Hello, One Zero, Three Zero, this is Zero Alpha. Collapse back to my location now. Blizzard callsigns twenty minutes out. Acknowledge over.' Tom looked to the east, where he could see the pinpricks of the Mastiffs in the distance, the column raising a great cloud of dust.

Just as they prepared to leave, a pickup truck appeared behind them and joined the gaggle of militia sitting smoking under the shade of a tree. Evidently it was someone to impress because the boy ran over to the craters and jumped into one, shouting anti-Taliban slogans that Solly translated for Tom. The lads didn't pay him any attention, and Tom only started to take any interest himself when the boy left the craters and ran at the orange-and-blue-gated compound, screaming at it.

'Solly, what the fuck is going on?' said Tom, his neck prickling.

Solly, bored, replied, 'Oh, usual stuff, boss. He's just saying that the guys in that compound are Taliban cowards. Saying that they planted the bombs that we blew up the other day.'

'I don't like this. Get him back. Now.'

Solly started shouting at the boy to get back. He was now kicking the gate and jumping around in front of it, completely lost in trying to impress his friends, who were howling with laughter. Tom seemed to hear every bit of noise now flushing away from the area and swirling into the boy, whose screamed insults and boot clanging on the corrugated metal were then erased by the explosion that suddenly flung him five metres in the air and blew the gate off its hinges into the compound.

'CONTACT! CONTACT IED!' screamed Tom.

Miller, who had been lying prone, scanning the area with his GPMG, rolled over, dug into his trouser pocket for a pack of cigarettes and lit one. 'Stupid cunt,' he said, louder than he meant to, as he took a drag from it.

Tom stood rooted to the spot, not knowing whether to go and help or stay put. In the corner of his eye he saw the pickup truck drive to the front of the compound, some militia get out of it and scrabble through the dust to find the boy. *The lads, think of the lads!* He screamed out to either side of him, 'Stay down, stay down, boys. Everyone OK?'

Already Trueman was running around them. He came up to Tom and said breathlessly, 'No worries, boss; all ours are fine. Get a sitrep up to Zero, tell 'em a green casualty.'

Tom fumbled with the radio pressel-switch and spluttered out, 'Hello, Zero, this is Three Zero. Contact IED compound 42. No ISAF casualties, suspected militia Cat A. Wait out.' He didn't know what exactly had happened to the boy, but he had to have been fucked. The militia were now inside the compound; he must have been blown over the wall. Soon they emerged carrying what from Tom's location fifty metres away looked like a mass of pink pulp with a few blue rags of uniform hanging off it. They heaved it into the back of the pickup truck and with the driver flooring the accelerator screamed past them and back to the HQ building. They didn't even stop to let Tom know what had happened, and almost as soon as it had begun the episode was over, and the silence returned, filling the vacuum of the explosion's echo.

Tom sent as full a sitrep as he could up to Frenchie, reassuring him that none of the boys had been hurt. During the exchange Frenchie interjected, 'Jesus fuck! Sorry Three Zero for swearing on the net. Very unprofessional. The, er, casualty has just arrived at my location in the pickup truck. I don't think there'll be an open casket at that funeral . . . He is definitely dead . . . Return best speed to my location now. Tread lightly over.'

'Three Zero roger. Collapsing now. Out.' He briefed the troop. 'Right, lads, collapse from here now. Let's go back. The boy is dead.'

No one reacted to the news; everyone just seemed relieved to be going. Trueman went up and down like a mother hen checking them one more time, and Tom, not daring to go any closer to the compound, looked through his binoculars into it, through the gap where the gate had been. He could see the corner where four days ago he had walked among the chickens and the goat. They weren't there any more. Even the straw on the ground had been raked up and removed. It didn't look as though anyone had been there for years. Clearly the family had moved away, and someone had left the IED for them should they come back. He wondered how many more were in the compound. He did a final scan of the area. Far away to the left he thought he saw a black figure with a white headdress nip behind a compound wall but couldn't be sure. He turned and led the boys back to the HQ building to get on the Mastiffs and leave Shah Kalay.

The next evening Tom chatted with Frenchie on the HLS in Loy Kabir. Again an orange sunset. It was the first of the heli moves to get the squadron back down to Bastion to take over the Scimitars. Frenchie, now showered and immaculate again after the five days in Shah Kalay, said, 'Well, Tom Chamberlain, your first taste of ops. What do you reckon?'

'I don't really know what to think. It all seems a bit of a blur, to be honest.'

'I know. Don't worry; that was pretty niche stuff out there. It won't always be as complicated. It'll get simpler when it gets more kinetic. That's the rule I use. The more rounds fired, the easier for the boys to cope with it – in a funny sort of way. The trouble with those five days was that no one got off even so much as a shot, and yet it still felt very dangerous, very morally . . . well, as I said to you guys, grey. And as for having to work with those militia clowns . . .' He looked into the distance, dragged on a cigarette and breathed smoke out through his nostrils. 'Well, let's just say I hope it's the last time. Uh oh, here comes trouble.' He turned away and shouted, 'Right, lads, hustle up. Heli inbound.'

Brennan placed them all in their chalks as the Chinook appeared out of the sun, thrashing the humid air with its double-rotor *whack*. The boys crouched in their lines as it circled the HLS, dropped and gently touched down on the gravel, hurling up dust. Two chalks streamed out of it carrying bergens and mailbags, spare parts and an assortment of other junk.

The dust settled, and Tom waved at Jules Dennis, who came off the helicopter after the CO, himself just arrived in theatre to take over the battle group. Jules saw him and ran over while the Chinook was still being unloaded. He shouted at Tom over the noise of the engine, 'Going already?! What's it like up here?'

Tom yelled into his ear, 'Good question. Pretty crazy, to be honest.'

'That's how we like it! See you when you get back up

here with the wagons!' He ran off to join the CO, and the loadie on the back of the Chinook signalled for the boys to come on.

They rose as one and ran forward, refilling the old work-horse. Tom was the last one on. He clipped himself into his seat and glanced over at Frenchie in the seat opposite, who gave him a thumbs up. And then his stomach left him as the heli lifted off the ground, dipped its nose and rammed through the dust and heavy air, flinging out white flares either side of it against any RPGs, the heat from its exhausts skewing the ground with a shimmering, hazy film. Tom looked out the tailgate, mesmerized as the heli jinked along, hugging the folds of the earth as it headed into the dying sun.

My tent
A warm night in Camp Bastion
Dear Mum,

I hope this finds everything really well at home, and that Zeppo isn't missing me too much. I miss him! There are some quite amusing dogs out here. One hangs around the front gate of FOB Newcastle. He has terrible scars on his face from the dogfights that the Afghan soldiers put him in. But he's terribly friendly, and puts his head on your lap and looks at you with huge, sad eyes. The boys have called him Augustus. I hope I see him again when we get back up north in a few days.

It's been great being back in Bastion this last week. It feels so different from when we arrived on the first night (Oh my God that feels an age away!). Back then you just felt so completely out of your depth, and the worst thing was that as you filed off the plane, getting used to the heat, and the dust that immediately infiltrates your ears and nostrils – which I don't think I'm ever going to get rid of – a column of guys who are going home pass you in the other direction, jeering at you and saying things like 'Here you go, fellas. Six long months – enjoy!' which was a bit dispiriting. But now we're the ones who are doing that kind of thing to the new guys, who turn up every day. They are so easy to spot; pale skin, clean uniforms, blank faces thinking what on earth they've let themselves in for. Of course we are all wildly unsympathetic.

Loy Kabir is certainly quite amusing! It's in the most beautiful scenery, almost biblical. The main town's about five miles from north to south, but only about 800m wide at its widest point, enclosed by the sides of a wadi that must have been carved out of the rock back in the last ice age. The western side of the wadi is pretty shallow, but the eastern one is huge, soaring up to 80m high at one point. And the sunsets are amazing. The dust is so fine and light that it always lingers in the air about six feet up, so when the sun is low it bounces and reflects off these tiny particles to create the most vivid colours in a sort of prism effect. It really is amazing. Everywhere you go here you are constantly amazed by the weird shift from normal colours.

Anyway, all the boys are really well, and they LOVED the brownies you sent out. Lance Corporal Miller – you know, from Gateshead with the badger tattoo – has pleaded that I ask you for some more.

Please send any news at all about what's happening back home; any gossip at all is awesome! Still don't know when R & R is going to be, but Sergeant Trueman keeps on making noises about the troop trying to get the Christmas slot. Now that would be good. But don't get your hopes up.

With all my love, Mum,
Tommy xxx

PS Give Zep a massive hug as well.
PPS Don't worry, Mum; everything's all right out here, I promise. And the boys are awesome, like I always said they'd be. Promise you, don't worry! Tx

Tom closed the bluey, leaned back in the canvas chair and took a draw of coffee. He rubbed his eyes and started another letter.

The C Squadron Troop Leaders' Tent aka 'The Playboy Mansion'
Dear Will,

Mate, am I jealous of you! I was gutted to miss you in Bastion. Oh well. We moved up to BG(NE) the day before you must have come off the ground. Anyway, I hope POTL is gleaming, mate; argh I hate writing that – it makes me green with envy.

So anyway I've managed to make it through a month. It's been pretty weird, to be honest. The BG has had its fair share of contacts, especially in the north of the AO, but we've been slightly out of it in this barking-mad town called Shah Kalay. You won't have heard of it; it's in the arse end of nowhere. This place was seriously spooky. It was riddled with IEDs and was controlled by this militia who we couldn't trust further than we could have thrown them. We were there for five days, and the only thing that we achieved was getting one of the militia blown up, dead. Proper fucked, mate. Quad amp, and most of his head as well; he was basically just a slug. Good look. And then we bounced back down to Bastion and started taking over the CVR(T)s which amazingly enough are in quite good order. It's good to be back with them, and the boys are really excited about taking them up north, as there's loads of open ground to the flanks of the town where we'll be able to cut about. Fingers crossed anyway. But you know what this place is like. We'll probably get issued Uncle Sam costumes tomorrow and get sent to Islamabad to march around Mullah Omar's house on stilts.

Back up north in two nights' time, the whole squadron – 25 ancient vehicles bimbling through forty miles of bandido country. Ooooh that sounds like fun. If we get there this side of Christmas I'll be amazed.

Mate, I can't wait to hear all your news. Also if there are any tips at all you remember then I am all ears! Thanks so much for the parcel — the salami and biltong went down a treat, as did the Beano. *Old skool but I like it!*

Already looking forward to pints when back,
TC

Tom got up from the desk, a wooden board perched on two stacks of old Javelin tubes, and got ready to go over to the post office. Clive, Scott, Henry and an engineer mate of Henry's didn't look up from their poker game. The tent was their home in Bastion. It had been lived in since 2006 and was full of kit: new, old, borrowed, stolen, sent out by friends, inherited from outgoing mates. A huge sofa had been constructed out of a Hesco frame upholstered luxuriously with camp-bed mattresses, and Jason lay on this, tongue out in earnest battle with the latest Dan Brown novel. A TV stood, altar-like, on another platform of Javelin tubes in front of the sofa. The walls of the tent were lined with posters of topless girls, psychedelic drapes, a Union Flag, a rainbow flag and a CND flag. A couple of lamps were fitted with red bulbs, making the tent look like a dive bar in Vietnam.

Tom loved it; in the middle of the order and rigidity of Bastion the tent shone as a beacon of nonconformity. He pulled on ironed trousers and shirt, adjusted his beret in the shaving mirror hung by his bed and went out into the night air. It was starting to get a bit colder now; he'd probably start wearing his jersey at nights soon.

He passed a few of the boys on their way from the Naafi and then chatted for a moment with Miller and GV, just back from the gym. The last tent was the senior NCOs'. He walked into the porch and hung back to look for a moment through the mosquito netting at the scene within. It was a different universe from the officers' tent. Sergeant Williams stood at an ironing board in tiny Y-fronts, ironing a shirt as if his life depended on it, biceps straining down onto the board as if trying to rip open the regimental crest tattoo on his arm. Where Tom's tent was all soft and mellow, here a thin bare fluorescent tube threw its light into every corner. Brennan, Trueman and two other sergeants sat on rigid plastic chairs in front of a television, watching the news on BFBS, each drinking a steaming brew. Above Brennan's bed were paintings that his daughter had sent out, and above Trueman's was an Oldham Athletic flag and a Grateful Dead poster. Tom walked in.

Trueman greeted him: 'All right, sir, how's tricks? How much money you lost in that poker game? If you've come to borrow some then no can do.'

'No, Sergeant Trueman, those other maniacs are doing that. I've been writing some letters. Off to the post office now. You guys have any letters that I can take?'

'Nah, cheers though, sir,' said Brennan. 'That's kind of you. Hang about, what's this?' He looked at the television, and they all watched the story, about a mother who had been driven to committing suicide along with her disabled daughter after enduring years of bullying torment by a gang of thugs on their council estate. Apparently the police had ignored all her complaints and calls for help. Pictures flashed up of the woman and her daughter, and the car that they had gassed themselves in. Tom sensed something come over the tent. Normally stories in the news attracted nothing but mild shrugs from the soldiers, who tended to view everyone else's sufferings as child's play compared to what they were going through in Afghan. But this was different; Tom could see Trueman and Brennan looking shocked at the news.

'Fucking cunts. CUNTS!' Brennan broke the silence and threw his mug onto the floor, where it smashed and sprayed coffee up the wall of the tent. 'How fucking DARE those pikey scum. If I got my hands on any of those fucking cunt cowards I'd rip their fucking cocks off and shove them down their fucking throats.'

He was screaming, red-faced and spitting at the TV, and Tom watched nervously.

Brennan steadied himself. 'I'm sorry, sir, but it's just fucking unacceptable. How are we meant to stand here and watch our fucking country be taken to the dogs by these feral little pieces of shit?' He was whispering his words at the end, grasping the reality that he was unable to look after two little girls and a wife five thousand miles away.

Tom looked at him, unblinking, and said softly, 'I know, Sergeant Major, I know, I know. It's not right.' At that moment he felt nothing but Brennan's anger, an anger even worse than he had felt in the weeks before deploying. Tom wanted to destroy those half-men and felt as pure a rage against them as he had at anything before in his life. But the rage was shackled to an impotence that made it futile. Without another word he smiled sympathetically at Brennan, who was now slumped back in his chair and distractedly watching the next news item, went to go and pat him on the back, hovered his palm over him, but didn't. He withdrew his hand, left the tent and walked the lonely dark kilometre to the post office.

The next two days were a whirlwind as the squadron prepared to move north. While Frenchie and the troop leaders
pored over maps and aerial photographs of the route, planning and counter-planning, developing actions on, locating
key vulnerable points and areas of high threat, Brennan mas-
terminded the physical preparation of the wagons. Four
troops' worth of Scimitars plus an SHQ of four vehicles
were parked up in immaculate rows on the Bastion football
pitch with just a metre between them so that munitions and
supplies could be passed easily from vehicle to vehicle. The
boys swarmed over the wagons like bees on honeycomb.

All the bomb racks were filled, chains of lads passing
ammo clips into turrets. They took mostly high-explosive as
opposed to armour-piercing shells. HE rounds, with their
bright yellow warheads, were designed to explode upon
impact; if they missed the target they would probably still kill
with shrapnel, whereas AP rounds would, if off target, just
drive into whatever they ended up hitting. Boxes of 7.62 for
the GPMGs were stuffed into every available turret space.
Schmoolies, grenade boxes, smoke-grenade boxes, bin bags
full of cyalumes and Claymore mines all found accommodation in nooks and crannies. Javelin tubes were strapped to the
back of the wagons.

Brennan was everywhere, encouraging and ticking off in
equal measure. 'Come on, fellas,' he shouted. 'I want more
ammo. There's shedloads here, and I promise you, you can
never have enough. We are going to take it all up with us, so

let's start finding some extra fucking space for it. If you hit an IED you're going to be fucked anyway in these death-traps, so you might as well make the wagon into an atom bomb and make sure you die and not end up in the Paralympics. If you want to be one-limb Jim or Billy the stump then crack on, but don't come crying to me when it happens. No half-measures.' The younger boys blanched at this. 'Come on, fellas; lighten up. If you can't laugh what can you do?' he would say as he bounced from wagon to wagon.

In the afternoon Frenchie took Henry, whose troop was going to lead the column north, on a helicopter recce of the route. Afterwards Henry came to see Tom, who was with his boys as they sat around a wagon, chatting about nothing in particular and smoking. Tom was on the turret, quietly cleaning his rifle and listening to Trueman hold court, reeling off impersonation after impersonation or regaling them with stories of previous tours. The boys were all cackling away, in particular GV, whose high-pitched almost girlish laugh completely belied his barrel chest, his white teeth flashing smiles. Henry bounded up to the wagon.

'Hi, mate; how was the flight?' asked Tom.

'Great, pal, really great. That's the way to travel. A bit gutting when you realize that we covered the route in twenty minutes when it's going to take about twenty-four hours tomorrow, but oh well.'

'What about VPs? What's the going like?'

'Like the maps really, mate. Pretty flat, a few wadis with steep sides but nothing the wagons won't handle. The only real drama is that the moment we break off Highway One it's immediately obvious we're going up to Loy Kabir, so any Talib worth his salt will start guessing where to put the IEDs.

'We'll be able to cut about off the main tracks pretty easily, but there's one or two places where we're going to be channelled. But we should be all right. The weird thing is, there's this massive town about two thirds into it that isn't on any of the maps. I tell you, mate, massive. Just about five miles by five miles of compounds sprawling over the area.'

'Can we not just skirt around it?'

'That's the thing: no one's gone through it in the last three years, so, by extension, Frenchie thinks no one's going to have IED'd it. Everyone who's skirted around it on the obvious bypass tracks has been smashed. You can see the craters of previous hits from the air.'

'Well, chum –' Tom grinned as he punched Henry on the shoulder '– just as long as you don't get us lost we'll be fine. Good luck with that one; I can't wait. Every time it all gets a bit too much I'll just think of you up front flapping about getting lost with Frenchie breathing down the radio.'

'Thanks, mate. It's going to be a nightmare trying to lead this thread of vehicles through the route, especially at night, and especially through that sodding town. And you jack bastards are going to be monging it in your wagons just following the previous vehicle. You lucky fuckers.'

'No probs, mucker; any time.'

That night in the tent they huddled round Clive's laptop to watch *Black Hawk Down*. They were all able to quote from it verbatim, and they found it amusing that even here they still watched war films. They were asleep by ten, their minds able now to switch off at will, knowing the next few days were liable to be completely sleepless.

The next morning the squadron mustered, and Frenchie walked around the wagons, inspecting kit, climbing into turrets, sniffing round like a search dog. Brennan, the SQMS and the tiffy trooped after him, and as the party came to each troop the troop leader and sergeant followed nervously on, hoping the wagons would pass Frenchie's high standards. He never cared much about cleanliness, a losing battle in Afghanistan, but if any moving part hadn't been oiled to within an inch of its life he would get very angry. He clambered over the wagons, jumping into the gunners' seats to test the smoothness of the elevation and traverse of the Rardens, making sure the GPMGs were dripping with oil, checking the running gear of the tracks to see that oil levels were correct and burrowing into the engines, twanging the generator belts for tautness.

After an hour he jumped off the final wagon, his coveralls filthy, and took them off to reveal his immaculate combats. He hated getting these dirty. Ever fastidious, he took his beret off, ran a comb several times back through his hair and then beamed at Brennan. 'Well, Sergeant Major; it looks like half of NATO's entire stockpile of ammunition is on these wagons. Bloody good job; very well done indeed. We're quite a force to be reckoned with, aren't we?'

'Too right, sir. Let's just say it's going to be a brave bastard who decides to mess with us on the way up.'

They held the O Group for the move. It was nothing that they hadn't talked through informally over the past week, and when Tom in turn delivered the orders to 3 Troop he didn't have to refer to his notes at all. As he handed over to Trueman for the casevac plan and CSS part of the orders he looked at the scene in front of him. The boys were sitting around in canvas chairs, shirts off, dog tags clinking softly on their chests in the steady warm breeze. They had lost their little rolls of puppy fat and were lean and hungry-looking, and the pumped-up look in their eyes rubbed off on him. He could tell they were excited about the move through the big town.

Frenchie thought that while they would avoid IEDs on this route, the move would inevitably generate a big contact from the local Taliban, who would feel impelled, almost out of pride, to put up a performance as twenty wagons trundled through their backyard. Tom noticed Miller and Davenport's contrasting reactions: Miller calmly taking in every word, Davenport a bundle of nervous energy, his foot tapping the ground and his head bobbing up and down as though he was listening to music. They were in the zone. *Christ!* Tom thought. *I'm in the zone too.*

In the afternoon everyone lined up in their crews on the football pitch, and Jason took them through a dozen scenarios, from the lead wagon hitting an IED, to the centre wagon hitting one, to a strike on the rear one, to a complex ambush being thrown at them with three wagons taken out in one hit. They rehearsed what would happen in a sustained contact from the left, from the right, from the rear, actions on a single shoot and scoot from a lone gunman. They rehearsed what would happen if Frenchie was killed, how they would move in mist or fog, bunching much tighter together. The midday sun beat down, but they were used to it now.

At one point soldiers from another unit walked past and sniggered at the sight of the squadron moving in their strange bundles of three. Brennan predictably blew up. Striding towards them so quickly that they started to run, he screamed after them, 'Right, you lippy cunts can fuck off. We're doing this not to look good, but so we don't end up with our fucking legs blown off. You fucking REMFs wouldn't know a thing about that, would you? You ballbags, get the fuck out of my sight before I rip your eyes out.' The fat rear-echelon soldiers scurried off as fast as their unworn boots would take them to a chorus of jeers and abuse, and Brennan said to Jason, 'Sorry, sir; please carry on.'

Just at the point where Tom could tell the boys were about

to lose interest, Frenchie called a halt; time was moving quickly. They rolled out at midnight, and it was 1700 now. Time for scoff, and then back to the wagons for last-minute tweaks until they struck out. He dismissed the boys and they ran to the scoff house.

They stuffed themselves with food as Brennan had told them all to, in case there was a major drama on the move and they found themselves on the ground and on rations for a week. Plates were piled high with curry and rice, stew and chips. Jason had the fullest plate and was about to further engorge himself with a chicken leg like a Roman emperor when he sniffed it, pulled a face and put it back down. 'Something's definitely not right with that.'

'I thought you were the human dustbin: eat anything animal, vegetable, mineral or metal?' said Clive.

'Yeah, not that though. It just smells weird – like off. The rest of it's all right though.' He started chomping through the rest of his plate.

Tom stopped eating and seemed to go green. He picked up the chicken on Jason's plate and held it up to his nose.

'You're right, mate. It reeks. And I've just eaten one of those bastards. I thought it tasted weird.' He prodded the mangled remains of the chicken leg on his own plate, pink ripped flesh hanging off it and watery fat beneath.

They stopped eating and looked at him. They all knew what happened when they got ill on tour: you were out for five days minimum, of no use to man or beast. To get ill on a big move like this one was going to be dreadful.

Clive chuckled. 'Well, mate, glad I'm not in your wagon. I don't envy Dusty.' He spotted Miller on another table. 'Hey, Dusty, hope you've got some Immodium on your wagon, cos I thing your boss is going to be shitting for Britain after that chicken he's just eaten.'

Miller shouted back to Tom, 'Oh cheers, sir; rookie error. You ain't heard the rumours about them chicken legs, did you? Everyone says they're a killer.'

Tom clicked his teeth. 'Bugger off, the lot of you. I'll be fine. I've got a lead-lined stomach anyway.' He started upon a bowl of apple crumble with studied nonchalance, praying inwardly that he wouldn't get ill. He glanced at the chicken leg. It looked rancid.

They finished and went back to the tent to pick up their gear. Tom felt sorry to be leaving the civilian comforts of the tent. He would miss the eight nights they'd had here, watching films, playing cards, writing letters home. The last one to leave, he turned out the red lamp and paused for a moment in the dark before running outside with his rucksack to join the others.

At the tank park there was nothing to do but wait. They knew the plan inside out. Leave camp at midnight, head north to Highway One, head east on that for ten kilometres, then leave the road to strike north again and thread their way up the seventy kilometres to Loy Kabir. Try not to hit any IEDs en route. All going well they'd be there by dusk the next day. All going badly it could turn into an epic.

Frenchie's philosophy on military operations was simple: plans either work perfectly or not at all. If one tiny thing goes wrong, he held, everything else unravels until what eventually happens bears no resemblance to anything that has been planned or even conceived of before the operation. All or nothing. It was vital to have a plan, he maintained, as it was useful, when things went awry, to be able to use a previous template to judge progress and inform possible decisions, but it was equally important to be able to depart from it without pride or sentimentality. That was why he spent more time on rehearsals than he did on orders. They constantly rehearsed and talked through every possible scenario or weird mutation of a plan, and he rammed his philosophy into the troop leaders as they gathered around his wagon for a last pep talk.

'Here we go, fellas. Henry, best of luck. Whatever you do, don't get us lost, all right? No pressure! Remember, lads: if one thing goes wrong here, the plan's going to disappear. But don't worry about that. Have faith. You've all got the grammar and vocab of ops by now. When things start to go wrong just apply them to the new situation, and you'll be OK. Forget the basics, and we're screwed. And at least we're not working with any Afghan muppets this time. Hopefully next time I see your ugly mugs this close will be in Loy Kabir. Here's hoping anyway. Right, back to your troops. Best of luck. And keep VP slick, whatever you do.'

By 2300 everyone was set in the wagons, snatching some sleep or lost in their own time-passing rituals. Davenport was fast asleep in his driver's seat. Dusty was plugged into his music reading a Bernard Cornwell book by the light of an orange cyalume. Tom had checked and triple-checked all the weapons and radios and had oiled everything inside the turret two times now, so he reached into his side bin and drew out a bluey. He'd write to Cassie. He folded it out, took a pen from his trouser pocket, thought a bit about how to begin, toying with various ways of opening up, and started writing.

Bastion
Dear Cassie,

I hope this finds you very well. I can't believe I am writing this, stuck in the desert a million miles away. At the moment I am in Camp

Bastion, and we are about to begin a move north to this town called Loy Kabir that we're working in. I cannot even begin to describe to you what it is like out here. And I don't mean that in a bad sense at all, but in an all-encompassing sense. It is quite simply the most over-whelming experience of my life. Everything is brought into focus to the sharpest degree. You cover the entire range of the emotional spectrum pretty much every day, from excitement to terror through boredom.

And there's a lot of boredom. But it doesn't really matter, as the boys are always there to chat to and get you through the dull times. And the most amazing thing about here is that you do everything against a backdrop of astonishing scenery. The sunrises and sunsets are something else. Like tonight. We had a bright red sunset, and as the sun dropped to the west the full moon rose as its exact mirror in the east. It hung on the horizon even redder than the sun, like some kind of blood orange. It's now fully back to its normal bright white, almost directly above us now. It feels quite friendly, just next to the good old North Star, our guide for tonight. This one star trillions of light years away which through some random intergalactic chance is our homing beacon. I promise you I haven't become a space geek in the past few weeks. But the sky is amazing out here, so much more intense that anything I have seen before.

I think about you a lot, Cassie. I hope we can still be friends. I think it's fair to say that I became a bit of a prat when I joined the army, a real puritan in many ways. The army gives you the opportu-nity to seize the moral high ground in virtually every situation, so that you look down on people and often actively despise them just because they haven't decided to join the army. It is not a good look, and I am not proud of it. When I get back I promise I won't be so bad. It would be great to see you when I get back on R & R. I'll let you know when it is asap.

Better go now — we roll out of here in about half an hour and my gunner is telling me it's my turn to make the brews on the little kettle we have inside the turret. What an impertinent wretch. I could spend *hours trying to close this letter, so I'll just take the easy way out and say that I am thinking of you, with love,*

Tom

He sealed the bluey and dropped down into the turret to plug in the boiling vessel. 'All right, Dusty, how do you want it?'

'Oh cheers, sir, thought you'd never ask. Usual please, tea Julie Andrews.'

'What?'

'Julie Andrews. You know, *Sound of Music*. White nun.'

'Oh, I see – white no sugar.'

'Exactly, boss.'

'What's black with no sugar? Black nun?'

'Yeah – tea Whoopi Goldberg. Do they teach you nothing at university?'

Tom made the brews and they sat on the turret breathing in the steam from the tops of their flasks. They were shivering, partly from the cool night air and partly because of the ticking clock, and their teeth chattered in curt machine-gun bursts. Tom drained his brew, jumped off the turret and trotted over to Staff Sergeant Grant next to Brennan's wagon. As the SQMS, Grant was based in Bastion and so could post the letter. 'Evening, SQMS; sorry to interrupt. You couldn't bung this in the post, could you?'

'Course sir, no dramas.' He looked at the address. 'Miss Cassandra Foskett. Interesting. What is she – out of ten, I mean? Any less than a four, mind, and I'm not going to send it, for your own good.'

Tom blushed and hoped it wouldn't show in the moonlight. 'She's just a friend.'

'Come on, sir; I ain't falling for that. No fella's *just friends* with any girl. You're having a laugh.'

'OK, hands up, guilty. Maybe she is more than a friend. As for the out of ten, I dunno, probably a two or a three. Face like a bulldog chewing a wasp. Only joking. Truthfully? I reckon a nine, possibly more. Way out of my league anyway. But you've got to dream, haven't you? But if you could get it to the post I'd be grateful.'

'Of course, sir, I promise. I'll do it first thing you lot bugger off. And, sir,' he said as Tom started to walk back to his wagon, 'best of luck for the move. I'll be thinking about you guys. Stay safe.'

Tom heard Grant's concern not in the words themselves but in the soft manner they were spoken. 'Thanks, SQMS, we will. We'll be good.'

Not long left now: twenty to midnight. Tom scrambled up the Scimitar's bar armour and into the turret. He carefully fastened his headphones and then put his helmet on top, did up his chinstrap and enjoyed the satisfying *pop* that said the button had securely hit its housing. He reached forward with his foot to nudge Davenport on the shoulder to wake him up. They tested the intercom. All good to go. He looked around him at the compact grid of wagons and the silhouettes of the gunners and commanders of each vehicle through the haze generated by the engines.

Ten minutes. Frenchie came up on the net for a final radio check, and in sequence all callsigns gave it. They had done this two hours ago in any case; it was more out of form than necessity.

Tom's watch struck out the final few seconds, its luminous tick like a drumbeat. It hit midnight, and as if on cue Frenchie came up again. 'Hello, all Tomahawk Callsigns, this is Tomahawk Zero Alpha. H-Hour. In order of march, move out. Best speed. Out.'

Henry's four wagons started to roll, and then Scott

followed on. SHQ moved next, in the middle of the column. As the final SHQ wagon left, Jesmond, the lead car of 3 Troop, moved, and Tom said over the intercom, 'Right, Dav, we're on.' Davenport put the wagon up through the gears and then they were moving, wordlessly sliding through Bastion. They passed soldiers at the side of the road, who threw them thumbs up and shouted good luck.

On Tom's left he noticed in the artillery camp the dark bulk of a GMLRS rocket system pointing into the sky, framed against the stars, and just as he was about to point it out to Dusty a plume of fire scorched from it into the night. Another and then a third followed in quick succession. Three phosphorus fireworks searing through the night and bathing their skin in white. Tom could see Dusty's freckles. Frenchie came up on the net. 'Fire mission for a contact in Sangin. Pity the folk who are going to end up beneath those thunderbolts. Out.' Tom kept watching, his neck straining up as the bright smoke trails lingered way above them, memorials to the targets of the missiles, who would be dead long before they disappeared. Space-age weapons used at midnight to kill men who didn't even have electricity in their homes.

Tom was taken back to when he was a boy, to when he watched footage of the first Gulf War, with Scud missile launches and rockets from aircraft carriers. He wasn't shivering any more. He was grinning. Finally he had come into his inheritance.

At dawn Tom took off his goggles, slugged some water, swilled it around his mouth and spat it out over the side of the wagon, filthy from the packed dust which clung to his gums and his swollen tongue. He took a photo of himself on his digital camera and examined it. He had huge panda eyes where his goggles had been, and the rest of his face was caked in the dust that had been thrown up by the column through the night. Everything on the wagon was covered by it. It was in his rifle, it was in his pistol, and when he snapped the elastic on his helmet a cloud of dust jumped up. He could feel it in his crotch, and it clogged up his fingernails and matted his hair. Every pore was stuffed with it, and he couldn't blink properly; his tear ducts had been blocked up even behind the goggles.

They were in a temporary halt, as 1 Troop barma'd the exit to a wadi that they had been driving up for a couple of hours. Tom rasped over the IC, 'Dav, use this – get some kip. I'll kick you when we're on again. Dusty, I'll stag on. Get your head down.' But Dusty was already out, slumped in the turret, mouth open, head resting on the sight.

Tom looked back to the wagons behind him and gave a thumbs up to Jesmond and Trueman in their turrets. He felt the kind of giddiness that only comes on after extreme lack of sleep, and he stuffed a chocolate bar from the side bin down his mouth, hoping for a tiny sugar hit. The chewed chocolate became clogged by the dust in his mouth and moved down his throat in a viscous lump, dragging sand

and mucus down with it. His legs ached – he had been standing all night – and so he sat on the turret hatch and stretched
them out in front of him, enjoying the creak of his muscles
and the blood flowing back into starved capillaries. He
moved his legs apart and then together and wondered what
they would look like as stumps, what they would look like
jagged and bloody after an IED strike. He had never before
thought about how big legs were, how much blood they must
contain.

He took his binoculars out and looked ahead of him. All
the wagons in front had just one figure standing out of them;
clearly everyone else was sleeping. The net was silent save for
the occasional sitrep from Henry, whose wagons were inch-
ing along behind his four-man barma team, the gunners from
his four cars, who were moving with brisk and purposeful
steps up the shallow exit of the wadi, now and again stopping to examine the ground where a Vallon had picked up a
reading.

One of the barma team called to the others to halt. He
had obviously found something. The other three crouched
down on their knees as he drew a paintbrush from his body
armour, lay down on his front and brushed away at the dust.
After a minute or so he picked up a small item, probably a
coin or a wheel nut, hauled himself onto his knees again and
dismissively tossed it aside. He gave a final cursory wave of
his Vallon over the area and then stood up. The others all
rose from their crouches and they continued their funny, deft
ballet. Tom found it strange not being able to hear them and
oddly lonely in his turret, cut off from the rest of the column
by an eerie silence. The radio was quiet too. Here they were,
a tooled-up violent caravan, all isolated from each other in a
strange archipelago. He could see every wagon but talk to
nobody.

After twenty minutes the exit had been cleared, and slowly every turret came to life again. Drivers were kicked awake, and water was thrown on sleepy faces. It only turned the dust into a cloying mud. The column started to move again, the sickly pale sun to their east shallow in a milky sky. Tom could feel its heat increase by the minute, and the desert sand lost its night-time greyness and paled into a white glare. The column rolled on. The horizontal light from the sun created shafts of rainbow prisms in the glinting, shifting dust, and Tom was surprised by his shadow imprinted on the haze of dust around him. He lost himself for a moment and looked more closely at the shadow, permanent against the ever-changing dust cloud. He waved his arm in the air, and the shadow copied it. He did it again and again, thinking of Cassie always being in front of him but then slipping away into the shadows. He drifted until his trance was broken by Dusty over the IC: 'You OK, boss?'

'Sorry, yeah, Dusty, I'm OK. Just remembering something, that's all.'

'No worries, sir; this lack of sleep fucks you up. For a minute there I thought you'd lost it. Here, have some gum.'

Tom brought himself back to the move; already it felt endless. They would be visible for miles and miles around; a pound to a pinch of salt the Taliban to their north could see the plume and were preparing to fight them. Forty minutes later they had their first dicker appear. To their left a pickup truck drove to the top of a low rise and parked, a silent sentinel. Frenchie called a halt, and as one turrets traversed as the car commanders used their sights to get a closer look at a figure in a dark purple robe, looking at them through binoculars. Quite obviously he was reporting on their progress.

Frenchie came up on the net. 'Charlie Charlie One callsigns, as you can see we have our first dicker. They know we're coming. Let's hustle up; expect contact.' Tom felt his stomach drop away. 'As much as we'd all love to give the good news to our friend on the hill, I'm afraid we can't do anything. We'll have to move on. One Zero, your ball. Out.' The column started moving again.

Dusty muttered, 'For fuck's sake. Why can't we just waste that dickhead? One shot, all I need. Fucking rules of fucking engagement.'

For the next four hours the journey continued its slow rumble in a now familiar pattern of driving for a couple of kilometres and then halting to clear a VP or to crest a rise and observe the area in front. They were still in the open desert, so Henry was enjoying the luxury of being able to pick a completely virgin route. Just on the horizon, though, Tom could see the low cluster of compounds that formed the town. Inevitably the Taliban were expecting them; the one thing they wouldn't be anticipating though was for the column to steam straight through the middle of it. It was the kind of trick that could be pulled just once.

Frenchie had cleared it with the CO two nights before, who thought it a good plan. Over the secure telephone link from Bastion to FOB Newcastle he had said, 'Well, Frenchie, it's ballsy, but if anyone can do it C Squadron can. Just don't cock it up. Bravura looks good when it succeeds, but when it goes wrong you look like a muppet. So, don't cock it up. Got it?'

Even Frenchie, whose self-confidence and faith in his own and his men's ability usually won through any moments of doubt, was chastened by this, and a sudden stop in his throat held him before he answered, 'Got it, Colonel. Don't worry. We'll do it.'

Slowly, inexorably, the column kept its course. For half an hour at midday they had a Lynx fly over them. The FAC in the back of Frenchie's Sultan talked to it, and the pilot over-flew the town and gave live feed of what he was seeing. So far activity was perfectly normal: on both the east and west of the huge sprawl people were going about their daily business. Farmers were in fields, couples rode on motorbikes and children played outside compounds. Frenchie relayed all this to the squadron and Tom was reassured, but he just wanted to get to Newcastle by dusk. He was starting to feel a little peaky and wasn't sure whether it was lack of sleep or something worse. He hoped against hope that it wasn't the chicken and withdrew into himself, and the banter in the turret dried up.

The Lynx was then called away to another task, and they were on their own again. Out on one flank, about two kilometres away, a motorbike tracked their progress, betrayed by the plume of dust thrown up by its rear wheel. *At least the desert's neutral*, thought Tom.

Closer and closer they came to the compounds. The Taliban would be expecting them to commit to the eastern or western bypass route at any point now and must be surprised that still they kept on heading for the centre. Tom drank some more water; he was getting a low throbbing headache. The sun, now at the height of its parabola, beat upon the back of his neck. The water, cold earlier, was now horribly warm and seemed to scour and burn his throat. With just five hundred metres left before the town, Frenchie came up again. 'Charlie Charlie One, Zero Alpha. This is it. Eyes peeled. Be prepared to engage enemy if fired upon. One Zero acknowledge over.'

Henry replied, 'One Zero roger. I'll thread a route through with my One Two callsign. Hope it's to your liking. One Zero out.' And so the column plunged straight into the cluster, the open desert now giving way to another archipelago of compounds, all fifty or a hundred metres apart, separated by rough tracks and ploughed fields, Henry's troop twisting and turning through the maze.

Progress was surprisingly rapid. For four miles they jinked their way through faster almost than they had raced through the desert. Far from the village emptying of all activity, the wagons seemed to be the biggest draw in town, and the boys exploited this to the full, throwing from their turrets sweets and pencils at every opportunity. If there was a halt due to the lead wagons trying to work out how best to skirt around an obstacle, children would come up to the vehicles and the crews would lift them on board and have their photos taken with them, letting the children wear their helmets and putting on their little hats. Three Troop's biggest draw was Trueman, who always had about twenty children clustered around his wagon. He entertained them by pulling faces and then pretending to be a monster chasing them away. Tom entered into the spirit of things only half-heartedly. He was now feeling really queasy, and could only raise a wan smile when Dusty started larking around with the kids. He was relieved when the wagons started rolling again.

With only a quarter of a mile before the lead wagon broke clean from the cluster there was another halt. Corporal Ealham, who had led all of the way from Bastion, halted five metres into a ploughed field which lay between a little conurbation of compounds. Farmers were in the field, and one of them looked angry. Ealham came up on the net. 'Hello, One Zero, One Two. I'm just going to reverse and take a route around this field. I don't think this fella's too pleased about me driving through it. Apologies. I'll get back on track. Over.'

'One Zero roger. Agreed. No dramas. Just get out of there and we'll go around. Out.'

The wagon was with its tracks parallel to the deep-ploughed furrows in the field, meaning that to its left and to their right were walls of soil. Ealham, exhausted after bearing so much responsibility for so long, looked over the side of the wagon and judged the depth of the furrows. He knew they should just reverse out but somehow found himself saying over the IC to his driver, 'Right, Mikey, let's get out of here. Neutral turn to the right.'

The driver, also drained by the stress of the move north, the lead man of the entire squadron, automatically and with no appreciation for his surroundings immediately yanked back the right drive stick to perform a neutral turn.

Behind them Henry could hear the splintering of metal on metal as the track was driven straight into the deep furrow, tearing it away from the wheels. 'The fucking twat,' he swore. 'He's thrown his fucking track.' He ripped off his ANR and in a fit of rage jumped down on to the ground and ran over to the wagon, whose occupants were peering over the side of the turret in horror at what they'd just done. Henry lost it, all the angst and fear of the past hours boiling over. 'Corporal Ealham, what the fuck have you just done?'

Ealham looked horrified, his dull, exhausted eyes slowly realizing what a mistake he had made. 'Boss, I'm so sorry. I can't believe I've just done that. I can't believe it. My bad, my bad. I just got too tired.'

Henry looked into his eyes, saw an almost dead glaze and knew he shouldn't have kept him on point for so long; he should have changed around the order of march ages ago to rotate the burden of responsibility. But Ealham had never ever, neither on exercise nor on ops, made this kind of mistake before and took huge pride in being lead callsign. Henry softened his voice. 'OK, OK. I know, Eals, I know. It's going to be OK. We'll get that track fixed back on again and then be on our way. I'll get on to Zero Alpha and we'll get one of the Samsons up here.'

He jogged back to his wagon to get on the radio. He had an uneasy feeling. Everything had been going so well up to this point. Putting the track back on should take all of half an hour, but somehow he didn't think it was going to be that simple. As he clambered with seasoned agility onto his own wagon he remembered Frenchie's dictum that the moment one thing went wrong, everything else followed.

Frenchie heard the news and ordered one of the Samsons forward to bring some REME expertise to bear. He said to the FAC, 'This is either going to be cured in two shakes or we're going to be here till hell freezes over. And I reckon it's the latter.' Sure enough, when Staff Sergeant Prideaux reported back, all was not looking good at all. The force of the turn had not just taken the track off the wheels but also sheared off the rear idler. What could have been a half-hour job was now, at best, a five-hour one.

'Fuck. Fuck fuck fuck,' cursed Frenchie. This was not good. If this had happened in the desert, then fine. No one was going to attack them in the open. But here, in the midst of the cluster, anyone could get up close to the vehicles, strung out as they were over a kilometre.

The Taliban obviously hadn't yet realized what had happened, and children were still coming up to the wagons. Frenchie ordered everyone to redouble their ambassadorial efforts. He needed to come up with a plan to protect them all; in the meantime they would continue to use the children as de facto human shields. He knew he was up against it. The moment the Taliban realized their predicament they could lock them into the area by laying IEDs to their north and south, blocking their exit routes. Frenchie had to secure the route out; that was imperative. He also had to secure the recovery zone while the REME boys struggled in the open with the track and idler. He briefed the squadron over the net. 'Charlie Charlie One, this is Zero Alpha. Here's the plan. We have to secure our exit route as soon as possible. To that end, Four Zero, I want you to leapfrog from the rear, push north past the stricken wagon and secure the edge of the cluster. Four Zero roger so far over.'

From the rear of the column came Clive. 'Four Zero roger so far. Understood over.'

'Zero Alpha. One Zero, you will provide all-round defence around the stricken wagon, and SHQ are going to come up next to it and make that location our HQ until we can move. One Zero roger so far over.'

'One Zero roger.'

'Zero Alpha, Two Zero remain in your positions, and Three Zero push up to take SHQ's place, where you'll be the rear of the column. Spread your vehicles as you see fit to prevent us being contacted from the south. Three Zero acknowledge over.'

Tom, now feeling worse and worse, his guts rumbling and his forehead damp with sweat, replied weakly, 'Three Zero roger. Understood over.'

'Zero Alpha. OK, that's the new plan. Move now to new positions. Out.'

And so the squadron reorganized itself according to Frenchie's instructions, with the centre of mass reforming around the stricken One Two, with the hapless Ealham cursing himself and wilting under Brennan's glare when his wagon parked up next to his. Tom moved 3 Troop up to where SHQ had been and fanned out the four wagons to face south. After half an hour everyone was in place, and Frenchie could breathe a bit more easily. They were still vulnerable, and he was sure that the Taliban would try something, but at least they had secured their exit for when they could move again.

Over the course of the afternoon the weather got worse. A low blanket of cloud came in, and the hot dry wind changed into a damp one carrying tiny specks of water. The air became humid and close, and in the far distance a low growl of thunder provided a sinister backdrop to their efforts to get out of the cluster. The children still came up to the wagons, but with less innocence than before. Trueman had seen this before on his previous tour, and radioed Frenchie to warn him that he thought the children were now being used by the Taliban to get information on the cars from close quarters and then report back.

Shadowy figures popped up at the corners of compounds all along the column, which, although now contracted, was still spread over three hundred metres. Often these men would come into the open and eye the scene before them, taking it all in before slipping back behind the walls. It made the boys feel very vulnerable, and weapons were re-oiled and likely firing points identified by the commanders and gunners, who practised dry-run shoots on them. Each wagon could see the one before it and after it in the order of march, so they could support each other in contact and could make sure there were no blind spots where IEDs could be dug in between them, but it still felt to the boys as though the initiative had slipped to the Taliban.

Tom by this point had completely succumbed to D & V, and was in and out of his turret, vomiting and defecating by the side of the wagon. His clothes soon stank, and when he hauled himself after each bout into the turret he just sat there, sweating and then shivering, his clothes stained with filth. Dusty made sure Frenchie and Brennan knew, but there was nothing they could do for him. He was the least of their concerns at the minute, and a few others in the squadron were coming down with the same thing. It was all, as Frenchie predicted it would, feeling as though it was unravelling very quickly.

Dusk came on and with it an increase in the cloud. Large raindrops fell and kicked up sand from where they bored their tiny craters. The wind picked up, whipping squalls of sand high in the air to mix with the rain into mud showers. The dust on the wagons turned into sticky paste, making the slick movement of machinery into a grinding mangle. Progress on the stricken vehicle was awful. The track took hours to tease off where it had been tangled in the running gear, and even with Brennan cajoling them on the boys were shadows of their usual selves after so long without sleep. Three had come down with D & V, and one of the boys even tore a hole in the seat of his trousers so he could defecate without having to take them down.

Night came on, still without any commitment from the Taliban. Frenchie sent round that there was to be no sleeping that night; everyone had to remain awake. He knew it would suit the Taliban perfectly to exploit the dark and the dust, using their knowledge of their own backyard to spring a complex ambush on the column. It was what he would have done in their shoes. So the boys sat in their turrets, trigger fingers poised for any movement. Although they were close to their friends, the gloom that separated them made each crew feel as though they were in the middle of nowhere.

Tom, now soaked from his own sweat as well as the steady rain, awoke with a start from a few moments' captured unconsciousness. Dusty, who had let him sleep and stepped up into the role of vehicle commander with aplomb, was wide awake next to him, steadily traversing the turret and watching to the south, the thermal imaging sight able to see perfectly through the rain and fog. 'Fuck,' said Tom, scrambling out of his seat. 'I need to go again.' He had barely lifted himself out of the turret before he puked again. His foot slipped on the vomit and he almost fell off the wagon, but he just caught himself on the bar armour at the last minute, ripping his hand open on a sharp edge. He looked at the gash, livid across his filthy palm, with numb acceptance. Tetanus, he thought, would be bliss compared to what he was feeling like at the minute.

He got to the ground and emptied himself in the hole he had dug at the side of the wagon. He had no energy left at all. The air fizzed with the dust and drizzle, wind howling between the vehicles. He stood, did his trousers up and saw shadows flit in the murk about twenty metres away. Curious, he walked away from the wagon into the gloom, soon being enveloped by it. The dust and rain swirled all around him, and he felt even colder than before. He felt he was stepping out of the war and into another world.

One shadow in particular seemed always in front of him, and with each step he took it receded back into the dark. He walked forward again, taking the pistol out of his holster. The shadow stopped. It was a man, just five metres away from Tom with his back to him. Tom raised his pistol, and just as his lips opened to challenge him, the figure turned. He was tall and thin, and dressed in black. On his head gleamed a white dish-dash, bright even in the dark. Tom couldn't speak. The pistol felt heavy, and his arms groaned with illness. The figure fixed him with an unblinking gaze. Tom's hand dropped and the pistol hung limp by his hip. The figure raised his hands to his dish-dash as if to reveal his face.

And then Dusty was next to him, and the man retreated into the shadows. 'Boss, boss. Relax. Relax. Put the pistol down. Please put the pistol down.' He felt Dusty's hand on his shoulder. He saw Davenport next to Dusty. 'What's happening, boys?' he asked, bewildered. 'What's going on?'

'Don't worry, boss. Just come with us.'

Davenport put his arm around his shoulders, and they took him back to the wagon, where Trueman was waiting with a stretcher that he had laid next to it. 'There you go, boss, there you go,' he said as he helped Tom lie down, took his helmet off and wiped his brow with a damp rag. It felt good. 'You've had a bad dream, boss. Christ, we were scared. You fucking off like that into the dark, what were you thinking? Dusty saw you go into the dark all on your own and came to get me from my wagon. Thank fuck we got you before you got lost in the compounds. If anyone got you there you'd be fucked. Christ, you gave us a scare.'

Tom barely heard Trueman but knew he had been saved from something by Dusty. He murmured thanks. Davenport sat by him all night. Mercifully the rain lifted, but the wind and the dust persisted. Tom kept soiling himself throughout the night, unable to move. Davenport took his trousers off for him, so he could shit at will. Tom seemed detached from his body. He felt no shame at all at his illness. He just wanted to die. His mind's eye couldn't escape the figure receding into the shadows and imagined its soft voice beckoning him into the darkness. Even when he closed his eyes he saw it on the inside of his eyelids, gently coaxing him.

Throughout the night they worked on the vehicle. The rain had turned the ploughed earth into shin-deep mud. The boys had to dig underneath the wagon to allow work to take place on the track. The more it rained the more the vehicle subsided into the mud. Slipping and sliding around it, their red head torches the only light in the dark, they moved with slow, lumbering steps, cursing their bloody and blistered hands as they dug and grappled with the track. Brennan moved among them, lifting them out of the mud, taking their spades off them and hurling himself into a digging frenzy. He didn't shout at them or swear and made sure there were constant brews coming from the BV in the back of his wagon.

Every effort to drag the vehicle out of the mire failed. At 0400 the REME Samson, trying to drag it out to allow the boys to work out of the field and on the slightly firmer earth at its edge, managed to throw its track as well. Staff Sergeant Prideaux, caked in mud and nearly crying with frustration, went to report to Frenchie in the back of the Sultan. Frenchie received the news calmly; he had personally prepared himself to be here for another week at least. 'Right, Sergeant P. Just come in here and have a brew. If anyone needs one, you do.' He poured a flask and watched Sergeant Prideaux, a bear of a man, slump onto the seat opposite him and drain the steaming mug.

Frenchie got onto the radio. 'Charlie Charlie One, this is Zero Alpha. Sitrep. We will be here for a few more hours yet, I'm afraid. Five One has thrown a track as well.' He could imagine the sighs from each of the turrets along the column. 'So we're going to be here for a while, and I reckon dawn is the time for the attack. Our Widow callsign,' he looked over to the FAC, who nodded back, 'assures me we're going to have an Ugly on station in the morning, but we're only going to have it from 0600 to 0800. And then who knows what will happen. I expect a running battle with shoot-and-scoot gunmen. Four Zero roger so far. Over.'

Clive, zombie-like, choked his response: 'Four Zero roger so far. Over.'

'Zero Alpha. All callsigns keep your sitreps coming in. As long as we have our route secured by Four Zero to the north we'll be fine. Keep your drills slick. Don't expose yourselves unnecessarily. Watch your arcs. Out.'

As the darkness melted away from black into morning Tom was still lying next to his wagon. He had started, slowly, to lose the hallucinations and felt a tiny measure of strength crawl back into his bones. Davenport sat next to him, now and again holding a water bottle to his lips. The water had had three sachets of diarrhoea powder in it, to get his salts and sugars up. His trousers were still around his ankles. He felt as if he had nothing left in him. His head was a bit clearer, and he had regained his voice.

Davenport shook his shoulder. 'All right, boss, we've got to get you in the turret. It's dawn now, and we're in the open here. Come on, let's get you up.' He pulled Tom's trousers up and helped him off the stretcher. Groggy, as he steadied himself against the side of the wagon Tom looked over to the east where the faint shape of the sun had appeared behind the thick purple cloud. He just wanted to sleep. It was all he wanted. Then above his head the crack of a bullet whipped past. He forgot all his weakness and a thrill shot through him.

'Contact! Fucking hell, Dav. Contact!' Like a ferret Davenport slipped into his driver's hatch in a single fluid jump as Tom scrambled up the side of the wagon, his hand, still oozing pus and blood, scrabbling for purchase on the congealed vomit on the bar armour. More rounds now winging over his head, he finally dropped into the safety of the turret, where Dusty was traversing desperately.

'Fuck, boss, fuck. Where the fuck are they?' Tom poked his head out the turret and looked to his left and right, the commanders of the other three wagons doing the same. Still helmetless, he strapped on his ANR. The net was going crazy. Trueman was sending a contact report up to Zero. To his left Jesmond's cannon roared, and tracer streaked from its barrel towards a compound two hundred metres away. 'Dusty, traverse left, traverse left!' The turret whipped around. 'Steady, steady. On! Compound with green door. You got it, you got it?' He looked through the sights to check what Dusty could see. Just over the lip of the wall a black shadow appeared, and then came a muzzle flash from it. The shadow dropped. He couldn't believe he had actually been looking at a man trying to kill him. 'I'm on, boss. I'm on!' Dusty screamed. 'Lasing. Two forty.'

'Loaded fire. Smash it, smash it!' Tom flicked the selector switch at the back of the gun from safe to automatic, and then poked his head out of the turret again. Dusty sent six rounds in a remorseless beat towards the compound as in unison Trueman and Jesmond both joined in, their cannons shredding the wall. Some rounds flew over the top, but most beat into it like pickaxes, dust and rubble flying. The guns pounded Tom's head even through the headphones. He was amazed at the speed of their response.

No return shots came, and silence settled again over the wagons, the last of the rain steaming from their Rarden barrels. Fumes filled Tom's turret and made him heady with adrenaline. His heart bounced up and down, and an ecstasy took him by the throat. His first contact. He heard a loud bang away to the north, and the net sprang into life again as Clive screamed, 'Contact RPG!' The first bang was followed by two more. It all fell into place. It was exactly as Frenchie had predicted.

For the next forty minutes the squadron came under concerted attack. Another gunman opened up at 3 Troop from the south but kept shifting his position before they could bring the turrets to bear. SHQ and the scene around the stricken wagons came under contact as well, rounds dancing over the heads of the working party, who sheltered in the hole next to the track. The rounds bounced off the wagons with flat *claps* as Prideaux and Ealham lay in the watery filth at the bottom of their hole, but despite everything they passed out, unconscious with exhaustion.

It took forty minutes for the Apache to come on station, when all contact stopped, the gunmen melted way, and the boys started the painstaking work on the wagon again. But when the Ugly left, the attacks started again and continued all through the morning. From tiny murder holes bored through the compound walls overnight, snipers rained a sporadic, harassing patter of bullets at the wagons with impunity. Whenever the turrets swung towards them they just moved to a new position. The Taliban moved like bees attacking a great clumsy bear, shifting from compound to compound, sometimes firing from a hundred metres, sometimes from four hundred. Once they had fired from one murder hole, they would move by motorbike to the next location, always covered by other buildings. Around ten of them kept up this petalling movement, never allowing the column to rest.

Frenchie and Brennan, in the back of the Sultan, flinched each time a round smacked into its side as Frenchie constantly tried to coax air support from Brigade. When he got some again the attacks melted away, and the helis hovered over the town with the whole squadron willing them to find a target to destroy. But none appeared; the moment a heli arrived the gunmen hid. Nothing was happening in the town that day. No farmers were in the fields, no children played. The place was completely given over to the contact.

Progress on the vehicles continued, even under fire. Frenchie himself helped out, leaving Jason in charge of the squadron to help fix the track of One Two. It started to rain again, and the shooting subsided a bit. The boys kept working, their dull eyes blinking over chain-smoked cigarettes.

In the south Tom gathered his car commanders in the lee of his wagon. He was still retching, still needing to shit twice an hour, but he felt re-energized. He looked at Trueman, Jesmond and Thompson, filthy, unshaven, all somehow still grinning. They all smoked and shared out some boiled sweets as Tom and Trueman discussed the stag roster. Tom decided he could sacrifice two guns. They had to get some sleep and agreed that two crews would kip for two hours while two crews would stag on, and rotate like that. The wagons were close together anyway. Tom could see the relief in their eyes at the prospect of sleep, any sleep at all. They had been awake now since the morning of the move out from Bastion – forty-eight hours without sleep for most of them.

They went back to their turrets, Trueman and Thompson to sleep, Tom and Jesmond to keep methodically scanning their arcs, firing now and again at the occasional muzzle flash. Two hours later they swapped, and Tom and Dusty slumped in their seats over their sights. Not even the distant RPGs or Trueman's cannon only five metres away from them could wake them. For a hundred and twenty minutes they fell into a coma, their brains completely shutting down, their mouths dribbling stalactites of drool.

Finally, in the late afternoon, things started to improve around the bogged-in wagons. After managing to fix the Samson, Prideaux, with his immense strength and unflagging determination, turned back to Ealham's Scimitar, finally replaced its rear idler, and the boys heaved the track on to it an hour later. They had been static now for twenty-four hours. Bullets still sang around them, but amazingly no one had been hit. At 1800 the column started to move again, and limped its way out of the cluster, the tracks of the wagons struggling to get going again, grinding through the mud that had glued the running gear over the past day. Three Troop at the back moved out with their turrets facing to the rear as deterrents against any final contact.

None came, and soon the column was back in the safety of the open desert, heading north. The town refilled with children and its normal bustle resumed as scared families emerged from their homes. The farmer whose field they had been stuck in took his plough again to the furrows and evened out the earth around the hole. By dusk he had levelled the field again. It was as though they had never been there.

The further they got from the town the worse Tom began to feel again. The illness returned after its slight abatement, and as the wagons went through the dark moonscape of the desert he had to shit over the side of the Scimitar, Dusty holding him by his shoulders and Davenport keeping the pace as steady as he could. Over the intercom Tom murmured, 'Christ, this is undignified,' and he and Dusty laughed deliriously at his wretchedness.

Eventually, with thinning clouds scudding across the moon, the exhausted thread of vehicles pulled itself over the final rise before Loy Kabir. FOB Newcastle was a beacon in the middle of the silvery town. Lit by floodlights, it stood out for miles. Around it was no light at all: no street lamps, no electricity in the compounds. It was as though no soul existed outside it.

At 0200 the column pulled in to Newcastle, where the CO was waiting. Laughing, he clapped Frenchie on the back. 'Well, you did it, you madman, you did it.'

Frenchie looked at him vacantly, his hair woollen with dust. 'Thanks, Colonel. I can't quite believe how, but we bloody did it. It's all down to that man really.' He pointed to

Prideaux, who was sitting on the front of his Samson wolfing a bowl of stew that the RSM had made sure was prepared for their arrival.

The REME staff sergeant noticed them, braced up in acknowledgment of the CO and raised his bowl. 'Never again, sir. I'm off to go and join the Taliban. At least those twats don't have any vehicles to fix.'

All around, the boys ate, the food not touching the sides of their throats, sitting beside their vehicles as though scared to leave them after the shelter they had provided during the contact. Their eyes blinked underneath the floodlights, making them look shell-shocked. Tom was the last to get out of his wagon, methodically shutting down the turret with Dusty, unloading the gun and switching off the radios. He wearily climbed down, and as the CO came over to welcome him he braced up to attention, then his legs buckled and he fell unconscious to the ground, face first onto the sand. The boys lifted him on a stretcher and took him to the medics.

For four days he was quarantined in a small compound at the rear of the FOB, which while still inside the wire felt as though it was miles away. Eight small rooms looked out onto a central yard, and he was alone. The others who had been ill were only there for a day; his cut hand had combined with the D & V into a full-blown illness. His room was furnished with a camp bed, a bucket and a jerrycan of water. In the middle of the muddy yard were four latrines. Tom lay naked on the camp bed, the bucket next to him for when he couldn't make it outside in time. He had his pistol with him, and a T-shirt and trousers were on a small ledge next to a few books left by previous occupants, but Tom didn't have the energy to read them and simply lay there, losing all concept of time, only registering night when he felt cold and had to get into his sleeping bag.

The doc and a medic came to see him every morning to take his blood pressure and temperature and bring him more water and a tiny bit of food. Tom lost nearly a stone, and on the fourth day he could see his ribs poking through his skin. Gaunt, with a week's beard, his muscles felt empty. That afternoon Trueman appeared, alone, unsolicited and against all the rules. He stood at the entrance to Tom's hovel. 'Knock, knock. Hi, sir. You look in a shit state. Like what you've done with the place. What is it, Helmand chic?'

Tom could only mumble weakly, 'Hello, Sergeant Trueman. What are you doing here? Don't come any closer; you'll get this wretched plague.'

'No fear, sir. I'm staying right here. Funny thing is, Dusty, who basically spent three days living a metre away from you, is absolutely fine. Constitution of an ox, him. Here's some post that arrived for you. He threw over a couple of e-blueys, and Tom's eyes lit up. 'Ha! Knew that'd raise your morale.'

'Thanks, Freddie,' said Tom, scrabbling up the letters from the dust next to his bed and seeing with delight they were from Constance and Will. He felt a pang that there wasn't one from Cassie. 'That's awesome. How are the boys?'

'Bored. We've just been on the wagons tinkering since we got back in. Rumour's going around we ain't going to use them much anyway and get on those Mastiffs. The leader's working out some kind of rotation, from Mastiffs to Scimitars.'

'What, so we go through all the hassle of getting those things up here, and we're not even going to use them?'

'I know. I know, boss. Everyone's pretty pissed about it. Anyways, I'm going to love you and leave you; don't want any more of your toxic fumes. When you going to come back to the fold?'

'Soon, I hope. As soon as I can keep some food down without vomming it up. I feel like properly jack lying here monging it.'

'Don't, boss. You can't help it. I had it on the last tour and was out for eight days. Just a matter of time before I'm where you are anyway; everyone gets it at some point. No hurry though, yeah? The Taliban ain't gonna run away within a day. They ain't going anywhere. Take care then, boss.' He looked around the dim bare room, lit only by whatever light came through the tiny doorway. 'Try not to go too stir-fry crazy in here.' And then he left.

Tom looked at the e-blueys with glee and read Will's first.

Dear Tom,

*Mate, it was really good to get your bluey a couple of days ago. I'm
glad things are OK and I really hope you guys are staying safe. It's
weird; just as you guys are getting used to being out there I'm finally
starting to get used to being back. It's been a hell of a lot harder than
I thought it would be. On tour all you looked forward to was
POTL – we would dream about it and have huge conversations
about what we were going to do, where we were going to go, what we'd
eat, etc. – but when it came to it, and we were free to go after the
medals parade, I just couldn't make up my mind what to do with
myself. It was ridiculous; six months of minute-by-minute
decision-making and there I was completely unable to make any
decision at all. In the end I went with two of the other subbies to this
hotel on Lake Como, the kind of place where honeymooning couples
go, so we looked a bit strange as a group of three lads. We basically
spent the entire week getting absolutely slaughtered every day. We
would open the day with a drink, drink through lunch, pass out for a
couple of hours and then smash on through supper. I don't think we
were model guests necessarily, but it helped us to unwind a little bit.*

*At the moment I'm back in Mum's flat in London, doing nothing.
I wake up at about ten, sit on the sofa watching Jeremy Kyle in my
boxers, watch about three DVDs, and then go out and get ham-
mered with whoever's around. It helps you remember. It's so strange
how quickly you lose stuff from tour. My tan has gone, and I've put
on all the weight that I lost. Essentially I now look as though I've
never been away at all. And you start to forget it all so quickly – the
heat, the dust and the noise. But when I drink, somehow it all comes
rushing back then. But don't worry; I'm not a complete dipso (yet!).*

*I go over to Headley Court quite a bit to see the wounded lads.
They're the only people I've seen since I've got back who you don't need
to explain anything to. I just sit by their beds and we read the
magazines that I've brought along in silence for about an hour.*

It's funny; the last time I saw them they were in pieces, bloody and mauled as we put them onto whichever MERT after whichever contact. And now they're in this anodyne ward, wearing tracksuits with their stumps and scars, looking immaculate as though they've always had them. At the moment the adrenaline is carrying them through, the adrenaline of coping with their new lives and meeting the new challenges of trying to walk again on their new pegs. But I wonder what happens in a few months, or years, when they can walk really well, or as well as they will ever be able to. They'll reach the point when they realize the exact extent of what it is they can do, and the huge unattainable expanse of what they can't do, and I wonder what it will be like to come up against that wall. Yeah, they'll go and do marathons and climb the Matterhorn or whatever, but it must be truly a lonely moment when they realize they'll never, never, never, be able to pick up the remote control for the telly again or play kick-around in the garden with their son.

The ones with wives and children I feel less sorry for, as at least they don't have to go and try to impress girls; they've already got a captive audience as it were. But the eighteen- and nineteen-year-olds in the wards at Headley? Some of them are triple amputees for heaven's sake. They still think like eighteen-year-olds — they still want to go to nightclubs and cop off with hot babes — but will they ever be able to do that? When they're back home out with their mates on a Friday night, away from the military, is any girl going to even throw them a second glance as they sit in the corner in their wheelchair? No, of course not. And then one day these boys lose their looks, their youth, their freshness, which is about the only thing they've got going for them, and it'll be ten years' time. We'll all have forgotten about Afghan, but these lads will still be triple amputees — fat, unshaven, jobless. And no one will care. I look at these lads in the ward and just think about the last few months, the ridiculous game of chance we played. Some of us, most of us, won; we came through. For these boys, they lost, and some of them have lost really big.

I'm not sure whether it would have been better for some of the really bad ones just to have bled out. To have had the medic overdose them on morphine, loosen the tourniquets and let them just slip away in peace, surrounded by their friends, instead of facing decades of pity that will give way sooner or later to apathy. People won't even give them a second glance; they'll look right through them. I do it myself already with old tramps. I look at them and see a ghost, a beardy, scruffy cripple. But I bet you when he got the injury that made him eventually wind up homeless he was fit and strong, a good lad, a hard worker. A somebody. That's going to be what happens to these boys once the music stops, once Afghan's over, and once we've stopped parading them out in public, presenting the FA Cup, being at the front row of film premieres, all that gubbins. It's almost unfair we're doing this to them, as when reality bites they're going to feel the drop dreadfully.

Christ, this is depressing. I'm sorry to unload on you like this, mate, but I know you'll understand. Just remember what I told you at that party when you smashed that bloke's face in: make sure they all come back. Please don't let any of your lads be injured mate, please.

I'll write again soon; POTL ends in five days' time and then it's back to Battalion in London. I'm looking forward to seeing all the fellas again.

Take care, mate. Thinking of you,
Will

Tom retched into the bowl again but could only manage to produce green saliva. *What's happening to Will?* The last few months, ever since he had arrived in Afghan back in March, had seen him descend into a spiral of depression. Tom knew he was hiding the extent of his drinking. He wondered what exactly Will was getting up to in London when he went out. He wouldn't be remotely surprised if he went picking fights with people, people who he'd accuse of cowardice for not being in the army, people he'd accuse of shirking because they'd decided to avoid the chance of getting their balls blown off in a Dark Ages desert five thousand miles away.

Tom picked up Constance's letter, and a surge of guilt came. Why had he not spoken to her for so long? He must get to a phone as soon as he could. He opened it.

My darling Tommy,

We are having the most glorious autumn back here. The trees are a fantastic colour, and already there are huge great piles of leaves beneath them that you would love to go and kick up. I wonder what autumn is like in Afghanistan. I hope it is as nice. I look at the BBC website to see what the weather is like in Kandahar and it says that it is 30 degrees. I hope none of you are getting sunstroke. There has been a bumper crop of blackberries and raspberries in the garden, and I have been making some jam for when you get back on leave. Sam has picked what seems to be the world's supply of sloes as well and is currently making sloe gin in great big glass containers to send some out to you. I hope it will remind you of home when you taste it.

It was so good to get your letter. Is it possible for you to send any pictures back in an email? It would be so nice to see what the country-side looks like and what your day-to-day life is like. And also it would be good to see how you are looking. I hope you haven't lost too much weight. Dear me, I do bang on! I will stop.

Zeppo is well, but he obviously knows you are away and so sometimes looks sad. I am keeping myself very well; there is all sorts of stuff happening in the village at the moment. It looks like we might soon be getting a new vicar, as Reverend Moore seems to be persona non grata for some reason with the archdeacon. Something about some kind of 'financial irregularity', whatever that means.

Why can't they just come clean and say they think he's been a crook? Honestly, why people never call a spade a spade is beyond me.

Everyone in the village is wearing their poppies with pride, you will be pleased to hear. And when I go into the village it is amazing how many people know you are away. I am getting all sorts of free stuff from the butcher, etc. and the newsagents sometimes let me have the papers for free! They all ask after you; I feel a bit like I am some kind of celebrity. The man in the delicatessen — Mr Booth — you know, big white hair — told me the other day that his weekly prayer group always says a prayer out loud for you and your soldiers.

And how are they? I hope they are well. You won't believe it, but I had a very kind letter from Lance Corporal Miller asking directly for some more chocolate brownies. He sounds like a nice boy, not like the mini-thug you sometimes say he is, what with all his tattoos. He sounds very well mannered. His spelling isn't great though; could you use the next few months to help him out with that kind of thing?

I am so looking forward to seeing you again, Tommy. I know your father will be very proud of you, and will be watching down on you. I do miss him and you so much.

I am so excited to think that you will soon be in the kitchen eating all this jam I have made; you will be sick to death of it by the time leave is up.

Take care please!
Your loving Mummy

Dusty! What an absolute wretch, Tom thought, then grinned at him going behind his back like this. He reached to the side of the camp bed, had six huge gulps from the jerrycan, laid the letters down on his chest and went to sleep. It was four o'clock in the afternoon. At dusk he woke again, pulled his clothes over his bones and wriggled into his sleeping bag. He was asleep again within a minute. As he slept a rat came into the room and sniffed the speckles of vomit around the bucket, unafraid of his steady, quiet breathing. Tom slept until the morning crumbled away the darkness. He hadn't dreamed a thing. He might as well have been dead. There was a surge of power in his limbs that he hadn't had for days. He was better.

November settled in with its longer nights, and squeezed the sun's warmth into fewer hours around midday. Rain and hail showers harried Loy Kabir, and a great three-day storm turned all the earth into mud, hour after sodden hour. The wadi rose as the rain from the mountains drained into it, turning the normally clear blue trickle into a clay-ridden milky motorway. After it subsided and the town got back on its feet the corn in the fields was harvested, and the green zone suddenly opened up. The eight-foot-tall corn packed together in serried rows which had dominated the fields over the summer gave way to flat brown earth. The only cover now available to foot patrols were the ditches between the fields, six feet wide with oily, filth-ridden water filming over a waist-deep ooze of mud and muck. The water infected open cuts and nicks in calves and thighs as the boys waded along, the freezing black paste sometimes up to their chests when they sheltered in the ditches during a contact.

As Tom emerged from his purgatory, he saw how much had changed in the military landscape as well as the physical in Loy Kabir. RHQ was now fully up and running, with the CO at the helm for three weeks now. He had bounced all over the AO, going on foot patrols, accompanying IED clearances, hanging at the back of night ambushes and joining in compound searches, as well as meeting every village elder, twisting every police commander around his finger and crucially winning over Gumal, who had been impressed by his ability to drink him under the table after a private drinking session between the two of them at which two bottles of Scotch had been the battlefield. He had barely slept since he had arrived in theatre, but still infused everyone, from the company commanders down to the youngest trooper, with a zeal that defeated the torpor that a dull autumn threatened to produce. With its keen new staff BGHQ buzzed with activity and purpose in Newcastle's ops room, a pregnant prelude to the focused maelstrom of violence that the staff were planning over the next few months, pushing at the FLETs in the north and south and expanding the bubble of security around the town's commercial heart.

Despite the daily patrols and compound searches, the tempo had died down into a welcome relative lull after the savage fighting that the town had seen over the summer. In both the north and the south of the AO the patrol bases found themselves in a kind of unofficial and uneasy truce, as the Loy Kabir Taliban downed arms; local fighters to help with the harvest and prepare their homes for the oncoming winter, out-of-area fighters leaving to rest, resupply and make contact with their families. On the British side all the soldiers who had fought in the area over the summer had finally been rotated back to the UK, and by and large, apart from the occasional firefight, their replacements were just concentrating on familiarizing themselves with their new homes.

In the north an infantry company from the Duke of York's Regiment, callsign Pilgrim, moved into PB Jekyll, placed on a low rise overlooking the outskirts of the town where it diluted into less densely packed compounds until finally petering out three miles away. In the south A Squadron of the King's Dragoons, C Squadron's great rivals, had their vehicles taken away from them and were in PB Eiger in a ground-holding infantry role. The compounds to the south of Eiger were tightly packed together, with high walls creating a complex interplay of alleyways. Over the summer heavy casualties had been inflicted on their predecessors, who had lost three killed and fifteen wounded, earning the area the nickname Satan's Grotto. C Squadron with their Scimitars were based out of Newcastle, in the middle of town along with a battery of artillery, a squadron of engineers, plus medics, clerks and a few Foreign Office staff.

Despite the relative quiet, there still came a bleed of casualties. During a compound search one of Clive's soldiers, Smiley, was shot in the hand by an old man with an ancient rifle, the bullet tearing off his thumb, leaving it dangling by a clean yellow tendon as he lay on the floor, white with shock and staring at the fizzing maw above his thin wrist. A Russian legacy mine placed in the 1980s blew the foot off a medic attached to Scott's troop as they scrambled up a hill on a patrol to get a better view of a motorbike that had fled at their appearance. In PB Jekyll a corporal was killed by a command-wire IED. It exploded four metres from him, and while he survived the blast the compound wall next to him was toppled and his neck broken by falling rubble. His face was dusty from the wall but his body entirely unmarked; when they brought his corpse to Newcastle for the angel flight to Bastion, he seemed to Tom as though he was just sleeping.

Tom and Trueman were struggling to maintain morale among the troop. The lottery for R & R had been held, and 3 Troop had got the last slot, in late February. This meant they would get back from the two weeks away and only have another four weeks to push until the end of tour. The only way it could have been worse was to have got the first slot, in early November. Scott drew that, and he and his troop left the day after they had casevaced the medic who had lost her

157

foot. He didn't look ready to go at all and stood forlornly on the HLS. Tom chatted with him as he waited for the heli.

'Have a good one, mate. You lucky fucker. What are you going to do?'

'I dunno, pal. It seems only yesterday that I was home anyway. I'll feel like a bit of a fraud. It won't seem as if I've been away at all. I'll go to Selly Oak to see Corporal Claydon, I suppose. I hope she's doing OK.'

'Yeah, man, I'm really sorry about that. What was it like?'

'Horrific, mate, horrific. I mean, it was a fairly minging injury anyway, but it happening to a girl was just awful, you know? None of the boys could really comprehend it at first. When we saw her there after the explosion, screaming her head off, none of us knew what to do. It was like seeing your sister. I just thank goodness she only lost her foot; she'll be able to live a normal life, and the important thing is that she'll look completely normal. But what if it had been worse? What if she'd quad-amped? It's just strange, mate, seeing that happen to a girl like that, you know, with dimples on her cheeks and who puts a bit of perfume on just before she goes on patrol to raise morale. It was like seeing a child. Would have been a lot easier if it had been one of the lads, you know. Anyway, I'll go and see her. Apart from that though, I'll just be hanging at home. Minding my own business really. It's going to be weird. Like some kind of limbo. I'll probably just be spending all my time on the MoD website, trying to get any news on stuff out here. Tragic really.' He trailed off as his ears pricked at the sound of the heli. 'Well that's me, mate. I can hear the beers already. See you in a few weeks. Take care, mucker.'

They shook hands and then, silently deciding this wasn't enough, hugged. Tom then watched as Scott and his boys got their gear together, filed into the heli and lifted off back to Bastion, none of them really ready to go back yet and knowing that they still had four months of tour to push. It was going to be a hollow homecoming.

The squadron had started the troops' rotation around the AO. There was a troop in the north based with the infantry at Jekyll, a troop working off the Mastiffs on route security, a troop on QRF in Newcastle, and a troop either on R & R or standing by for the other jobs that came up from time to time. The worst job was definitely route security, and 3 Troop were on that for four weeks. It was tedious, thankless work, and more dangerous for being so dull, which encouraged the soldiers to take risks when they shouldn't.

The job was to keep the routes to the PBs clear so supply convoys could pass easily. Every day one of the routes would be swept. There were three main ones: Bristol, Glasgow and Canterbury. Route Bristol, the route from Newcastle into the desert, was only used once a month for the great eighty-vehicle-strong Operation Tulip convoys from Bastion. But its totemic value was such that it still had to be cleared; if they couldn't keep that artery clear they were essentially cut off in the town. On the route at roughly kilometre intervals were small checkpoints manned by ANA and ANP. In theory they had eyes on the entire route, and there were no blind spots where devices could be planted. Too often devices were found on it, however, leading to the inevitable conclusion that the ANA didn't bother patrolling by day or night. The Afghan forces were chastened by news from Babaji of Taliban sneaking into a police checkpoint at night and slitting the throats of its sleeping occupants, but the CO knew he couldn't really trust the integrity of Bristol.

Route Glasgow went north through the town to Jekyll. It also had a few checkpoints on it; some manned by ANA and others by a couple of sections from Jekyll. But the route was too long and winding to be covered fully, and the track, just wide enough for a Mastiff to squeeze through with its bar armour scraping against compound walls, was riddled with blind spots. By and large though it was clear, as the Taliban stayed further out to the north and seemed unconcerned. Route Canterbury was another matter. No matter how many patrols were sent from the checkpoints along it, no matter how many night-time lurks and ambushes were put out to get bomb-layers, devices always found their way onto it. It was the CO's single greatest concern. If it was shut, Eiger was isolated. The route had to stay open.

Tom didn't mind doing Bristol and Glasgow; they were usually clear runs, not too draining on nerves, patience and fingernails. But Canterbury was dreadful. Progress was tor-turous. Local children were paid by the Taliban to drop nails, nuts and bolts in the sand to slow the barma teams. The more often one of the barma boys came up with a reading and found a nail, the more likely he was to assume the next reading was also a nail and ignore it. But then that was the intention, and it was actually a bomb. It was a war of patience, pure and simple.

Tom let the barma team take things at their own pace, using their own instinct, judgement and skills, and knew he had to try to devalue the concept of time. Every reading had to be treated as a potential bomb, even if they had just found fifty nails. Sometimes it wasn't intentional Taliban decoys; when-ever they passed a crater where a wagon had been hit they would be slowed by bits of metal debris in the ground. The only advantage about Canterbury was that it was a route through open fields, with nowhere near the same number of bottlenecks as the other routes.

The drills became well worn, slick and unspoken. The barma team selected by Tom was Ellis, GV, Livesey and

Acton. Livesey and Acton were add-ons from SHQ on loan to the Mastiff troop. Tom didn't really know much about them. He liked Acton, whose broad moon-shaped face sat atop an ungainly torso and who had a friendly and vacant grin to go with a soft Black Country accent. Everyone knew him as Yam-Yam. Livesey, with his small pinched weasel face, was sly-looking and had an unpleasant joyless cackle. His breath stank, and none of the others liked him, but he was excellent at barma, and in this, if not anything else, Tom trusted him implicitly.

He was loath to rotate the other boys in the troop into the barma team because this foursome quickly established a good working relationship, and, as was the case all over theatre, despite the extra danger of the job and the lack of extra money for it, those who did it enjoyed a feeling of quiet pride that their mates were relying on them. They were protective of their kit and hated letting the others use it. Tom once tried to help, to show that he wasn't shying away from the job. He did it for ten minutes but was so much slower than the others that he realized he should concentrate on letting them carry out the job themselves and stop tinkering with their way of doing things. Trueman and Tom had asked them if they wanted resting or to have the other boys help out, but the answer had been an emphatic no. This suited everyone, and Tom could see Dusty and Davenport's relief when he told them they wouldn't have to be part of it.

The barma team would gather at the front of the lead wagon at a VP and go forward in their formation, with the only noise above the hum of the Mastiff's engine the synthetic yelps of the Vallons as they sent down their radar beams and caught the ones that bounced back at them. When a Vallon sang really loudly it meant it had picked up a significant metallic reading in the ground. They would halt, all kneel, and the man who had picked up the reading would place his Vallon behind him, take out a screwdriver and paintbrush from the front of his body armour, and chip and brush away at the earth to see what it was. Most of the time it was a bolt or nail, sometimes a spent rifle cartridge. Sometimes, though, they would come to the plastic sheeting that covered the pressure plate of a device or the garish yellow plastic of a fertilizer container containing the main charge.

And then everything got complicated. If there was a way around the bomb, they would mark and avoid it, but if not Tom would get on the radio up to battle group and begin the long process of getting a search team and ATO out to them to blow the device and take any forensics from it. The wait was mind-numbing. Often they would have to sit around for six hours while a team was flown up from Bastion and then driven out to them. If they were lucky, there would be a team already in Newcastle, and they'd be there quicker. The boys would just doze in the wagons, reading magazines or playing on their PSPs. In Tom's Mastiff Dusty would dig out one of his Bernard Cornwell books. He was becoming daily more obsessed with medieval England and planning to get a tattoo of a crusader knight on his back when he returned from tour. He told Tom about it.

'It's gonna be gleaming, boss. I've already got a sketch from the artist. On my left shoulder blade, about A4 size. It's this knight just after a battle, dressed in white, kneeling at an altar and holding out his sword in offering to it. He's got this jagged cut on his arm, which is the only bit of red in the picture. It is going to be fuckin' mint; I can't wait.'

Tom really liked Dusty. He liked them all, but Dusty and Davenport were his favourites. He had the greatest bond with Trueman, but Tom was still a bit overawed by him and by his talismanic presence in the regiment. But with Dusty and Dav it was different. They were both younger than him, Dusty twenty-two and Dav nineteen. They were becoming like younger brothers, and there was no hiding anything from them: they saw, whether they were in the Scimitar or the Mastiff, his every doubt, every fear, every moment of bravado and recklessness. His personality and his command were stripped bare in front of them. The other members of the troop usually felt his presence over the radio, where he sounded authoritative, calm and detached. But in the turret with them there was no hiding.

On one particularly bad day on Canterbury they found six suspect devices in one field alone. When they finally got back to Newcastle, having marked them so the locals wouldn't drive over them, Tom was greeted by the CO. 'Well done, Tom. Good work. I can only begin to imagine how tedious that was.'

Tom managed to fight down his frustration; he had spent most of the day almost weeping with it. 'Thanks, Colonel. The boys were all over it. They're getting damn good at barma. But our luck's going to run out sooner or later. There's just so many of those things. One day we're going to miss one.'

The CO nodded. 'Don't you worry. I've got a plan to solve Canterbury once and for all. We're getting a REST up from Bastion, and they're going to come out with you in a few days to blow all the devices in that field.'

'What, all of them?'

'Yep. I'm sick to death of this route. We're going to clear it, and even better we're then going to put a nice big checkpoint slap in the middle of it. Well, not massive, but enough for a section. Brigade have just given it the go-ahead.'

And so three days later they were sent back to the field with a Brimstone team to clear it. While the ATO was on one of the devices Tom chatted with the RESA, an officer from Nigeria who spoke at a thousand words a minute and had a nervous tic of wrinkling his nose every few seconds. He soon explained it. 'I can see you noticing my nose, buddy. Don't worry about it. Think I'm going to get cured by a shrink who they're getting out to Bastion in a few weeks. Not just for me; there are a few other guys apparently as well. It's weird; it just developed a couple of weeks ago. I don't notice I'm doing it until I see people looking at it. Hope it's not permanent.' He paused as Dusty handed him a brew. He sipped from it, the steam billowing around the cramped wagon where they sat among the search team's kit. 'Christ that's good. Thanks.'

'No worries. Lance Corporal Miller dishes up the meanest brews in theatre. Don't you, Dusty?'

'Bugger off, sir. I swear your brew obsession is killing me. When I joined the army I thought it was going to be all about slotting people. But all I actually do here is get the fucking kettle on.'

'Poor old Dusty. I offer to do them, but apparently my brews are awful, so he won't let me anywhere near it. He loves it really.'

'No I don't, boss; I hate it. Having said that, better than having to drink the rancid filth you produce. What is it with officers and brews? It's like drinking cat piss. All I'm gonna be able to do is work in sodding Starbucks when I leave the army. Ridiculous. Officers all leave and become barristers; me and the lads leave and become baristas.'

The RESA laughed and continued, 'The thing is, this tic makes me look like I'm a cocaine fiend. I'm going to go back home and everyone will think I've been on a drugs binge all the time out here. Come to think of it, wouldn't be a bad idea. Probably make everything a hell of a lot easier.'

Tom nodded. 'I know. Everything might start to make some kind of sense, for one. Because who knows what kind of fucked-up reality this is out here. When did it first happen?'

'About a day after we lost two of our lads. Well, one of them. The other's an amputee – left arm. Down in Sangin. Messy. There was nothing left really of Danny, one of my staffies. Staff Sergeant Thorburn – hear of him? Epic bloke. Just the best.'

'What happened – IED?'

'No, never. That would never have happened to Danny; he was the best searcher I ever met. Sixth-sense kind of good. He just *knew* where and when there was stuff in the ground. Like a sniffer dog. Incredible talent. And in this team, not wanting to brag, we're all good.'

In the corner of the Mastiff one of his team, who was dozing, didn't bother to open his eyes but just mumbled, 'Too right, boss.'

'There you go, ringing endorsement. No, no IED. Well, not one in the ground anyway; suicide bomber. Bloke dressed as a woman. Because of all this cultural-sensitivity bollocks and the fact that the lads are so scared of offending these twats by even looking at their women, the infantry boys on the cordon for our search job just let this bomber through, too scared to look at her – I mean him – let alone stop and search him. Anyway, suddenly he just runs at us, this fucking burka bloke, while we're monging it in the shade of this compound wall, and before any of us can do anything he just evaporates in this massive bang. Next thing you knew there were just blokes everywhere, and bits of blokes. I thought we were all dead, all eight of us, but it was just Danny and Phillips, one of the new lads, who got it. The clean-up was fucking dreadful.'

'Christ, mate, I'm sorry.'

'Thanks. Anyways, the tic started the next day.'

Dusty said, 'Fuck me, sir; that sucks.'

'Yeah, pretty bad day at the office. All that was left of the bomber was his spine. It was picked almost clean. Looked like a finished spare rib. That was all I could think about when I saw it. That night we were back in Bastion, and after I'd been to the hospital to see Phillips I went to the scoff house. And guess what?'

'Spare ribs?'

'Exactly. When I saw them I started crying and had to leave. Luckily it was dark outside so no one saw me.'

'I'm sorry, mate. I really am.'

'It really pisses me off, this cultural stuff. I've told my lads to ignore it. All this shit about having to sit cross-legged when you talk to the locals and not being allowed to use your left hand, or right hand, or whatever one it is when you shake their hand or point. Who sits cross-legged anyway? It's ridiculously uncomfortable. Last time I did it I was listening to my teacher read *Thomas the Tank Engine* at primary school. And they expect us to do it as fully grown men with all this body armour on? They're having a laugh; you need to be some kind of contortionist or sex pest to do it.

'I mean, it's not as if we're going to go into a room, sit cross-legged with some greybeard, and he's suddenly going to be like, "Hey, this bloke's just like me, brother from another mother." Bollocks he is. You're still going to look like an alien to him. It's like Martians coming to invade London, and their cultural adviser telling them that they can blend in seamlessly and hide the fact they're ten-foot-tall intergalactic five-headed mutants by wearing a bowler hat, carrying a copy of *The Times* and calling everyone old bean. It's just bollocks. And all because some tosspot in the MoD says we've got to do this shit. He'll probably get an MBE out of it. And because of all this crap no one stops this suicide bomber, and Phillips gets his arm blown off. Nice one, Whitehall. Thanks a fucking million.'

He finished the drink and broke into a broad grin. 'Still, if you can't take a joke, you shouldn't have joined, right?' He clambered out of the wagon, and Tom joined him as they watched the ATO complete his work on the bomb and prepare to blow it.

Tom had lost count of the number he had seen being blown, but he still loved it, never able to resist craning his neck out of a wagon or over a wall to see the explosion and feel the shock wave buffet his face. This one was a hundred metres away, and so he didn't even make a nod to taking any cover; he and the RESA just stood there in the open. He saw, almost in slow motion, the great plume of dust soar into the air, dissipating out a hundred feet up, a moment of creation. He saw the shock wave ripple over the dust towards him, go under him, and at the same time felt it pass through him, and then a split second later the boom hit his ears. He found it a purification, blowing away his imperfections, a kind of elemental purging of his body. A little death and then a rebirth.

They worked on the devices all day, and by evening they had cleared the field. At dusk a troop of engineers arrived to build the new checkpoint and a platoon from Eiger came up to help guard the build, through the night and into the next day. The new PB was called Yukshal, after a farmer who had been killed by an IED in the field three days previously. Three Troop headed off back to Newcastle to deliver the Brimstone team back to another tasking.

Tom and the RESA sat together at scoff that night, eating beef stew and rice. Tom was sad to see him go.

'Take care, will you? I don't know how you boys do your job. I mean, for us, sure we're out on the ground every day, but when we come across a difficult situation, there's always people to help. Like in a contact I can get a fire mission or an AH strike. If we find a bomb, we phone you guys up. But you guys, there's no one above you to help out. You have to do the job yourselves. I take my hat off to you, mate. I really do.'

'I'd never thought of it like that. I know what you mean; it's quite lonely not being able to get a grown-up to come and help. That's why I love it, I suppose. Better go and get the gear together. Heli leaves in half an hour. You take care, yourself; you've got quite an AO up here. And those IED-layers know their stuff. They're good. Tread lightly.'

'Shall do. Thanks, mate. You do the same.'

They got up to go. Outside in the frosty dark they breathed sharp, painfully cold breaths. They split, the RESA to go and pack and Tom to see the boys. Tom called out to him, 'Hey, what was your name again?'

'Kwekwo. Michael Kwekwo.'

'Got it. Well, really good to meet you. Safe journey.'

An hour later he was in the boys' tent, heard the heli come in and felt the canvas of the tent get beaten by the down-draught. He hoped his new friend would be all right.

Three nights later, at the daily battle group six o'clock conference, broadcast to all the PBs, Tom sat at the back of the crowded ops room as Jules Dennis read out the events of the day in theatre. 'In Battle Group Centre South this morning, two kilometres north of PB Majid, there was one KIA from a daisy-chain IED and two Cat A casualties. The KIA was the RESA who was with us a couple of days ago work-ing with Tomahawk Three Zero. Captain Michael Kwekwo.'

Tom didn't so much as flinch. He looked ahead, calm and impassive, fixed on Jules' lips as he carried on his update. The news wasn't somehow a surprise. Standing behind him, Trueman put his hand forward and squeezed his shoulder.

Dear Cassie,

Thank you so much for the parcel. I can't tell you how good it was to get it. The Christmas decorations are hung up in my tent. Talking of which, it's quite a pad, I have to say. There will be thousands of student digs back home that won't be a patch on this. One of the engineers here knocked up a bookshelf with about a hundred books on it, left here from previous tours. Some of the lads come in to borrow the books; it feels as though I'm the librarian in The Shawshank Redemption. *But I haven't got a blackbird for a friend. Nor am I going to hang myself. And top work with the Christmas pudding. That didn't really last long; we absolutely wolfed it.*

*   What's really strange, on the book front, is that I've hardly read a thing all tour. I had thought I would read voraciously, especially given the fact that there is a lot, and I mean a lot, of inactivity out here. So often you're just waiting, waiting, for ever, for something to happen, and you desperately need something to pass the time. My gunner Miller reads his historical novels every spare second. Sergeant True-man's working his way through all of Nick Hornby. But I just haven't so much as picked up a book. I mean, I read half of one about Robin Hood, but that's no great claim really. If you'd asked me before tour I would have said that I was going to read all the great novels at this seminal time in my life, blah blah. But it just hasn't worked out. And I did English at Cambridge! I brought out* Paradise Lost *to read on tour. Cringe! In fact all I read are the newspapers that Mum sends out and lads' mag after lads' mag. You would be appalled. I read them all:* Loaded *(old school),* Front

(the best one, as it uses girls with no, um, how do you say it, 'enhance-ments'), GQ *(a bit poncy, takes itself far too seriously),* Bizarre *(just plain weird) and of course the infamous* Zoo *and* Nuts. *I reckon I could take an* NVQ *in Lads' Mags Studies at the end of tour, I have read that many. We have a stack about a foot high in the front passenger footwell of our Mastiff (basically a big armoured truck), and in the Scimitar (a kind of little tank) we're about to move into there's a place behind my head in the turret that we've already earmarked as storage space.*

Oh my God! I have reviewed what I have just written. This is just ridiculous. How can I be talking about this! I have had the finest literary education in the country and here I am reading articles like '100 greatest abattoir accidents', 'Tangerines that look like monkeys' or pieces about naked Bulgarian mud-wrestlers. This has to stop.

And it is freezing out here. I'm sleeping inside two sleeping bags at the mo, and fully clothed as well. During the day it never gets above freezing, and we're not even at Christmas yet. Luckily it hasn't snowed yet, and I hope it never will, as it'll be a nightmare finding IEDs, *and when it thaws and melts the ground will just turn to glue. It's quite busy out here at the moment – we're bouncing all over the area – but largely I'm keeping myself out of trouble so don't worry about that.*

I am sorry this is so short; it's written in the back of the Mastiff, and we are just outside a school that I've driven my boss to so he can chat with the local elders about education provision in the area. How random is that?

So pleased you are around in Feb for my leave; can't wait to see you again.

All love,
Tom xxx

Mate,

Quick one, written outside a school where the CO is having a shura with some greybeards. We're guarding the cordon in Mastiffs. Utterly, utterly bone. We've been on route clearance/security for a month now, and we swap over back onto Scimitars thank goodness in a week. It's actually been all right this last month, ups and downs but generally OK. It's been good to bed into the AO fully and get accustomed to the town itself before we start to push out at the FLET for the rest of tour. And that's what's going to happen; you can feel the lift in tone. Basically since September there's almost been a de facto truce, or at least a slight lull, and it's about to seriously ramp up. Just in the last week there's been a change of tempo. For one, there's been a hell of a lot more drone assets given to us; almost as indicative of a scrap oncoming as it would have been in WWI when extra ladders were delivered to the trenches. You can feel it in the ops room. A few weeks ago it was quite chilled in there, but now Ops and Int are running around like blue-arsed flies, and when you try to catch them for a moment they evade all your questions. So basically all the boys know something's about to kick off.

To be honest I'm looking forward to getting back onto the Scims. The Mastiff is a great, great bit of kit, don't get me wrong, and is about the only reason we've still got freedom of movement in the AO, but the thing is its invincibility makes the boys complacent after a while; they know they're not even going to get so much as a scratch if they hit an IED, and so their drills start to lapse. We've kept ours up pretty well so far, but you know when they start to drop off. Yesterday I had to bollock one of my best lads, Jesmond, for slack drills. He should have barma'd a VP but just drove over it, saying 'Risk it for a biscuit' over the net. Luckily there was nothing in the ground. I lost it with him. He's an awesome soldier but I think I just let my frustration get to me. Your reserves of patience can only take so much. In a sense the reason I went so mental with Jesmond is because I was angry at myself, as I know I'd have done the same thing as him.

I don't know what it is, but in the Scimitars you are definitely more switched on. Obviously because the danger is that much greater; if you hit something you're going to know about it. But I also think it's to do with the fact your head and torso are stuck out of the wagon in the open. You can sense stuff so much better like that. But in the Mastiffs you have this disconnect from the ground, and from the locals too. They see the Mastiff and they might as well be looking at the Starship Enterprise, *but in the Scimitars you can reach down and shake their hand, and they can see you're normal human beings. That said, if we didn't have Mastiffs I reckon casualties would be double what they are now.*

Anyway, you're boring me now. I think the CO and the rest of Tac are about to want to leave anyway; it's nearly dusk. It's so weird. Today's job is possibly the dullest one I've done this tour, and I am treating it with all the trepidation I would photocopying some docu-ments back at home. But that's because the bar is so high out here that jobs like this pale into insignificance. There is still a massive chance that something will go wrong. I'm sitting behind a grenade machine gun for Christ's sake; we found an IED earlier today just near the school, and we currently have two Apaches in the overhead for some reason, but basically this feels like the most normal thing in the world. When I get home I wonder if I'll look at times like this and actually realize that even this dull day in theatre would be the most exciting thing ever for someone in civvy strasse. Who knows? Who cares?

Looking forward to seeing you, mate. It's amazing how much you miss people. I can't wait to see Mum again; that's the hardest one. I know you know.

Tom

It was a beautiful morning, the first proper winter's day. Cassie walked out of the house with her scarf wrapped tight around her neck and lower face and welcomed the icy air that tingled the tip of her nose. She turned down the street and felt the scrunch of the new grit that had been spread the night before. A curious dog sniffed at some that had gathered in a pile beneath a kerb as a sullen Filipina housekeeper yanked at its lead, eager to get on so she could hurry back inside and away from the cold. Cassie walked down to the King's Road and weaved her way through parents taking their children to school, wrapped up snugly in their smart uniforms, some looking nervous and others breathless with excitement at the sudden cold. She crossed the road and walked down Beaufort Street, past the always-mute queue at the bus stop. The milky-blue sky shone before her over the river beside the Chelsea Embankment, and she walked along it, the low sun sprinkling over the green water.

The scarf in front of her mouth was now looser and damp with breath. As she stepped carefully along the pavement she took the letter from her coat pocket and read it again. She could see little bits of dust on the dried gum that had stuck the letter together, and she thought, maybe, that she could smell the desert on it. She had read the words twenty times already and her lips, moving in solemn silent incantation, betrayed this as her eyes pretended they were reading the scrawl for the first time. The letter puzzled her. She loved it, just as she loved all his letters, but she knew he was massaging the truth, that he was leaving out a huge amount to protect her. But how much? And what? She felt briefly annoyed with him for trying to exclude her.

She folded the letter up and put it back inside her coat. She crossed the Albert Bridge, dodging the cyclists pushing north towards their work from Clapham with their usual impatient self-righteousness. The river felt as friendly as it had done when she and Tom had said goodbye, the only difference being the bracing, enriching cold. She went to the spot in the park where they had parted, to the bollard, stout in its shiny black paint, next to which he had kissed her on the forehead, and performed her ritual. She touched it once with her woollen-gloved hand, then again, and then tapped her foot twice against it. She had done this every Friday since September. She didn't know why she did those particular things, and this time she chuckled at how ridiculous she must look to those walking past. She closed her eyes and thought a brief wordless prayer, then turned and walked back over the bridge to the Tube and then on to work.

On the journey she tried to think of his face, but she couldn't ever quite capture it. Just when she thought she could grasp him he slipped away back into the base of her brain, never willing to come out and be caught in the crystal light of her mind's eye.

She got off at Mansion House. She always smiled involuntarily when she walked out of the station, remembering the stupid riddle Tom had once told her. It wasn't even a riddle, merely an annoying piece of trivia that he had obviously learned in a cracker at Christmas. 'What makes Mansion House so special compared to all the other Tube stops?' he had asked her with a smug glint in his eye while they were going around Europe, about a week before they had had the argument.

She feigned ignorance and looked vacant for a minute or so, before saying, apparently frustrated, 'All right, David Starkey, what is so special about it?'

'It's the only Tube station to have all five vowels in it.' He didn't need to smile; his eyes danced at his pathetic victory, and she had grinned dutifully at how proud he was.

But then she had foiled him with, 'So I suppose South Ealing doesn't count then? And that one doesn't repeat any vowels. Just saying.' She remembered his expression as she had said it and laughed through her scarf.

As she walked from the Tube through the winding streets of the City to her office she recalled their argument in Graz. She still thought that what she had told him had needed to be said, but she wished she hadn't been so violent about it. But then maybe that was what Tom had deserved. He had seemingly been so blind, so unquestioning, about what he was going off to do.

She walked into the building, passed the group lurking by the lift, brusquely pushed through the fire door and sprinted up four flights of stairs to her floor, feeling the blood hurtle into her fingers and her cheeks blush with a deep red as she did so. When she walked into the office, already a hive of activity, all the men looked up. They always looked up. She knew there was something about her that cast a spell over men, and she always found this funny. Just as quickly they looked back at their computers and Bloomberg Terminals, but she caught it every time.

She had been at the investment management company for a couple of months and was loving it. She had been headhunted from her previous job at a hedge fund, and although she was the only woman there, apart from the receptionists and PAs, she had found that the only difference this made was that tiny fraction of a split-second look she induced as she walked in. No one had even so much as tried to ask her out, knowing that she would only – politely and charmingly – rebuff them. None of them knew about Tom, though her boss, a friendly corpulent man who had the air of an Anglican minister and the razor-sharp brain of one of the City's finest and most ruthless operators, had more than a few times caught her looking at the BBC website listing fatalities in Afghanistan. An ex-army man himself, he knew that he should not encroach. She probably had a boyfriend or relative out there.

Outside work there were a few other boys popping up and down on her horizon, but only a handful, and she allowed none of them closer to her than a couple of drinks, or supper, or maybe the theatre. She had lately realized that she had throughout her life cultivated quite an air of mystique. Evidently most boys were scared of her. She had suspected she had this trait at university, but it was only when she split up with Tom that she properly realized that she had a knack of unintentionally intimidating people. She usually didn't mean to, but she didn't really mind being able to. It was good sometimes not to let people get too close.

The day went quickly, as it always did. She loved having to use her brain so much and so intensely, and she was glowing with health. She had never felt so good or in a way so happy. Tom being away seemed to have given her a stable emotional centre around which she could throw herself into work and weekends, meaning that she would never stray too far or too wildly. She was still in denial, to her friends and certainly to her parents if not quite to herself, that she and Tom had rekindled their friendship, but when she thought about him or read an article about the war or blinked and fleetingly saw him on the inside of her eyelids, she felt a tiny lightness in her stomach. She wondered if it would last. For the moment, however, she didn't mind it at all.

As she left work that night she looked at her phone for the first time since lunch. There were no messages. She knew there were parties happening tonight, that she could have rung a few people and got herself invited to any number of things, but she didn't. She walked all the way back home from work, handrailing the river. She enjoyed the expectant Christmas air, which had finally been augmented by wintry weather, and the pregnant broiling Thames, which her walk caught right at the fulcrum between high and low tides. An hour and a half later she reached Albert Bridge. She thought about crossing to touch the bollard again, but she was cold and wanted to get inside the house and watch television and chat with her mother over a glass of wine. She left the bridge uncrossed but, as compensation, again in her head went over her prayer for Tom.

Two days before Christmas Frenchie brought the Scimitars back into Newcastle. SHQ and two of the troops had been on the ground for three weeks, roving around in the far north of the province, interdicting Taliban supply routes and providing a mobile punch to prevent out-of-area fighters coming in from the north. It was the kind of role the boys loved, recalling the Western Desert and the Long Range Desert Group.

As they rolled in Tom looked on with envy. All the boys had wild, unkempt beards, had each lost at least a stone, and their clothes hung off them. Dust was ingrained in every pore, and it took each of them at least ten minutes in the freezing showers to get remotely clean. Some of them had frost nip on their earlobes; all had cracked lips, cut fingers and a dry cough. Skin was stretched over sallow cheeks like parchment. None of them had had any fruit or vegetables for the whole operation. Tom felt guilty that he hadn't been on the ground with them.

They greeted Tom and his boys with friendliness but with an undercurrent of sanctimonious resentment that insinuated that 3 Troop had somehow deliberately chosen the easier path. As ever, Frenchie read the situation correctly as he chatted with Tom in the scoff tent in the evening and heard all his news.

'Don't you worry. I know you're jealous of what we've just done. But fear not, my son, because you're now back with the gang. Two more days, and you're in the Scimitars.'

'Was there much scrapping?'

'Not really. I mean, nothing major. Nothing worse than that retreat-from-Moscow-style debacle we had back in the cluster when you were shitting through the eye of a needle. I mean, the boys will bang on about a few contacts here and there, especially up in the north, but they weren't exactly the tractor factory at Stalingrad. The main thing was the conditions, which were horrendous. Whenever we leaguered up during that rainy period it was like the Somme. On to you. I've heard great things about you boys back here.'

'I don't know about that; it hasn't exactly been rocket science. Clearing routes, clearing routes, waiting for ATO, waiting for ATO, all day long.'

'Don't knock it. If it's dull then you're doing it well. I'd rather dullness and steadiness over cutting corners and me then having to write letters to a couple of parents telling them how sorry I am their son's been ripped into constituent parts. Dull is good. It means good drills. Capiche?'

'I know, Frenchie,' Tom said apologetically. 'But I can't deny we're not keen to get back on the Scimitars.'

'That's the spirit, sunshine. And I think we're about to be in the hot seat. Every bit of gossip I hear about this op tends towards the idea that whatever happens in it, wherever in the goddamn AO it is, we're going to be pretty high on the billing.'

He got up to go back to the canteen, and returned with a bowl brimming with more carrots and peas. 'That's better. First fresh veg I've had in weeks. Anyway, tell me more about living it large back here in slipper city.' He waited to see Tom's nostrils flare. 'Only joking. Christ, you're highly strung! It's like when I tell my wife that she's looking nice, and she bursts into tears and bangs on about how that means I think she looks fat. You know what women are like. Just like troop leaders. If your egos aren't massaged every minute of the day you end up suicidal. Women and troop leaders. Peas in a pod. And both the banes of my life.'

'How is your wife?'

'So so. I spoke to her a couple of times on the satphone while we were on the ground. But we keep it businesslike, just sorting out boring stuff like school fees. Doesn't really do to dwell on it really. It's fine. I mean, we've been married for eight years, and this is my third tour since then. We cope. Certainly a hell of a lot better than other marriages do. But where it's really hard is with the children. That's who you really miss.'

'How are they?'

'Fine. Fine, I think. Alex misses me terribly, I know. Apparently when he gets home from school he goes and finds a bit of my army kit and puts it on, as though he's the guard of the house, and then patrols the garden. I think he took my instructions that he look after his mother a bit too literally.'

Frenchie paused, and lost in thought pushed some peas around with his fork. Tom could see the creases around his eyes. He looked exhausted.

'I have this daydream. Whenever we halt or whenever I'm on the brink of sleep, for some reason all I think about is me and him, next summer, at the first day of the Lord's Test match, watching a game of cricket on a boys' day trip to London. I've got the whole thing planned. I just can't stop thinking about that day. I suppose when it finally happens it will signify the end of tour proper. I mean, psychologically. You always take a few months to wind down.'

He scooped up the final peas in his bowl and poured them into his mouth.

'And you know what? I bet you, I bet you, that when we do go and watch that match it's rained off.'

Christmas Eve was 3 Troop's last day on the Mastiffs and they were tasked to ferry two bits of cargo down Route Canterbury to PB Eiger. Trueman's wagon carried a generator to replace a broken one, and in Tom's wagon was the padre, going to Eiger to conduct a Christmas Eve carol service for A Squadron.

A man of considerable girth, short and with thick round glasses that gave him the air of Mole from *Wind in the Willows*, the padre barely fitted into any of his clothes and Tom thought he might struggle to fit inside the back of the Mastiff. He chain-smoked little Hamlet cigars, of which he had an inexhaustible supply, had white hair and looked far, far too old for the job. Everyone suspected that he had lied about his age, and there was a rumour that he and an old chief of the general staff had been at school together or some such, and that strings had been pulled to get him out on the ground. He had been vicar of a slum parish in Liverpool, and after the Iraq War started he had volunteered for the Territorial Army. He had done a tour in Iraq, where he had taken a shot in his helmet. He had a calm, soft voice and a bookish air.

The boys loved him, and even the most taciturn and tough of the nineteen-year-olds would open up to him. For that reason the CO made him one of the busiest men in the AO, and he was always visiting the troops on the ground, to his obvious delight. He never carried a weapon, and when Tom asked him before leaving if he wanted a pistol, he reached inside his pocket and patted a dog-eared Bible. 'Not to worry, Thomas;

this is all the defence I need. Well, and this, I suppose.' He drew out a huge hip flask from his other pocket, unscrewed the top and took a glug before offering it to Tom as though he was administering Communion.

Tom gleefully swigged from it. 'Christ, Padre. I mean, bloody hell, Padre, what on earth is that? Rocket fuel?'

'Not quite, Thomas. Napoleon brandy. On the few occasions when God can't save me, then that French bastard might just.'

The four wagons left camp and headed south. Jesmond led with the barma team, then came Tom, then Thompson and then Trueman. Over the past few days a heavy frost had settled. The puddles on the route were glazed with ice that nearly held the weight of a soldier, even with all his kit. While barmaing one of the VPs Acton, to amuse the others, had jumped up and down on one without realizing how deep the puddle was beneath him, broke the ice and plunged in up to his thighs. The earth turned into rock-like chunks, and to dig into the ground to investigate a metal reading required several minutes of chipping away with screwdrivers.

As they trundled down the route Tom waved from his turret to farmers trying to get ancient tractors to defy the petrol-freezing cold. About a kilometre from Eiger two children appeared from behind a compound, a boy and a girl, and ran alongside the wagons, waving at them. They kept up all the way to Eiger, and once the Mastiffs were safely inside the camp and Tom had caught up with the news from down there he walked to the front gate, where the sentry was laughing with the two children. Tom recognized him. 'Morning. Borrowby, isn't it? How's tricks?'

'Aye not bad, sir, but it's fucking shanking out here.' He blew on his hands, and his breath enveloped his face as he hacked away a cough. 'These kids are the best bit of it.' He laughed as they pulled faces and chased each other around. 'They always come down here, every day. They're brother and sister.'

He broke off suddenly to pretend to chase them away, and the children, squealing with delight, ran off and hid behind a dead tree, smirking as they peeked out from behind it. The girl was about thirteen, with high cheekbones and a beautiful smile. Her long hair was wild and shiny, and her immaculate yellow dress stood out, violent saffron against the frosted brown earth and the milky grey sky. The boy was the only other source of colour in the dead land, his blue dish-dash dirtier than his sister's dress but still strikingly bright.

They regained their courage and tiptoed back up to the gate in comic fashion, lifting their legs exaggeratedly high and placing their feet back on the earth with over-the-top softness. 'Wait,' said Tom to the sentry. 'Pretend to look the other way.' So they did, and the children came closer, unable to suppress their giggles. 'Wait for it, wait for it . . . When I say, we turn and chase them, OK?'

The sentry was also laughing. 'Got it, sir.'

The children came up almost to their backs, and at the last minute Tom whispered, 'Now!' and they both turned with a great roar.

The children screamed and ran away, Tom and Borrowby chasing them for forty metres over a field next to the route. Tom was breathless with joy as he sprinted after the little boy, who laughed and skipped over the furrows. He stopped and bent over, choking with laughter. Taking a chocolate bar out of one of his pouches, he held it out to the boy, who shyly took it from him, ripped the corner open and gnawed at the hard chocolate. Tom turned and almost bumped into the girl, who looked up at him with huge eyes, hurt that she hadn't also got a present. Tom patted his pockets apologetically to show he had none left.

She looked crestfallen, and so he took a spare pen and notebook from his thigh pocket and handed them over. Her delighted eyes moved from the pen and book to Tom with a wide smile, and she said something in Pashto. Despite the freezing cold and her thin dress she didn't shiver, and Tom held out his hand to shake hers. She looked up at him. He realized that he must look like an alien to her, towering in his body armour and helmet.

He knelt down, took off his helmet and put his rifle on the ground as her brother sidled over, still munching on the chocolate. Again he held out his hand and left it there as they both looked at it. After a while the girl held out hers, very daintily grasped Tom's fingers and shook them up and down. The boy then did the same. Tom saw that the boy was about the age he had been when his father had died. They stayed there in their little triangle, the girl testing the pen on the paper and the boy's jaw the only sounds in the bitter breeze. Tom got up and walked back to Eiger. He turned back to watch them run away up Canterbury and gazed as the blue and yellow dots receded into the distance.

They stayed in Eiger for most of the day. The generator was quickly replaced, but they had to wait for the padre to do his rounds. Tom wanted to leave in good time to do the home journey in daylight, and so the padre held his carol service at four o'clock. A Squadron gathered in a hollow square, 3 Troop mingling with them. They were to sing a couple of carols with a CD player providing a tinny accompaniment. A first, mumbling attempt at 'O Come, All Ye Faithful' was stopped halfway through the first verse by the squadron sergeant major, irate that none of the younger soldiers was singing.

He strode out in front of the padre, who looked on with a wry smile as the SSM screamed at them, 'Right, you cunts.

It's fucking Christmas, and you'd better start fucking enjoying it. Yeah, we all want to be home. Yeah, we all miss being on the fucking piss. Yeah, we all miss Christmas dinner with the family. Yeah, we don't want to be in Afghan playing Mary fucking Poppins to the ANA. Well boo fucking hoo. Dry your eyes, sweetcheeks, and get with the fucking agenda. We're here whether we like it or not, and if our mums and dads could see us they'd be sure as shit hoping we were singing our hearts out. So grow a pair and start sparking. Over the wall is Terry fucking Taliban. If he hears this fucking excuse for a carol service he'll piss himself laughing. So let's belt out these fucking carols and show him we've got some balls, yeah? Right. Take two.' He turned to the padre and said politely, 'Sorry about that, Padre; that should have done the trick.'

'Thank you very much, Sergeant Major,' he replied. 'I'm afraid my sermon later isn't going to be quite so colourful. Right everybody, let's have another go at that.' He pressed the play button and the boys shouted the carols till their voices were hoarse. After 'Hark the Herald Angels Sing' the boys looked at each other grinning at how loudly they'd all sung and the padre began his sermon. Already the first hints of evening had come on and he noticed some of the boys beginning to shiver.

'Well gentlemen, I can see the last thing you need is to hang around listening to an old codger like me bang on, but if you will give me two minutes then I would be most obliged. I just want to say that, as the sergeant major so . . . elegantly alluded to, this is a time when your thoughts will more than ever turn to your families. You will all be thinking about presents, about teasing your brothers and sisters, about desperately hoping to avoid being sat next to mad Great Aunt Doris at lunch. You will all be hoping to watch an episode of

Dad's Army on the telly; you will be thinking about making snowmen with your children, about the solemn rituals that every family has at this time of year. I'm afraid that I can't promise you any of that here.

'But I can promise you two things. Firstly, I can promise you a surrogate family. You may not realize it, but look around you now, at the men and women you have lived with, worked with and fought with over the past months. Who you have cried with. Bled with. Laughed with. One day, although you may not realize it now, you may, just may, look back on this group, gathered here far away from home, as a kind of family. I know I do. Goodness me, I miss my own children, although they probably do not miss me, snoring in front of the television and giving them books about Church history as presents, but when I look around me at meetings in HQ, on patrol when you let me come out with you, or when I see a barma team prepare to sweep a VP, I see something that is definitely a kind of family. So there, promise number one. You do have a family out here.

'And secondly, I promise you this. You will all go home. One day all this will be over, and you will go back home and this will all seem like a dream. A vivid dream at first, and one that may take years to shift. For some of you it will be as firmly fixed in your mind's eye in seventy years' time as it was when you first got back. But the point is you will be looking back at it from home. And, even though some of us may not make it back whole, or indeed alive, none of us will be left out here. Everyone will go home and leave this strange and foreign place. So the home you are missing at the moment is a home that you will not be apart from for ever. I hope you manage to find some kind of peace in that thought. I am not going to stand here and bore you rigid with stuff from the Bible or any of that claptrap – though I can if you want – but

I just thought that at this time, when our hearts tend more than ever towards home, we should all remember those two things. We do have a funny sort of family out here, and we will all go home. I hope that brings some comfort to you. I know it does for me. A very merry Christmas to you all.'

He said a blessing and the huddle dispersed. Many soldiers came up to him to say thank you, and Tom let him stay and field their questions as he and the boys got the wagons ready. As they started the engines A Squadron's 2ic Adam McAllister came out of Eiger's ops room and beckoned Tom towards him. Annoyed at the delay, Tom got out the back of the Mastiff and jogged over. 'What's up, Adam? Could slightly do with getting a move on, mate.'

'I know, I know, Tom. Chill your beans. We've just picked up some ICOM chatter that says that the Talibs might try to spring something at you on the way back.'

'What? But we're going to be inside the PB ring all the way. It's a milk run. What are they saying?'

'The usual. Stuff like "Get the big one ready for the big trucks." That kind of thing.'

'But they pull this all the time. They know we're listening in. They'll be saying it to get on our tits. You know what they're like.'

'I know, mate, I know. I'm only saying, that's all. Just take care.' He looked hurt and Tom regretted his peevishness. 'Look, Adam, I'm really sorry. I'm being a tosser. I really appreciate it, mate. I know you're looking out for us. Sorry, pal.'

'Forget it, Tommy; no hard feelings. You'd better offski, schnell machen. We'll keep you updated on the net if there's any more.'

'Thanks, bud.' Tom was already trotting back over to the Mastiff. 'And merry Christmas!'

The Mastiffs rolled out, stopping for the padre to tear himself away. In the back of Tom's wagon Dusty hauled him in as they trundled out the gate and back up Canterbury. Tom briefed the others over the radio on the ICOM news. The red sun sank lower and lower on the horizon. Tom looked at his watch. An hour until dark.

The wagons bumped in and out of the puddles in a bid to outrun the dark. Twice they had to stop to barma VPs where they were bottlenecked. The barma team swept over the first area with their customary thoroughness, and they were four hundred metres shy of Yukshal when they came to the second VP. After this they could trust that the route north, completely in sight of Yukshal and other checkpoints, was clear. It was now very gloomy; the sun had disappeared and its residual light was being dragged away after it.

They halted at the VP, and the barma team spilt out of Jessie's wagon. Tom's wagon pulled up twenty metres behind them, and he watched with pride as the boys clinically and thoroughly swept the area, found nothing and then returned to their wagon. They relaxed at the doors, their tension melting away. That was the last barma in their capacity as the Mastiff troop; now they'd be back on the Scimitars and able to leave the role behind. Tom felt the strain drain away from him as well. After this VP all that remained was a clear run north. They'd be back in thirty minutes.

Tom dropped inside his wagon and saw with amusement that both the padre and Dusty were snoozing in the back, lulled into sleep by the motion of the Mastiff as it bounced up the route. Over the intercom he bantered with Davenport, who was cocooned from the world in his driver's seat.

Tom got back up into the turret, and everything started to happen in slow motion. The barma team were still standing at the back of Jesmond's wagon. About to shout forward to them to get on board and stop dallying, through the shadows to his right a movement flashed in the corner of his eye, and Tom swivelled the GMG out of an animal instinct more than any rational judgement. A dart of light blazed from about a hundred metres away; he saw a figure standing next to a compound wall, and he realized at once that it was an RPG man. He registered a huge explosion as the rocket hit Jessie's wagon, garish white phosphorus shooting up into the early-evening sky.

Still Tom kept the GMG turning, and suddenly he was looking down its sights at the man. Immediately and without thinking, he felt his freezing fingers switch the gun to fire and then his hand squeeze the trigger handle as he sent a hammering burst of eight grenades towards the gunman. They exploded all around him in firework-like flashes. Tom saw the man fall, pitching straight forward onto his face, and a spear of adrenaline fizzed through his brain. He realized at that moment what it was he had done: he had killed a man, and he had done it subconsciously, as an automaton. He wanted to scream with delight.

He dropped down inside the wagon. 'Dusty, Dusty, contact, contact! I just wasted an RPG man!' Dusty was out of his seat. He popped open the hatch at the rear of the wagon and slickly unslung the gimpy strapped inside. Tom's earphones sprung into life. It was Jessie.

'Hello, Three Zero, this is Three Two. We have a casualty from the RPG. I say again, casualty. My Alpha Charlie call-sign. Don't know what's wrong with him exactly. Over.'

Tom's throat went dry, and he looked out of the turret. His eyes struggled to readjust to the dark after the yellow light of the Mastiff's interior. He couldn't see Jessie's wagon properly but could only make out in the dark a commotion at the rear of it. Over the intercom he said calmly, 'Dav, headlights on.'

Davenport flicked on the headlights and the scene in front of them appeared in surgical white. Three of the boys were kneeling down around another sprawled out on the ground. Through the earphones again came Jessie, panicked this time.

'Yeah, Three Zero, Three Two. We've got real trouble here. Confirm Zap number Alpha Charlie Two Six Six Five. He's bleeding really badly.'

Tom felt his stomach leave him, and everything seemed to become silent. *Acton.* Acton was hit. Tom didn't even really know him. He paused just for a second, which seemed to stretch over minutes. He felt a tiny bit of bile rise from his gut; he swallowed it down and then hit it, hit the zone. Things started to happen very quickly. He dropped back down inside, ripped his headphones off, grabbed his rifle from its slot, screamed, 'Cover me, Stardust, cover me,' pulled his way past the padre and jumped out the rear doors on to the frosty ground and turned to sprint up the track.

He ran out of the dark into the light thrown by the headlights and came to the back of Jessie's wagon. As he broke into their group GV looked up at him and said, 'It's all right, fellas. Boss here, boss here.' Acton was lying on his back, his large round face pale with thin streaks of blood trickling from his nostrils. The boys had already put two dressings on his legs, which looked horribly torn. Blood oozed out of wounds where his trousers had been shredded away, but Tom could tell that they weren't life-threatening; the blood was dark not arterial, and wasn't coming out quickly. But he couldn't work out why Acton was so white. He was convulsing in spastic, violent spasms, and was hardly responding to the boys' efforts to get him to stay awake.

Tom looked around him and saw Livesey vomiting and crying. 'Hey, GV, get that cunt back in the wagon. Get him away from here.' GV got up and hurled the cowering Livesey into the wagon. Tom focused back on Acton. *Where was the blood coming from? Why did he seem to be so badly hurt?* 'Fellas, we need to strip him down, get his body armour off.' Tom and Ellis tore off Acton's Osprey, which revealed his saturated under-armour shirt. When Tom pulled this up a great flood of blood spread out from his torso, washing over the white ground and, unable to soak into the hard earth, drenching their knees.

'Where the fuck's his wound? Where the fuck's the wound?' said Tom as he ripped his shemagh from his neck and furiously tried to dab away the blood to see any sign of skin rupture. He felt like an art expert feeling a piece of silver which he knew, somewhere, had a dent in it. But where was it? 'More light, we need more light.' The headlights were helpful but they kept on throwing shadows over the convulsing torso. One of the boys flicked his head torch on. 'Good lad. Keep that light there, keep that light there.' Tom kept mopping away the blood. And then he saw it. It was a cut, only about an inch long, where Acton's ribcage met his right armpit. Blood, frothy and scarlet, was pouring freely out of it. 'OK, OK, we've got the bleed, we've got the bleed. Someone give me a fucking hemcon.'

Again the boys' drills showed. All the lessons and reruns that Tom and Trueman had insisted on back in the summer in the green Pembrokeshire fields paid off, and Ellis whipped out a hemcon from his med pouch. 'Ell, get that in there.' Ellis went to work, and Tom was able to step back from the bleeding and shivering torso, the white flesh stark against the black around it. Acton's mouth was now frothing blood, and he was choking. Tom realized he was about thirty minutes, max, away from death, if he was lucky. He had no idea how long he'd been over the body; he had to get on the net to start the casevac. If Acton didn't get to a MERT within half an hour he'd bleed out. Tom had no idea of the extent of internal bleeding. He climbed into Jessie's wagon.

'Jessie, here's the plan. I'm going to get Yam-Yam back into my car; there's too many lads in yours and Three One's got the generator in it. Send this to battle group while me and GV get Yam-Yam to mine. Get Minuteman Nine One on the line and tell him that we've got a Cat A and we're going to get him best speed to Newcastle. Tell him to get the MERT moving to Newcastle's HLS. Roger?'

'Got it, boss.'

'Also tell him that if he can, get the QRF to crash out with the doc in it, and see if we can meet him on the way. He desperately needs a doc and I reckon a shedload of blood and IV. The sooner he can get an expert the better. Clear?'

'Clear, boss.'

'Right, GV and I will get Yam-Yam back. When he's in my wagon GV will run forward to you, and when he's back, that's your signal. Hell for leather all the way home. Stop for nothing until we RV with the doc. OK?'

'No dramas, boss.' Jessie switched to the battle group net and started sending to BGHQ: 'Hello, Minuteman Zero, this is Tomahawk Three Two. Reference that Cat A casualty, plan from my Sunray. Over . . .'

Tom jumped back out onto the ground and briefed up the boys. Snow now swirled in the headlights. Acton was breathing softly and shivering as they tried to keep him warm and his wounds plugged. 'Boys, on the wagon, now. GV, you're good to take Yam-Yam back to Three Zero, aren't you?' He had to be. GV was the only person in the squadron of even remotely comparable size to Acton, and they had no stretcher.

'Yeah, boss, I got him. It's good. It's good.'

'Let's do it.'

They hauled Acton up and heaved him onto GV's shoulders, who panted under the weight. He set off but slipped on the dark blood congealing on the ground and dropped his cargo. He lay there sprawled, his limbs intertwined with Acton's.

'Fuck fuck fuck. Sorry, boss. I slipped. Let me try again.'

Acton moaned with pain. They picked him up again and this time GV was all right.

'GV, let's go! GV, let's go!'

The boys got back on board as GV stumbled down the track, Tom hustling behind him, still in the headlights of Three Zero and with no cover at all. And then, above the hum of the engines from their left, automatic fire came at them, and shafts of tracer pummelled into the earth at their feet and fizzed between them. 'Fuck fuck fuck!' said Tom. He switched his rifle to automatic and on the run, from the hip, unloosed the entire magazine in a three-second burst back in the direction of the muzzle flashes.

He had no idea whether the rounds were on target, but it felt good to send some back. His ears rang with the beat of his rifle and his nostrils filled with cordite. Still the rounds came as they continued their now painfully slow waddle. One of the yellow bolts passed between GV's legs, and Tom felt a round whistle past his nose. And then the hammering of a .50 cal came from Trueman's wagon in the rear of the column. Dusty on the gimpy also started to engage, unfurling a carpet of fire to cover them.

It took an age, but with Trueman's .50 still belting out a

staccato beat Tom and GV reached the cover of the Mastiff and escaped the glare of its headlights. They reached the back, where the padre was kneeling inside with open arms to drag Acton aboard. With surprising strength he pulled him in and laid him down on the seats, and Tom, standing on the tailgate, turned to GV. 'You can't go back in this fire. Get aboard.'

He tried to yank him onto the wagon, but GV turned to him, his bright honest eyes gleaming with adrenaline. 'No, boss. No room on wagon, innit. Yam-Yam gotta lie down. I'm too big to fit in, innit.' He turned to run back towards Three Two.

Tom called after him, 'No, GV! Come back!' But to no avail. GV raced down the track and passed once again into the open killing ground of the ambush. 'Dusty, Dusty, give GV some cover!' Immediately Dusty opened up again, burst after burst flying into the dark. Tom looked back up the track, willing him to make it. A beam of tracer slewed into GV's head, and he went down like a rabbit, his great lumbering form reduced to a rubber-limbed doll. 'GV!' Tom screamed, and the world collapsed in on him; this was now an unmitigated disaster. A chill swept over him; were any of them going to escape this ambush?

Just as he gulped down his fear and his muscles tensed to begin the lonely sprint over to GV's corpse, Tom saw GV rise again from the ground, totter and then continue his run all the way to the back of Three Two, where he was dragged in by friendly hands. Jessie's wagon immediately started moving. Tom got in his own Mastiff and clambered over the padre, whose fingers were now deep inside Acton's ribcage and who was up to his elbows in blood. Tom grabbed the net off Dusty. 'Hello, Three Two, this is Three Zero. Tell me about the Golf Alpha callsign. What's wrong with him? Over.'

196

Jessie's voice came back, drunk with joyful shock, his VP going out of the window, 'Yeah, boss, it's OK. It's OK. GV's just been hit on the helmet. Bounced clean off.' He started laughing. 'But he's all right, he's all right; the big ox is up again. Not even a scratch. He says he hasn't even got a headache, but he's sure as fuck going to go spastic on the next Talib he meets! Over.'

Rounds slammed into the Mastiff's side, flat thuds that reverberated around the cab. Tom yanked Dusty down from his hatch, screamed forward to Davenport to follow Jessie and said to Dusty, 'Stardust, get on the GMG. I need to be in the cab talking to Zero.'

'No probs, boss.' Dusty sank back down into the Mastiff's body with the gimpy, unloaded it, rested it on the floor, swerved around Tom and got back on the GMG in the main turret. Tom could hear Trueman's .50 behind him laying down a valediction to the ambush site.

'Hello, Minuteman Nine One, this is Tomahawk Three Zero Alpha. Has my Three Two callsign updated you on our situation and plan? Over.'

Immediately the reply came back from Jules Dennis, friendly, understanding: 'Roger. Tomahawk Three Zero understood. Your Three Two has briefed me up. We're crashing out the QRF down Canterbury now, with the doc callsign. Going to make best speed to you. When you RV the doc will jump aboard and you'll continue north to Newcastle. Roger so far over.'

Tom felt a surge of optimism. Maybe they could win this race. 'Tomahawk Three Zero roger so far over.'

'Minuteman Nine One, the MERT is on its way from Bastion to the HLS at my location. We're going to need a MIST for them. We've got Mike and the India, but we need the Sierra and the Tango. Please send. Over.'

'Tomahawk Three Zero roger. Wait Out.'

He put the headset down and looked at Acton. He was hanging in there but only just. His eyes were flickering open and he was trying to speak. His lips were moving, first quickly, then slowly. The padre remained with his fingers inserted resolutely inside his ribcage.

'Padre, doc's on his way down. I need to get his signs and his treatment for the MIST. What are you thinking?'

'I've been around enough hospital wards in my time to know a thing or two about wounds. I think I've got the external bleed, but he's really badly hurt internally. One of his arteries is pouring blood somewhere into his trunk and I have no idea where. I don't know if he's going to make it, Thomas. How long have we got to go?'

'About fifteen minutes till we meet the doc.'

The padre paused, and his voice lowered to a whisper. 'Then it's touch and go.'

Tom pressed two fingers gently against Acton's neck, and counted over ten seconds the faint pulse trying to throb blood into his brain. They were very far apart. Three beats per ten seconds. Pulse rate of eighteen. He leaned closer to him, put his ear over his mouth and counted his breaths over another ten seconds. Deep inside his lungs he could hear a frothy wheezing. Two breaths over ten seconds. Breathing rate twelve. Not as bad as the pulse. He looked over the whole body and saw the FFDs on his legs, the hemcon the padre was holding in place in his side and the letter M scrawled in blood on his forehead, after Ellis had whacked him with morphine. At least he was out of pain.

'Hello, Minuteman Nine One. Tomahawk Three Zero reference that MIST serial Sierra: pulse eighteen, breathing twelve. Unconscious. We think he's got a severe internal bleed in his torso. His lungs sound very bad, frothy and bubbly. Roger so far? Over.'

'Minuteman Nine One roger.'

'Tomahawk Three Zero serial Tango: two FFDs on either leg, hemcon in his torso wound, one times morphine. End of MIST. Over.'

'Minuteman Nine Zero roger. That's understood. Over.'

Then another callsign butted in. 'Minuteman Nine One, this is Minuteman Eight Two.'

It was the doc.

'Understood all that. Tomahawk Three Zero just keep that bleeding plugged. I'm on my way south with saline for your Alpha Charlie casualty. Over.'

Yes. Tom felt the whole battle group's weight kick in behind him. Maybe they could save Acton after all.

Tom looked at him more closely. His breathing remained torturous and slow. The convulsions had stopped in the warm Mastiff, and Tom noticed his chest, with barely a hair on it, was heavily tattooed. A dirty film of blood lay dried over his skin. He mopped Acton's brow and stroked his hair. 'There you go, Yam-Yam. There you go. We're going to get you home.' He looked at his watch. Twenty past five. Christmas Day in a few hours. He thought about the news that Mrs Acton was about to get. *Christ!* He didn't even know if Yam-Yam was married or had any children. Ever since Acton had arrived he had always meant to interview him, to find out more about him, but had never got round to it. Did he even have a family? Any siblings? He must have a mother. He felt ashamed that he hadn't bothered to find out.

His eyes welled up and, not wanting to show any weakness in front of the padre, he opened the hatch that Dusty had been firing out of at the ambush and stuck his head out into the sharp, biting air. He drew it deeply into his lungs. The wagons drove at a frantic pace through the snow. He looked down inside the wagon at the wound, with the padre's fingers stuffed inside it. The skin around it was black and scorched by the heat of the shrapnel as it had passed into him. Where was that piece of shrapnel? There was no exit wound. It could be lodged anywhere – in his heart, in his lungs. In his spine? He looked up again out of the wagon, and there, in the distance, he saw headlights coming towards them. The QRF. The doc. Through the IC he shouted, 'Dav, foot down, foot down. The doc's here.'

And then they were there, and he was kicking open the back doors and the doc came aboard carrying two bags of saline and with another medic. The wagon was now ridiculously crowded. 'Padre, get forward to the front cab!' The padre squirmed his egg-like form forward to free up space as the medics went about their work immediately and wordlessly, and then they were on the move again. Only ten minutes now till Newcastle.

Over the radio came Jules. 'Hello, Tomahawk Three Zero, Minuteman Nine One. Understood you have the Eight One callsign. MERT inbound and eight minutes out of Newcastle. Best speed over.'

'Tomahawk Three Zero roger. QRF RV seamless. Doc now on the casualty. We'll get him to the MERT, don't worry. Out.' He turned to the doc. 'Doc, what do you reckon?'

The doctor looked up, his face spattered with Acton's blood. He shook his head. 'I'm sorry, Tom; I just don't know.' Acton started spasming, and the doc muttered, 'Bollocks. He's arresting.' Every jolt of Acton's torso seemed to rock the wagon as much as any pothole in the track. The doc gave Acton CPR, inflating his broken lungs with his own breath. Tom saw Acton's chest slowly reinflate. Twice the doc did it.

Then a third time. And a fourth. No response. And then a tiny choke, a tiny splutter. Finally the chest started moving by itself, slowly, painfully slowly. The doc looked exultant. 'I think I got it! I think I got it!'

At last the column rolled into sight of Newcastle. When they were two hundred metres away a great black shadow studded with lights swooped overhead, barely fifty metres off the ground, and Tom shouted to the wagon, 'It's the MERT; the MERT's here!' The dark shape of the Chinook braked over the HLS and spiralled down to a soft landing.

The wagon came through the gate and into camp, Tom opened the doors and Brennan was there with a stretcher party. 'Don't worry, Mr Chamberlain, we got him.' He patted Tom on the back as Acton was carried out of the Mastiff and put onto a stretcher.

The boys set off at a run up the low hill to the HLS, the doc next to them carrying the saline bag. Tom jogged behind and noticed tiny drips of Acton's blood spill from his chest onto the shuffling boots of the stretcher bearers. The doc yelled, 'Faster, boys, faster; he's arresting again.' On the stretcher Acton started his second cardiac arrest as his heart cried out for more blood, his writhing and juddering slowing their dash through the camp.

Soon they felt the warm blast of the exhausts as they neared the heli. They ran on board into the dark womb of the MERT; the doc shouted some information to the emergency physician on board, then they were off again, and the bird rocketed back into the sky, lights flashing in concert with the stars above it as it lifted way up into the clear night and back to Bastion.

Tom stood there dazed as the doc, Brennan and the stretcher party left him alone for a couple of minutes to gather his thoughts. Enveloped by the sudden silence, he walked back down the hill to the 3 Troop Mastiffs and found the boys gathered around his wagon. Blood was everywhere: on the floor, on the walls. Spent cases from the gimpy studded the floor, the tank park floodlights picking out their brass against the dark red.

Tom reached the group. He wished he had had more time to compose himself, but now would have to do. He felt fierce and proud. 'Fellas, Yam-Yam's on the heli; he's with the docs now. I don't know if he's going to make it.' They looked down at the ground. No one spoke so he continued: 'I just want to say that I am incredibly proud of every one of you. I can't believe we managed to turn that around. Every man of you stepped up. And you,' he turned to GV, 'you absolute fucking madman. You ever do that again I'm going to court-martial you. You gave me a heart attack, you great ox. Come here.' He went forward and gave GV a bear hug. 'How's the head?'

'OK, boss. Just glancing blow, innit. Had worse on rugby pitch. Fuckin' Taliban chippy cunts. Can't even shoot straight.' Tom hugged him even closer and then remembered himself and awkwardly pulled away from the embrace. He couldn't believe he was doing this; he would never have acted this way with the men even a month beforehand. He tried to correct himself. 'Anyway, Sergeant Trueman, we'd better get these wagons squared away again.' Trueman and the rest of them laughed at his self-consciousness; it was a running joke by now how he tried in vain to be formal with them.

'Yes, sir. Fellas, start getting these fucking wagons cleaned up. I want a full clean-up, full ammo resupply. And Dusty, get Yam-Yam's blood out of your wagon, will you. It's minging in there. And boss,' he said to Tom, 'I think the padre has something for you.'

The padre sat inside the wagon, his clothes drenched in

Acton's blood, his eyes smiling behind his glasses. One of the lenses was shattered. He held out his hip flask and said softly, 'Thomas, if anyone does, you deserve a drink.' Tom took it and drank gratefully.

They cleaned up the wagons all thinking about Acton. The adrenaline of the contact and the race to the HLS wore off quickly, and they filed dismally into the scoff tent. They sat apart from the others, and no one spoke during supper. They went to the troop tent, Tom, the padre and Trueman with them, and waited anxiously for news. A few of the boys flicked through magazines; some just sat staring ahead at the dirty white walls of the tent. Dusty hummed to himself, foot tapping on the ground, and Davenport twirled a pen around his fingers, clicking his teeth. Even Trueman was subdued. Tom found he had no words that could ease the wait. Outside they could hear the patter of footsteps as soldiers moved around camp, but nobody came to the tent. And then, at nine, some footsteps did come closer, and they collectively breathed in as the flaps of the tent opened and Frenchie and the doc came in.

They could tell immediately that it was good news. The doc wore a broad grin and shook Tom's hand. He didn't know what to say and in a daze listened open-mouthed as the doc addressed them. 'Well, 3 Troop, you did it. Acton's going to make it. He's going to be OK.' Tom could see the tension lift from the boys' shoulders as he went on: 'That was a very, very close-run thing. The MERT went pell-mell back to Bastion, and they stabilized the bleed during the flight. And then he went straight into theatre at the other end. They found the shrapnel. Lodged in one of his ribs. Really badly cut up his lungs. He was bleeding badly internally, very badly. That's why he was arresting.'

Dusty interrupted: 'You promise me, sir, you promise us?

We're not going to hear in an hour that he's slipped away, are we?'

The doc smiled, understanding and patient. 'No, Corporal Miller, no. I've just spoken to the senior surgeon. He operated on him himself. Acton is going to be all right, I promise you. I promise you. No brain damage, no paralysis, nothing. He won't be playing football any time soon but he's going to be OK. Who was it that treated him when he was hit?'

As if afraid to do so, Ellis and GV put up their hands, embarrassed.

'Well done, you two. Really well done. Without you guys and –' he glanced at Tom and the padre '– the work in the wagon on the way up, he wouldn't have made it. That's some work. Goes to show those lessons in the summer paid off, doesn't it?'

The doc and Frenchie left. Three Troop looked around at one another. Still Tom didn't know what to say. He sat down, exhausted, but the boys started cheering and hugging each other. Davenport came over to Tom and sat next to him on the camp cot. 'Nice one, sir, nice one.'

Tom looked up, surprised. 'Oh, thanks, Dav, thanks a lot. Well driven yourself.'

'Nah, sir. That was all you. Happy Christmas!'

Later that night Tom, Henry, Clive, Scott and Jason sat round an upturned cardboard box in their freezing tent drinking the contraband alcohol that had been sent to them. In defiance of regulations friends and family had posted out shampoo bottles full of whisky, mouthwash bottles full of vodka, sometimes even hidden miniatures inside hollowed-out books to evade the censor at Bastion. Sam had sent some of his thermonuclear sloe gin in a bottle of Ribena, merely one weapon in the arsenal of spirits in front of them. They hadn't been together as a group since Bastion and were thrilled to be united again. After Christmas Day they'd be split up once more, Clive to take over Tom's Mastiff role and Tom his Scimitars to prepare for the big op in the New Year.

They were listening to Tom's – already embellished – account of that evening's ambush when from outside the tent came a quiet 'Knock knock?' They froze. If they were caught drinking they'd be in a world of trouble. Ashen-faced, they sat like dummies as the flaps of the tent opened and Brennan's head poked in.

Clive shot up, flustered. 'Good evening, Sergeant Major. This isn't what it looks like.' He looked down at the table. Covered in half-empty bottles it was exactly what it looked like. 'I mean, we just decided to have one or two drinks. To celebrate Christmas, you know.'

Brennan didn't reply, just watched him dig himself deeper.

'Well, I suppose it may have been slightly more than one or two. Maybe three. Possibly four. But we're not drunk.'

Brennan flashed his gold teeth. 'Sir, stop flapping like a nun in a brothel. We thought we'd invite ourselves over with some good tidings of our own. Room for a few wee ones?' He came into the tent followed by the other sergeants, laden with bottles themselves.

Trueman was last. 'Oi oi, here are the jolly boys! Evening, sirs.' He picked up a bottle of gin from the table and eyed it contemptuously. 'Fucking hell, sirs, you lot don't half play it lame. It's like an episode of *Loose Women*. Next thing you'll be smoking Silk Cut. Well, here's the good stuff.' He plonked a litre of absinthe down on the table. 'Merry Christmas one and all.' They didn't stop drinking until four in the morning, and then retreated to their camp beds to wake up three hours later feeling very sorry for themselves.

The CO had designated Christmas a low ops day. In every base patrols stayed in camp and the boys across the AO tried to foster some sort of festive cheer. In Newcastle they had a carol service at midday. The padre gave another sermon, but this time Tom didn't listen, concentrating on trying not to vomit from his hangover. He looked across during the singing and saw Trueman looking green as well. The rest of 3 Troop were struggling too. That morning when he and Trueman had gone to wake them up and say Happy Christmas he thought he had smelt alcohol in their tent. Even Frenchie looked the worse for wear; he must have been boozing with the CO.

Only Brennan seemed unaffected. Amazing, Tom thought, given that he had seen him sink half a bottle of vodka in one go at three in the morning. He looked as sober as a maiden aunt. Pretty much the entire battle group had clearly got drunker than skunks the previous night but were now trying to maintain the fiction in front of each other that they were models of temperance.

The padre wound up his sermon, and afterwards Frenchie got the squadron together and had a photo taken of them all wearing their Father Christmas hats. At Christmas lunch the officers served the boys, as was the regimental tradition. When he and the officers sat down Tom inhaled his turkey and potatoes, welcoming anything to soak up the absinthe still swishing round his guts.

At 1400 the news came that Op Minimize had been lifted. There had been a KIA down south late on Christmas Eve, and the dead man's family had now been informed, meaning that people were finally now allowed to phone home. Brennan produced a rota prioritizing the phones: first the fathers, then the marrieds and finally the singles. Tom thought only in passing about how the glee with which the boys ran to the phones would contrast with the scene back in Britain at the home of the KIA that day. He flicked it from his mind.

There was a bank of five phones each in a little wooden booth with a hessian cloth for token privacy. Brennan monitored call lengths. There was every chance that Minimize could be called again any minute with news from elsewhere in theatre so he religiously limited each one to five minutes. He stood outside the booth and when the soldier went in started a stopwatch he had taped above it. When it hit four minutes he would put his head in and say sympathetically, 'Sorry, lad, one minute left,' and allow the boy to wind up the conversation before another was allowed in.

Tom took his place with the other troop leaders at the back of the queue, happy to kick his heels and to chew the fat with the other boys. Finally Tom's turn came. He settled into the booth on the grimy white plastic chair, took a few deep breaths and called home. He looked at his watch. Four o'clock. Half eleven back home. Would Mum be back from church? The phone rang and rang and then hit the answer machine. His heart sank. He hung up and tried again. On the eighth ring came her voice: 'Hello, Chamberlain?' His throat went dry. He couldn't speak.

'Hello? Hello?'

Come on!

He croaked, 'Hi, Mum. Happy Christmas.'

It took a while for her voice to reach him over the line.

'Tom! Tom! How are you! Are you OK? Where are you?'

'I'm fine, Mum, I'm fine. We're all allowed to ring home today. I know I promised not to, but I just decided on the off-chance. I'm fine; don't worry. I promise you. We're all fine.' He thought about Acton and decided not to mention him.

'Tom, it's so good to hear your voice. I've literally just this minute got back from church. I was going to stay and go to drinks with the vicar afterwards, but I decided to come home and feed Zeppo early for some reason. How funny! What are you doing today? Are you going on patrol?'

'No, Mum; we're in camp today. It's been great. We had a carol service and Christmas lunch and everything, and the rest of the day is pretty chilled – nothing planned. And then it's New Year, then three more weeks, and then that's me on R & R. I can't wait! How's Zeppo? What's the weather like?'

'He's well, but he's getting fat; I spoil him. You're going to need to take him on some long walks when you're home.'

'Ha! Poor Zep. Give him some extra turkey today.'

'Hmm, OK. The weather's so-so – cold and crisp and frosty – but the drive is so slippy. I've managed to get a man from the council to come and grit it. How is it with you?'

'Freezing! The nights are about minus ten at the moment. But we're OK. We're all OK, Mum. Can't wait to come home though. And thank you so much for all the parcels.' He looked at his watch; not long to go. 'Tell Sam that we had his sloe gin. It was pretty toxic!'

'Will do. It is so good to hear you. Everyone in the village has been watching the news about Afghanistan. Everywhere I go I'm like a celebrity.'

'More free drinks for me the next time I'm back then. Mum, I'd better go in a bit. We're only allowed five minutes.'

Brennan put his head around the hessian and whispered, 'Sorry, sir; one minute left.'

Tom nodded, and continued to Constance: 'Ma, we're about to go into the desert for a bit so I won't be able to ring for a while. Please still write though. And I will too. Have you been getting my blueys?'

'They're stuck up on the noticeboard in the kitchen. I'm looking at them right this second. Please keep sending them. It is so good to hear your news. And remember I want photos!'

'I know, Mum, I know.'

'Well you'd better go. I am so pleased you called. This has made my Christmas. I'm off to lunch with Sam and Florence. They'll be delighted you rang.'

'Say hi to them from me.' He felt the time slipping away and desperately wanted to stop it and to continue this fragile link for ever. But he had to go.

'Ma, Happy Christmas. And I'll see you in a month any-way. I can't wait! Not long.'

'I know, Tom. Take care, darling, will you?'

'Always do, Mum, always do.' He had to end this. 'I'll write, I promise. Great to speak. Bye, Mum.'

'Bye, Tom.'

They rallied farewells at the end.

'Bye.'

'Bye.'

'Bye.'

And then the phone went dead. Tom hung up and walked away from the booth past the remnants of the queue and back to his tent, trying to look brave. He passed Dusty, who paused to speak to him but then noticed Tom's face and let him go on his way.

He went into the tent, empty bottles still on the table stinking sweetly. He lay on his camp cot and tried to take everything in, not sure whether his numbness came from either the night before or from the phone call. A helicopter's downdraught beat against the roof of the tent; absent-mindedly he recognized the sound of a Sea King. Maybe it carried some mail. Music came softly from Clive's speakers, and he started to lose himself in its calming, cathartic beat. He realized then that he was very tired, and turned over the events of the night before. It seemed so long ago. Because Acton was fine, or at least would live, everyone had slightly forgotten about him. If he had died, and Tom knew just how close that had been, the whole day would have been spent writing reports of the action for the coroner, being interviewed by the CO, being grilled by Frenchie and having his every move pored over, every detail of the ambush brought up from the thrilling fog of memory into the stark white light of an inquest.

He knew there had been many, many things wrong with how he had conducted the action. Why had he been so blasé about the ICOM threat? He had forgotten about it the moment they left Eiger. Why hadn't he made the barma team get back into Jessie's wagon more quickly? Why had he even bothered to barma that VP in the first place? They'd been over the ground five hours before, and in that hard earth it was impossible to dig in an IED. But most of all he wondered why on earth he had run forward to Jessie's wagon and then back with GV through the tracer gauntlet when he could just have told Davenport to drive forward and put his bumper at the back of Three Two. That way they could have done the casevac in the cover of his own wagon.

He was sweating. It was so simple. Why hadn't he driven up to the wagon? And why had none of the lads asked him about this? Surely it was blindingly obvious that that would have been the safest thing to do.

Tom leaned over the side of his camp cot to his Osprey folded neatly beneath. He unzipped it, reached behind the front plate to the envelope he kept there and opened the letter from his father. He cast his mind back, far away, to the little boy in the den at home reading it for the first time. He didn't need to look at the words; he knew them by heart. He ran through them all in his head, lips mouthing every one, until they reached 'Nothing in excess,' where they stopped moving and felt dry. He knew deep down then, in that instant, that he had run across the gap not because he wasn't thinking clearly but because he was, because he wanted the thrill, and when it had come, he had loved it.

The run back through the bullets with one in front of him passing between GV's legs? That was why he had joined the army. His heart started racing, his pupils dilated, all these thoughts whirling through his skull in seconds. He had to get out there again. He couldn't wait for it.

What was he becoming? Or had he always been this, and the weeks out here were just stripping away the layers draped over him and drawing them back to reveal the raw violence inside him?

Clive walked in, and Tom shook himself out of his dream. 'There you are! Looking for you everywhere. Look what I've got!' He dangled a piece of paper over Tom's eyes, which struggled to focus in the dull afternoon gloom. An e-bluey.

Tom snatched out at it, but Clive whipped it away at the

last second. 'Not so fast. Who's this from?' He looked at it theatrically. He'd already read the sender's details on the outside. 'Cassandra Foskett!? Oh I see! The Doris.'

'Give it here.'

'How much?'

'Nothing. Give it here.'

'How about I read it out aloud? Like a bedtime story. With the whole squadron listening.'

'Give it here. Or else.'

'Or else what?'

'Or I'll shoot you in the face.' Tom reached beneath his bed and suddenly found his pistol in his hand. He just stayed his arm from pointing it at his friend; instead it hung limply from his wrist, but his eyes blazed.

'Jeez, OK, OK. Whoa, boy. Just joshing.' Clive threw the letter onto the cot and trying to mask his shock left the tent quietly. Tom didn't notice and ripped open the envelope.

Christmas Eve

Half two in the afternoon. After one too many lunchtime gin and tonics. Hic!

Tom paused. She would have written this just as they were driving Acton back to the MERT. He carried on.

Dearest dearest Tommikins,

Only joking! I knew that would annoy you. Big rough tough soldier little Tommikins! How are you, my Afghan warrior? I cannot begin to imagine what it must be like to have Christmas out there; I bet you it is a world away from here. We are in London, and it has been snowing and magical and it is like a ghost town and just like those stories we used to read as children. Frosty windowpanes, breath steaming like clouds as you walk and snowmen all over Battersea Park. Oh Tom, it is so, so lovely here and yippee I have a week off work and I'm going skiing on Boxing Day with Jasper Smith and Charlie De Groot – remember them from Cambridge – out to stay with, yes you've guessed it, Jonty Forbes in his chalet in Wengen.

Tom had to stop. *She what?* While he was out here, she was running off with two of those tossers from Cambridge? He vaguely remembered the Jasper one as a tall sneering embodiment of everything he had resented about his time there. As for Charlie Grotbag, who knew what rock he had crawled out from under? And they were staying with that utter wanker Jonty. He lapsed into dreaming about the Taliban opening up a second front in Wengen and laying IEDs on its slopes. He'd defect and join them.

I know, I know. You'll hate me for it, but as I told you, Mum and Dad are best friends with his, etc., and I couldn't refuse a free invitation, could I? You know me; yes, there is such a thing as a free lunch! Anyway, it's only for four days or so. I come back on New Year's Day. I wonder what you will be doing then.

Probably with Dusty pummelling seven shades of shit with my 30 mil into some poor Afghan.

But Tom, I want you to know something. Can we talk when you're back? It's just that, well, I don't know. It feels weird this, keeping whatever's going on between us going on by letter. I mean, it all feels a bit like a Jane Austen novel.

He braced himself for the hit. When it came though, it wasn't as bad as he expected.

Tom, I don't know what is going to happen between now and when you're back on leave. I mean, I don't really know what I mean. Oh bollocks, I shouldn't have had all that gin. It's just that I can't wait to see you, but I don't want to keep my life on hold for all the while you're gone. It feels like I'm a war widow sometimes, for Christ's sakes, and we haven't even slept together for two years.

Two and a half.

Tom, I think I'm just trying to say in an incredibly clumsy way that I really want you back here. Every day there's news about soldiers dying in Afghanistan and every party I seem to go to is in aid of some sort of army charity, and there are wounded boys who are all smiling and pretending to be having a good time but it must be just so awful.

And I bet your mate Jonty's on the committee for half of these parties, crying crocodile tears every time he hears of another death.

I didn't even know where Afghanistan was, I realized at one of these parties when someone stood up to make a speech about it, an officer who reminded me of you. He had your hair and your eyes, but he had his sleeve pinned up at his shoulder where he had lost his arm. He was very cheery and kept on making lots of jokes about himself. I talked to him afterwards and he was so nice. But I felt embarrassed when I got home, so I (how pathetic is this) looked where it was in the atlas. So there you are! Right next to Iran. And just south of Tajikistan. Wouldn't it be fun to go to those places travelling some time?

I can think of better ones.

I'm rambling. I'm going to press send straightway, otherwise I'll look back at this in half an hour, realize it is all embarrassing gobbledegook and delete it. But I hope something of the above has made sense.

Clear as mud.

All I want is for you to be back safe, and I want to see you. But all I'm saying is that I don't know if you and I are boyfriend and girlfriend, or friend and friend, or nothing at all, or what. I can't promise you anything, Tom. Nothing. Apart from the fact that I <u>will</u> see you when you're back, and I am counting down the days till then.

Tommikins, I am going to miss you, my little Christmas bunny. Hope you're a good boy and that Father Christmas is nice.

From Cassie the Red-Nosed Reindeer xxxxxxx

Tom rested the letter on his chest. He really wanted to see her. He lay on his cot in silence, eyes open and vacant. Finally he sighed, heaved himself up and tried to throw her out of his mind. She could wait. He needed to see the boys. He got up and went out into the dark to find Trueman. As he left he bumped straight into him. 'Hi, sir. I was looking for you.'

'What's up?'

'You're wanted in the ops room. They didn't say why. The leader asked for you and all the troop leaders.'

Tom's heart lifted into his mouth. *The op was on.* 'Christ. This must be the op.'

'Dunno, sir; think it's a bit more panicked than that. Some duty rumour going around that Shah Kalay might be about to fall. Apparently the militia are surrounded in that compound of theirs.'

'What do you reckon?'

'Like I do with most ops. I'll be shitting myself until we're 'mongst it.'

'And then?'

'And then –' he paused, and the sides of his mouth turned up '– well, it'll be gleaming.'

About 30 km north of Loy Kabir
12th January 2010
Will,
Haaaaaappy New Year!

If this doesn't find you neck-deep in a barrel of grog somewhere I am going to find you and kill you. You should see me at the moment; we've been on the ground, in the ulu, living off the wagons for more than two weeks now in the freezing, freezing brass-monkeys cold, and I look like a frostbitten Patrick Swayze from Point Break. *Well, that's what I think I look like, but the lads say I remind them of Compo from* Last of the Summer Wine. *Impertinent bastards; I'll have them all flogged when we're back. Apologies for the length of this letter, mate; it's going to take about eight blueys or so to get all this down and you'll probably get them all on different days and in the wrong order, so I'll number them at the end. We're having a maint day in the desert, and my wagons are in pretty good order, so all the boys are just getting their heads down. I thought I'd write and give you the low-down. Bugger all else to do.*

It's been a busy old time since Christmas; I thought winter tours were meant to be chilled out. Not this one, it's been madder than a dog in a bag. I don't even want to know how much 30 mil we've got down range in the last days. I think the squadron's on something like fifteen confirmed enemy KIA. Basically, the much-heralded op that we were going to do came good just after Christmas. Op Tor Barcha IV, aka Op Certain Death. There's this town I told you about beforehand, I think, Shah Kalay, which is where the governor of Loy

216

Kabir lives and his militia rule over it. They'd completely fucked up and on Christmas Day were holed up in their compound, being attacked from all sides by the local Taliban. The town was about to fall, and so on the evening of the 26th, after a manic day of battle prep, we sent out this relief column (that makes it sound like Mafeking!), C Squadron with all our Scimitars and then loads of infantry crammed into Mastiffs, with the plan to drive deep into the desert in a massive feint to the north overnight, and then in the morning swing south to appear on the ridge line overlooking the town. Then four Chinook loads would bring BG Tac and a company of ANA and we'd go through the town together, the infantry clearing the objectives and us in intimate support through the alleyways.

The town was split into five objectives around compounds that we thought the enemy would base in, Objectives Bardot, Budapest, Alabama, Khrushchev and Princess Grace. So called because our Ops is a massive Cold War nut and they're all names from 'We Didn't Start the Fire'. Bardot was the northernmost, and was the police station. We'd secure that, link up with the militia, and then move south through the town, clearing each objective over the day. We'd hang around for a couple of days afterwards, leave the ANA company and the OMLT there as a bolstering force, and then come back for tea and medals. Sound simple? It was a total clusterfuck.

We set out at dusk on Boxing Day. The sight was pretty impres-sive, about twenty vehicles storming through the sunset up this wadi, plumes of dust streaking into the sky and each looking like that pillar of fire that guided the Israelites in the Bible, with the sun bouncing off them. Except that everyone for miles around could see them too; I'm surprised you didn't notice them back in London. We might as well have had a man in a clown suit flying a plane trailing a banner over us that said HI GUYS, WE'RE COMING TO RESCUE THE MILITIA IN SHAH KALAY for all the subtlety we were displaying. And they guessed our feint. At night, at about 2100, we broke up out of a wadi into the open desert, and had to go through this VP between a couple of compounds. No biggie, we just had to barma it. So Clive's troop, who had just taken over the Mastiff job from me and so had to barma for the squadron, had to do it. It was their first time doing a proper barma and they were taking for ever. We watched through the BGTI (that thermal sight we have on the Scimitar; it's epic – you can see anything and everything), and my gunner and I were going mental at how much time they were taking. And then the weirdest, weirdest, most horrible thing. Before I heard it, I saw the explosion in front of me on the thermal screen. On the BGTI, if it's warm then it appears black; if cold it's white.

So there they are, the barma team, picked out black against the white, and then this massive black blot appears as the IED explodes, and then disappears. And then we see the four boys again, but this time it looks like there's five of them. We soon realize that what we thought was a fifth man was the blown-off legs of one of them, Trooper Ransome, and suddenly the net goes mental with the casevac. We watched as the legs kept on getting yellower and yellower, until by the end you couldn't see them as they had lost all their warmth. Both at the thigh. He's twenty-one. Good lad as well. Really good. A real scallywag – mischievous, LOVED scrapping. And now, well, whatever awaits him. The MERT came in to get him out and we got ready to crack on.

But then behind us, at the very back of the column, there's this massive other explosion; one of the Mastiffs at the back has been hit. No one's hurt, and we don't know what on earth it was. Pressure plate? Command wire? Legacy mine? Either way, it fucked the Mastiff. And every one of the Scimitars had been over that spot. If that had hit one of the Scims then that would have been three KIA, no doubt. Turret ripped off and everything. But yet again the Mastiff sailed through. So we had to wait for another six hours for the SVR to recover the wagon, take it back to Newcastle and then come back to rejoin us.

So it's now four in the morning, and we're still in the wadi. The leader decides to ditch the feint to the north and just head straight for the town. H-Hour was at 0600, and that's when the helis are inbound, so we race hell for leather to the north of the town. But the ground is awful, dunes set solid by the frost, and even the tracked Scimitars are slipping and sliding. It's the dark of the moon, and no lights allowed, so the column's a nightmare to control. The Mastiffs on their wheels are all over the shop, and one of them nearly overturns traversing a slope. It is a total, total nightmare, and we're all exhausted when we finally get to the LOD.

So we get to Shah Kalay at dawn, and there's now a white flag over the police station; the Talibs are in it. So we're going to have to fight from the get go. The helis land with Tac and some of the ANA. The helis go back to pick up the rest of them from Newcastle, and the plan is that when they're all here we'll start the advance. So the CO comes up to my wagon with the Ops, and we're looking over the ridge at the town, when suddenly the ANA start running down the hill, about a platoon of them. Before we can do anything the Talibs at Bardot open up on the ANA in front of us, and they're butchered. Like the opening of Saving Private Ryan. All hell's breaking loose, and it's going to be twenty minutes at least until the next heli load appears. So the CO gets Frenchie to get us onto the ridge, and we all just start blazing hell into Bardot as Clive's troop goes forward in his Mastiffs to get the casualties out. It was 0630 now, and there's already four ANA KIA, and ten Cat As and Bs. All momentum had been totally pissed up the wall. The CO is going spastic at the ANA.

And so the infantry re-org behind the ridge, as we keep pummelling away into the Talibs as they stick their heads up to fire at us, and then as 2 Troop sit on the ridge giving us covering fire, the infantry and my troop go back down into the bowl, this time with a wall, and I mean a wall, of fire over us. It felt like the end of the world was happening above our heads. And then the infantry start *running, and we reach the wall of Bardot. They blow it with a mousehole and then storm through it. I turn the turret round to protect the 30 mil and ram the wall, and then we're through as well, expecting to walk into a hell load of fire. But there's nothing; the Talibs have slipped away at the last minute. The CO's there as well, and he's thrilled as their absence means we're going to squeeze them into the middle of the town. Oh yeah, I should have said, the Warrior company were seconded to us for the op, and they drove over from Musa Qala for it, and are lined all along the ridge to the south of the town, so no Talibs can escape.*

We had a short halt in Bardot, and swept the militia station in the middle of it for IEDs. I'd been in that building about three months ago, and it gave me the creeps. An evil place. And when we went in there we found five of the militia hung up from the ceilings by wire, their ears cut off and stuffed in their mouths, stripped naked and covered in whip marks and burns. Good look.

But the advance south continues. The next two objectives, Budapest and Alabama, follow a similar pattern, with token resistance around the clusters of compounds, a few bursts from an AK that slows the advance, but then they leg it and by 1200 we've got back on track and hold about two thirds of the town. The governor's driven over from Loy Kabir by this point with a load of ANP, so we've now got Brits, ANA and ANP cutting about the area. My troop's at the head of the push, with the infantry crowded behind my wagons as we go over the fields between the objectives, which is ace as it's all a bit Normandy 1944, but when we get in among the compound clusters it's terrifying, as the tempo is too high to barma properly and we're channelled wherever we drive. And with the advanced notice they've had, I just know that they're going to have laid IEDs in the alleyways for the Scims, so every metre south we drive I'm wincing, expecting an explosion at every moment. Dusty and I are standing in the turret ramrod straight, like pencils, so if we do hit something we'll just fly out like missiles from the turret and hopefully land on a pile of straw somewhere. Yeah right. Probably land in a compound and get hacked to death by some mental family.

And then we're on Khrushchev, and this is where they're standing to scrap. As it turned out later, they'd prepared it as a defensive position amazingly, and it takes the infantry a good two hours to clear it. At one point the CO and the Ops are in the lead assaulting section, and as my wagons are outside the compounds we can hear one hell of a firefight inside as they go through the position, grenading and mouseholing. But then it's clear, and there are six enemy dead and two prisoners. And then, in a final stand, two RPGs come at us from Princess Grace, one of them I swear going straight between Dusty and me, and so we just blitz it. No more fire comes from it, and when we push south and get to it we find a final two dead, torn to shreds by our 30 mil.

It's odd, but I didn't feel anything. Nothing at all. When I saw the bodies I felt anodyne. All I had done was to remove a threat. That was all. I know the dead enemy had families, I know they had nicknames, had jokes and rivalries. But when I looked at them I saw them as one step closer to going home. I had this strange thing earlier in the tour, a dream about a man dressed in black with a white headdress, as I thought I'd seen him when we were in Shah Kalay back in September. One of the dead in Princess Grace was wearing exactly that, and when I saw him I felt like something had been lifted from me.

By evening we had the town secured, for the loss of three Cat B GSWs from the infantry lads and two further ANA KIA as well as about a dozen Cat Bs and Cs. So it was a hell of a fight really. No holds barred. No IEDs at all until the very end, when the Warrior company started to move off from the southern ridge and hit one. We saw the dust plume from about 2 km away. A lad in the back, a lance jack – can't remember his name – was killed. The angel flight comes in for him, they self-recover the vehicle, which wasn't even that badly damaged, and then suddenly they're off, and it's just Tac, the ANA and C Sqn left in the town.

The squadron hung around Shah Kalay for four days or so, trying to get the ANP who are replacing the militia to get out and patrol the town. But they were dreadful. You couldn't fault their enthusiasm in the mornings, but by afternoon they'd lost all interest. And while their fighting spirit is good, their kit is just non-existent, and they were begging us for anything – clothes, water, food, batteries. It's their own country for Christ's sake. It's like having someone to stay in your own house and then asking them for washing-up powder, soap, keys and the code for the burglar alarm.

I remember what you wrote back in the summer – how on earth are they going to be trusted to fend for themselves when we're gone? I've got a theory about this actually, that Dusty and Dav helped come up with. Here goes. At the moment we're playing a tennis match, us v. the Taliban. We're pretty good and have much better tactics and kit than they do, but they're playing at home and know their way around the court better. So it's pretty even. The problem is though that there's someone on the sidelines who's going to have to replace us halfway through and carry on the rally for us when we leave. Now imagine – and stay with me on this one – that this someone isn't a bloke at all, but a monkey (Alan Partridge's Monkey Tennis finally gets a series!!) who's never wielded a tennis racket in his life. And so we, at the same time as continuing the rally, have to teach this monkey not only how to play tennis, but then how to win some points and eventually the match. So sometimes we let him do a shot or even a whole rally on his own, and sometimes he wins a point with an amazing cross-court dipping forehand that he's plucked from nowhere, but at other times he just lies down and goes to sleep and we have to rush in and save the point. On other points he just starts smoking crack, or throws his racket away, and in the worst instances he actually starts attacking us with the racket – did you hear about that green on blue down in Gereshk last week? Mental, mate, mental. Now, give us a few years, until 2018, say, and I reckon we can give you a monkey who'll take on anyone – Borg, McEnroe,

Federer – but we ain't got that long. It'll be a wonder if, by the time
we leave, the monkey will be able to sustain a rally. I don't think
that's going to work its way into any counter-insurgency manuals, but
you get my drift. They're great scrappers, the ANA, but we both
know scrapping's the easy part; it's everything else that's hard.

After four days we finally left Shah Kalay, hopefully for good. I
hate that town; it gave us all the spooks. It came at a hell of a cost.
Ransome's legs, the lance jack (Latimer, that's his name) and all
those ANA dead and the Cat As and Bs. And the sight of those
dead militia hanging there. Mmmm yep, that'll be a nice memory for
the rest of my life. 'So, Daddy, what did you do in the Afghan War?'
'Well, little Tom junior, I actually had to cut down five naked,
tortured dead guys who'd had their ears and noses cut off and then
throw them in the back of a pickup truck.'

Since then though, we've had the best bit of tour so far, two weeks
of cutting about as a squadron way to the north of Loy Kabir,
completely self-sufficient, living and sleeping off the wagons in the
desert, interdicting TB supply routes and doing proper old-fashioned
recce stuff like going into villages where no ISAF have been before
and getting the local gen. It's been great, and Frenchie, the leader, has
given us a load of autonomy. Three Troop have been operating miles
and miles way from SHQ sometimes, and it's like being in the
LRDG way back in the Western Desert – gleaming!

Sometimes we regroup back as a squadron and go and try to pick
a fight if we know where there's a build up of TB in an area and
BGHQ want us to go and take it on. The other day we had this
massive firefight over about ten hours on the outskirts of this town in
the north, Tuzal. My wagon almost got rid of a whole bombload –
Dusty was absolutely loving it – and SHQ had the works called in:
guns from Newcastle, Apaches, American A-10s. We've got this
legendary USMC FAC team with us at the moment, centred on
SHQ, and these guys have walked straight out of a comic book. The
officer, a lad called Rob Martinez, spends the entire time chomping on

a cigar and in his spare time reads a copy of the Iliad *that he has with him. In the original Greek. Berserker. And he loves to do nothing more than, as he says, 'bring the rain'. He always bangs on about it. It's a squadron joke now that whenever guns or air get called in someone sends over the net, 'Charlie Charlie One, get yer brollies out; rain is forecast.'*

We're out here in the ulu for another ten days or so, and then . . . drum roll . . . it's back to Newcastle for a few days and then . . . uh-oh . . . lock up your daughters . . . it's R & R! Finally, finally 3 Troop get to the promised land. I should land back home on the 31st Jan or thenabouts. I. Cannot. Bloody. Wait. Please say you'll be about. I'll try to phone or email from Bastion or Kandahar. Ah yes, Kandahar. I've been hearing about that place all tour. It sounds like the land of milk and honey. The boys who have been out here before say it's almost the best bit of R & R, as though it's better than being home. Can't wait to see for myself.

Anyway, you're boring me now. Oh, one turn-up for the books before I go: very, very slowly, it's getting a bit warmer. Hopefully by the time I'm back from R & R I'll be just in time for a bit of Op Bronze before the end of tour. Oh, and just in time for the fighting season to kick off again. Yippee. Mind you, if the last three weeks has been the low season I'd hate to see the summer of love out here.

All best mate,
T

Just before dawn they began their routine, established over a month now and formalized into a rite. Ellis, on roaming stag, walked around the four wagons, put his head into the canvas shelters at their sides and prodded the sleeping bag closest to the entrance. In Three Zero it was Dusty's, who levered himself out of his cocoon to lean over and shake Tom in the middle and Davenport beyond him. They lay there for a minute, in the cold damp of the shelter, dank with the frozen mist of their snores, then scrambled out of their bags and out of the shelter into the glowing purple of the pre-dawn desert.

Davenport switched the engine on, and the Scimitar juddered into life. Dusty got into the turret, and Jessie, who'd been on the last radio stag slot, got out to amble back to his own wagon. Dusty oiled the gimpy and switched the BV on to heat up the boil-in-the-bags he'd placed in there the night before. Tom and Davenport packed up the shelter, teeth chattering and grey fingers fumbling in the cold as they rolled up the sodden canvas and fixed it onto the bar armour with bungees. Tom chuckled at something Davenport had said the previous night just as they were about to drift off to sleep, their sleeping bags pulled tight high over their heads: 'Fucking hell, boss, it's always bags around here. All the time. Bags, bags and more bags.'

'What do you mean, Dav?' Tom had mumbled, waves of sleep crashing against his eyelids.

'Well, think about it. We sleep in a bag, we shit in a bag, we eat out of a bag, and then when we get slotted we get carried home in a bag. Might as well just rename Op Herrick and call it Op Bag instead.' They had trickled off to sleep giggling and exhausted.

Tom walked round the wagons. In the distance, about half a kilometre away, he could see the emerging silhouettes of SHQ at the centre of the 'death star' formation the squadron adopted each night, with the three gun troops the points of the star protecting its four wagons. Trueman was sitting on the front of his wagon drinking a brew, its steam spiralling into the air and catching on his thick dark beard, his cut calloused fingers poking through fingerless woollen gloves. He greeted Tom cheerfully.

'Well, boss, we done all right, ain't we? Six hours' time and I'm going to smash my wagon straight into the scoff tent. I am desperate now, desperate, for some fresh. My body's screaming out for some proper vit C. Any more of this and we'll all get scurvy. Here, want some?'

He held out his flask and Tom sipped from it. Hot chocolate mixed with coffee. It was delicious.

'I know. I can't wait. None of my clothes are going to fit me when I get home. Look at me.' He tugged at the waist of his torn and oil-stained trousers, which billowed around his scrawny legs. 'And my ribcage is even worse.' He ran his hand up his left side and felt the undulations over his bones, and his gaunt face with its straggly beard grinned. He took another sip. He changed the subject, knowing that now was the time to ask. He had been sitting on this for days but now felt ready. It was a bit like when he had first asked Cassie out.

'Um, Sergeant Trueman, I was wondering if it wouldn't be a good idea if we, er, met up over R & R, if that's OK, to go and visit Ransome and Acton in Selly Oak. I know it's a bit irregular, but I think it would be good for them.'

Tom tried not to laugh at his own stiffness. He thought in that moment about how Trueman had seen him grow over the last few months. His sergeant had known him for almost a year now. They had become great friends in that time, and yet they still both liked to maintain the gap between them, both slightly scared of admitting the depth of their friendship and nervous that they might become too close and then have it all crash down if they disagreed about something. Tom knew it was the right way for him. When they disagreed any awkwardness was taken away by being allowed to fall back on the rigidity of the army's hierarchy. The matey-matey approach could work – Trueman had been close to Jules Dennis in Iraq – but it had proved a disaster for 4 Troop with Clive and Sergeant Leighton, who had started the tour all lovey-dovey and were now hardly speaking to each other.

Trueman said, 'Yeah, sir, that'd be great. The lads would like that. Who knows, we might even go out for a drink afterwards. I know Brum quite well; there's a few good places in and around the area.'

Tom smiled at the strangeness of their stiffness with each other. 'Christ, Sergeant Trueman, we'll have to see about that drink. Pretty revolutionary stuff that. What would people say? No, that'd be good. On me.'

'Fuck that, sir. No one's going to serve you; you look barely out of nappies.'

'Bollocks. I look like a steely-eyed dealer of death.' He proudly tugged at the straggly down on his cheeks and neck.

'You look like Compo. Hate to say it.'

'No, I look like Patrick Swayze.'

'He died last year, sir.'

'Yeah, I know, the new Patrick Swayze. The second coming of Swayze.'

He left Trueman shaking his head into the dregs of his

brew and went on to Jesmond and Thompson's wagons as a gold film hovered in the east, and the dead land started to come to life again.

At midday the squadron arrived back in Newcastle. They had been out on the ground for four weeks without fresh food, showers or washing their clothes, which now hung off them like curtains. In their ragbag collection of civilian quilted jackets, woolly hats underneath helmets, and gloves and mittens meant for tobogganing but in fact used to pull triggers, disassemble guns or fix thrown tracks, they looked like tramps. With dirt driven deep into every pore and crevice they had christened themselves the Dust Devils.

Tom had loved living off the wagons in the desert; it had been so simple. He didn't have to think about what to wear, about what time to get up, about how to get to work, about any of the hundreds of trivialities that encumber the minds of billions of people every day. It had been a pure, austere existence of the most brutal simplicity. Keep warm, eat when you can, try not to get killed. Sleep when you're not doing anything else. In the four weeks he had changed his boxer shorts twice and had kept the same trousers throughout. In the turret the gimpy dripped oil onto his upper thigh, so the permanent dark stain made him and all the other car commanders look as though they had wet themselves.

He always wore two pairs of socks, two T-shirts, his combat shirt, then his woolly jumper, and on top of that his CBA. It was too cramped to wear the Osprey inside the Scimitar, and so all the squadron wore the older flak jacket-style CBA. This offered far less protection but was lighter and, crucially in the boys' eyes, looked far allyer, as it marked them out from everyone else. Scimitar crews were the only people in theatre for whom the army had managed to get an insurance waiver for not wearing the better Osprey.

Behind the front plate of the CBA, which covered his heart and left breast, Tom had his father's letter, transferred from the Osprey.

Around his neck dangled his dogtags and the St Christopher he had taken from home. Every morning in the desert he had kissed it and in his sleeping bag said one of the prayers he remembered from the booklet the padre had given them at the start of tour: 'O Lord, you know how busy I must be today. If I forget you, do not forget me.'

The squadron parked their wagons and clamoured to go to scoff, but Brennan ordered them to wash, shave and change beforehand. 'Look at us,' he chided them, as he addressed them after Frenchie had congratulated them on the epic, violent and, amazingly, since Ransome, casualty-free patrol. 'We look like Fred Karno's Army. And no one in that scoff tent is going to thank us Dust Devils dragging in our filthy clothes and putting dirty hands onto serving spoons. Think again, fellas. Plus, we stink to high fucking heaven. So, we all wash. No man goes in unless he's looking immaculate.'

And so to a chorus of moaning the squadron traipsed back to their tents and took freezing showers, the dust mixing with the water and forming trickles of mud down their white bodies. They tore their faces to shreds as razors blunted themselves on thick matted beards. Eventually they were clean and shaved with pink if bloody rash-ridden faces, their bodies luxuriating in fresh clothes as they sat in the scoff tent and stuffed themselves with fresh food, heaping piles of vegetables into their mouths. They spent the afternoon tending to the wagons, rebombing them, cleaning them up, getting them good to go again. And then they all went to their tents and slept for twelve hours straight.

Tom lay on his cot in the tent, almost feeling guilty that he wasn't with the squadron back up north but then quickly suppressing that thought and glorying in the soft duvet. It had been only twenty-four hours since they had arrived back in Bastion, having cabbied a lift with a Chinook mail flight, but already he was getting used to it, and the month in the desert seemed an age away.

Jessie poked his head through the door. 'Hi, sir. Dunno if you want to join us, but me and the sarge thought it'd be a good crack to go over to the American scoff house tonight over in Leatherneck and try out their burgers and stuff. You keen?'

Tom weighed up what he should do. *Bugger it.* He'd spent the last four months with these men sweating, shivering and bleeding. Of course he'd go. 'That sounds great, Corporal Jesmond. Are you sure I won't cramp your style though?' *I sound like his grandmother.* 'Give me two minutes and I'm with you.'

'No dramas, sir; we'll be in the wagon.'

Tom pulled on some trousers and a shirt, adjusted his beret in the mirror and went outside to the Land Rover, lights on, that the boys had requisitioned. *Where had they got that?* Well, ask no questions, hear no lies. He got in the front passenger seat next to Trueman. Five of the boys were in the back, and he picked them out by their bickering and laughing: GV, Jesmond, Dusty, Ellis and Thompson. He immediately felt happy.

Trueman drove the Land Rover through the silent Bastion while the boys chattered in the back. In the American camp they parked the wagon up and went into the cookhouse.

It was like Disneyland – burgers, free Cokes, ice cream, more ice cream than they'd ever seen before – and they ran amok through the food on offer. As they ate Tom looked at the boys, watching their intricate set-in-stone interactions and smiling at the bizarre little family that he and Trueman had fostered over the last few months. They argued with each other; they laughed at people outside their group; they talked with disdain about some regiments and with great respect about others. They ate more than they had all tour and a couple of hours later piled back on board the wagon.

Trueman turned to Tom and, with a mischievous glint in his eye picked out by the bright white lights outside the cookhouse, said, 'Right, boss, fancy some fun?'

'What do you mean?

Jesmond said from the back: 'He means, sir, fancy some fun?'

A spark of fear ran up Tom's spine. Did they mean fun as in brothel fun? He had heard rumours about ISO containers in various corners of Bastion that were run as brothels by camp rats. Were the rumours true? He couldn't possibly go along with it if they were.

Sensing Tom's discomfort, Trueman steadied his nerves. 'Relax, it ain't that bad; just a game we used to play when we were back in Bastion on the last tour, that's all. A bit of a war against the REMFs.'

'I don't understand.'

'I mean, sir, that we go around Bastion fucking up some fat REMFs. Watch, it'll be fun.'

Tom, intrigued now, said, 'Well, OK then, but I still don't know how this is going to work.'

Trueman laughed to himself and reversed out of the parking space. 'Just watch.'

They drove through the sprawling camp, dark and lit only by the occasional flashing lights of a plane or heli landing over on the runway. They passed soldiers walking to and from various places, who would hold their thumbs out speculatively, hoping that a wagon would stop and give them at least a tiny bit of a lift. Trueman ignored all of them until they saw ahead of them a pair of large, scruffy soldiers. He sprang into life, delighted. 'Here we go, sir; classic Bastion rats! Look at them fat fucks. Shirts untucked, waddling around. Wouldn't know a rifle if it hit them in the face.' He shouted back to Jesmond, 'Here you go, Jessie; some custom for you.'

'Gotcha, Freddie. Right boys, get ready. REMFs coming up.'

Trueman slowed and pulled up alongside them. They were indeed pretty woeful specimens, fat, scruffy, with bulbous flesh drooping over their waistbands.

Trueman wound down his window and said, as though talking to an old lady on his street back home, 'You must be knackered, fellas. Fancy a lift?' Tom started to cotton on to the plan and giggled. Trueman elbowed him in the ribs to shut him up, but they'd bought it.

'Oh cheers, mate. Nice one,' they said, licking their lips at not having to expend any more calories wandering around the camp.

The two soldiers walked to the back of the wagon, and Dusty pushed down the tailgate. 'Hop in, fellas.' He smiled, and the fatter of the two heaved his leg on board. Just as he stepped up, Dusty whispered, 'Now!' and Trueman floored the accelerator, pulling away from the REMF, who fell off the tailgate flat on his back in the dust to howls of laughter from the boys as the wagon sped away.

GV shouted back at them, 'That's right, get some fuckin' dust down your necks, you fat chippy cunts.'

'Again, again!' said Dusty, like a little boy asking to go down a slide at a playground.

'OK, OK, just let me get some distance from those lads. What do you reckon, sir? Good crack, eh? Sir? You all right?' He looked to his left and saw Tom shuddering with laughter, bent double in his seat, unable to say a thing.

Trueman raised his eyebrows. 'Fuck me, it's funny, but it ain't that funny. Officers! I'll just never understand you lot.' He looked ahead, and a hundred metres away his headlights picked up another waddling group. 'All right, Dusty, round two coming up, dead ahead. Get ready!'

The next evening they were ready to go. Their kit was packed in the tents and their flight to Kandahar was at midnight. They spent the day bouncing around Bastion, having brew after brew with mates from other regiments and hearing how things were going in the rest of theatre. Tom had forgotten how cocooned they had been up in Loy Kabir; he loved hearing all the stories from the friends from Sandhurst he bumped into, and their take on the past months.

At dusk they gathered with other units on the Bastion football pitch for a memorial service for a corporal who had been killed four days before, whose body was about to be repatriated to the UK. A chaplain ran through the brief formulaic service, six hundred soldiers dutifully listening to words about a man they had never met, but still polite and attentive, feeling as though they ought to have known him. He had been killed by an IED near Babaji in an explosion that had wounded three others. Tom listened to proceedings with his nose scrunched up in denial. He didn't want to think about this any more. All he wanted was to go home.

The corporal's platoon commander stood up to give the eulogy. It was standard stuff – about how good he had been at his job, about what he had done in his career – and the lieutenant was no orator. He kept fumbling his words; he hadn't even bothered to learn them off by heart and read shakily from a piece of paper, which fluttered and rasped in the wind. It was an entirely forgettable speech, and Tom felt sad that this was all the send-off the man was getting from

Afghanistan. But after the officer came a lance corporal who introduced himself as the dead man's best friend; they had joined up together and had served all over the world living out of each other's armpits.

The lance corporal's speech was short and seemingly off the cuff. He needed no notes, and with a series of jokes and memories rammed home to the entire assembly how special this man had been to him. He ended with 'I just wanna say that Carl was the kind of bloke that glues a platoon together. Without him a platoon falls apart. Look among you now. You know who the guys are in your own unit. The ones that make you laugh. The ones who are never down. The ones who always start the banter. The ones always first through the door, first to help with the barma. Well, Carl was that bloke. And we only ever realized it after he was killed. Look around you now and think who that bloke is in your platoon. And when you've found him look after him. Because you won't realize how important he is until he's gone.' His voice, which had started clear and booming, was faltering. 'I mean that. Just look after those guys.' He broke off, composed himself, turned and walked smartly back to his comrades, who dragged him close and hugged him.

The chaplain finished off the service and then two 105s blasted blank rounds into the sky in violent salute. The assembly broke up, and 3 Troop went to their tents to get ready for the flight. Tom walked back alone, having lost the lads in the crowd, and thought of Trueman, how he was just the person described in the speech. He'd never really thought about it before.

At midnight they flew the short distance to Kandahar. As they walked off the Hercules, all around them was the hum of a huge airfield. Two jets scorched their way into the sky, and immediately they felt the change in atmosphere from the restrained, almost austere Bastion to the military baroque of the American base. They were corralled into buses and driven to a huge warehouse sixty metres long packed with bunk beds. There was room for maybe four hundred soldiers in there, and it was about half full. They stumbled through the half-dark to find an area to bed down in, climbed onto some bunks and fell asleep using their daysacks as pillows.

They awoke disorientated and dehydrated, and stepped out into the mayhem of daily life in Kandahar. Bastion, they immediately realized, was a masterpiece of military planning: neat ordered rows of tents with wide roads and drainage ditches immaculately dug, almost Roman in its symmetry and order. Kandahar by contrast was a jumble of sprawling huts and winding roads, like a shanty town, with huge warehouses and hangars strewn randomly around. American soldiers and marines mingled with civilian contractors with huge paunches and bull necks wandering around behind sunglasses grafted onto their faces. Trueman and Jesmond immediately and entirely true to form bridled at the American scruffiness and made sure all the boys looked smart, like mothers at school gates doing up ties and combing down fringes. All the while in the background jets took off; an A-10, teeth painted on its nose, buzzed the airfield.

Even this little bit further south it was ten degrees warmer than Bastion and felt amazing to be back in some sort of sunshine again. The troop went down to the Boardwalk, a great wooden hexagon built around a basketball pitch lined with coffee shops, T-shirt shops, doughnut shops and burger bars. It was indeed the paradise that Tom had heard it to be, and the boys fell upon it. Tom walked around on his own, enjoying the feeling of being in transit and not required to do anything or think for himself save only when to eat and sleep. They were to fly out at 0200 the next morning and so with the whole day to waste he mooched through the Boardwalk shops, amused by a lot of the stuff available.

Clearly the Americans hadn't yet fully got to grips with the delicacies of local-population-centric counter-insurgency. One T-shirt featured jets with Gothic script beneath clamouring, LASER-GUIDED DEMOCRACY! GET SOME! GET SOME! Another had the Grim Reaper riding atop a tank, a third a skeleton chomping a cigar and shooting a machine gun from the hip. Yet another had the cross hairs of a rifle overlaid on a Taliban silhouette; TALIBAN HUNTING CLUB OPEN SEASON, it proclaimed. One echoed a phrase from Vietnam, shouting out, again in Gothic script, YEA THOUGH I WALK THROUGH THE VALLEY OF THE SHADOW OF DEATH I SHALL FEAR NO EVIL, FOR I AM THE EVILLEST SON OF A BITCH IN THE VALLEY. Another posed the delicate question, HEY TALIBAN, HOW ABOUT I OPEN A GREAT BIG CAN OF WHOOP-ASS . . . IN YOUR FACE?

Tom went to the counter and handed over a torch he wanted to buy. Fumbling for dollar notes in his pockets, he looked at the shop assistant. She was about his age with black hair in a neat ponytail and a small slightly upturned button of a nose, deep-brown skin and the kind of smile he hadn't seen in months. 'There you go, sir. That'll be nine dollars fifty.'

He couldn't speak at first. He hadn't spoken to a girl in weeks, and he stared at her, eyes on stalks.

'I'm sorry, sir; are you OK?'

Tom went red and blurted out, flustered, 'Yes, sorry, quite all right, quite all right. Away with the fairies, I'm afraid.'

She laughed.

'What's so funny?' said Tom, trying to claw back a shred of confidence.

'I don't know.' She had a chirpy, happy voice with maybe a

tiny Southern drawl in there. It was beautiful. 'I guess you English are just kinda funny, that's all.'

'Funny peculiar or funny ha ha?'

'What do you mean?'

Christ! What an idiot. 'Um, I mean are we funny like we're strange funny, like a monkey might be funny, or funny like in joke funny? Oh, forget that; I suppose a monkey might be both types of funny.' *What am I saying?* He was behaving like a total prat. He couldn't believe that the sight of a girl had reduced him to this state.

'I mean funny both ways.' She smiled and then, tilting her head to one side inquisitively at Tom's own laughter, said, 'Now why am *I* so funny then?'

'I don't know. You're not funny. I mean, you might be funny ha ha but not strange funny. You're very nice. It's just, well, I haven't spoken to a girl in months, and it's quite a weird feeling.'

'Oh really, where you been?'

'Up in this town in Helmand called Loy Kabir. It's in the middle of nowhere. I wouldn't go there. Pretty overrated as a holiday destination.' *Why can't I just shut up? This is utter bilge.* But he carried on: 'The locals aren't terribly friendly. Weather's awful. No galleries, exhibitions, theatres, no nothing. And the food? Don't get me started. Dreadful.'

'You can say that again. You ain't carryin' an ounce of fat. You look like a skeleton.' She paused as if to try and pluck up the nerve. 'A nice-lookin' skeleton, but still a skeleton.' Tom looked to his right and caught his reflection in a mirror. She was right. He was very, very thin. He looked like a brain on a stick.

'Crikey, you're right. Do you know, I'd never realized how thin. We don't have any mirrors up there. Might break one and get bad luck, you see.' *Oh Lord. This is risible. And did I really just say 'Crikey'? This is terrible, terrible.*

'Well you better get yourself some burgers!' Tom thought he recognized a glint of something he had seen before, and he took a moment to place it. It was when he had seen Cassie the day he had left. This girl was just like her. He drew a breath, and behind him the bell on the door tinkled as some other customers came in.

'Um, I know this is all a bit sudden, and you probably get this from every soldier who walks in here, but I wonder if when you get a break you might, er, you might want to come and get a burger with—'

He broke off as a shout came from across the shop: 'Oi, boss, so this is where you been!'

Bugger. He turned around. Dusty, wearing an LA Dodgers baseball cap and aviator sunglasses, was with Ellis. He was holding aloft one of the LASER-GUIDED DEMOCRACY! T-shirts. 'What do you reckon? Suit me?'

If ever a moment had been ruined this was it. Tom looked at the shop assistant apologetically and her eyes met his. He smiled, and she winked and turned back to the till to pretend she was examining a receipt. Dusty and Ellis looked at Tom and realized they'd interrupted. Dusty stage-whispered, 'Oh sorry, boss; didn't realize you were *on duty* as it were. Did we disturb anything?'

Tom walked over to them, turned the baseball cap on Dusty's head back to front and clipped him gently around the head. He sighed, 'Nothing, Corporal Miller, nothing at all. Come on, brews on me.' They laughed and left.

That night they boarded the plane. They hadn't slept all day, too excited about going home. The plane was two-thirds full and also taking home an RAF Regiment squadron which had been guarding Bastion. Trueman shepherded the boys away from them, pushing them towards the back of the plane as if scared that they would catch something from the REMFs. 'Don't want to be associated with that filth, sir,' he told Tom as he patrolled the rear of the plane like a mother lioness, snarling when one of the RAF Regiment lads even so much as dared to intimate he was going to sit near them.

As they were taxiing to the runway Jessie got out of his seat and made an announcement. 'Well, fellas, we've got this far. Who'd have thought it? Just wanna say, everyone have a crackin' leave.' He reached into his pocket and pulled out a little white plastic bottle. 'We all wanna be in fine fettle when we get back home, so I went to see the Dutch doc in KAF, told him some bollocks about how I was suffering from PTSD and had trouble sleepin'. Well, you know what the Dutch are like. He gave me the strongest, most hard-core sleepin' pills around.' He looked at the bottle proudly. 'Here the fuckers are. Called Schleepz. The quack said they knock you out like a light. He said no more than three at a time though. Otherwise you die.'

He passed around the bottle, and they all took one. Dusty was next to Tom, and when the bottle reached him he looked with contempt at the pills. 'What? They're mini, these. Only three? Bollocks to that.' He poured at least six onto his palm and before Tom could stop him gulped them down. 'Bet you they're fuck-all use. Sleeping pills are a complete joke. Always are. We'd be better off having a spoonful of Calpol.'

Five minutes later, as the engines roared into life and they shot down the runway towards home, Dusty was fast asleep, mouth wide open and a stream of dribble dripping from it.

A cold and frosty late-January dawn was breaking when they touched down at Brize Norton eight hours later. They emerged from the plane drawing great gulps of air. It was the first time in months they could breathe without dragging dust down their throats. Tom and Trueman stood at the bottom of the steps and heaved great breaths of clean, pure Atlantic air. Behind them at the top of the stairway Ellis and Davenport struggled out the door, supporting a comatose Dusty still fast asleep. They staggered down the staircase and Trueman led them over to a fire hydrant, where they rudely woke Dusty up with a high-pressure blast of icy water to his face. Cackling with laughter, they went inside to pick up their bergens.

A bod from rear party met them with a minibus outside the terminal, and soon they were speeding down the motorway towards Aldershot. They looked out the windows in silence, mesmerized by the green and brown countryside, wet with thaw and with spindly trees spreading their bare fingers into the sky. Winter had never looked so beautiful.

Through the drops of drizzle clustered on the train window Tom looked, resting his forehead on its cold surface. The train followed the route he had taken into London when he had last seen Cassie. Back then the river had shone and the city had looked fantastic; four months on, it had shed that coat and lay naked in its greyness; grey buildings, grey pigeons under the eaves of the stations they stopped at, grey sky arching overhead.

Tom got off at Clapham Junction and walked north to Victoria. He was wearing his uniform. There were some civvies in his room in the mess, but he had decided to stay as he was. For one, he couldn't bear to take his deserts off; they had become almost a part of him. For another, he wanted to walk through London pushing his uniform into people's faces, to show them what men who fought in Afghanistan looked like, to rub their noses into the fact that the war wasn't just on the news, but something fought and lived by real Britons. As he walked he glared at everyone he passed, as if daring them to say something hostile.

He tried to grow used to the sensation of the city and its unaccustomed background hum. In Afghan there was no such thing as ambient noise. The only thing that you heard, ever, was what was going on right in front of you. It was strange having these new layers of sound impede his senses. He walked up Albert Bridge Road and stopped where he and Cassie had split in September. It looked different. The river then had sparkled; now it seemed old and dull, the only brightness coming from the reflection of passing headlights on the wet road.

He crossed the river and walked up to the King's Road. He had wanted to come there specifically; he might bump into Cassie, but also he couldn't imagine anywhere on earth more different to Loy Kabir. It was raining heavily now, but he didn't make any concession to it and puffed out his chest in defiance at the freezing drops streaming down his neck. He looked with contempt at grown men scuttling like beetles down the street, or cowering under awnings afraid to step out into the wet.

Scum. None of them were fit to lick his boots. It was Sunday lunchtime, and here they were, masters of the universe, wallets heaving and all clearly doing something clever with money, and Tom hated them. Some looked at him with curiosity, and Tom hoped that they felt a piercing, emasculating shame. Digging his fingernails into his palms he realized how angry he was and told himself to chill out and enjoy himself.

He stopped at a delicatessen to satisfy a sudden urge for a cake; he hadn't had a cake for ages. But when he went inside he couldn't decide what to choose from the array of pastries before him, and he sensed the queue becoming impatient behind him. He found the shop bewildering, and everything seemed to swirl around: the bright cakes, the thick make-up on the women's faces behind him. Two children were screaming at a table a few metres away, an incompetent nanny trying to get them to behave. Tom found this infuriating and began to feel hot. He hurriedly and awkwardly left the shop to continue his arrogant snarling march up the road.

In Victoria he queued for a ticket and then stood in front of the departures board, becoming tenser as the world moved around him and the board flicked its changes from right to left until his train appeared. He went to the train and found a seat, bolt upright and with his daysack on his lap, feeling scared by his anonymity. An old lady came to sit opposite him and smiled. He smiled back and then shifted his gaze.

The train left the station, and they crossed back over the river again. The old lady was wearing a black fur hat and an elegant dark-blue coat; she had perfect skin, if heavily wrinkled, and bright, piercing blue eyes beneath shining white hair. She leaned towards him conspiratorially and said, as though not wanting anyone else to hear, 'Bet it's strange to be back.'

Tom looked surprised. 'How did you know?'

She laughed with a rising, girlish peal. 'Young man, look at you. It doesn't take Einstein to work out where you've been. Besides, you look like my son did when he came back from the Falklands. Wound up like a coiled spring. Is it very bad out there?'

Tom was taken aback. He found that he wanted to tell her everything. He had never thought about how he would explain it. In a few seconds he scanned back in his mind's eye over the entirety of the last months in crystal-clear review, and then, in barely more than a whisper, he replied, 'Yes. Yes. It is very bad out there. It's . . . unforgiving. I don't think I've learned so much in all my life. There are horrible times, but, do you know, there are some rather wonderful times as well.' His muscles loosened and he settled back into his seat. 'I suppose . . . that, well, I suppose . . . I never really thought properly about coming home, the whole time I was out there. You just blank your mind off to it. I think . . . I think that in a funny sort of way I never thought I was going to come back. And now I am back, it feels strange. I mean, I've only been back in the country for what –' he looked at his watch and noticed it was still on Afghan time '– seven hours, and

244

this city doesn't feel like home at all.' He flicked his hand contemptuously towards the suburbs as they sped by. 'It sounds strange, I know, but I've sort of found a home from home with my soldiers.'

He broke off as if he'd said too much, and to fill the gap she stepped in: 'And where are you off to now, if you don't mind me asking? To your parents? A girlfriend?'

'No, home. To my mum. My pa died when I was young. I can't wait to see her.'

He saw a tiny glint of moisture in her eye. 'Yes. Your poor mother, she will have been worried sick about you. Do you have to go back out again?'

'Yup, but only for four weeks or so. Peanuts really. And most of that will be taken up with handing over our kit to the guys replacing us. So I'm basically home and dry, to be honest. I mean, fingers crossed and all.' He grinned, and with his smile felt the last of his tension ebb away. He began to enjoy being where he was. In a comfy train heading home, shooting past familiar fields now, fields he used to tick off in his head whenever he was heading home from Cambridge or Sandhurst. He lost himself in the late afternoon, and the old lady let him be for a while as he sat contentedly watching the countryside.

A drinks trolley came, and despite his protests she bought him a gin and tonic. He sat and sipped at it like it was the most delicious thing in the world. She looked at him approvingly. 'There. That'll take the edge off. Where are you getting off the train? How are you getting back home?'

'Probably just get the bus from Teynham station to my village and then walk home from there.'

'Nonsense. You'll catch your death of cold. My car's parked at Sittingbourne. I can give you a lift to your home, if you would like.'

He looked at her, overcome with gratitude. 'Are you sure? That'd be great, but . . . but you don't even know me.'

She looked indignant. 'Young man, I may not know you personally, but I know your type. You are just like my son and his friends when they were your age. And, to be honest, just like my husband after he had just come back from Korea.' She stopped frowning and beamed at him. In that moment he felt as though he had never been away.

'Well, if you're sure . . . '

'Of course I'm sure. It's the least I can do. Tucked up back here in a nice warm house while you and your soldiers are fighting for your lives. And don't worry; you don't have to talk in the car. Just tell me where to go. I won't press you for conversation.'

He tried to say thank you but felt his eyes welling up with tears.

She stepped in. 'Don't worry. Get some sleep now. You need to be in good form for your mother. I'll wake you when we're there.'

A minute later he was fast asleep.

The final trace of the sun was dipping beneath the trees at the back of the Old Mill when the car pulled in at the top of the drive. He got out and looked back in through the window. 'I don't know how I can possibly thank you. For everything. For the lift, obviously, for the drink too, but also . . . ' he tried to work out how to express himself ' . . . for teaching me to enjoy being back.'

'Young man, my pleasure. Just one favour, that's all I ask.'

'Anything.'

'When you hug your mother, hug harder than you have ever hugged her before.'

'I promise.'

'Righty ho, best be off. I have to get back to feed the dogs.' She put the car into gear and started off.

'But wait, I don't even know your . . . ' he trailed off as the car sped down the narrow lane, leaving Tom to darkness and himself.

The silhouette of the house loomed in the gathering purple. Tiny flecks of white lined the drive, guiding him home, as snowdrops pierced their way out of winter, leading the charge towards spring. He set off down the drive, glorying in the cold air.

He knocked too quietly on the wooden door to the kitchen, and when he pushed it open he saw Constance standing by the sink, chopping carrots. Zeppo was lying on his beanbag and didn't even stir.

He stood in the doorway and said softly, 'Hi, Mum. It's me.'

She looked up, dropped her knife into the sink and blanched as though she had seen a ghost. And then she was hugging him harder than she had ever done before. Tom felt as though he was a little boy again. He remembered his promise and made sure he hugged back harder.

The train was pulling into the station, and as the car screeched into the car park Constance held him back as he tried to get out of the car and pecked him twice on the cheek like a woodpecker. He squirmed away and shouted back as he ran to the platform, 'See you on Tuesday, Ma. I'll ring when I know what train I'm getting.' He just made it onto the train, and as it pulled away to London he pushed the window down to wave again.

Constance shouted to him, 'Behave yourself, Tom! Don't get into any trouble!'

He pointed to his ears and shook his head, laughing as the train picked up speed. 'Can't hear you, Ma. Can't hear you!' He watched her recede, tiny and alone, and when she was out of sight he flopped onto the seat, restless with excitement. After five days at home he was heading into London to see Will and Cassie. He had put on a tiny bit of weight in the past five days; Constance had pushed food down his neck from morning to night. He had finally got rid of the last dust in his skin, and after six bouts with a shampoo bottle had managed to rid his hair of it as well. He would spend ages in the bath amazed at the velvety water and the bubbles against his skin.

He went for long walks with Zeppo, lost in the newness of the world around him. It was like he was seeing a colour world after previously being able to view it only in black and white. As though he had had a second birth. At nights he sometimes thought about Afghan, looking into the fire, lost in the roots of the flames and with a glass of whisky in his hand steadily rising to his lips. He would see all the past weeks in the flames until the fire died.

One night he shifted from the fire and stared fixedly at a photo of his father when he was Tom's age now. It was of Leonard and his platoon in Northern Ireland. He was standing at the back with his crooked grin and looked so young, younger than all his soldiers. Tom looked hard into the photo until a tear fell on to the glass, and he remembered himself and embarrassedly wiped it off. He put the frame back on the mantelpiece and went upstairs. He stood outside Constance's room, made sure he could hear her heavy breathing through the ajar door and went to his room to sleep in total peace for ten hours, his body and brain now back into home life.

On the train he sat and scrolled through the messages on his phone. He was going out for supper with Will tonight and then tomorrow having lunch with Cassie. Will was going to give him keys to his flat in Primrose Hill. There were a few other guys kicking around town on leave from A and B Squadrons, so he might bump into them as well. He watched the fields go by and felt a million miles from Loy Kabir.

Sunlight streamed in through the windows to prise open his eyelids. A bolt of pain tore through his head. His mouth was dry; his tongue felt too big for his mouth. He fell off the sofa, staggered to his feet, tripped over the coffee table, which was littered with empty beer bottles and cigarette butts, and crashed onto the floor. He stumbled to the loo, threw some water over his face and locked his mouth around the tap. In the mirror he saw huge bags under his bloodshot eyes. He looked at his watch. Nine o'clock. He was meeting Cassie at one, more than enough time to get ready and sober up.

He stood in the shower for twenty minutes, seeing alcohol steam from his body. He smelt a whiff of tequila and had to gulp down a retch. He came out, shaved, and then brushed his teeth and tongue. He left the bathroom and smelt bacon in the kitchen. Will was there, already dressed, over a frying pan brimming with sausages, bacon and mushrooms.

'Here he is! The dead man riseth. Wow. Do you feel as dreadful as you look?'

Tom rubbed his head. 'Worse. It feels like someone drove a Scimitar over my head. What happened last night?'

'Well, apart from you almost getting us arrested five times and then drinking me out of house and home, not an awful lot.'

'I can't remember anything after supper.'

'Well, we then tried to get into every bar in London, but you were so lashed that no one was letting us in. Every bouncer who refused us you then had a stand-up argument with, calling them war-dodging REMFs.'

'Oh God, really?'

'Yeah. It wasn't very conducive to getting in anywhere. So we just came back here and got on it. You passed out at about one on the sofa, and I threw that duvet over you. Impressive, mate. After five months away you can still take down some grog. When I came back from tour I was in pieces after a pint.'

'I don't feel so clever now.' He smiled, but a thought nagged him. 'Mate?'

'Yeah, pal?'

'I didn't say anything weird last night, did I? I mean, apart from hurling abuse at some bouncers. Did I talk about Afghan?'

'Why do you want to know? Surely you know what you think.'

'No. That's the thing. I don't know what I think about it – under all the layers, if you know what I mean.'

'Yeah, I know, mate. You talked about your lads a lot. Like, a lot. Jesus, it feels as if I know them as well as you do, the amount of time you spent on them – Trueman, Dusty, Dav, GV– whoever those crazy cats are. I could write their reports myself.'

'Anything else?'

'Not much. Banging on about how Mickey Mouse the ANA are, but that ain't exactly revolutionary.'

'But was there anything else, like more deep-rooted? Like, about fear and stuff?'

'Well. You talked about contacts and IEDs blah blah, but all pretty normal, mate.' He broke off, remembering something. 'There was something else actually. You were talking about it on the walk back here.'

'What, what?'

'You were talking about the Taliban lad in black and white you killed in that town. Again, just what you wrote about in the bluey. How you kept dreaming of him, having nightmares about him and how when you killed him you felt invincible.'

'And?'

Will looked back into the pan and flipped some slices of bacon. 'I don't want to say, mate.'

'No. I need to hear this.'

Will got some plates out of the cupboard and the noise cut between them. He sighed. 'You said how you were scared that he was still alive, that you hadn't actually killed him even though you had seen the body. Like he was still around, like a ghost.'

'Really?'

'Yeah.'

A couple of hours later and feeling somewhere approaching normal, Tom was waiting for Cassie in the Italian restaurant just behind her house at the kink in the King's Road. He was early, she was late, but he didn't mind and sat recovering some strength with a hair-of-the-dog vodka and tonic. She came breezing in, squealed and as he got up hugged him, lifting her knees up behind her and making him take all her weight, in front of the whole room. Tom would have felt like a film star had he not then almost lost his balance and knocked into the table next to theirs.

'Well hello, hero. Look at you! You look amazing.' She stroked his arm and exclaimed, 'My, what big arms we have!'

'No, I don't. I look like a skeleton. You look incredible though. Where's the tan from? That skiing trip?'

'Yep. Four weeks old but still got it.'

'How were Pongo, Bongo and Mongo?'

'Fine, fine, since you ask. Better than ever really.'

'What about my old mate Jonty – was he there?'

'Yes.'

'And?'

'Not too bad. Slightly chastened whenever I mentioned you. Still don't think you're number one on his Christmas-card list.'

'Yeah, I didn't get one.'

They ordered, and the food arrived. She talked on and on, telling him all about London, about her new job, about Christmas. After twenty minutes she stopped herself. 'I'm so sorry. I can't believe it; all I'm doing is banging on about me. How are you? What's it like? Or is that not the kind of question I'm meant to be asking?'

'No, no. It's great to talk about something that isn't Afghan, to be honest. Seriously. You get so blinkered by it.' He then unloaded on her all the events of the tour, and she sat rapt, half through shock, half through interest.

He was in a really good mood, left out all the bad stuff and concentrated on the funny moments. She laughed at all the right bits, looked tense at all the right bits, and when he was really milking the stories for all they were worth leaned forward and grasped his forearm.

Around the restaurant sat people huddled up against the winter, with pasty and sun-starved skin, sniffling and coughing into their food and drink. Cassie shone out against them. She had changed her hair since the summer; it was shorter, more businesslike. Tom had always thought of her as a girl, just as he had always thought of himself as a boy, but, watching as she whispered about the other diners and flirted with the waiter, he realized she had changed. He still felt like a boy around her, though.

She noticed him drift away and kicked him under the table. 'Tom! Pay attention!'

'Ow! I am.'

'OK, what was I just saying?'

'Um, er, what were you saying?'

She kicked him harder. 'You are such an oaf. You've been staring at my breasts for about a minute, you utter perv.'

'No, I wasn't.'

'Tom, everyone in the restaurant could see you drooling over me. Have you not seen any women in the last five months?'

'Let me think.' Tom thought about the American girl in Kandahar but decided it might be best not to mention her. He remembered Corporal Claydon, way back in September, getting her foot blown off. Best leave that aside too. He was desperate not to talk about casualties as he knew that when those floodgates opened there'd be no stopping him. 'I suppose there are a few artillery girls in our base, but they're all like East German shot-putters. All the Afghans are covered up in burkas. It's a shame really, because you can tell they're utterly beautiful. But you only get that from looking at the young girls, before they're taken away to work in the house. There's this girl, maybe twelve or thirteen, down at this base we have called Eiger. She has the prettiest face of any-one I've ever seen; you can just tell she's going to grow up into an absolute babe. Sorry.' He grinned. 'My lingo's shock-ing. I mean beautiful woman. Blame the lads for that.'

'Well at least try to be a tiny bit more civilized than a drib-bling caveman. Come on, let's go.' She winked at the waiter for the bill.

'Where to?'

'Surprise. Come on, slowcoach.' As they left she looked at him disapprovingly. 'Oh dear.'

'What?'

'You haven't got a coat.'

'I know. I'm fine.'

'I promise you, where we're going you're going to freeze.'

'Oh no. Please don't say we're going ice skating. I'll just break my wrist and end up in Selly Oak next to properly wounded lads from Afghan.'

'No, somewhere else. But you will need a coat. We can go home for one. You can borrow one of Daddy's.'

The thought of meeting her father was less than thrilling.

'Don't worry,' she said, recognizing his reluctance. 'Mum and Dad are out skiing themselves at the moment. They're not back until Wednesday.'

They went to her house. Even in the bright afternoon sun-shine it still cast a menacing shadow over the street. Detached and huge, with its dark brickwork it reminded Tom of the kind of place where one of Sherlock Holmes' enemies might live. He smiled as he remembered how scared he had been of her father when he was a student. In a way Tom was dis-appointed he was going to miss him. He now seemed a pantomime figure of fun, to laugh at instead of run away from, with his snobbery and disdain for the army.

They went in and he chose a ridiculous ankle-length coat made of a thick herringbone tweed in an almost white grey, with a black velvet collar perfectly in keeping with her father's peacocking. He put it on and nearly drowned in it. But it was very warm, and he wished he had had it out on the desert patrols in Afghan. He started out the door.

'Leave your bag here.' She pointed to his rucksack.

'Oh yeah, we'll be coming back to drop off the coat.'

'No, I thought you were going to stay here tonight. I mean, you can if you want.'

Ah. Right. This is promising. Play it cool, Tommy, play it cool. 'Er, I was just going to stay at . . .' *Come on, Tom. Come on, mate; for once in your life buck up!* 'I mean, no, yeah, that'd be great. You sure?'

'Of course I'm sure.'

'Great.'

As they left the house and walked down to the river his heart was racing.

They reached the river, full now in the early afternoon and bouncing with sunlight, just like when they had parted back in the summer.

'So where are we going? I promise you if it's ice skating then I'm going to run away.'

'What ice rinks do you know around here?' She stopped at the black iron gate to Cadogan Pier, punched in a code and opened it. She went behind him, put her hands over his eyes and guided him down the gangway. They came to a halt and she said, 'Are you ready?'

'Think so.'

She took her hands away. 'Oh Lord.' In front of him was what he could only describe as one hell of a speedboat. 'What's this? It's amazing!'

'It was Daddy's birthday present to himself.'

Of course it was.

'He keeps it here and gets someone to drive him to work in Temple once or twice a week.'

Sounds like him.

'He sent me on a course, and now I'm qualified to drive it. So, I thought we'd go for a spin. This is my welcome-home present for you!' She jumped on board. 'Come on, make yourself useful. Start untying it.'

He wrestled ineffectually with the ropes, and she had to help him. Two minutes later they were pulling out into the Thames. She eased the throttle out and the speed increased. 'Go on.'

'What?'

'Well we can't exactly talk.' She was right; the engine made an almighty racket. 'Go and sit on the front and smoke and just watch the sights.'

Tom made his way up to the front of the boat and sat there, smoking cigarette after cigarette, wrapped up in his lovely snug coat, as London shot by, nothing in front of him as spray flicked up to lash his face.

Finally they stopped just beyond Westminster and sat there bobbing around. She shouted from the cabin, 'Open that cabinet at the back, will you?'

'Sure.' He clambered to the rear of the boat and opened it up. Inside was a magnum of champagne on a bed of ice. He started laughing. 'This is just taking the mick.'

She was buckled over with laughter. 'Go on, crack it open.'

He took out the bottle, ripped the foil and cage off, aimed the cork at a passing seagull and tried to hit it. He thought back to Afghan almost a month ago, when Dusty had shot a Taliban on a moving motorbike with the Rarden. It had been a hell of a shot. But he put that thought away.

She produced two glasses from the cabin and he poured. And then they were kissing. Tom missed her mouth completely on the first go, but then his lips hit hers.

That night they went to a pizza place for supper and then to the cinema. They walked back, and Tom tentatively held her hand, and she didn't take it away. When they got inside the house they sat on the sofa, pretending to be interested by the telly. Cassie got up to go to bed and they tidied up downstairs and went up. She stopped outside her bedroom and turned to kiss him again. They stayed there for a minute, and Tom made to step into her room.

'No, Tom, no. Not tonight.'

'OK, no probs, no probs.' He sounded hurt.

'Just not tonight. It's too . . .'

'Strange.'

'Yeah. It's just quite a lot to take on board, having you back. I'm so sorry.'

'No, no. No problem at all,' he said earnestly. 'I don't want you to feel under any pressure at all.' He went on: 'But you don't mind if I stay again tomorrow, do you? I promise you, I don't want to make you feel uneasy.'

'Of course you can stay.' She was whispering now. 'Just not in my bed.'

'I understand. Besides, my snoring is horrendous at the mo, so you've got off lightly.'

'Thanks, Tommy. I knew you'd understand.' She kissed him again, this time on the cheek, and shut the door behind her.

He remained in the corridor, smiled wryly and padded down to the spare room.

The next morning they had a quick breakfast and left the house, she for work and he for Euston. It felt like they were a married couple as they walked together to the Tube. When they parted at Sloane Square she kissed him again, and as she did so he relished the envious glances of the passing commuters. *Jog on, REMFs*. He made sure he held the kiss that little bit longer to rub it in.

He walked all the way north to Euston, slowly getting used to the city and starting to resent it less. On the train to Birmingham he read a newspaper, drank some coffee and then watched the countryside speed past the window as he enjoyed the feeling of being at ease with home again.

As he went through the barrier at Birmingham New Street a familiar voice greeted him: 'Oi, fancy-pants! Nice coat. Where d'you get it from? A polar bear?'

Trueman.

'It's actually my bird's father's.'

'What, he give it you?'

'No. I sort of nicked it.'

'Nice touch. Come on, boss, get to the car. If anyone sees me hanging out with you in that coat they'll think I'm a raving bender.'

Tom laughed. They did indeed make for an odd couple as they walked through the station, he in his ridiculous coat and Trueman in his jeans and tracksuit top.

In the car they couldn't stop talking, catching up on what they'd done in the last few days. It was great to see him. Tom remembered that back in the desert he had thought that when they met up it might be a bit awkward, like when holiday friends find that when they meet afterwards they have lost the one thing that they had in common. It wasn't like that at all.

As they got close to Selly Oak Trueman said, 'Right, boss, how do you think we play it?'

'Who are we seeing?'

'Ransome, definitely. Yam-Yam's in Headley now, though. And Mr Lanyon obviously.'

'What?'

'Mr Lanyon. What, did you not hear?'

Scott. 'No, what happened?' Tom had no idea, and his mouth was dry.

'He got hit a couple of days ago.'

'IED?'

'No, shot. Through the shoulder, I think. Not dead anyway. Cat B though.'

'How did you hear?'

'Just through the grapevine. I'm sorry, sir; I thought you'd know. I'd have said before otherwise.'

'No. No probs. Just a bit of a shock, that's all.'

As they pulled into the car park Tom's jolliness left him and he was very nervous. Trueman sensed it and said, 'Don't worry, sir; you get used to it after a couple of minutes. Won't lie though; your first time in here's a hell of a shock. Just remember, don't stare at their injuries. That's exactly what they hate. Just look them in the eye and talk to them like they ain't got anything wrong with them. That is, if they still got eyes. If they don't, it doesn't matter where you look, I suppose.'

Tom laughed.

'And don't say you feel sorry for them. They fucking hate

that. Just treat them like they've got flu. That's what I always do, anyway. It seems to work OK. If it all gets too much, then we'll go and get some fresh air.'

'Thanks.'

They approached the hospital in the midday sunshine, frost icing the grass around them. Tom felt scared. 'Here you go, sir; the famous Ward S4. Operating theatre of dreams. Come on, ain't that bad. Christ, it's like trying to get my little girls onto a roller coaster!'

At the entrance to the hospital there was a boy in a wheel-chair. He had only one leg and one arm, and with his good hand was lifting a cigarette to his mouth. His face was band-aged heavily, and with his one visible eye he looked at Tom, his lips curled contemptuously. Tom smiled back awkwardly, mumbled, 'Good morning,' and hurried past him, heart racing.

They were directed up the stairs to S4 and booked in as visitors. As Tom handed his coat to one of the nurses, he had to press himself against the wall as a trolley shot past him surrounded by a cluster of doctors. 'Out the way, out the way – just in from Bastion.' They rushed the stretcher into an operating room, and Tom peered after it.

One of the nurses in its wake said, 'No hope, I'm afraid. All gone below the navel. He'll probably go tonight.' Tom felt sick.

Trueman grasped his shoulder. 'All right, sir, this way.'

They went further into the ward, all around them boys in wheelchairs, limping down the ward or lying on their beds. Some had families and friends around them, some were con-scious, others comatose, others tripping in and out of morphine doses. Often the families were laughing with the boys; some were crying. There was one boy lying uncon-scious draped in a sheet that was much flatter than it should have been. He looked peaceful. Above his bed were all sorts of get-well cards and drawings. He was surrounded by flowers, and a middle-aged woman sat reading him a story, now and again leaning forward to wipe away dribble from his mouth, just as she had sat by him when he was a child and in bed with a cold. As Trueman guided him down the ward Tom couldn't speak. All he wanted to do was to get out. He had no idea this was the cost. In Afghan every night over the net he heard the casualties from the rest of theatre but had never translated them into this butcher's bill.

They came to the end of the ward, and there were Ransome and Scott, in opposite beds. Both looked up with sheepish grins. Tom saw with relief that Scott did still have all four limbs. His left arm was in a sling, and his upper torso was swathed in bandages. Ransome's stumps in the other bed looked just like Will had said they would, as though they had always been there, neat and permanent.

Tom went to sit by Ransome and Trueman turned to Scott. Tom pulled up a chair and took a box of chocolates from a carrier bag with some magazines he'd bought at the station. 'Here you go, Ransome. Thought you might like these. Usual stuff, I'm afraid. *Zoo, Nuts, GQ.*'

'Cheers, sir.'

'How are you?'

'So so. Could be worse, I suppose.'

Tom looked at his stumps, ending cleanly about six inches below his hips, and wondered how it could possibly be worse. He didn't answer, and Ransome, sensing his discomfort, eased him into it. 'I mean, still got my arms. And my bollocks. Still gonna slay all the birds. And the nurses here are hot.'

Tom laughed, and soon they were both back in Afghan mode, joking and taking the mick out of each other.

After twenty minutes they switched over and Tom went to talk to Scott, who had a wild look in his eyes as though he wasn't yet accustomed to being back home. Tom realized it was probably the look they all had when they were out there. He must have had it himself. He might still have it.

'Hi, bud. I'm so sorry. What happened?'

'I got hit up near Jekyll, about half a K north of it, near the Farad gardens. AK round. In under the collarbone and out through the shoulder blade. No internal damage, clean through. So lucky. Hurt like fuck though. I passed out when it happened. Next thing I knew I was in a ditch with the boys after someone had dragged me back. The boys pumped me full of morphine, but it didn't seem to work. I was in agony, mate. Promise me one thing.'

'What?'

'Don't get shot. Massively overrated.'

'I'll try to remember. Thanks for the tip. Why were you even up there? I thought you were meant to be on the wagons?'

'We were. But the day after you boys went down to Bastion it all kicked off in the north. Every day Pilgrim up in Jekyll were getting whacked. Shoots and scoots, ambushes on their patrols, daisy chains, everything. Massively kicking off. They took a lot of casualties. There's a few of them in here now, actually, in the other wards.'

'What happened?'

'Battle group think a shedload of out-of-area fighters came in, sort of mid-January time. Twenty or so of them, Pakistanis. Fucking good shots. And their IEDs are good too. There was a rumour that some of them were Chechens.'

'Great.'

'I know. Those lads are mentalists. So I went up with the troop to help out. We left the wagons at Newcastle and went out on our feet to bolster their patrols. We were doing OK as well. We'd been up there for four days and had five firefights, and then this happens. There was this contact and I ran out of a ditch where we were taking cover to try to get to Frenchie for a face-to-face as my comms didn't work. And then some knobber shot me. The burst went all around me. I saw all the rounds kick up the dust, almost in slo-mo, and then the last one whacked into me. Like someone thumping you with a sledgehammer.'

'And then?'

'One of the boys – don't know who – dragged me back into the ditch, and they casevaced me all the way back to Jekyll. They were amazing. Absolutely amazing. Before I knew it I was back in Bastion, and now I'm here.' He looked around, his eyes shifting nervously. 'Feels really strange, to be honest.'

'Jeez, mate, I wish I'd known.'

'The CO's trying to get on to brigade to whack the area. Big op planned. And I mean big.'

'When?' Tom started feeling excited.

'Dunno, not for a couple of weeks anyway. But definitely before the squadron goes home. Smash time, mate, proper smash. Plan is to push all the way up and clear the whole town. Apparently the brigade commander's pretty keen for it.'

'Yeah, he would be. Another chance to move his drinks cabinet closer to Russia. One step closer to his DSO,' said Tom.

'What do you mean?'

'I dunno, mate. Just something that really gets me about tour.'

'What?'

'Just that the more lads that die, the greater the chance the bigwigs get a medal at the end of it. It's an unwritten rule, isn't it? If the brigade gets fifty-plus KIA, the brigade commander gets a DSO, and climbs another rung to CGS. Forty-nine KIA and you only get a CBE. I thought that's what everyone said. Brennan and Trueman say it the whole time.'

'Well, he'll get his casualties. If the op does go ahead it's gonna go spastic up there. Those guys don't muck around. They'll fight tooth and nail.'

'But there's an appetite for it?'

'Hell yeah. They've already got a name for the ops box – Ops Box Republic.'

'Sounds like a nightclub. As in Plato's *Republic*?'

'No, as in "Battle Hymn of the". Named by Jules, surprise surprise.'

Tom looked away, remembering.

'What?'

'Nothing, mate. Just that hymn was my school song.'

'Nice.'

'Yeah, but you know the fifth verse? "As he died to make men holy, let us die to set them free."'

'That sucks.'

'Too right it sucks. How are the boys?'

Scott ignored him and clicked himself with more morphine. He suddenly seemed far away but after a minute came back to Tom. 'Sorry, mate. Sorry, had to get rid of some pain. That stuff is so good.'

'Mate, you were saying about the op?'

'The op? Oh yeah. Sorry, mate. All I know is they want to clear the whole village.'

'But that's two miles at least. And how many enemy? Twenty? Thirty?'

'At least. God knows, really. But a lot. And they're good

too. I was in the open for all of about a second, and they got me.'

Tom lowered his voice. 'Did you tell Sergeant Trueman?'

'Yeah. Was that wrong?'

'No, no. I'd have told him myself. But it does mean it'll be round the whole troop by tonight, if I know him. Bollocks. I thought we were going back to wind down and basically just hand over kit.'

'Doesn't look like it, bud. Is that bad?'

'No, not bad, just . . . unexpected. I mean, I'm terrified, obviously. But, and I can't believe I'm saying this, it sounds like an epic op.'

'Too right, mate. Front-row ticket to the end of the world.'

'All right, chill out. Christ, nothing like a smack addict for melodrama.'

They stayed for a couple more hours and sought out the wounded guys from the company up in Jekyll to get any tips about what to expect. It was the one PB in the AO that 3 Troop hadn't worked around yet. They found four of them, dotted over the ward. Three had their families beside them and so they didn't interrupt. One was alone though, on his bed, pristine save for a bandage over his eyes. The lower part of his face was streaked with grazes and dried cuts. They sat next to him.

Tom let Trueman do the talking. 'Hi, fella, it's two guys from Loy Kabir. Tomahawk callsigns. We're on R & R and came to see some of our oppos here. We just want a favour.'

'How can I help?'

Tom watched the interchange with fascination. Trueman was a sergeant with ten years' service but talked to this boy, no more than nineteen, as though they were exact contemporaries.

'Yeah, no dramas. What d'you want to know? I'm Costello, by the way. Jordan Costello.' He held out a hand and both of them shook it.

Tom stepped in. 'Just a bit about the AO north of Jekyll. When we get back there's a big op planned in the north, and we want to know about the ground up there, what the local Taliban are like and stuff.'

'You're an officer, ain't ya?'

'Er, yep. How did you guess?'

'Cos that is without doubt the dullest question I've had in my time here. Just kiddin'. No worries, boss. Nice to think back, in a way.'

For half an hour he told them all about it: how he thought the Scimitars could be used, the tactics of the local Taliban, how the fighting had escalated massively at the end of January with the influx of foreign fighters. He was astonishingly lucid and spoke beyond his years, getting more and more into his role as storyteller, enjoying his audience's attention.

As they thanked him and got up to go he said, 'You're probably wondering what happened to me, aren't ya?'

Before they could answer he went on.

'IED. Next to me. Got me mate. He's in the operating theatre at the mo. Shredded his leg. But it's still on; they say he'll keep it. Got me in the eyes though. Not the shrapnel, just loads of grit. Wasn't wearing my safety specs. Tell your lads to wear theirs.'

Tom glanced at Trueman guiltily. Neither of them could be bothered with their protective glasses.

Trueman said, 'Are you gonna be all right, mate?'

He answered bloodlessly as if talking about someone else: 'Dunno. Too early to say, the docs told me. They say a 20 per cent chance I'll see again. But they don't know the full damage yet.'

'Mate, I cross my fingers. I really do.'

'Ta. Well, see you later, I hope!'

Trueman only managed to whisper back, 'Yeah, mate, yeah. Get well soon.'

'Cheers. Take care out there. You're going into a shit storm if you try to clear the whole town. Rather you than me.'

They left him, and with both Ransome and Scott now asleep escaped the ward and went back to the car. Tom was about to speak but glanced at Trueman and saw he was weeping, so he kept quiet. It was the first time Tom had ever seen any vulnerability in him, and he thought it must be like when a little boy sees his father cry for the first time. They got into the car and drove to a pub, and soon Trueman perked up and was back to normal. They had a drink and then drove to the station for Tom's train back to London. He sat alone, watching out the window as the day faded into dark.

He arrived in London during rush hour. On the Underground passengers crowded like cattle onto the platforms, jostling shoulder to shoulder in the fight to get on board. It took Tom three trains before he could get on to one.

As the train headed south he wriggled himself away from the doors and into the middle of the carriage. He looked at the people who had managed to get a seat. Three in a row were youngish men. One was a builder, grizzly with days-old stubble, clothes flecked with paint and dirt, clearly exhausted. The middle one was a tourist, confused and obviously lost, his spectacles misted with the breath of those around him. The third was about Tom's age, in a smart suit underneath a camel-coloured coat, plugged into his music. Tom immediately hated him. He looked around. An old man wearing a flat cap and a thin shabby grey jacket was standing, swaying

267

into other passengers, too short to reach the rail above his head and clearly in need of a seat.

Tom remembered something Frenchie had once told him. 'Thing is, Tom, there are three things you need to do in life. First, never stand on an escalator; always walk up the bastard. Second, never unfurl an umbrella unless you are doing so to prevent a girl getting wet. Just man up; it's dry between the drops. Step out, don't open your brolly, take it on the chin. Heck of a lot smarter, and it confuses the hell out of people. Third, never let me catch you ever, and I mean ever, sitting on the Tube when it is more than half full. It is the most contemptible activity conceivable to humanity. Whenever I see some prat sitting on the Tube, especially when there's a girl there, I go up to him and tell him to do one. Works every time. Sitting on the Tube is a plague on our society, Tom, and it must be crushed. Crushed.'

Tom went for it. He stepped forward, bloody anger surging up his neck, and reached to tap the city slicker on the shoulder and tell him to move it, but something checked his arm at the last moment.

No. No. Let it be. You cannot be this angry all the time. You cannot let it destroy you.

He didn't make his move. They pulled into Victoria, where he got out into the evening rain, cheerful. He was going to come out of this all right.

And then, somehow, that night it all worked perfectly. He met Cassie for a drink at a bar on Pimlico Road, and afterwards they walked arm in arm to an Italian restaurant. In the soft light and with wine warming him Tom told her all about the day – about Ransome, about Scott, about Costello. He mentioned the Tube too, speaking about the quashing of his rage with the pride of a rehabilitated alcoholic.

Cassie listened to all of this in silence and at the end she said, 'So when you go back you're going into a big battle.'

'Yes.' There was no point lying, not this late on.

'And?'

'And what?'

'Are you excited?'

He used the wine in his glass as a prism to look at her. 'I think I am. Yes. I am excited about it. But also terrified. It's always like that. There's always this fight going on between these different parts of you.' He paused and drank some wine, trying to savour every drop. 'Basically, there's three people in your brain, and they're all scrapping for control. Stay with me on this; if it gets a bit weird then just say.'

'OK.' She smiled, tilted her head slightly and twirled her hair with her fingers.

'So, these three people. First, you've got ten-year-old Tom, who just loves the fact he's carrying a gun. He thinks the whole thing's a dream come true. And then you've got the rough-tough army officer, who's trained for this for two and half years now. He loves it too because he's applying what he's been trained to do to reality. He feels no fear, sees everything ruthlessly and bloodlessly. This guy can't wait to get out there again. Believe me, he's properly mental.' He sipped from his glass again.

'And the third?'

'Well, the third is a twenty-six-year-old graduate who read poetry at university. He's got a ma, who's on her own. He's not violent; he never even watches horror films. He still has his teddy bear on his bed. He finds any violence horrific. And he's really squeamish; he hates blood. He looks at what's happening around him and thinks it's madness. Utterly horrendous; boys and girls getting turned into meat. And he wants to scream and run away. But he can't because the other two guys are stopping him – the ten-year-old and the professional. So there's this constant battle, but the third guy always loses. I wish I could pretend I hated it, I really do, and I do sort of hate it, massively hate it, but more of me loves it. Loves it. And I wish I could be ashamed of that. I know I should be ashamed of it. But I'm not. And that really scares me.'

She sat back in her chair. 'Thanks, Tommy. I've never heard anyone speak like that before.'

'You must think I'm some kind of psycho.'

'Yes, obviously. I've always thought that. But no, it's incredible to hear you talk about yourself like that. I had no idea.'

'I didn't know I even thought like that myself until I was saying it. But it's true. Weird but true.'

Tom paid the bill and they went out into the drizzle. They were both wrapped up warm and went down to Chelsea Embankment to walk along the river. There was no traffic; they had the city to themselves. They didn't talk, and walked along in silence. There was nothing that needed to be said. Tom clasped her hand and felt her fingers tighten around his through her soft woollen gloves. They passed the Albert Bridge and remembered their parting back in September, when neither of them knew what was going to happen. Cassie thought about telling him about her Friday-morning ritual, but decided not to. She didn't want to somehow jinx it.

They turned up towards her house and stopped at a bar for a final drink. At midnight they left and went to Cassie's. She fumbled with the keys, and they giggled as she clumsily unlocked the door. They went up the stairs and then kissed again outside her room. This time she let him in.

He had been awake for a few minutes and was examining her bare back. Her shoulder blade stretched her skin, tanned and freckled. He kissed her on the back of the neck and then put his arm over her and tried to coincide his breaths with hers so as not to wake her. She carried on sleeping, and he stayed there as the morning breached the curtains.

He looked at his watch. Ten to eight. She needed to be at work for nine. He slinked out of bed as quietly as possible, pulled on his boxer shorts and eased open the door. He went down the stairs, the cold air goose-pimpling his chest, and in the kitchen switched on the kettle and rubbed his arms, trying to get warm.

In the bedroom Cassie had pretended to be asleep and heard him leave. She lay still for a minute, lost in the fog of morning, and then reached over to her bedside table for her phone. It flashed with a new message, and she dragged herself up onto her elbows to read it. Straining her eyes at the screen, she discovered three missed calls and three messages. All the calls were from her mother's mobile. So were the messages. She read the most recent one: 'At Heathrow. Now in taxi. Xxx.' She flicked to the oldest one, sent last night at ten o'clock. 'Hi Cass darling, we've had the most FANTAS-TIC time out here – wish you'd been with us. Dad just received news of a big case and has to come back to see big client tomorrow for emergency meeting. A day early – drat! Getting red-eye Geneva tomorrow morn; back 4 breakfast. Mummy xxxxx.'

Cassie looked at her watch. Eight. She looked back to the message from Heathrow. Sent at 7.15. In a panic she ripped away the bedclothes, suddenly thinking completely clearly and her brain shedding the previous night in an instant. Still naked, she ran down the stairs to get Tom.

Tom had finished making the coffee. One mug in each hand, he pulled open the kitchen door with his foot and, using his other heel to pivot, rocked himself forward through it. As he did so, to his left the front door opened and people started coming in. His momentum carried him out from the cover of the kitchen into the hall, where he stood framed in the light flooding through the open door. To his right Cassie was on the stairs for some reason, completely naked. He froze, his first thought being that he wasn't wearing any boxer shorts. He remembered that he was, but his fear just transformed into something greater.

The two figures in the doorway were looking at him, or at both of them. He glanced in horror back to Cassie, who shrieked and, rather skilfully Tom thought, used both her arms to cover herself up and then ran back up the stairs. That left him with her parents. Her father looked like a dying fish. Tom could have sworn that Lavinia was eyeing him up. No point denying it; well and truly caught red-handed. Drawing from the Frenchie school for these kinds of situations Tom beamed a thousand-watt smile and said, 'Lavinia, Jeremy, welcome back. Welcome home. Here, coffee. Great to see you both again. Long time.'

Four days later, at home, Tom's alarm went off at 4.15, and after a cup of tea he and Constance got into the car to drive him back to Aldershot. He had to be there by seven to get the minibus with the troop up to Brize. In the darkness on the drive he felt fine, and he and Constance chatted happliy. He remembered when they had driven to Sandhurst and how nervous he'd been then. This drive seemed so much easier; he was going back to the familiar and, no matter how terrifying that was, at least he knew what its face looked like. Back then he had worried about the length of his hair; now he was proud of his shaggy, unkempt mane. He thought of the Grade 1 he'd had in Bastion at the start of tour; now he looked like a hippy. His sideburns were just within regulation length, but they were pushing it; he planned to grow them into mutton chops out on the ground.

They drove into the barracks, where the boys were by the guardroom, hanging around a white minibus. He smiled as he saw them in their characteristic poses. Dusty was reading a book in front of the bus, GV and Jessie were smoking, and Trueman was making the others laugh. 'Mum, come and meet them. I promise they won't bite.' Tom felt very proud that he was able to introduce Constance to the lads. As the car pulled up and he got out the boys started heckling him.

'Oi oi, boss, what time do you call this?'

'Aw, boss, no haircut? Standards, sir, standards.' Then they saw Constance and instantly became more formal.

Tom led her over, and cigarettes were stubbed out and clothes straightened as though they were getting ready to meet a general. 'Well, Mum, here are the pirates I've told you about. Lads, this is my ma. The one who's kept you all, and particularly you, Lance Corporal Miller, in chocolate brownies all tour.'

The boys laughed politely but genuinely. Trueman was the first to break the ice and thrust his hand out to shake hers. One by one they did the same, and Tom was amused to see them all become paragons of clean language. He excused himself to go to the mess for his body armour and helmet, and when he came back, as he knew would be the case, he found that Constance had them all wrapped around her finger, telling them stories about him when he was young. He stood off for a moment and smiled at the scene. Then he went in to break it up, and they all laughed at him. After a few more minutes Trueman looked at his watch and said, 'Sorry, boss, we'd better get a move on. Don't want to miss the plane.' He grinned at Constance. 'Well, we do, but it ain't really the done thing.'

'Sure. Right fellas, let's go,' said Tom. As they got on the bus he turned to Constance for one final hug. 'Bye, Mum. Get in the car now and go before we do. I promise you, it'll be easier.'

'OK, Tommy, OK.' She wanted to make this as short as possible too. She extracted herself from the hug but then pulled him back one more time and whispered into his ear, 'Take care, darling boy. I'm so proud of you all. Look after them, but look after yourself, please.'

'I will. See you in a month. Just a month. I'll hardly be away.' She pulled away, blinking more than was natural, got into the car and drove out of the camp, leaving Tom waving after her. He turned to get on board. Jessie held his hand out and hauled him on, his eyes meeting Tom's and saying all that needed to be said. And then they too left camp and headed to Brize.

The helicopter came in low, skimming over compounds. Tom looked out the tailgate, gazing down at battlefields already famous in regimental lore as they flew over Eiger and then up Route Canterbury. They approached the DC, and the heli slowed, gained some height and then spiralled down to touch onto the HLS, and they ran out. Some infantry guys ran on to take their place, off for their own R & R, and the Chinook lifted off again, leaving 3 Troop in the warm mid-morning sun. They were exhausted after two days in transit: from Brize to Minhad in Dubai, up to KAF and then to Bastion, where they were hurried off the plane to pick up their rifles and then driven over to catch the heli. They had only just made it and cursed that they did; if they hadn't they would have been able to spend a day in Bastion sorting themselves out and getting some kip. None of them felt ready to come straight back into the thick of things. Tom put his kit in the tent and went into the ops room. Frenchie, Jason and Jules pored over a map of the AO.

'Well well well, look who it isn't!' Frenchie smiled, and Tom immediately felt back into the zone. 'How was it? You look well, my boy.'

'Gleaming, Frenchie, gleaming. Sorted me right out. Best two weeks ever.'

'Welcome back to the suck, Tommy,' said Jules.

'*Jarhead*. Very nice.'

'You know me. We've got some news for you.'

'What about, Ops Box Republic?'

Jules frowned. 'How do you know about that? Who told you?'

'Scotty did. I went to see him in Selly Oak.'

Frenchie laughed. 'So much for opsec. How is he?'

'All right. High as a kite on morphine, but he told me all about what's been happening to Pilgrim.'

'Is he going to keep his arm?'

'Oh yeah, definitely. Smashed up his collarbone but the docs say he'll be back to normal in a few months. Lucky boy.'

'Too right. Did he tell you about it?'

'Bits of. Not all. What happened?'

'When he got hit the sergeant major ran out to drag him out under a massive weight of fire. I was about fifty metres away when it happened. Bravest thing I've ever seen. I'm putting him up for a gong. With any luck he'll get an MC.'

'Awesome! Does he know?'

'Don't think so. As you can imagine he's being fairly blasé about the whole thing, but the CO's going to give it his full backing. Anyway, what did Scott tell you about Republic?'

'Just that it was all kicking off. Bigger than *Ben Hur*.'

Jules butted in. 'You could say that. It's been frantic up there. Pilgrim are getting smashed every time they go out the gate.'

'And so?'

'We're going to sort it out. That's where you come in.'

'OK, hit me. Don't beat around the bush, please. Am I on point?'

Frenchie and Jules looked at each other as if debating who should break the news. Frenchie decided he would. ''Fraid so. The CO wanted our best troop, so I told him that the Chamberlain and Trueman show wouldn't let him down.' He watched the news sink in. 'No pressure then.'

Tom's throat was dry, but his brain was racing. 'Well,

276

that's um, flattering, Frenchie. Thanks. But we've only just got back in.'

'Don't worry; D-Day's not for a week yet. Plenty of time to bed in. O Group in five days. We're just doing shaping stuff at the mo and bidding for brigade assets.'

Jules continued: 'And we need a shedload of them – UAVs, Chinooks, Uglys, the works. Brigade are being OK about it.'

'What do I do in the meantime?'

'I imagine the sergeant major's sorting Trueman out already. Your lads are going to get the Scimitars ready this week.'

'I don't like the sound of that – sounds like something else for me.'

'You're good, Tom. Just for three days or so you're going to take over Scott's troop. Sergeant Williams has D & V, and I don't want Corporal McMaster to have to troop-lead; he's too crow. So you're on the Mastiffs, troop leading Two Zero till Willie's better.'

'Roger. Are we doing anything today? Please say no.'

'No, low ops today. But tomorrow you're going down to Eiger for an admin run. Milk run, just to ease you in.'

'Where have I heard that before? Yeah, sure, of course. It'll be good to get back into it. But I can kip today?'

'Fill your boots, whatever floats your boat.'

'I'd bite your arm off for it. I'm knackered.'

Frenchie chuckled. 'Then crack on, son.' Tom went to leave, picked up his rifle and helmet and pulled away the hessian over the doorway. 'Oh, Tom?'

'Yeah?'

'Nothing. Just it's good to have you back, that's all.'

'Thanks. Can't believe I'm saying this, but it's actually quite exciting to be back.'

Jules replied, 'There you go, mate, like I always said. You bloody love it out here.'

The next day the Mastiffs went down to Eiger, carrying a replacement generator. A Squadron had managed to break another one. It was a clear run. They barma'd the usual VPs but came up with nothing. The whole of the AO's focus had shifted to the north since Christmas; it was as though the troubles down south had never happened.

Tom enjoyed being back amongst it and working with Scott's troop. They were good lads, and their drills were immaculate. Their banter wasn't as good as 3's, but then they'd never had Trueman, and their sergeant, Williams, while solid and a decent soldier, was pretty dour. It took them an hour, and when they got there he chatted with the A Squadron officers, swapping stories about R & R and hearing how since it had all started happening up in Jekyll their own contacts had completely dried up. They made a show of complaining about it, but he could see relief etched into their faces. They themselves only had five weeks to go and were clearly content to moan about a lack of action while actually revelling in it. He didn't blame them.

At the front of the PB was the same soldier Tom had talked to on Christmas Eve, standing before the red and white corrugated iron gate. It was dirty, and riddled with bullet holes that the sun sent shafts of light through on to its shadow. Borrowby was wearing lance corporal rank now. 'Congratulations, Corporal Borrowby; when did you pick up?'

'Cheers, sir, about a month ago. The boss did it out on the ground. On patrol, he came up to me, told me I was going to be charged for being improperly dressed and then tossed me the rank slide. It was a good crack, actually.'

'Well done. How are things here?'

'Same old. A bit quieter than last time you were down, sir, but I ain't complaining about that. I've had enough contacts to last me a lifetime to be honest.'

'How are those two little kids?'

'What, Jack and Jill? That's what we used to call 'em. Yeah, they were good crack.'

'Do they not still come down?'

'Nah. Fucking sick, sir. About three weeks ago, like, we hadn't seen the girl for ages, just the lad. So we asked the locals what had happened to her.' He looked away into the distance.

Tom could guess what he was about to say. 'Go on.'

'She got married to some bloke in a village ten miles to the south. Arranged by her parents. She was taken off and given to him. She was only thirteen. Sick, sir. Fucking sick.'

'Christ.'

'What are we doing out here? These people are barbarians, sir, you know?'

'Well, we can't judge, Corporal. It's their culture, and they've got their way of doing things.' Even as he said the words he realized they sounded idiotic.

'Fuck off, sir; we don't have to swallow all that cultural bollocks. We can still judge by our own standards. If that kind of shit happened back home, back in my town, some pervert raping a girl like that, he'd get his balls cut off, no questions asked. It just ain't right, sir, it just ain't right.'

Tom made no reply as they stood there, lost in their lonely thoughts. *What kind of reality is this? What are we doing here?*

Borrowby coughed, shook off his anger and asked Tom politely, 'How was leave then? Heard you guys were away.'

Tom was grateful for the new conversation. 'Awesome, thanks, really awesome. You had yours yet?'

'Yeah, but it was shit. Over the New Year. Went home and

me missus had been shagging some other fella from Aldershot. Some electrician. So we split up. We had this blazin' row and it's all over.'

'Jesus. I'm sorry.'

'Fuck it, sir.' He grinned sadly. 'More fish in the sea, all that crap. And then when I got back here I discovered about Ransome.'

'He your mate?'

'Yeah, joined up together. Been mates since the off.'

'I saw him in Selly Oak last week.'

Borrowby's eyes lit up. 'Did you? How is he?'

Tom didn't reply immediately. 'He's . . . doing OK. He's bloody brave. But I'm afraid what's done is done. He's going to have a long hard struggle for the rest of his life.'

'But he's cheerful, is he?' Borrowby looked at him as if desperately needing reassurance.

'Yes. Yes, he's cheerful. But he's going to need a lot of support.'

Tom thought back to Ward S4 and his ghastly journey through it, and was quiet for a few moments.

Again Borrowby broke the silence: 'I dunno how those boys do it, to be honest. We've got this thing down here, some of the lads. This informal pact thing that if one of us gets fucked, like truly fucked, then we're just going to pump him full of morphine so he dies of an overdose. Better that than what comes after.'

'No. No, I don't agree with that.'

'Come on, sir; better than a lifetime of shit.'

'No. Honestly, maybe a couple of months ago I'd have agreed with you. It's a valid view. But, personally, since I was in that hospital, I disagree. It was horrible there, but it made me realize that what you have is so precious that if there is a tiny chance to save a life and keep it going, it has to be taken. I don't expect you to agree with me. That's just the way I see it.'

'But what if you've had your balls blown off?'

'Even then, I think.'

'Really?'

'Yeah. And anyway it'd be cheaper.'

'Eh?'

'Well you wouldn't have to bother taking girls on dates.'

Borrowby smiled. 'Fair one. Boss, that's your guys hot to trot.'

Tom looked over and saw 2 Troop milling around the Mastiffs. He held out his hand. 'Well, good to see you again, Corporal Borrowby. And congratulations.'

They shook. 'Cheers, sir. Will I see you boys again?'

'Dunno. We're back to Bastion in about three weeks, and I think most of the time till then we're going to be up north.'

'On this mental op?'

'Yeah. You heard about it?'

Borrowby grinned and lit a cigarette. 'Too right. Sounds like the circus is in town for that one. Clown cars, lion tamers, the works. Sounds Mickey Mouse to be honest.'

'I'm inclined to agree.'

'Take care, sir. It's too late on for any funny business now.'

'I don't know about that. Always room for funny business. Remember, if you can't take the joke, Corporal Borrowby, what shouldn't you have done?'

Borrowby's creased and dusty face grinned back through the smoke from his cigarette. 'Shouldn't have joined, sir. Shouldn't have joined.' Tom jogged off, hopped onto his Mastiff and the troop rolled back out northwards, leaving

Borrowby at the gate like a statue, like he had always been there, like he was always going to be there.

Through the week the tempo picked up. Sergeant Williams got better, and Tom was able to rejoin 3 Troop. Newcastle became crowded as platoons and sections were stripped away from across the AO and formed into composite units for the op. D-Day was Tuesday. Full orders would take place on Sunday in Newcastle, and on Monday they would leave Newcastle and forward-mount around Jekyll for the next day's drive. They were going in with sledgehammer force.

The company at Jekyll, the Pilgrim callsigns which had fought so hard throughout the month, were to be the lead sub-unit. In support of them they had two companies of ANA under the supervision of the OMLT. Two troops from C Squadron, Clive's and Henry's, were on their feet under Frenchie, with a platoon of US Marines also under him. BG Tac were coming out; Sergeant Williams commanded the Mastiff troop and 3 Troop were in their Scimitars as intimate support for the infantry. They also had a REST from Bastion with one of the best ATOs in theatre heading it up. Even the mortars from Eiger came up for it. They had lorries loaded with Hesco, and diggers from the engineers, who would build the new patrol base.

The force had two and a half miles of the town to push through, which would take about three days, BGHQ thought. Int said there were forty or fifty Taliban in the area. The plan was simple: to push north, clear and destroy all enemy in boundaries until they reached the edge of the town and then establish a new patrol base. The town had round-the-clock UAV surveillance to watch for any IED activity. Opsec had gone out the window. With such heavy ANA involvement it was a foregone conclusion that most of the details would be leaked, but the CO didn't mind. He wanted the Taliban to know they were coming, to intimidate them into leaving. Better that than they stayed and fought. But the downside was that the Talibs had had weeks to prepare defensive positions, and weeks to guess approaches through the town.

The operation had been calculated with two things in mind. First, it would provide a real buffer to the north of the brigade's entire area and make it impossible for the Taliban to infiltrate down into the town. Second, and more immediately, it would be a massive and emphatic show of strength, a chance to show that ISAF ruled the town, no questions asked. For that reason, and unlike the assault through Shah Kalay, there was to be no cut-off force to the north. The CO wanted the Taliban to be able to escape if they wanted to, and, even better, to be seen to be running.

Every day helicopters arrived with more supplies: more artillery shells, mortar shells, 30 mil ammunition, ladders, water, all in great underslung loads. One box was being carried off a heli and the soldier carrying it tripped and the box burst, spilling pristine bodybags out onto the ground. The humour became even darker than usual. The Scimitars heaved with water and ammunition, Trueman making sure every available space was filled with HE, gimpy link, schmoolies, LASMs. Even before the big O Group, bergens and daysacks were already packed. Link, extra tourniquets and FFDs filled every pouch. Every GPS, every torch, every head torch had new batteries inside, and spares taped to it. Marker pens renewed faded and dusty Zap numbers and blood groups written on body armour and trouser legs. Everyone carried spare batteries for the Vallons. Their operators, almost surgically attached to them, let no one near the detectors, recognizing by now every single variation in the tones of their beeps. Everybody knew that while grenades, rifles and gimpys would win the fight, the Vallons would determine its cost.

On Sunday they had the O Group, with the CO and Jules conducting it around a giant model of the town in front of fifty officers and NCOs. The OC of Pilgrim, who had cabbied back in a Mastiff for it, gave a presentation about what they could expect north of Jekyll. He had lost three KIA and eleven wounded in the last six weeks, and despite his tired eyes a blazing energy still burst out from his gruff, weary countenance. The RSM and the doc outlined the resupply and the casevac plans; the ATO gave his piece about devices.

They went from the orders to wargame it for three hours, ignoring the heat, now about thirty degrees, all fixed intently on the planned dance of the battle group's players through the town. Ops Box Republic had five objectives. Jules had named them after code words for American nuclear defcon states, which delighted the US Marine contingent. The first objective, four hundred metres north of Jekyll, was Fade Out. Objectives Double Take, Round House and Fast Pace lay beyond it, with Cocked Pistol the final one at the edge of the town. The CO had insisted on a bit of Britishness in proceedings, and the controlling phase lines for the op were named after the equipment from the second verse of 'Jerusalem'; Phase Lines Bow, Arrow, Spear, Chariot and Sword were all traced onto maps and memorized.

At the end, with the sun now low in the west, the CO spoke to them. He spoke loudly and slowly, to allow the interpreter next to him to translate for the ANA, who somehow were still looking keen and sharp.

Sweat gathered on his forehead beneath his tight-cropped hair, a faint pepper of grey dusting his temples. 'I don't do eve-of-battle speeches as a rule. They overblow things. But this one is justified, I think. This is our defining operation this tour. Its importance lies in the seizure of the north and what that will mean for Taliban supply routes. If we can get these northern compounds we cut them off all the way to Baghran.

'But you all know it's more than that. It's the symbolism. We've been on the back foot here since the start. I'm a cavalry officer; movement is my stock-in-trade. Without it I'm nothing. Our movement has been clotted by their IEDs all tour, down to a trickle at one point. Back in November, with all the dramas on Canterbury, we were on the verge of failure here. No matter how many of them we kill, no matter how good our drills, equipment and vehicles are, if we cannot move with impunity, and are seen by the locals to be unable to move, then we lose. Simple as that.

'We can change that now. We can show the entire population that we own the town with one bold stroke. And then once we've shown them that, we give it to them, and then they can breathe commerce into it. And then we all get to go home. But we must, I say again must, be seen to win this in the clearest, most unequivocal way. We steamroll them. This is going to be annihilation. Any Talib unwise enough not to take the hint that we are coming and who stays and fights, gets blitzed. We will unleash on him an overwhelming, ruthless, focused application of raw, savage violence. And that responsibility rests on every trooper. Everyone with a rifle in this battle is my personal representative. Tell your boys that, and tell them that well. Whatever they do in the coming days, if they do it with the honest belief that they are doing the correct thing, they can count on my support to the hilt. To the very hilt. But remember, the moment the enemy run, and some of them will run when they see what we are bringing, then we let them run and we let people see them run.

'Perception in counter-insurgency is everything, and we will propagate the perception, because it will be true, that we own the town. We own it by day, and we own it by night, and we will show the world that the Taliban and their brand of business have no place in a town that looks not to the rule of fear, but to the rule of law, that looks not to rule by the gun, but to rule by the ballot box. And we guard the law, and we guard the ballot box, with our lives. End of story.

'So go to your men and tell them this message. Just as we will win this fight, so we will win this war. There will be casualties; this is going to be a hell of a fight. I will not hide that from you. But it is worth the flame. That I can promise you. God speed, and for God's sake tread lightly.'

The ensemble broke up. The C Squadron officers and seniors went to Frenchie's tent to run through the plan once more. Afterwards Tom and Trueman briefed up the troop, who wrote down all the information in their notebooks as if savouring every last drop of the final operation they would conduct on this long tour. It was as though, somehow, they were already starting to miss it. They went to scoff and got an early night. They were moving out at midday.

The force was gathered on the wagons in the tank park, a mass of men and machines. They had been good to go for two hours already, and the boys on the Scimitars sat on their turrets or the front decks, smoking and chatting. The Mastiff crews and their passengers hung about outside them sharing brews and reading magazines. Tom was with Clive and Henry beside his Scimitar. They were all in the zone, raring to go. This tour had been odd for their relationship. They had spent so long with their soldiers rather than with each other, unlike when back at home, that their friendship had almost been put on ice.

Tom looked at his friends as they argued about who had the better helmet cover. They both looked so much more grown-up than they had a few months ago. They didn't flap about anything, had much easier laughs and had shaken off the insecurities that had bugged them all at the start. Driven into their faces were hardness and austerity. He looked at his watch. 1130. He leaned forward and flicked Henry's ear just like they always used to do to annoy each other back in Aldershot. 'Lads, you're boring me now. I want to bonnet-brief the troop.'

'Bonnet-bore them more like,' hit back Henry. 'Here we go. Just when there's any danger of morale breaking out Thomas Chamberlain crushes it mercilessly. Captain Fun to the rescue.'

They sloped off back to the Mastiffs, and 3 Troop gathered themselves around Tom's Scimitar.

Tom took a moment to study them, the eleven boys clustered around his front deck. They looked at him, keen and expectant. He had feared that it was going to take them some time to get back into the swing of things, but now it was as though leave had never happened. Tanned and lean, they shared the flint in their gaze that he had just seen in Henry and Clive. 'Lads, you all know the plan. I just want to say the usual stuff really. Nothing revolutionary, just me teaching you, as ever, how to suck eggs. Just watch your arcs, that's all. Watch your arcs, and watch the ground. It's nothing we haven't done a thousand times before. Just remember how we moved and operated in Shah Kalay, and we'll be fine.' He turned to Jessie. 'When we get into those alleyways, you're my eyes and ears. Anything at all you don't like just let me know. If necessary we can always break out into the desert, OK?'

Jessie replied breezily, 'Hey, boss, what's not to like, threading a fifty-year-old vehicle through a medium-density minefield? I'm just waiting for the insurance payout for my legs so I can get me a Lambo.'

The boys laughed, and Tom continued: 'Just three days, lads. Three days. I wish I could say it wasn't going to kick off, but we all know it's going to. Just keep it calm out there, OK? I know you will, but it's never worth forgetting that. I'll see you all tonight. Christ, I don't know why I'm doing this really, but it never hurts. Take care on the drive up and I'll see you in Jekyll. You can crack on now. Lecture over.'

They split up and mounted their wagons. Tom, Dusty and Davenport strapped on their headphones and did some final checks in the turret. The CO came down the line and shook the hand of every vehicle commander, and then at 1200 on the dot the long column, twenty vehicles crammed with soldiers and kit, started out of the gate, snaking its slow course up Route Glasgow.

By the evening they were set in their positions for the next morning. Jekyll was packed full, the infantry there clearly resentful of the newcomers invading their home. It was a ramshackle base with no comforts. A stream ran through the middle of it, used for washing and bathing. The base was on the fringe of the green zone. Only four hundred metres north was the first objective, Fade Out, centred around an area known as the Farad gardens. This was apparently where the old governor of Loy Kabir's house had been, and the area was densely planted, featuring cypress trees that rose fifteen metres in the air, far higher than the normal scrub of the green zone. Pilgrim had had contacts from the gardens all tour. In the late-afternoon sun the gardens looked like a lush oasis from Jekyll, and Tom, watching from a sangar with Trueman, was intrigued about what would be there. The walls around it, he could see through his binoculars, were studded with holes from mortars and strafing runs from hel-icopters and A-10s.

At 1800 the barrage began. The CO wanted to scare the Taliban away and had ordered a massive show of force. There was a prominent hill to the north, three kilometres from the town and visible for miles around. It was barren, completely empty. On cue the guns from Newcastle and mortars from Jekyll started a five-minute bombardment. Shells crashed down on the hill, the flashes of the explosions visible amid huge plumes of dust, *thumps* reverberating back down the wadi. The guns fell silent, and a minute later their battered ears picked up a rumbling from the south, and then up the valley, right on cue, streaked two American F-16s, flying brazenly low, shooting up the wadi, flinging out flares as they went and then at the end of the town pulling up and barrel-rolling into the darkening sky, before wheeling around to do their run again.

The boys on the ramparts of Jekyll whooped and cheered, holding up their cameras in delight as the jets switched on their afterburners to break the sound barrier over them. Trueman looked at Tom and said, 'That will have sent the fear of God through 'em. Talibs should run a mile after that little lot.' Tom was about to agree but then remembered Castlemartin back in the summer, when he had said the same thing to Trueman after a similar display and the sergeant had poured cold water on his overconfidence. Tom knew deep down that no Talib was going to be cowed by the display, that all the jets in the world weren't going to stop IEDs and shoot and scoots. He was going to remind Trueman of what he had said but checked himself at the last minute. He didn't want to appear a smart arse. He just nodded and said, 'Too right. That'll show them we're not mucking about.'

They climbed down from the sangar and walked through the base to the wagons. All around was quiet, loaded, battle prep. Soldiers fiddled nervously with their rifles, endlessly cleaning them in a well-worn ritual. Some read, sitting against the walls of the compound in the space where they would sleep that night. The CO was walking around, talking to the boys and getting an easy smile from everyone he talked to. He would cadge a cigarette from a young private soldier and then the next moment earnestly quiz a grizzled corporal about what he thought about the op and its chances of success. He called all the platoon and troop leaders to him, and Tom, Clive and Henry, the Vixen callsign OMLT officers and the three Pilgrim platoon commanders gathered around him at the back of an ISO container.

He looked at them fondly, like a father about to tell his sons how to behave at a party. 'Chaps, game face on.' He gestured behind him to the men scattered all around the compound. 'These boys'll be looking to you for the next few days. Keep smiling, keep calm and keep thinking. If you get into trouble just call us for help. I'll be right behind you with Tac, and we can get you all manner of things to come and help. I will be on your shoulder from here until Cocked Pistol. You know as well as I do it's going to go noisy from the off. I'm not going to treat you like imbeciles.

'You know,' he said, stepping outside his tough shell, 'when I look at you I think back to when I was your age. What you boys have done for the last few months has been way beyond anything I did as a young lieutenant. When I joined, in the early 90s, the most action I could hope for was a good old-fashioned riot in Ulster. Which was good, but it wasn't daily warfighting, like you've done. But you lot? You volunteered knowing full well you were going to get to sandy places. And so you're different from me. And I just want you to know that I admire you hugely. You won't realize the enormity of what has happened to you out here until you get back, but let me assure you what you are doing now is years, and I mean years, beyond what anyone your age, even my age, back home could ever do. Just remember that. I take my hat off to you.' As they all seemed to puff out their chests and carry themselves a little bit straighter he put back on his spartan shell. 'But that doesn't mean I'm going to let you off this op. I will drive you into the ground if I have to. We must make this succeed. But then, soon, we'll all get to go home, and we can forget all about these charming environs.' They laughed, and he sent them away. 'Go to your lads. I'll see you tomorrow.'

The CO went back to the Jekyll ops room and the rest of

them returned to their men. Tom hung around the wagons with the boys until it was pitch black, and then they crawled into their crew shelters at the sides of the wagons and went to sleep.

The sun was high in the sky, almost at its apex. Tom looked down at his shadow, tiny and barely spreading beyond his shoes. He was standing beside the wagon, spent 30 mil shells scattered over the front deck. He swigged from a water bottle, took off his helmet and poured some over his forehead. Dusty was in the turret. To the north all was silent; the advance had stalled since the early success of taking Fade Out in the morning.

It had been a two-hour contact to take the gardens, but they had done it after the Scimitars had pummelled its walls from the fields while the infantry stole up along hedgerows and broke through with mousehole charges. Tom and Jessie had surged up to follow them, crashing through a gap in the wall and helping out in the close-quarters fighting inside. Rounds had whacked off the wagon as they stormed through the breach, Tom and Dusty stuck firmly inside the turret knowing that if they put their heads out they'd be taken off.

Tom directed Dusty onto targets less than a hundred metres away in the rich green surroundings of the gardens. When he saw the infantry get close to enemy positions he stopped firing as they went through the bushes and ditches with grenades and bayonets until the position was declared clear at 0830. The infantry recocked, the ANA now taking the lead as Pilgrim reorganized themselves. Two hours later Pilgrim headed off again, leaving a section as security for the gardens.

It had been a blunt use of the wagons, as brutal as it had been unorthodox. The Taliban were used to the Scimitars being long-range sniping platforms, but in the gardens they had been used as battering rams. Now though the CO held them in the rear while the road was cleared up through the town to Double Take. Occasionally a contact broke out, but then died down again almost as soon as it started, as the Taliban sniped from the green zone at the REST searching the road for IEDs. Progress was painfully slow. They were finding a lot of devices. At times the road was so narrow they couldn't mark and avoid, and the ATO had to go forward to blow them in place.

Frustration seeped into everyone. They knew the infantry could easily find a route over the compound walls to get to the objectives, but there was no point them doing so unless they had a secure route along which they could be resupplied and get casevacs out. They were tied to Route Glasgow, as the REST made its painstaking, nervy way northward. By evening they were still four hundred metres short of Double Take and couldn't even see it amid the web of compounds. The CO came over the net. Tom could hear the disappointment behind his voice, even though he tried to sound upbeat. 'Charlie Charlie One, Minuteman Zero Alpha. All callsigns to go firm in their current positions tonight. Pilgrim Zero Alpha, Vixen Three Zero Alpha, Tomahawk Zero Alpha acknowledge over.'

For the next thirty minutes the net rang with acknowledgements and orders as commanders all along the route prepared to guard their positions for the night. Another jet was ordered in, again filling the valley with its roar and barrel-rolling its way up to the stars, but the boys watched it with indifference this time. The day had been a stalemate at best. They had lost all momentum, and now that they knew the extent of the IED seeding to the north, each of the three hundred stomachs north of Jekyll felt empty that evening.

As the dusk descended, the gardens started to feel chilly and gained a strange, ghostly air that spooked the boys. None of them wanted to leave the safety of the wagons, as though fearing some kind of evil spirit. None of them slept well that night, their imaginations fearing what would happen if they lost consciousness.

The next day progress was better, as the CO decided to sacrifice security for momentum. The REST remained on Route Glasgow, but he ordered the infantry from the route and they headed over the open fields for Double Take, which they found unoccupied but riddled with devices. There were no locals in the area; there had been none since the operation began. Three Troop were now called up to help with the push north to Round House. They drove away from the gardens, glad to be leaving the eerie shadows.

As they moved onto Route Glasgow and drove up it, Tom realized how draining the day before must have been for the search team. The route was impossibly narrow at times, and he counted eight craters where devices had had to be blown. Given how much time this normally took, it was amazing they had made the progress that they had. In the north there was a contact going on as a sniper harassed some ANA callsigns, but in general all was quiet. Again it was a clear and beautiful day, and Tom felt excited. He knew how potent the wagons were and how scared the Taliban were of them, and he felt like a prizefighter walking out into the ring.

They came to where the CO had broken away from the route, the place marked by one of the Mastiffs, and Tom could see the REST still sweeping away with their Vallons up the road. They turned off and drove over the fields, new crops ankle-high and bright, vivid green, and picked their way towards Double Take. Tom took his rifle out of his side bin, dismounted and, leaving Trueman in charge, walked up the safe lane marked with yellow spray-paint into the compound.

BG Tac were in a corner of the compound. The FAC was on the net to an Apache high above, the RSM was talking to Newcastle about resupply that evening, and Jules, looking up from a map, beckoned him over. He had taken off his helmet and Tom could see how tired he was. Tom went to him, making sure he stayed in the safe lane, a mere two metres wide and parallel to the wall. All around lads were sweeping with Vallons and extending the area of the safe zone in the compound. Looking over the wall Tom could see the REST emerge from the cluster of compounds around Glasgow and push towards them. This was good. Once the search team got here they would be balanced and could push on. Jules pointed out Round House to Tom. 'There you go, Tommy. Got it? Large compound. Orange door.'

'Seen. Looks nice.' Tom couldn't miss it. On a low rise, the compound dominated the landscape. It was in open fields, with other compounds a hundred, two hundred metres away from it. The route there would be easier; at least they wouldn't be tied to Glasgow.

The CO said, 'I want you in intimate support of Vixen. Just like you did at Shah Kalay. Pilgrim are knackered so I'm going to use Vixen and Frenchie for this one, with Pilgrim as rear security. I'll be with you all the way. I want us in there by tonight. Now where's that search team?' He looked over to the south. The REST were only two hundred metres away. 'Good. All going OK. Right, Jules, what I want now is—'

An explosion threw them against the compound wall. Tom hit his head and blacked out for a couple of seconds. Ten metres away dust and smoke flew into the sky, and a pile of straw was vaporized around them. 'Contact explosion, contact explosion!' came a scream from nearby as Tom, Jules and the CO picked themselves up, checking themselves for wounds. They had none, but the blood pounded in Tom's head. The CO made to run over but was held back by Jules. 'No, Colonel, stay here, stay here. Stick to the cleared area.'

Through the dust as it settled and as he struggled out of his concussion Tom saw what was happening. Two bodies lay surrounded by people tending to them. He could see blood flowing freely from the stump of a leg, while the other casualty seemed to have lost his entire face. Someone was screaming, a sickly, high-pitched shriek that cut through the smoke and dust. The three of them picked their way along the safe lane back to the radio at Tac. Jules got on to BG Main in Newcastle and, as if completely disconnected from the explosion, organized the casevac. Tom, not sure where he should be with the safe lane blocked, stayed next to him in a kind of trance.

He watched with a detached gaze as the casualties were put onto stretchers. The one who had had his leg blown off he recognized as a sergeant from the infantry who was friendly with Trueman. He had lost his leg at the knee, and the bone blinked out of the stump beneath the tourniquet wrapped tight around his thigh. He was white with shock and his teeth were chattering as he was carried out of the compound to an HLS being cleared for the MERT. The other stretcher had a tarpaulin over it, which fell away from one side to reveal a naked and bloody arm covered in tattoos.

The MERT soon arrived, landing outside the compound, its downdraught throwing up bits of straw. Tracer came over their heads as the Taliban fired at the Chinook. The stretcher party ran on to the heli, dropped off the casualties, and the Chinook lifted away again, sending more straw into the air as though it was a ticker-tape parade for the dead boy. As it disappeared down the valley, the contact continued. Tom climbed a ladder on to a roof to join some of the infantry, and lay alongside them firing with his rifle. A few metres down from him one of them was setting up a Javelin. Once it was ready he scanned the horizon.

His platoon commander shouted across, 'You on, Kez?'

'Yeah, boss. Two gunmen in the treeline. Three metres apart from each other. I've got 'em clear as day.'

'Then Jav 'em. Jav 'em.'

'Roger. Firing now.' He pulled the trigger and the rocket popped out, its motors fired and it flew high into the sky before crashing down into the treeline with a sharp bang. Some of the boys on the roof cheered; others kept firing until the platoon commander told them to stop. Tom left the roof, jumped down into the compound and almost landed on Tac.

The CO turned to Tom and said calmly, as though the last thirty minutes hadn't happened, 'Right, Tom boy; back to your wagons. We move out of here in twenty minutes. I want to take Round House by nightfall.'

'No dramas, Colonel.' The safe lane back to the door was clear again, and so Tom left the compound. He passed the crater from the explosion and noticed dried blood splattered over the wall. In a corner one of the infantry was crying; the others just looked exhausted. They still had to clear the rest of the compound, and were doing so nervously and slowly. They had found four devices already, each now marked with red spray-paint and fenced off with tape. Tom wanted to get out of the compound as quickly as possible and ran back through the field to the wagons. GV looked down from his turret and said, 'Fuckin' shit, boss, eh?'

'Too right, GV.'

'We'll fuck 'em up proper when we go up. Those Talib chippy cunts gonna pay.'

'Yeah. Yeah. They're going to pay.'

He hopped on to each of the wagons to brief the crews, and when he jumped back into his own Dusty looked at him. 'Fuck me, boss, what the hell happened in there? You OK? You look pretty spaced.'

'I'm OK, Stardust, I'm OK. Banged my head, that's all. No one knows what happened. No one knows. They think one of them stepped outside the safe lane. Either that or the safe lane hadn't been swept properly. I just don't know.'

'Fuck. And now?'

'We take Round House.' Tom clenched his teeth. 'And we destroy them.'

Dusty patted the back of the 30 mil. 'We like the sound of that.'

Twenty minutes later they set off. The REST had linked up with them now, and so the engineer tractors were able to start work on the new PB. The Pilgrim callsigns stayed put, and now the ANA company took the lead, with Frenchie's squadron in reserve. Three Troop led the advance over the fields, and immediately another contact started from the cluster of compounds around Round House. The Apache had been called away off station, so they had no air support. The Scimitars picked out targets and poured fire onto them which the ANA used as cover to work through ditches and get closer. Tom's turret was soon filled with cordite as he and Dusty laid down round after round. Often they fired just for the sake of firing; it was impossible to see anything of their targets other than muzzle flashes.

Tom was lost in the contact, and his concussion meant that he only caught brief moments of the afternoon. Two hundred metres before the objective there was a lull, and

Tom saw BG Tac in a ditch, the CO and Jules having a face-to-face with Frenchie. Jules again called him over. Tom left the turret, ran across and slithered into the ditch next to them, finding himself up to his thighs in filthy water. They all looked at him and smiled. Frenchie punched him on the shoulder. 'You OK, Tom? Quite an afternoon!' He was smoking, serenity personified.

'Yeah. Yeah.' Tom couldn't help grinning back. 'It's a hell of a day.'

Over their heads came an RPG, quickly followed by another, which both smacked harmlessly into a compound wall fifty metres behind them. Above the ditch Dusty's 30 mil barked back. The contact was on again. The CO crawled up to the lip of the ditch to get eyes on and clicked his fingers for the FOO, who gulped and then squirmed up next to him. Tom, Frenchie and Jules stayed at the bottom of the ditch, and Frenchie offered his cigarette to Tom, who took it gratefully and drew three long drags. Above them he could hear the FOO jabbering to the CO.

'Yeah, I've got them. I've got them, I think. Fire coming from the base of that white-painted tree.' He called the mortars at Jekyll. 'Hello Pilgrim Five Five, this is Witchcraft One Two. Fire mission. Over.'

Next to them in the ditch was the CO's interpreter, ridiculous in a Liverpool football shirt underneath his body armour and wearing a pair of aviator sunglasses that made him look like Hunter S. Thompson. He was listening to his ICOM scanner, and Tom could hear the chatter from the Taliban on it, excited at some points, calm and businesslike at others. 'What are they saying?'

The terp looked up, smiling. 'Nothing much at the moment. One of them just boasted about firing the RPG, saying he killed two of us with it.'

'Bollocks they did. Christ these guys are jokers.' Jules laughed. Five sharp cracks flew over their heads, and the CO and the FOO quickly ducked down into the ditch again.

'Bloody hell, someone's angry up there. That's an RPK,' said the CO with an almost detached amusement. They put their heads up again over the lip and continued the fire mission. Three large *crumps* came as the mortar rounds hit. The firing stopped.

The ICOM came alive, and they all looked to the terp again. 'They're asking Rashid if he's OK.' Another voice. 'Yes, he says he's OK. He's laughing and saying, "The idiots are firing at the white tree a hundred metres to my left."' The interpreter was interrupted by more firing. A round pinged off the Scimitar above them and whistled into the sky.

The FOO looked delighted. 'Well, is he now? What a good lad, helping us out. Hello Pilgrim Five Five, Witchcraft One Two. Correction. Left one hundred.' He waited for their read back, and then said gleefully, 'Three rounds, fire for effect. Out.' Again the mortars tore into the treeline. They all looked at the terp.

'They're asking for Rashid again.'

'And?'

'No reply. I think you got him.'

Frenchie reached into a pouch, took out another cigarette and lit it. 'What a legend. Bringing the rain onto his own position. With enemies like that, who needs friends?' They all laughed, long and loud.

The advance continued. In a blur the next two hours disappeared, and then suddenly, in the late afternoon, they found themselves in Round House. It was a collection of several compounds all deserted earlier that day. The last embers of a fire burned in the middle of one of them, but apart from that it was as though no one had ever lived there.

The CO briefed them over the radio. Even after two days' solid fighting his voice sounded fresh and keen. His instructions were simple: at dawn they would push on to Fast Pace; Tom was to hold his Scimitars in Round House until the contact started and then bring them forward to help out. They were to be in Cocked Pistol by evening. Meanwhile Tac and Frenchie's company were in the northernmost compound with the ANA company. Tom and Jessie's wagons were in a compound with a platoon from Pilgrim which had come up, and Trueman and Thompson's Scimitars were to go to another one. As they split that evening Tom walked with Trueman over to his wagon as O'Shea gunned the engine, anxious to get to the new compound and sleep.

They shook hands, and Trueman climbed on board to get into the turret.

'Not long now, boss. Sleep well; see you in the morning. You gonna be all right without me? Don't let the bedbugs bite.'

'Course I'm going to be all right. You're not that good, you know.'

'Yeah, I am. Without me, boss, you're like a car without an engine.' His teeth flashed through his dry lips, his heavy stubble darkened with oil and cordite.

Tom wondered how he would ever manage without him but shot back, 'I don't think so. You're more like the fluffy pair of dice hanging from the mirror. I mean, quite good banter but pretty superfluous really.'

'Fighting talk! Nah, boss, I'm the engine, mirrors and the driver. You're the annoying kid in the back asking if we're there yet.'

'Ha! OK, OK, you got me. See you in the morning.'

Trueman changed his tone. 'Yeah. Shall do. We're going to be all right, boss.' He buttoned on his helmet, gave a final smile and then drove off with Thompson behind him, leaving Tom outside the compound waving after them.

Tom and Jessie made sure their wagons were good to go for the morning and then started to relax. There was nothing much to do after scoff and putting up the crew shelters, so Jessie organized a left-handed throwing competition in the compound to pass the time. Soaking with sweat, Tom took off his body armour, sat on his turret and watched them as they played it, feeling happy as the sky turned red and a warm breeze fluttered and dried out his T-shirt. He took out a few blueys from his side bin and started to write a letter to Constance. He wanted to sum up what he was feeling. He sat for half an hour writing away, and when it got dark he wound it up.

At eight, just as night was about to envelop the town, Sergeant Williams and his Mastiffs came up the newly cleared Route Glasgow to resupply them and dropped off some 30 mil shells, gimpy link and a few jerrycans of water. As he was leaving Tom opened the back door of his Mastiff. 'Sorry, Sergeant, are you going back to Newcastle now?'

'Yes, sir. We're dropping some stuff off with Freddie, but then we're going down and ferrying stuff back up all through the night. Gonna be a long one.' He looked absolutely broken. The Mastiffs had been on the move all operation, carrying supplies and people up and down Glasgow. He hadn't had a wink of sleep.

Tom held out the letter. 'Can you pop this in the postbag when you get there? It's for my ma.'

Williams looked at him kindly, took it and put it carefully into his thigh pocket. The oldest of the sergeants, while he lacked Trueman's spark and charisma, he was a steady, avuncular figure. 'Sure thing, sir. No problems. I'll make sure it gets in there.'

'Thanks, really appreciated.'

'No dramas. We've got to go. No rest for the wicked.'

'Safe journey.' Tom shut the door and the four Mastiffs rolled away, their headlights flicking and bumping over the fields. Tom went back inside the compound and found Dusty and Davenport next to the crew shelter. They got inside, wormed into their sleeping bags and within a minute had all passed out.

Do not forget me.

Do not forget me.

Please don't forget me.

Tom and Jessie's wagons pulled out of Round House and screamed up the track in a race to Fast Pace. Two hundred metres to the right were Trueman and Thompson, tearing over the fields, flinging up sand behind them. The sun in the east threw a golden halo around the wagons as the light bounced off the dust around them, and the sky above streaked with orange and purple cirrus as the day opened. Trueman raised his arm in salute to Tom as they charged north across the fields together. Tom felt adrenaline surge through him. Ahead, even above the roar of the engine, he could hear the beat of machine-gun fire as Vixen engaged the Taliban.

Tom leaned over the sights and bent his knees to the jolts and rhythmic rocking of the wagon. 'Stardust, you ready?'

Inside the turret Dusty traversed the Rarden from left to right. 'Ready as I'll ever be, boss. In it to win it. This is going to go large.'

'Too right. When we get there, and I get you on, I want six rounds automatic at the first target we get. Nothing like a dose of 30 mil to wake these fuckers up.' The firing sounded closer now and Tom tightened the chinstrap on his helmet. 'Right, Dav, down you get.'

'OK, boss,' replied Davenport, who lowered his seat and drove using his periscope.

'I've got you. Keep going, keep going.'

They rounded a compound and there ahead of them was Fast Pace. Tom could see ANA around its southern side preparing to assault and muzzle flashes beyond it. He felt a fizz above his head and ducked down into the turret.

'Right, that's contact, that's contact. Dav, stop there, stop there.' The wagon halted abruptly, and twenty metres to his left Jessie's did the same. 'Dusty, we're in business. Traverse left, traverse left, steady, on. Base of tree, muzzle flash.' Every movement he did now was automatic; all fear had been swept away by the action.

'On. I got him, boss. I see him. Base of tree. Lasing. Six fifty.'

Tom flicked the switch at the back of the Rarden to automatic. 'Loaded fire. Six rounds automatic. Fuck him up.'

'Firing now,' came Dusty through the intercom, sounding a thousand miles away even though his and Tom's arms were touching. Through the sight Tom watched the six rounds hammer into the treeline where he had seen the muzzle flash. He slammed six more rounds into the feed tray, scraping the skin from his knuckles as he did so. 'And again, Dusty. Loaded fire.'

'And again, boss. Firing now.' Again six rounds ploughed into the trees.

Tom put his head out of the turret. 'Target stopped. Well done, Stardust. We got him, we got him. Right, Dav, let's push up.' They drove up to the south of Fast Pace. Inside the compound he could hear grenades but he felt safe, as though what was going on inside was a different war, self-contained and miles away.

Frenchie and Brennan were talking in the shelter of one of the compound walls, and next to them was an ANA soldier who had had a finger shot off. He was screaming and thrashing about as the medics tried to restrain him.

Eventually four of them pinned his limbs to the stretcher; one stabbed him with morphine, and the screaming died down. Tom jumped down and sprinted over to them. He crouched next to Frenchie, who looked at him proudly. 'Hey there, John Wayne. That was some gun show you gave us there. Nice one. You get him?'

'Yeah, we got him,' Tom replied, getting his breath back. The ANA soldier on the stretcher was now just gurgling.

Frenchie glanced at him briefly. 'Don't worry about him. He's going to be all right. Big girl's blouse. It's just his pinkie. Doesn't even need a MERT. What I need from you, Tommy, is more important.' He pointed over to the east, to the ridge that skirted the town. 'CO wants you up there. I agree with him. Get up there, and you can give cover for the entire rest of the day. Four Scimitars on that will dominate the town and give us an easy run-in all the way to Cocked Pistol. You got me?'

'Yeah, I got you.' Tom couldn't help feeling relieved to get out of the green zone with its unseen threats and to spend the rest of the op in the open. 'No dramas. When does he want me there?'

'About ten minutes ago. As soon as you can. Schnell machen.' Inside Fast Pace two more grenades exploded and someone started screaming.

Next to them a sniper shot into the treeline, shattering the comparative quiet outside the compound. Brennan asked him, 'You get him, Sammy?'

'Yep. Head shot. Pink mist.'

'Good lad.' Brennan looked at Tom and said cheerily, 'All right, sir? Barrel of laughs this, ain't it?'

Tom broke into a huge smile. He got up and ran back over to his wagon. By now Trueman and Thompson had joined up with them, and he briefed his three crew commanders in the lee of his wagon. Still in the background was the contact.

'Right, lads. Our ticket out of here. Higher want us on that ridge. We get there, and we can pummel the Talibs from the high ground so the infantry can sweep through. We'll go as four wagons, hell for leather, and get there asap. Jessie, me, Thommo, Freddie. As per. Jessie, you happy?'

Jessie put his head up over the front deck and scanned the ground. 'Yeah, boss, I reckon. I'll keep us on fields, but we'll have to do a bit of time on that track to break out into the open and get up on the ridge. You all right with me just going for it?'

All four then poked their heads up like nervous rabbits sniffing the air outside their warren. Tom looked at the ground in front of them. They could mostly stay on the fields, but they were going to be channelled for a bit of it. 'Yeah, sod it. We can't waste time with barma in this contact. And there haven't been any IEDs since Fade Out. I reckon they never thought we'd bother to come up this far.'

'Hell, boss, if you're happy I'm happy.' Jessie smiled. 'Risk it for a biscuit, yeah?'

Tom looked at Trueman, who winked at him and nodded. The plan was good.

They got up and went back into their turrets. When they were all in, Jessie looked back at Tom. Tom held his thumb out and then turned to Thompson and Trueman. Even as the final Talib was killed inside Fast Pace they started out for the ridge.

Jessie traced his way over the fields for four hundred metres until a ditch meant they had to break off onto the track. Tom winced as he realized they would be channelled more than he had thought. Jessie's wagon hesitated ahead of him but then turned onto the path and started up it. The sand was deep, and his tracks laid down two ruts that were easy for Davenport to follow. As long as they stayed in the ruts they would be all right. Tom could imagine the tension inside the lead wagon as it crossed the unknown ground.

Just when Jessie was about to break back out into a field there was a sharp crack and his wagon disappeared in a huge plume of dust. 'Contact IED, contact IED!' came Jessie over the net, shouting so loud that the radio almost cut out.

Fuck. Tom's heart dropped away, but when the dust settled the wagon was still there, apparently intact. Over the radio Jessie came again: 'Hello, Tomahawk Three Zero, Three Two. Contact IED but we're OK, OK. No casualties.' He sounded delirious, almost joyful. 'I don't know what happened. I don't know what happened. We've hit something but I don't think it went off properly. Over.'

For Tom everything started to move as though he was always meant to be here. Dusty's wide eyes looked at him. 'What are we going to do, boss? We're fucked here in the open.' Even as he said it he traversed the gun left so that it was pointing towards the north.

'I need to get up to Three Two to see the damage.'

'No, boss, don't go. Stay here, stay here.'

'No, I need to see it to work out how we're going to get the hell out of here. I need to get forward.' Before Dusty could stop him, Tom lifted himself out of the turret, picked up his rifle, stepped down on to the front deck, patted Davenport on the helmet as he was wriggling out of the driver's compartment to take a piss and then jumped down onto the track. He was pleased to be in the open and to feel his ears free of the sweaty headset. He ran down the path to Jessie's wagon, staying carefully in the track marks, and hopped on board, climbing up the back of the wagon. Jessie and GV looked shaken in the turret. 'You OK, boys? You OK? Are you sure you're OK? You promise me no injuries? You promise me you've checked all over?'

'Yeah. We're fine, boss, we're fine. I dunno what happened,' replied Jessie, pale even beneath the dust that stuck to his face.

Tom walked forward on to the deck and looked down into the crater to the front right of the wagon. The Scimitar's track had had two teeth ripped off, but the crater was small, only about a foot deep. In it Tom could see the top of a yellow container. 'Fucking hell! Your lucky day, lads. It's only partially blown.' He thought for a moment. 'Right. Here's the plan. You stay here; I'm going back to Three Zero and get on the net. There's no way we can continue to the ridge without the REST sweeping this track. We'll be here for a while yet. I reckon this is our battle over.'

Just as he spoke, a treeline erupted to the north and gunfire screamed towards them, bouncing off the turret. GV and Jessie dropped inside and immediately traversed towards the contact as Tom lay over the turret hatches, trying to stay as low as possible. He felt ridiculous, almost comically vulnerable. He reached down and hit Jessie on the helmet. 'Right, Jessie, I'm going back. You cover me!'

'No, boss, no! Stay until GV starts firing.' Tom sweated as GV seemed to take forever to find a target. He looked to his left and saw all three other wagons searching with their turrets, trying to sniff out where to aim. And then Dusty started firing. *Good lad.* Davenport was firing his rifle from behind the wagon.

Inside the turret beneath him GV shouted, 'I'm on, I'm on,' and Tom saw Jessie flick the selector switch to fire.

'Loaded fire. Firing now!' Tom's ears exploded as the gun spat a shell into the trees. Jessie looked up. 'Go, sir, Go! Go! We'll cover you. Get out of here!'

Tom jumped off the turret and crouched behind the Scimitar. He checked his rifle magazine, yanked his helmet strap tight and took three big breaths to prepare for the run back to Three Zero. Jessie and GV were now firing steadily, and Tom's head pounded with each shot. For a moment he seemed to step outside himself; he saw himself there, brain racing behind a calm face, eyes set, unblinking. A thrill leaped through him. This was awesome. He snapped back and looked down the track.

Davenport was firing his rifle with careful, aimed shots. He stopped, looked over at Tom and screamed, 'Come on, sir; I'll cover you.'

The seconds stretched into minutes; everything became slow motion. The world assumed an order and clarity that Tom hadn't felt before; everything he did, every muscle he moved, felt predetermined.

He shouted, 'I'm coming!' even though over the noise of the firing no one could hear him. He left the shelter of the Scimitar and set off down the track, his legs propelling him like wings. He glided along, borne by the adrenaline that swamped his head and soaked every sinew. He started to laugh, a child's laugh at the sheer sense of movement, like a five-year-old running down a hill delighting in his speed and his defiance of the bumps and clumps of grass that tried to trip him.

Closer and closer the wagon got. Davenport, now firing bursts into the trees, shouted, 'Come on, sir! Come on!'

Tom was almost there now, but then in front of him the ground opened up as though a zip had been drawn along it as a crease of bullets stitched a line. Instinctively he veered off the track rut that he had so far religiously kept to. The bullets stopped, but he was now outside his safe lane. He was still laughing. He was now just five metres from the Scimitar and felt as though he could almost touch Davenport. Just five more steps. And then *bang*.

There was a flash beneath him, a white, pure light, and he wanted to touch this light but felt sad that it vanished almost as soon as it had appeared. *Where had it come from?* A cloud of dust was thrown up at his feet and enveloped him, and a warm wind brushed his face. He liked this cloud – it felt like a blanket – but now he was out of the dust, and he seemed to have risen above the Scimitar, as though he was a bird. He thought how funny it was that he was flying away from the battle, how easy it had been all along to fly home. He would go home, and now here he was; he had left Afghan and was running up the path, and his father was at the gate, crouching and holding his arms out, like he had when Tom was learning to walk. 'Come on, Tommy! Come on, Tommy! You can do it!' Tom smiled. To his father's left he could see Constance, smiling over a basket of flowers that she had just picked. The sun bounced off the flowers and threw a rainbow over her face. He giggled. He left the path and swerved into a field, and was running through wildflowers, laughing with the joy of limbs moving faster than ever seemed possible. His tongue flicked his teeth and for some reason they felt sore and jagged.

The IED was a large one, intended to destroy one of the Scimitars. It had been dug in early that morning while it was twilight, just as Tom had been waking up. The pressure plate had been set on the left edge of the track, and Jesmond's wagon had missed it by a foot. It was a wonder that there was anything left of Tom at all. The explosion had ripped his legs off, the left one just below the hip, the right just above the knee. His rifle was flung up into his face to shatter his nose, while the blast had torn away his left cheek and some of his forehead to leave it a fleshy, bony pulp. His white left eye flashed huge against the scarlet mush, unenclosed now by its socket. His left arm was taken clean off at the shoulder, though his right one remained on, without even a bruise. His ribcage was kept intact by his body armour, but there was so much grit and dust shot through his abdomen that a thousand dark comets streaked incipient infection through him. His left buttock was taken off, and while he had kept his genitals, a jagged gash ran from them up to his navel. He was lifted four metres in the air, and his torso landed just a metre away from Davenport. One of his legs cartwheeled onto the front deck of the Scimitar, the other one remained by some strange inertia in the crater that the IED had punched into the earth.

Davenport was blown back by the blast, hurled against the Scimitar's tracks, the impact breaking three ribs and slicing his right bicep. Dazed, ears ringing, when he got up he saw Tom. When he saw that both Tom's legs were gone and with them the tourniquets in his trouser pockets, Davenport reached for his own and with a speed and calmness that he never thought he had yanked them both tight over Tom's spraying stumps until the flow of blood stopped to a trickle. He hadn't realized it would be so easy; the tourniquets worked just like they had said they would in the lessons at Bastion. The maw at the boss's shoulder was going to be harder to deal with, although the blood vessels there appeared to have been almost cauterized by the blast.

Dusty must have sent a sitrep on the radio, as Davenport soon saw Trueman's wagon race up the track, having leap-frogged Thompson's in the order of march, and screech to a halt behind theirs, dust flying forward off it as it braked. Davenport wondered if there were more IEDs in the area but realized that as long as they stayed in the track marks they should be all right. He just wanted to get the boss out. He looked at his own sleeve and with more curiosity than alarm noticed that it was soaked in blood from his own wound. But it was not as red as his trousers or his face, both of which had been spattered with Tom's arterial bleed as he had put the tourniquets on.

Davenport saw Trueman leap off his wagon and scramble over. Freddie stood over Tom for a tiny moment, his face collapsing at the sight before him, before reaching down, squeezing Davenport's shoulder and then kneeling by Tom. He looked at him as though pondering how to pick him up, like a father who doesn't know quite how to pick up a newborn baby from its mother's chest, and then with one huge heave he swooped him up, cradling him and putting him gently on the front deck of his own wagon. He jumped onto Dusty's turret.

For Trueman every minute of his long career had led to this moment. Rounds tearing the air around him, he dipped his head into the turret and spoke to Dusty in a calm, measured voice. 'Right, Dusty, you stay here. I'll give you Ellis to drive you. I'm taking the boss and Dav to an HLS to get them the fuck out of here. You and Jessie's wagon hold this track. When we've got the boss away we'll set about getting you guys back. Fucking pump that wood full of shit. Nothing survives in there, OK?'

'No probs, Sarge. How's the boss looking?' Dusty yelled back. Trueman was silent; his eyes said everything. Dusty nodded, slammed six rounds into the feed tray and screaming and swearing with every shot ploughed round after round into the wood until the turret was full of cordite and the tears he never realized he was crying mixed with sweat and black powder.

Trueman stepped from Dusty's back on to his own wagon and screamed to Ellis, 'Ell, Three Zero needs a driver. Get the fuck out and drive for Dusty. I'll be back for you once I've taken the boss back.'

Ellis gulped, looked out of the turret, saw the boss and Davenport on the front deck and felt a round wing past his head. White with fear, he gathered himself and cross-decked, picking his way over the two casualties and then on to the front wagon and finally slithering into Davenport's empty driver's compartment. He put on the ANR and over the intercom screamed, 'Fuck fuck fuck! Dusty! You there?'

'Yeah, mate.'

'Then keep going spastic! Fuck them up!'

'What do you think I'm fucking doing!' screamed back Dusty as rounds poured out of the Rarden, covering Trueman's casevac wagon, which was now picking its tortuous way back down the track towards the HLS, Trueman peering out and keeping the driver in the ruts, wincing at every bump, which he knew must be loosening Tom's tourniquets.

Davenport lay next to Tom on the front deck trying to shield him from the tracers that kept darting out of the wood to skim over their heads. He didn't feel scared and kept shouting to Tom over the noise of the engine, 'Stay here, sir. Stay here, sir. We're going to patch you up. We're going to patch you up.' He looked back up the track and saw the two front Scimitars firing pitiless salvos into the treeline. The long grass was now ablaze after dozens of HE shells had spat fire into it; smoke and dust kicked up by the Rardens shrouded the wagons in a fuzzy hue. Davenport leaned over Tom and felt for a pulse with two fingers jammed against his neck. It was terribly weak. He stroked Tom's head, spitting on his hands and trying to wash away a bit of the blood from his face.

Finally they were through the killing zone and reached the cover of the compounds, and after another three hundred metres arrived at a field behind Fast Pace mercifully away from the contact. A stretcher party prepared by Brennan lifted Tom off the wagon. One of the medics calmly asked Davenport to keep his knee pressed into Tom's shoulder as he deftly unwound a drip and started putting needles into him. Another shouted his pulse and breathing rates to Trueman, who was sending the MIST up through battle group.

Ten miles away this information was relayed over the roar of rotors to the MERT. This was their second call-out today and their second triple amputee in as many days. The doctor shouted to one of the nurses as he heard the report come over the radio, 'This bloke sounds fucked. With that pulse and that bleed he's not going to make it.' The nurse, a girl of eighteen with freckles and dimples in her cheeks looked at him and nodded through sad eyes.

Back on the ground Trueman kept looking into the sky and shouting, 'Where is this fucking MERT? Where the fuck is it?' while Davenport kept his knee pressed into Tom and shivered as he felt his kneecap scrape against what was left of the shoulder blade. He wiped Tom's brow with his sweat rag; someone had passed him a bottle of water, and he dabbed at the skin on the broken forehead as the medic tried desperately to bring Tom back from the brink. The medic had punched a line into his sternum to give fluids direct into his bone marrow as vein after vein at Tom's extremities shut down and closed off its flow.

'There you go, sir, there you go. We're going to get you home now,' Davenport said over and over, hoping that Tom could hear him and at the same time not feel any pain. Tom was making gurgling noises from his mouth, and the caught, laboured breaths from his exhausted lungs had now steadied into near-imperceptible rises and falls of his chest far too many seconds apart from each other.

Tom shook off his dream and woke up. He saw everyone around him and wondered why he was getting so much attention. *What had happened? Aren't we still in contact? Why are we back here and not on the track?* He looked up and fixed Davenport with his one-eyed gaze; *Dav would know.* 'Where are we, Dav? Where are the boys? How are the boys?'

'They're all right, sir. We're all OK, we're all OK. We're just going to get you back. You've had an accident but we're going to make you better.'

Tom grunted his thanks. He still didn't understand why they were making this fuss. His head hurt; he must have banged it. Had he tripped running back down the track and hit it on the front of the Scimitar? He could see Trueman above him now, who then pulled the pin on a smoke grenade and threw it. *Why is he doing that? He must be trying to mark an HLS or something. Ah yes.* He could see the helicopter now. The rotors pulsed in his ears and made the blue smoke whirl around him and then dilute into the brown dust whipped up by the downdraught. Tom liked the breeze. The heli flared thirty metres away from them, as though it were a surfboard cresting a wave, before gently touching its belly on the ground.

Again Davenport knelt over Tom and hugged him. Then Tom felt himself being lifted up and carried into the dark womb of the Chinook, where more people, wearing clean, undusty uniforms, crowded around and helped him. Davenport was with him on the heli as well; he must have been hurt too. With his right arm he pulled Davenport towards him; he couldn't move his left one.

'Are we going home, Dav?'

'Yes, sir, we're going home. You're going home to your mum, sir.'

A warm surge swept through Tom, and he just wanted to close his eyes and take a nap. He wanted to sleep in his own bed through, not a hospital one. He murmured quietly to Davenport, whose ear was now pressed against his lips to catch his faint whispers, 'Take me home, Dav. Take me home. I want to go home.' He squeezed his hand; Davenport squeezed it back.

Tom was back in the garden. He reached out to his father, whose arms folded around him and whisked him up off the ground with a throaty great laugh. Constance ruffled his hair. He was home.

Davenport squeezed his hand again. No return came.

Two minutes later, after a frenzied effort to resuscitate the pile of splayed and shattered meat and bone that the IED had created out of Tom, the emergency physician pronounced him dead.

The helicopter slowed its frantic pace.

THREE

They lined up in three ranks behind the church, immaculate in their service dress. Their drill boots were polished harder than they had ever been. The whole squadron was there; they had come down by bus from the barracks that morning. They had had their medals parade the day before and after today would all be going on leave. As the rest of the congregation went in the front in dribs and drabs the younger soldiers thrust out their chests to show off their first medals. Frenchie and Trueman were inside the church with Constance.

Brennan went down the ranks. His long rack of medals gleamed in the sunshine, and when he spoke to one of the boys it was not with parade-ground harshness but quietly and kindly. He came to Dusty and Dav. Davenport's arm was still in a sling, but he had struggled into his uniform for the service. Brennan looked down at them, both even shorter than he was. Dusty's eyes blazed defiance, as if willing tears to dare to come. Brennan smiled. 'You all right, boys? Stay strong for me in there. Stay strong for the boss.'

'Yeah. We're OK, sir.' Davenport spoke for both of them. Dusty found that no words came from his mouth. 'We'll be fine. Just, just I never been to a funeral before.'

Brennan nodded. 'I understand. They're shit, fellas. Not going to lie. People take them the wrong way. People stand up and try to speak as though it's a celebration of life. Which is bollocks. The whole thing's a fucking tragedy. So listen, if you get in there and you want to cry, then crack on. I ain't gonna stop you. In fact, I'll probably be joining you.' He broke off and looked at the ground. 'I'm proud of you boys. I'm proud of what you both did that day. My little lions. Remember. For as long as you live or as long as you're in this man's army, remember that day and use it. Use it so that one day you will be able to rescue other boys from being carried away in coffins. Remember Mr Chamberlain. He was one of the best.'

Dusty was still unable to speak, and scrunched up his freckles against crying. Davenport gulped but was still resolute. He managed to whisper back, 'We will, we will, sir.' Brennan walked on down the line and picked off pieces of fluff from forage caps or smoothed out creases in jackets. He finished and stood in front of them. He spoke firmly but not loudly.

'Well, guys, I wish we weren't here. But thank you. Thank you all for looking so smart. It means a lot. You look smarter than I've ever seen you. Mr Chamberlain would laugh to see you now like this, dolled up to the nines. Last time he saw you all you were the Dust Devils, up to your nuts in scrapping. And that was one hell of a scrap. I ain't seen many days like them ones. Not even the Iraq invasion. I know this ain't very profound, but I take comfort from knowing he was surrounded by us when he was taken. That's a proper soldier's death.

'I wish we weren't here, fellas. But since we are, I want you to sing your hearts out when you get in there. Raise that roof. Mr Chamberlain would want it that way. I've known a lot of guys die in my time. Most of you lot think I've been in uniform since the Crucifixion. Well it ain't quite like that, but I've seen a bit over the years. And I ain't seen many officers like Mr Chamberlain. So let's do him proud. Right, fall out.'

They turned to their right, marched three paces and then in a gaggle filed around to the front of the church and went in to take their seats.

The inside of the church was cool. In the front row was Constance. On one side of her was Sam, on the other Trueman. Trueman's wife was also in the church with their daughters, a few rows back. Just behind Constance sat the officers, Will with them. A Mentioned in Dispatches oak leaf gleamed on his Afghan medal ribbon; he had just been awarded it for his actions the previous summer in PB Mazeer. In the middle, in front of the altar, was the coffin. It was shrouded in a Union flag and had a simple bouquet of daffodils on it next to his Afghan medal, which had been inscribed '25186816 Lt TLR Chamberlain KD'. The coffin was weighed down with bags of sand to make it feel like there was a whole body inside; missing its limbs, his cadaver was far lighter than it should have been.

A quiet, nervous chatter filled the church as the last mourners arrived. Just as the padre, who was officiating with the local vicar, was about to shut the door he saw a taxi pull up at the gates to the churchyard, a girl jump out of it and in high heels run awkwardly up the path. She was wearing a simple black dress, with a long black woollen shawl and a black hat. The padre smiled a greeting and everyone watched her as she walked in.

Cassie was mortified to see there was only one space, almost at the front. A soldier with gold teeth and a completely bald head shuffled along to make room for her, and she sat next to him. She glanced around her, the doors now finally shut and a hush settling on the congregation as the service spiralled towards its start. She looked to Constance in the front row, who stared forward from behind her veil, stony-faced. She was watching the coffin and didn't seem able to take her eyes off it. And then she looked back and caught Cassie's eye. Cassie didn't know what to do, but Constance's face lit up and sparkled a smile at her. Cassie started to cry.

The service began. They sang 'Abide With Me' but Cassie wasn't able to manage any of it. The man next to her, who introduced himself as Adrian Brennan, let her hold his arm. Halfway through the service a good-looking, dapper officer went up to give the eulogy. She wondered who he might be.

Frenchie climbed the stairs of the pulpit and looked out over the congregation. He was almost directly above the coffin, and Tom's medal caught his eye and fixed him for a moment so that he had to catch his breath. He looked down at Constance, smiled weakly and nodded. He began.

'Good morning. My name is Chris Du Boulay or, as Tom would have called me, Frenchie. I was Tom's boss in the army. There are many things that one has to face up to doing as a soldier, but saying goodbye to your friends is definitely the hardest. It is the price you pay for an extraordinary privilege. You get to work with the finest people, and get to know them in a few short weeks and months better than people you have known for years, and you get to share with them in discovering life at its most fun, at its most savage, at its gentlest and at its most awful. I was able to know Tom for only one short year of his short life, but feel that in that year I came to be rewarded by an extraordinary proximity to the best officer I ever worked with and one of the finest men I have ever met.

'He was a model soldier, Tom. His soldiers loved him, and when I say loved I do not mean he was merely popular; I mean that they showed him a reverence that bordered on the religious. He never saw it – he was far too modest – but I saw it from the very start. The men who make up his beloved 3 Troop are a closed, fiercely tribal group of soldiers who it is almost impossible to break into, and yet I lost count of the number of times they came up to me and praised their leader behind his back. The most telling point, I think, came in the darkest days of Afghanistan, just a day before his death. In

324

the middle of a firefight I was talking to Lance Corporal Gatunakanivu and I asked him how he was doing. By that point we were two days into a very hard and fierce battle. Lance Corporal Gatunakanivu just looked at me as though I was mad, and said, "Why do I need to worry, boss? We have Mr Chamberlain. He gets us through everything." His soldiers loved him. And he loved them.

'But Tom must be allowed to speak for himself. There is little I can say that will augment the image you already have of him. A lot of you will not have known him in a military context at all. A lot will have shared schooldays with him, or holidays, or university days. A lot of you will simply not really know where you know him from; just that you do know him and you liked him and you wanted to come and honour his memory and say thank you to him for lightening up our lives.'

He took a piece of paper from his pocket. His fingers trembled, but as he smoothed out the folds of the letter he grew calmer. 'Constance, Tom's mother, wants me to read something to you. It is a letter that Tom wrote to her the evening before he was killed. It arrived at Tom's home ten days later. I have it here, and Constance has said I should read it out to you. It is all Tom's voice, and I will only add to it that this letter sums my friend up so much better than any words I could ever say. So I will just let him speak.'

Objective Round House (Basically a run-down compound, neither round, nor indeed much of a house if we're honest.)

Dear Mum,

This will get home after me, knowing how slow the post is, but I want to write now just to capture this one moment. It's a really good one and I thought that a letter would do it justice.

Ever since we got back from leave it's been pretty busy, and we're now two days into this operation up in the north of Loy Kabir. We started it at dawn yesterday, and it's been quite a lick. We've done a mile and a half and have got one mile to go tomorrow. It's been a long grind, without any sleep at all, but we're having a lull at the moment in a compound before we head off tomorrow to complete the mission. It's dusk and yet again we have an absolutely beautiful sunset. Spring is well under way and the evenings are getting warm again. I'm writing this in a T-shirt, which would have been madness a few weeks ago. The air is getting thicker and you can smell the blossom and flowers among the dust.

The wagons are parked up, and there's not really much to do. I'm watching the boys conducting a left-handed throwing competition. The rules are fairly basic: all you have to do is throw a rock as far as you can with your left hand. Clue's in the name, I suppose. Every time they play it I am in hysterics. I'm watching them now. They are squabbling, arguing, always with a smile or grin while doing so. They are the best of friends, and it has been my great fortune to have been accepted into their tight-knit gang. They are from all over the place, all ages, sharing neither background nor future, just the present. At the moment Jessie is chasing GV around and throwing stones at him for mocking his northern accent. Two guys who had not the slightest thing in common, from opposite sides of the globe, now like brothers who have known each other for years. And that is the really strange thing. You know I've never minded being an only child, and I don't, I really don't. I have always just enjoyed it being you and me, with Dad watching over us, as our little gang. But now I'm with these guys, it has been like giving me the chance to have brothers, for a tiny, finite, six-month period. And in a few weeks it will all be over and we'll be split up again. After the medals parade we'll go on leave, come back and then immediately move on to different jobs, and we'll never be together as a troop ever again. We'll see each other obviously, but never

*in this simple group of twelve. And so I know it's not going to last,
but it's still wonderful, this little family we have fostered over the tour.
In a kind of alternate reality way, this has become another kind of
home. The padre said something about that back at Christmas, and
now I know what he meant. I used to think out here that I'd never
been so far from home in my life, but now I realize that I never really
left it.*

*And while I'm on my soapbox, I think, looking at the lads now, I
might have come to a tiny, tiny, bit of a firm idea about the whole
question of what we're doing here. I think it is what I think, anyway.
Here goes.*

*This war out here has cost huge, huge sums, in treasure and blood.
We've spent a lot, we've lost a lot, we no doubt appear – and probably
are – arrogant beyond belief in the way we have assumed we can step
in, from our rock in the North Atlantic, and teach these guys how to
run themselves better. I cannot argue with that. But, but, but, and
this is a big but, one that studying the lads over the past months has
helped me to reach, there is one argument, however illogical, in our
favour.*

*You just have to bring the whole thing down to a street and liken
Britain to a bloke, a perfectly normal bloke, walking down it. He's a
bit rough, he's a bit cocky, but essentially he's a decent guy. Across the
street he sees a little old lady getting mugged. Despite himself and
against all logic, the man runs across the road (probably getting
knocked down by a car while doing so) to help her. And when he gets
there, the muggers start beating him up. After five minutes the fight
breaks up, and he leaves it bloody and bruised. The granny is more or
less OK, and probably doesn't even say so much as thank you (in fact
she most likely whacks him over the head with the handbag he's saved
for her). He crosses the road again and carries on down it.*

*The point is that, despite losing his own wallet, getting a black
eye, a broken nose and some cracked ribs, the man would do*

exactly the same thing the next time he saw it happening. And that is how to see Britain in all this. The kind of mug who sees another country in trouble and while probably completely misunderstanding or misreading the situation (Oh dear, Iraq) or underestimating the effort needed (Step forward, Afghanistan) nevertheless steps up and goes to help. This is the kind of mindset the lads have. They swear, they fight, they're not necessarily saints, but when it comes to it, they step forward every time. That is why I am so proud to know them.

And that character they have is exactly the same character that Britain as a whole has. When someone else is in trouble, no matter what the cost, we'll end up rolling up our sleeves and going to help out. And, and this I do know for sure, I'd be a citizen of a country like that a hundred times out of a hundred.

Well. There you go. Show this to me when I get home and I will probably laugh and deny I wrote any of it!

It's getting dark now, and I can't really see to write.

Only five more days on the ground and then we start getting ready to go back to Bastion to hand over to the lucky, lucky lads taking over. I never thought I'd say this, but a little bit of me is going to miss it out here. But I'm looking forward to coming home more than I could ever miss this place. I am so, so excited about the end of tour.

With all love, and don't worry – nearly there.

Tom x

Frenchie stopped reading and said nothing more. The seconds seemed to stretch into minutes. Then the vicar dragged the congregation out of their thoughts, and they stood up to sing the next hymn, 'Lord of the Dance'. Cassie was now feeling terrible. Memories came whirling around her, and the organ music drummed inside her head. She felt dizzy and nauseous, and she wanted a drink of water. Somehow she kept standing. Some of the soldiers were crying. Even the man next to her seemed to be choking back tears as he sang. They came to the penultimate verse.

> I danced on a Friday when the sky turned black;
> It's hard to dance with the devil on your back.
> They buried my body and they thought I'd gone;
> But I am the dance and I still go on.

Cassie swallowed down some bile that had risen from her stomach. She felt feverish and at the end of the hymn sat down exhausted. The service passed in a blur, and she was carried along in a kind of trance for the rest of the morning. Someone else seemed to be operating her limbs and directing her like a puppet on a stage. She walked out of the church behind the coffin; she walked to the grave, into which Tom was lowered by six soldiers, and then she was walking along the road to Tom's house for the wake.

None of it she could remember later in any detail. Tiny fragments of the morning stayed with her, but nothing else. She remembered very clearly Constance's hands when the first shovel of earth was thrown down on to Tom's coffin, snug in its grave, tighten and whiten around Frenchie's arm. She remembered a group of soldiers take themselves away from the graveside and stand in a circle, where they were led in prayer by the oldest-looking, who stood taller than the others. She was escorted to the wake by one of them, who introduced himself as Lance Corporal Miller. He dragged her towards reality, and she stepped out of her funk as she talked to him.

They didn't talk about Tom but concentrated on the weather and what Miller was going to do for his leave. He told her about a tattoo he was going to have, of a crusader knight, on his shoulder blade. When they got to the Old Mill a marquee had been put up in front of it, and there were waiters serving wine and plates of sandwiches. Cassie and Dusty gratefully fell upon them, and each drained a glass of wine in one without anyone else noticing. Then Cassie started to see things more clearly and was able to start remembering things. They were joined by another soldier, who introduced himself as Trooper Davenport. As they talked she realized these were the boys she had heard so much about, who had shared Tom's wagon with him. They didn't seem anything like Tom had painted them; they looked as though they couldn't hurt a fly. Both were so young.

The sandwiches did her good, although she continued to feel a deep sickness that she couldn't escape. All around were little groups like theirs, talking politely and, if they laughed, doing so in a qualified manner and quietly. She thought about how funny Tom would have found it, this peculiar study of manners. She saw a steady flow of people coming up to Constance. The bald man, Adrian, who had supported her through the church service, was talking to Constance and making her laugh. Cassie smiled. She went over and joined them, and she and Constance talked for ages.

The time came, and all the guests realized that they had better be on their way. As Cassie prepared to go she remembered the rose bush at the bottom of the garden which Tom would take her to when they visited his home from Cambridge. It was his favourite place in the garden, and she felt that she should see it once more. She walked out of the marquee and through the garden, and there, at the foot of a weeping willow hanging over a stream, was the rose bush. A soldier was there, and he looked up, startled that he had been discovered. He was not crying, but she could tell that she had disturbed him. He looked tough, this one, and had a wild, angry look in his eyes.

'Hello, sorry to disturb. It's just that Tom always liked this spot, and I thought I should come here.'

The soldier replied gruffly, as though unaccustomed to talking about his feelings: 'Yeah. He mentioned this place a lot when we were away. I thought I might be able to remember him better down here. His mum pointed the way.'

'How long have you been here?'

'Ten minutes or so, I think. Could have been an hour, I suppose. I simply don't know. Are you Miss Foskett?'

She was surprised. 'Yes. Yes, I am. How did you know? How did you know my name?'

'Tom – I mean Mr Chamberlain – used to talk about you a lot when we were away. Said you were beautiful, so it wasn't hard to spot you when you came into the church.'

She blushed and didn't know how to answer. They stood there, looking at the rose bush, neither of them knowing what to say next. He broke the deadlock. 'Sorry, I should have introduced myself. My name's—'

'Sergeant Trueman?'

Now he was surprised. 'Yeah. How d'you know that?'

She smiled. 'Tom used to talk about you a lot too. Said you were the rock that his troop was built on. So it wasn't that hard to guess when I saw you leading that group away after the burial.'

Now he blushed. 'What kind of stuff did he tell you about me? All the bad stuff, I suppose.'

'No. He didn't.'

'What did he say then?'

She didn't answer immediately. She looked again at the rose bush. The buds were thick now, just days away from bursting into flower. She saw their thick resin reflect the sun in tiny pinpricks. At the foot of the bush a few daffodils sagged down to the earth with drooping necks as if grazed by a plough. Almost silently she spoke. She still felt sick, and she felt her eyes welling up. 'He said that he couldn't have got through it without you. He said . . .'

'What?'

'He said you were like his older brother.'

They stood together as the stream behind the bush darted flashes of gold through its leaves.

The sun was out, and the last traces of spring had made way for summer. The leaves had settled into their greenness, less violent now than a few weeks ago and less fragile, and the Old Mill had eased into long days and warm, still Kent nights. Constance was downstairs in the kitchen. Sunlight streamed in through the windows, catching dust floating in its shafts. A vase of flowers was on the oak table, roses and lilies, and next to them was a bunch of wild flowers picked from the garden.

A photo of Tom stood on a side table as though it had always been there, in a tarnished silver frame. It was not a new frame; behind Tom's photo was a picture of Leonard as a young man. The photo was from just before Tom had come home on leave, taken of him as he sat on the front of his Scimitar eating a boil-in-the-bag. His hair was thick with dust; he was looking cheerfully at the camera, and his eyes sparkled. It had been taken by Dusty at the end of a long day's patrolling. The picture was in black and white, but somehow the brown and yellow tan on his skin from the sand still shone through.

Constance was humming to herself and brushing her hair when the phone rang. She hesitated for a moment and let it ring four or five times as though scared to pick it up and receive more bad news, even though she knew that no news now could ever really be terrible. She felt sometimes that there was nothing left to live for. Her hair, all her life a golden blonde, had lately started its descent into grey around her temples and at the top of her scalp. She was very thin, and her clothes seemed to hang off her. She picked the phone up. 'Hello?'

'Constance, hi. It's Frenchie,' came the reply, friendly and lively.

'Frenchie!' She perked up immediately. Ever since the funeral he had been a rock. 'How are you?'

'Well, very well indeed. In the big smoke, actually. I'm with Alex, off to watch the Test match. First day of the Lord's Test in an Ashes series. Can't get better than that. I just wanted to ring to say that I am, as ever, thinking of you, and Tom.'

Already her eyes were filmed with tears, and he could tell by her silence that she wanted him to continue. 'It's just that, back in December, Tom and I chatted about daydreams and how we passed the time. About what we used to think of to get through the day. I told him that for me all I could ever think about was this day, taking Alex to the cricket. I remember laughing with Tom that I thought it would probably be rained off.'

'And? It's a lovely day here.'

Frenchie chuckled. 'Here too. It's glorious.'

'How's Alex?'

'Hyperactive. I've shunted him off into a queue to get a book signed. I just wanted to ring you to let you know I'm thinking of you, and to say how lucky I feel to be with Alex.' He paused. 'And this makes me realize more than ever how lucky I am. How I don't want anything to happen to him.' He paused again. 'I'm sorry, Constance; you don't want to be hearing this.'

'No, no, Frenchie. No. It's great to hear. It's what I need to hear. Are you going to spoil him today? Please say yes.'

'Ha! I think so. We've got these great tickets, and we're going to this burger joint for lunch that's basically his favourite place in the world. But he doesn't know it yet. The thing is, Constance, when I talked to Tom about all this, I remember saying to him that this would signal the end of tour proper for me – when I would be able to draw a line under the whole thing. But the problem is, at that point we hadn't had anyone killed or really seriously injured yet. And when Tom was gone I realized that actually, try as I might, the tour will never go away. I'll always be stuck there, part of me.'

Frenchie now had tears in his own eyes and was willing Alex's queue to move slowly. He didn't want to be seen crying. Alex, inevitably, then chose that moment to turn round to look at him, excited about getting his book signed. Frenchie waved at him, somehow managing to blink away his tears and summon up an encouraging smile.

Constance's voice came back, calm and firm. 'No, Frenchie. You cannot think like this. What's done is done. You cannot chain yourself to the past. Of course you will remember Tom, but I promise you the pain will one day numb into a dull ache, and then might even go away entirely. Just look back and see a tiny bit of him in Alex, and he'll live on somehow.'

'And you?'

'Don't you worry about me. I always knew when we only had one child that I was going to be vulnerable to something like this. And now it's happened. I look to the future and, you know, I don't know what I see. Most of the time I think about how lonely I'm going to be.'

'But people will always be there.'

'I know, I know. But they're not there in the nights. They're not there in the early morning when even if he was still asleep I knew that the house was alive, waiting to hear him stumble down the stairs into the kitchen. No one's ever there when you're doing nothing; that's when you need them. But as I said, don't worry about me. Just look to your own.'

'You know I'll never forget you, Constance. Oh my God. Action stations. Alex has got his book signed. He's about to come back. I'd better go.'

'Go, go! Frenchie, go and have a great day, OK?'

'I will.'

'Just look to the sun, remember him and just carry on.'

'I will. I will.'

'Oh, one thing.'

'Yeah?'

'Thank you. Thank you very much. More than you could ever know.'

'No problem. My pleasure. No problem at all.'

'Bye.'

'Bye.'

'Bye.'

Constance put the phone down and finished brushing her hair. She picked up the bunch of flowers from the table and left the house. In the garden she found Lee, a local man who helped her with the garden once a week. He was almost hidden in a flower bed as he knelt down to mulch some roses.

'Lee, that's me off. Shouldn't be long.'

'Where you goin', Mrs Chamberlain?'

'Just to the churchyard.' She nodded down at the flowers. 'To give these to Tom.'

'Oh. Yeah, no probs. I'm here for another two hours at least so no hurry. Say hi to him for me, will ya?'

Constance smiled sadly. 'Of course, Lee. I shall do that.

Thank you. See you in a bit.' She turned to walk down the drive and on to the road towards the village, small and alone, moving with girlish sparrow-like steps.

The taxi pulled in at the top of the drive, and Cassie got out and paid the driver.

'Thanks. I'll ring you when I know when I want to go. I don't know when that'll be though.'

'No probs. Just buzz the office. Might be me that comes to get ya, might be one of the others.'

'Thanks.'

He drove off. Through the leaves and shrubs she could just see the house. She took some deep breaths and walked towards it. She came closer and remembered all the people crowding around outside after the funeral. There had been so much chatter then, so much forced cheerfulness, which had shrouded the house in a false veil of good feelings. Now it looked alone and vulnerable. She went up to the front door and again hesitated. She didn't know what on earth she was going to say.

A voice interrupted her thoughts. 'Morning. Can I help?' It was polite but had an undercurrent to it. She looked round and saw a young man standing in the middle of a flower bed. He was big and burly, and had a crew cut. He was quite intimidating, and Cassie didn't know how to reply at first. 'Um . . . er . . . I'm here to see Mrs Chamberlain.'

'Not in.' He knelt down, getting back to his work. He wasn't giving anything away.

'Do you think you might be able to tell me when she'll be back?'

He looked at her suspiciously, stood up and walked over to her slowly and deliberately. 'I might do. Depends who's asking.'

'What do you mean by that?' She was offended.

'Well, I mean just that. Depends who you are. If you're from the press, then you can jog on.'

She snapped back in a flash of anger, 'I'm not from the press. I'm not a journalist. I'm not here to terrorize Mrs Chamberlain. I have a very important message for her and I need to see her. I was a great friend of her son and I resent being spoken to like a bloody liar.'

He softened and looked embarrassed. 'Don't I recognize you? Weren't you at the funeral?'

'Yes. Yes, I was. I was Tom's girlfriend.'

'Oh. I'm sorry.' He looked genuinely contrite. 'It's just that, you know, we all want to protect Mrs Chamberlain now she's on her own. Been a few reporters around lately, that kind of thing. Want to talk to her about some kind of documentary about Afghanistan. Vultures. She doesn't want any part of it, but still they keep pestering her. It's just, well, you look a bit like they do. City girl and all.'

He said it with a twinkle in his eye and she laughed. 'No. No, I can promise you I'm not a journalist. I can't write for toffee, I'm afraid. Do you think Mrs Chamberlain will mind me waiting here? Is she going to be back soon?'

'Yeah, I reckon. Maybe only an hour probably. You can go and find her if you like. She's just gone to the graveyard to take some flowers to Tom.'

'No. I couldn't possibly. She'll want to be on her own.'

'Not necessarily. I go along with her now and again. She likes the company. Go on, go. It'll do her good. It'll give her someone else to remember with.'

'Are you sure?'

'Yeah. I'm sure. You know how to get to the church?'

'Yes. I remember from the funeral. Just left at the gate and about half a mile down the road.'

'That's the one. Should take you about ten minutes. She only left ten minutes ago herself. Go now and you'll catch her.'

'Thanks. Oh.' She held out her hand. 'I'm Cassie.'

He shook it. 'Nice to meet you, Cassie. I'm Lee, Mrs Chamberlain's gardener.'

'And bodyguard too, by the sound of things.'

He grinned. 'Yeah. You could say that. We're all looking out for her, that's all.'

'I understand. I think that's great. Tom would be grateful.'

'I hope so. He was a good man. Never knew him that well meself. But he was in the top year at school when I was small and was always nice to me.'

'Yes. He was nice to everybody. I'd best be off.'

'See you in a bit then.' But she was already walking back down the drive to the road.

As she walked she caught glimpses of the steeple through the hedgerows. Lazy, fluffy clouds hung in the sky, and some cows in a field watched her idly. With every step she lost her nervousness, and a glow came through her, spreading from the bottom of her back and reaching into her fingers. *Everything is going to be all right.*

Cassie lifted the latch of the mossy gate and walked into the churchyard. A rabbit started at her appearance and bolted down its hole beneath an old gravestone. Cassie paused, tugged up her jeans and ran a hand through her hair. She peered around the side of the church and saw Constance, who was standing at the foot of Tom's grave, staring down at the headstone. Cassie walked towards her as if in a dream. Everything now seemed to make sense. She came closer and noticed that, even just two months on, Tom's grave had started to blend in with the others. The turf was greener than that around it, and slightly raised, but the edges of the plot

338

were blurred, and soon the grave would look as if it had always been there. At the foot of the headstone was a bunch of blue wild flowers, and around it were some jam jars of other flowers: roses, tulips and a couple of poppies, their fragile, crêpe-paper petals waving slightly in the breeze.

Constance turned towards her and smiled, politely at first and then with delight. 'Cassie! What are you doing here? What a surprise!'

Cassie gulped. They hugged, and she kissed Constance on both cheeks. She felt tiny and frail in her arms. *Not just yet.* She lied: 'I was just passing through and thought I'd drop in. Lee said I would find you here.'

'Well, what a lovely surprise.' Constance looked down at the grave. 'Tom would be so thrilled that you came. I've just been chatting a bit to him and making sure he's looking smart. He always loved wild flowers.'

'They're lovely. I wish I'd brought some myself.'

'Don't be silly. It's just wonderful you're here.' She looked away and spoke as if Cassie wasn't there. 'Sometimes I wonder how he's doing, and I worry about him. But then I just come over here, where I know I'll always find him. And even in the rain, or in the wind, or even when it's night or a lovely day like today, it always feels as if he's next to me when I come here, and every time I look at the gravestone I feel him there, grinning cheekily and telling me not to worry.'

Cassie found herself crying. She couldn't find the strength to speak, and they stood there in silence. A cloud hid the sun for a moment, and when it reappeared she felt its rays on the back of her neck and saw their shadows flung over the grave. *Now is the time.*

In the evening the sun shot red over them, and in the turret Dusty traversed left to right, desperate to pick up any target. He had never felt so angry. The Scimitars were on the high ground giving overwatch. They had barma'd their way up in the afternoon. Cocked Pistol had been taken, and already the engineers' diggers were filling the Hesco walls, turning it into a new PB. It had fallen without much of a fight in the end, and now the battle group held the entire area. There was no jubilation; immediately it came over the net that the final objective had been cleared everyone realized how tired they were, and a heavy, leaden exhaustion came over them all.

The boys were sitting in the lee of the wagon. No one spoke. Jessie cried a single tear which cleared a line down his dusty cheek and hung on his jaw, refusing to fall off. Trueman stood over him. He didn't say anything.

In the turret were Dusty and O'Shea. Just as the sun dipped out of sight and evening started to sink into night, through the sight Dusty saw a pickup truck come to a halt outside a compound to the south. 'Fuck, we got something,' he shouted, and the others all stood up and looked back down the valley. Dusty watched the unfolding drama. From the compound two men came, supporting a third. Dusty started a running commentary. 'Three enemy conducting casevac. Looks like a wounded fighter. He's properly fucked. Black trousers. Looks like a white dish-dash wrapped around his stomach like a bandage. Lots of blood on it. Proper fucked.'

Trueman was on top of the turret now, scanning south with his binoculars. 'Got 'em, Stardust. Good spot. Clear as day. Keep watching, keep watching.'

O'Shea babbled excitedly in the turret. 'Can we engage? Can we engage? We've PID'd, clear as you like. We can just say we saw some weapons on them. Quickly, before they go.' He turned to Dusty. 'Come on, mate! Before they go!'

The fighters placed the wounded man in the back of the truck and went to get in the front. Dusty lined up the sights on them. 'Lasing. One two fifty. I've got them.' He flicked the gun to automatic and his finger stroked the trigger as he made some final, perfectionist tweaks to the elevation. He looked up to Trueman, who nodded, his face pitiless.

Again O'Shea jabbered: 'Come on, Dusty. Fuck 'em up. We've got 'em, we've got 'em. Waste them, waste them. For the boss. Do it for the boss!'

Dusty flicked the selector switch back to safe. The gun stayed silent. The pickup drove off. Tired and with a weary calm, he said quietly, 'No. No. The boss wouldn't have wanted it. He wouldn't have engaged. We don't do that stuff.'

GLOSSARY

10-liner. Document filled out upon the discovery of an **IED** or suspected device, consisting of ten serials such as location, time found, what kind of device it may be, to give the **REST** and the **ATO** the best possible information for when they come to investigate.

105. 105-millimetre calibre artillery piece with a range of up to eleven miles.

2ic. *Second in command.*

30 mil. 30-millimetre calibre ammunition for the **Rarden** cannon, the main armament of a **Scimitar**.

.50 cal. 0.5-inch calibre heavy machine gun. Fires bullets capable of tearing limbs off.

7.62 mm. The calibre of the bullets fired by the **GPMG**.

9-liner. Nine-serial document to be filled out to conduct a casualty evacuation by helicopter. Accompanied by a **MIST**.

A-10. US Air Force close air support plane, often called by troops to assist in a firefight. The rasp of its 30 mm cannon is very distinctive.

AH. *Attack helicopter.* Any helicopter, in Afghanistan typically an Apache, that provides fire support for ground troops. *See also* **Ugly**.

Ally. British army slang meaning 'cool'.

ANA. *Afghan National Army.*

Angel flight. Flight sent to pick up a fatality and take him or her back to Camp **Bastion**. Less urgent than a **Casevac**, it usually took place about six hours after a death.

ANP. *Afghan National Police*. The civil counterpart of the **ANA** and usually less well disciplined.

ANR. *Active noise reduction* headphones used in **CVR(T)**s which block out engine noise, allowing the wearer to listen to the radio better.

AO. *Area of operations*. The name given to the territory a group of soldiers is responsible for.

ATO. *Ammunition technical officer*. Bomb disposal expert whose task it is, once an **IED** is discovered by a **REST**, to collect DNA evidence from it and then either remove or destroy it. Probably the most dangerous job in the Afghan conflict; this was reflected in their shockingly high casualty rates.

Bar armour. A cage-like metal skirt fixed around a vehicle, intended to stop **RPG**s exploding on its skin and so prevent penetration.

Barma. The name given to the process of sweeping a vulnerable area, comprising four soldiers moving in concert with **Vallons**. Became a blanket term for any activity with a **Vallon**.

Bastion. Camp Bastion, the main UK base in Helmand and adjacent to the American Camp **Leatherneck**. Troops would arrive into Bastion by plane and typically spend a week there doing **RSOI** before deploying out to the bases in the rest of the province.

Battle group. A unit formed around an infantry battalion or armoured regiment (as in the case of the King's Dragoons) and commanded by a lieutenant colonel. The battalion/regiment also provides the HQ element of a battle group, which is typically furnished with three or four infantry companies or armoured squadrons, a battery of artillery, a troop of engineers and assorted other logistics, signals and medical personnel. In Afghanistan there were roughly eight hundred people in each battle group. The King's Dragoons battle group is called

BG(NE) – Battle Group North East – and is based in the fictional town of Loy Kabir.

Bergen. Army rucksack.

BFBS. *British Forces Broadcasting Service*. In Afghanistan in the **FOB**s and **PB**s there were televisions with a handful of channels provided by **BFBS**, usually screening BBC shows and high-profile sports matches.

BFPO. *British Forces Post Office*. The address for personnel on **Op Herrick** was BFPO 792.

BG Tac and **BG Main**. *Battle group tactical* is the commanding officer's team deployed with him when he is on the ground, comprising operations officer and others. *Battle group main* runs the operation from the rear in a **FOB**, making sure logistics and casualty evacuation are in order.

BGHQ. *Battle group headquarters*.

BGTI. *Battle group thermal imaging*. Thermal sight in the turret of the **Scimitar** that can detect body heat up to five kilometres away. It provides great night surveillance capability and accuracy for the **Rarden**.

Bleed out. For a casualty, normally a double or triple amputee, to die by catastrophic blood loss.

Bluey. Light-blue letter that can be sent to and from troops. Divided into three segments, it folds up and can be licked closed by gum strips around its edges. *See also* **E-bluey**.

Bod. Army slang for 'soldier', usually a private.

Brimstone. Callsign of the **REST**s.

BV. *Boiling vessel*. Electric kettle inside every **CVR(T)**, holding about two litres of water.

Casevac. *Casualty evacuation*. Used as both a noun and a verb.

Cat A/B/C. Casualty categories. Cat A is the most serious, meaning life-threatening injuries, through to Cat C, which means walking wounded.

CBA. *Combat body armour*. Flak jacket-style body armour, with a ceramic plate in front of the heart and a second one over the centre of the back. Replaced by the much better although much heavier **Osprey**. By 2009 the only personnel wearing **CBA** were **Scimitar** crews, as they could not manoeuvre in their cramped turrets with the more cumbersome **Osprey**.

CGS. *Chief of the general staff*. The commander of the British Army.

Chalk. A group of soldiers lined up and about to get on or off a helicopter or other transport.

Charlie Charlie One. A radio message directed not to one specific callsign but to every callsign operating on that **Net**.

Chinook. Twin-rotor helicopter, the workhorse of the UK helicopter fleet. Much loved by soldiers, it can carry supplies and/or up to thirty soldiers. Also used to carry a **MERT**. With the **GPMG** arguably the soldiers' favourite piece of equipment.

Chippy. Derogatory term for someone from a regiment which a soldier thinks is less professional than his own.

Civcas. *Civilian casualties*.

Civvie/civi/civvy. Different spellings of the abbreviation for *civilian*. 'Civvies' is also the nickname for civilian clothing.

Claymore. An anti-personnel mine placed to defend a position, comprising a box filled with ball bearings. When detonated it scatters the ball bearings out with lethal and staggeringly violent force.

Clip. To be 'in clip' means to be in a dreadful state. Used to describe someone particularly hungover, absolutely exhausted or very badly wounded.

Command wire. The means by which a command-wire **IED** (CWIED) is triggered, usually a couple of hundred metres long and buried in the ground, connecting the device to the site where it is detonated. A large part of any **Barma** was directed to finding command wires, which were often very shallow or covered by just a sprinkling of sand.

Comms. *Communications.*

Compound. The generic building found in rural Afghanistan. Built of mud and pebbles, and very often with no electricity or running water, a typical compound is about the size of a tennis court, with a high perimeter wall enclosing a cluster of small buildings used to house a family and its livestock.

Contact. A firefight, although troops could also have a 'contact explosion'. Used both as a verb and a noun.

Crow/crowbag. Novice, rookie. Typically applied to young officers and new recruits.

CSS. *Combat service support.* Another name for logistics. In an **Orders Group** the **CSS** section would be delivered not by an officer but by a sergeant, and would detail the **Casevac** and resupply plans.

CVR(T). *Combat vehicle reconnaissance (tracked).* A family of vehicles including the **Scimitar, Sultan**, Spartan, Samaritan and **Samson** which share the same chassis but have different top halves depending on what role they are designed for. Designed in the 1960s, many thought them obsolete, but they proved their worth time and again in Afghanistan, particularly the **Scimitar** with its intimidating and accurate **Rarden** cannon.

Cyalume. A 'glowstick' that when snapped provides a degree of fluorescent light, normally enough to read by. Lasting for about four hours, they performed a plethora of functions, from route marking at night to makeshift room lighting.

D & V. *Diarrhoea and vomiting.* A bout of mild dysentery that usually keeps a sufferer out of action and quarantined for a period of four to five days.

Daisy chain. A collection of **IED**s joined together to detonate at the same time when triggered. Normally placed along a compound wall. Not as nice as it sounds.

DC. *District centre.* The middle of a larger Afghan town, with its shops and bazaars.

Dicker. A name, first coined in Northern Ireland, for an enemy scout who reports on friendly forces' movements. Usually unarmed, they are very hard to spot and impossible to engage as to do so is a breach of rules of engagement.

Dish-dash. Colloquial name given interchangeably to the scarf used as a shawl-like headdress and the robe-like garment worn by Afghan males. When worn by British troops, the scarf was known as a shemagh.

DSO. *Distinguished Service Order*. A decoration awarded for outstanding command performance as opposed to an act of gallantry.

E-bluey. A subscription email service for British personnel. Emails were printed out in Afghanistan and then sent on to addressees.

ECM. *Electronic control measures*. Devices used to jam electronic signals that set off radio-controlled **IED**s (RCIEDs).

FAC. *Forward air controller*. A soldier trained to talk to aircrew in order to direct their weaponry on enemy positions. Either junior officers or especially talented NCOs, they typically accompany the senior officer of a unit or sub-unit.

FFD. *First field dressing*. Standard issue bandage. Capable of absorbing a lot of blood, every soldier in Afghanistan carried at least three or four.

Fire mission. Task given to an artillery piece or mortar to provide support for troops in contact.

FLET. *Forward line of enemy troops*. The line which if crossed by friendly forces would almost certainly generate a contact with the enemy.

FLOT. *Forward line of own troops*. Friendly forces' front line, denoting the limit of their sphere of influence.

FOB. *Forward operating base*. Usually home to a **BGHQ**, there was one in every major town. Around it were several smaller satellites, known as **PB**s.

FOO. *Forward observation officer.* Just like a **FAC**, but instead directing ground-based artillery and mortars. Usually sourced from the Royal Artillery, whereas FACs were from a variety of regiments.

Full screw. A corporal.

Gimpy. *See* **GPMG**. Pronounced with a soft 'g'.

Gleaming. Army slang for 'excellent'.

GMG. *Grenade machine gun.* Mounted on the top of a **Mastiff**, and capable of firing bursts of grenades at targets with devastating effect. An excellent weapon.

GMLRS. *Guided multiple launch rocket system.* Unit on a tracked chassis loaded with twelve rockets with a range of seventy kilometres. Based in Camp **Bastion** they provided cover for most of the British bases in Helmand Province.

GPMG. *General purpose machine gun.* Belt-fed **7.62 mm** calibre machine gun carried by infantry or mounted on vehicles. Easy to assemble and clean, accurate, with a good and intimidating rate of fire, it gained iconic status among troops.

GPS. *Global positioning system.* Devices used to pinpoint to the nearest metre the location of either oneself or a contact or an **IED**. Every officer in Afghanistan wore one on his wrist and would have a spare, if not two, in his kit.

Green zone. The fertile area of dense vegetation and crops that hugs any river or canal in Helmand Province. Elaborate irrigation systems enable water to reach fields sometimes several miles from a waterway. Beyond this zone is desert. Most of the Helmandi population live and work in the green zone, and therefore most of the fighting took place there.

Ground sign. Clue giving away the presence of an IED, such as disturbed or sunken earth, or soil of a different shade to that around it. Some soldiers became astonishingly good at finding devices through a sixth-sense-like awareness of ground signs.

GSW. *Gunshot wound.*

H-Hour. In military operations the time that troops are to cross the line of departure. Expanded now to refer to the start of any significant action.

Harbour. The night-time location of a group of soldiers, not permanent but organized with sentries, a central administrative point and intended to provide a degree of comfort and rest.

HE. *High explosive.*

Headley Court. Hospital in Surrey where British casualties from Afghanistan went to rehabilitate and receive advanced physiotherapy after having had their wounds initially treated and operated on at **Selly Oak**.

Heli. *Helicopter.*

Hemcon. *Haemorrhage control bandage.* Applied to stop severely bleeding arterial wounds. Very effective.

Hesco. Hesco bastions are used to create defensive walls in a very short time and at low expense. Every single **ISAF** base in Helmand was either built purely from them (why Camp **Bastion** is so called) or was in a pre-existing **Compound** heavily augmented by them. Made of sackcloth surrounded by a wire lattice cage, with the right digging equipment they are easy to erect and fill with sand or stone, and provide a thick bulletproof wall in hours.

Highway One. Name of the road that circles Afghanistan, one of the only metalled roads in Helmand Province.

HLS. *Helicopter landing site.*

IC. *Intercom.* The internal radio of an individual vehicle which can not be listened to by others. Conversation on the IC is accordingly less structured and pays no attention to **VP**.

ICOM scanning. The practice of listening into the Taliban's insecure walkie-talkie communications to get intelligence about their plans and tactics. The Taliban however soon discovered that **ISAF** could do this, and so would send false messages. On some occasions they would hurl abuse, which the interpreter would then pass on.

IED. *Improvised explosive device.*

Illum. Pronounced 'illume'. Illumination shells fired from a mortar or a **105** to light up a battlefield at night.

ISAF. *International Security Assistance Force.* The collective name for the NATO mission countries in Afghanistan, ISAF troops could be British, American, Canadian, Danish or any of the other nationalities that made up the coalition.

Jack. Selfish, letting others down when they need your help. So to 'jack on your mates' could be to withhold food from them if you had spare and they didn't, or to not tell other troops about dangers in an area. 'Having a jack brew' was to have a cup of coffee but not make one for anybody else.

Javelin. Man-portable anti-tank missile that also proved effective at destroying Taliban fire positions and bunkers.

KAF. *Kandahar Air Field.* A huge, mostly American camp in southern Afghanistan, around the airfield on the outskirts of the country's second city.

KIA. *Killed in action.*

Kinetic. Used to describe a period of heavy fighting.

Lasing. The practice of using the laser range finder on the **Rarden** cannon to get the distance to a target.

LASM. *Light anti-structures missile.* Lighter and less accurate than the **Javelin** and requiring no special training to use, this shoulder-launched missile also proved effective at destroying bunkers.

Leatherneck. American base adjacent to Camp **Bastion**.

Legacy mines. Name given to the tens of thousands of Russian landmines left behind from the 1970s and 80s. They were particularly feared as to be killed by one would be the legacy of someone else's war. As a rule high ground was avoided due to the Russians having liberally scattered these weapons around in such spots. Often dug up by the Taliban and re-used.

Link. Belt of bullets, usually **7.62 mm** for a **Gimpy**.

Loadie. The RAF crewman on a helicopter who mans the machine gun and helps troops and supplies on and off.

LOD. *Line of departure*.

Loggy. Affectionate term for a soldier of the Royal Logistic Corps.

Lynx. Helicopter used by the RAF for reconnaissance and for carrying small groups of soldiers.

Mastiff. Vehicle ushered into service with a degree of urgency during the Iraq War to combat the **IED** threat in Basra. It also proved brilliant in Afghanistan, and was for a few years about the only vehicle in which troops were likely to be safe in an **IED** strike due to its V-shaped hull and thick armour. It was often driveable even after one of its six wheels had been blown off. Armed with either a **.50 cal** or a **GMG**, it became the work-horse of the army's operations as a fire-support platform, protected mobility, or as a logistics vehicle.

MC. *Military Cross*. Awarded for individual acts of especial brav-ery in the face of the enemy.

MERT. *Medical emergency response team*. Team of doctors and para-medics, usually carried in a **Chinook**, which treated casualties during the journey from the **HLS** to the hospital at Camp **Bas-tion**. Feats of astonishing surgery were conducted by such teams, often under fire.

MiD. *Mention in Dispatches*. Award for bravery in the field signified not by a medal but by a little oak leaf worn on a campaign ribbon.

MIST. Four-line card filled out and sent with the **9-liner** to arrange a casualty's evacuation. **M** stands for *mechanism of injury* – **IED**, **GSW**, fall, etc. **I** denotes *injury type* – double amputation, bullet wound to the arm, broken collarbone, etc. **S**

is for *signs* – heart rate, breathing, whether the casualty is in shock, etc. **T** stands for *treatment given* – tourniquets, morphine, **FFD**, etc.

Murder hole. Aperture bored into a **Compound** wall just big enough to shoot through, thereby offering a sniper protection and concealment.

Naafi. *Navy, Army and Air Force Institutes*. Soldiers' shop, café or bar on a base or in a barracks.

ND. *Negligent discharge*. The unintentional firing of a weapon by its user. This is a grave sin punishable by the loss of up to a month's wages and one that can destroy a soldier's reputation. Soldiers are terrified of being killed not by enemy fire but by the mistake or slackness of one of their own friends.

Net. The radio channel being used to communicate.

OC. *Officer commanding*. The officer in charge of any group of soldiers smaller than a battle group, such as a company or a platoon. The officer in charge of a battle group is known as the commanding officer.

O Group. *See* **Orders Group**.

OMLT. *Operational mentoring and liaison team*. Pronounced 'omelette'. Small groups of British soldiers embedded with the **ANA**, responsible for the coordination of their operations with **ISAF** forces. A demanding and challenging role guaranteed to give excitement and plenty of action.

Op Bronze. Slang for trying to get a suntan. 'I'm just deploying on Op Bronze' meant one was off to sunbathe for a few hours.

Op Cat Flap. Escaping from a party without being detected.

Op Herrick. The code name of the British operation in Afghanistan. There was an iteration every six months: summer 2006 was Herrick 4, winter 2006/2007 Herrick 5 and so on.

Op Minimize. Procedure initiated in the event of a fatality or very serious injury and applied to all troops on **Op Herrick**. To ensure that the family of the victim discovered the news through official channels and not through rumour generated through emails or phone calls, all compassionate communication with the UK was suspended until the casualty's family had been notified.

Ops room. *Operations room*. The place in battle group or squadron headquarters from where operations were run. In **BGHQ** this could contain up to twenty people, and was always teeming with activity. Only for a few hours at night would it ever be quiet.

Ops/Int. Operations and intelligence officers, both senior captains. The two closest advisers to a commanding officer, responsible for drafting his plans of attack and the picture of enemy forces respectively. Perhaps the two busiest people in **BGHQ**.

Opsec. *Operational security*. The attempt, often forlorn in Afghanistan, to keep details of operations secret.

Orders Group/O Group. Formal process following a rigorous format by which a plan is verbally delivered to soldiers to be acted upon.

Osprey. Body armour worn by UK soldiers in Afghanistan, replacing the earlier **CBA**. Two heavy ceramic plates one each on the chest and back.

PB. *Patrol base*. A base smaller than a **FOB** accommodating groups of soldiers ranging in size from a company down to a platoon. Anything smaller was usually designated a checkpoint.

PID. *Positive identification*. To identify someone not only as an enemy fighter but as one with the intent to attack friendly troops. Only once a target had been PID'd as being such could they be engaged.

Pink mist. The immediate aftermath of a head shot, when the brains and blood of the deceased spray out from the exit wound to create a fine mist.

POTL. *Post-operational tour leave*. Pronounced 'pottle'. Leave after a tour to Afghanistan, lasting about five weeks.

PTSD. *Post-traumatic stress disorder.*

QRF. *Quick reaction force.* Group of soldiers kept in a **FOB** or **PB** on standby to help other troops already on the ground should they suddenly need help.

R & R. *Rest and recreation.* Two-week break in the middle of a tour when soldiers could return to the UK.

Rad Op. *Radio operator.*

Rarden. The main armament of a **Scimitar**, firing **30 mil** shells either automatically or in single shots. An excellent weapon with great range and accuracy, in the hands of a skilled gunner it could hit targets up to three kilometres away.

Rear idler. Part of the running gear of the track on a **CVR(T)**.

Rear party. Elements of a unit deployed overseas remaining in the UK for administrative functions.

Rebomb. To reload with ammunition.

REME. *Royal Electrical and Mechanical Engineers.* The British Army's experts on vehicles and technical equipment. In Afghanistan each squadron in an armoured regiment had about five of them attached, under the command of a **Tiffy**. They were the hardest worked of any squadron personnel; while everyone else slept they would be up repairing vehicles.

REMF. *Rear-echelon motherfucker.* Derogatory term for those not deployed on the ground.

RESA. *Royal Engineer search adviser.* Commander of a **REST**.

REST. *Royal Engineer search team.* The part of a **Brimstone** team tasked with sweeping an area for **IED**s and marking them for the **ATO** to deal with. Close-knit and dedicated, **REST**s were admired by every soldier they came in contact with.

RHQ. *Regimental headquarters.*

RPG. *Rocket-propelled grenade.* Fearsome if inaccurate weapon used by the Taliban.

RPK. 7.62 mm light machine gun from the Kalashnikov family of weapons. Used by the Taliban.

RSM. *Regimental sergeant major.* The senior non-commissioned officer in any regiment, who has served for at least eighteen years. Feared and respected by everyone.

RSOI. *Reception, staging and onwards integration.* Week-long period in Camp **Bastion** at the start of deployment to Afghanistan, allowing troops to acclimatize to the weather and environment, conduct exercises and learn final lessons before deploying on the ground.

SA80. Standard-issue rifle used by Britsh troops. With a magazine of thirty rounds it can be fired either in single-shot or fully automatic mode. If looked after and cleaned well, a fantastic weapon.

Samson. **CVR(T)** variant used by **REME**, equipped to rescue and repair damaged or broken-down vehicles.

Sangar. Fortified position in any base used to watch for enemy activity and to act as a main firing point. Protected with a mixture of **Hesco** and sandbags.

Schmoolie. Handheld rocket flare which, when fired, shoots about sixty metres into the sky, bursts and floats down on a parachute, brilliantly illuminating the surrounding area for thirty seconds or so. An excellent piece of equipment.

Schnell machen. German, meaning, 'Move fast.' A legacy from the British Army's long Cold War association with Germany.

Scimitar. **CVR(T)** variant armed with a **Rarden** and **GPMG**, used for reconnaissance and fire support for dismounted infantry.

Scoff. Food.

Scrapping. Fighting.

Selly Oak. Hospital in Birmingham where casualties from Afghanistan were treated.

Shoot and scoot. Typical and effective Taliban tactic of engaging troops with small arms and then swiftly retreating from the area, often by motorbike, to avoid being decisively engaged.

SHQ. *Squadron headquarters.*

Sitrep. *Situation report*, usually delivered over the radio.

Slipper city. Slightly derogatory term for any area away from the fighting.

SQMS. Pronounced 'squimce'. *Squadron quartermaster sergeant.* The second-highest NCO in a squadron and responsible for rations, water, fuel, etc.

SSM. *Squadron sergeant major.* Senior NCO in an armoured regiment squadron. Equivalent to a company sergeant major in the infantry.

Stag. Sentry duty.

Sultan. Command variant of the **CVR(T)** family, used by the squadron leader and the **2ic**, equipped with powerful radios and map tables.

SVR. *Support vehicle recovery.* Large truck capable of lifting and removing damaged or destroyed vehicles from the battlefield.

TB. *Taliban.*

Terp. *Interpreter.*

Threebar. Sergeant. From the three chevrons that denote the rank.

Throw a track. On a tracked vehicle, to have a track come off its wheels (known as the running gear). Usually a disaster, as it requires at least an hour to shoehorn it back on. Also used to describe an outburst of anger.

Tiffy. *Artificer.* The soldier, usually a staff sergeant, in charge of a squadron's **REME** detachment.

TTPs. *Tactics, techniques and procedures.*

UAV. *Unmanned aerial vehicle.* Drone, used to deliver ordnance or for surveillance.

Ugly. Callsign for an Apache helicopter.

Ulu. Slang for 'jungle' and broadened to mean 'the field'. Amazingly, this is probably derived from the ancient Greek *ule*, meaning 'forest'.

USMC. *United States Marine Corps*. By the time of Tom's tour of Helmand, the USMC was about to surge into Helmand in force, relieving the pressure on the British.

Vallon. Metal detector issued to troops and the primary equipment for finding **IED**s.

Vehicle docs. *Vehicle documents*. Each British Army vehicle has a plethora of documents that must be assiduously gone through and signed before it can be handed over to another individual or unit.

VP. *Voice procedure*. The correct way to talk on the radio, obeying certain conventions such as never using full names (*see* **Zap number**), not swearing, keeping messages accurate, brief and clear, only using the word 'repeat' when calling in artillery, and a host of other rules.

VP. *Vulnerable point*. Any obvious place to site an **IED** or mount an ambush, such as a bottleneck in a road or a doorway that troops would have to pass through.

Widow. Callsign for a **FAC**.

Zap number. The number used to make it easy to identify soldiers over the net without using their name, in an attempt to increase security and also to depersonalize injuries. Formed of the first two letters of a surname and the last four digits of a soldier's army number. So, Tom Chamberlain's Zap number (given that his army number is 25186816) would be CH6816, spoken as 'Charlie Hotel Six Eight One Six'. This number was also written all over clothing to enable quick identification should a soldier be disfigured by a wound.

Zero. Term used on the radio to describe any commander. 'Get me Zero' is a request to speak to the senior commander on that net.

Author's Note

All events in this book are fictional, and its characters bear no resemblance to anyone living or dead. Loy Kabir and Shah Kalay are fictional too, though if they were to be put on a map of Helmand Province they would be somewhere between the towns of Musa Qala and Kajaki.

Real experience was, however, father to the fiction.

My sincere thanks to the many people without whose advice and encouragement this book could never have appeared. In particular I am grateful to Johnnie Standing for championing it when it was at its most fragile. My wonderful agent Annabel Merullo, Laura Williams and the team at Peters Fraser & Dunlop have been brilliant to work with. Tim Binding intervened decisively to steer the book when it was a bit rudderless; a crucial help for which I am indebted. Hugh Davis copy-edited the book with great delicacy and surgical precision. Jedge Lewin gave his hard-won and lightly borne Afghan medical expertise. At Penguin Random House Beatrix McIntyre and Jess Jackson have been fantastic, and my great thanks to my editor Rowland White for his belief in the book, his inspiring enthusiasm and his sensitivity with the text.

I had the privilege in my Army career of serving with men and women from all across the Armed Forces. Great strength of character, innate human decency and selfless commitment were ubiquitous. I would, though, like to single out for special mention the Household Cavalry, the small part of the Army that I was fortunate enough to call home. I was welcomed into it by soldiers who have become lifelong friends. Every day I think about the time I spent with Household Cavalrymen, the lessons that I learned alongside them and those I learned from them. It was an extraordinary education.

I want to pay tribute to the men and women of Her Majesty's Armed Forces who served in Afghanistan.

I heard a country calling. Many others did too. So we went.